I0749597

WAITING FOR AN ECLIPSE

Book 2: Wounded Warriors Series

Newly Revised and Reissued!

by

Karen Wiesner

Women who have faced pain, loss and heartache.
They know the score and never back down.
Women who aren't afraid to love
with all their passion and all their strength,
who risk everything for their own little piece of heaven...
Men who live their lives on the blade's edge.
Knights in black armor.
The only thing more dangerous than crossing these men
is loving them...

http://www.karenwiesner.com

Waiting for an Eclipse **is available in electronic formats from Uncial Press, an imprint of GCT, Inc.**
http://www.uncialpress.com
electronic isbn: 978-1-60174-081-6

Waiting for an Eclipse by Karen Wiesner
© 2009, Karen Wiesner
paperback isbn: 978-0-578-03152-1

2005 EPPIE Award Finalist!
Romantic Times Reviewer's Choice Award Nominee!
Lories Best Published 2nd Place Winner!

4 ½ Stars! "This poignant book reflects on the complex dynamics of drug addiction and the profound impact it has on the lives it touches. Wiesner's ability to delve into her characters' psychological makeup to depict the sensitive topic of drug addiction makes this an exceptionally powerful story. This is a must-read." ~*Romantic Times*

5 Angels! "While I normally prefer escapist romance fiction to nitty-gritty reality, I found myself riveted by this very unusual romance story. It is neither insipid nor sweet nor aggressively erotic, and yet it is a compelling read. The bittersweet story is so well-written that, although the true sadness and horror of Steve's situation is clearly described, the reader feels sympathy and hope rather than despair, and comes away with the satisfaction that the characters have finally found their way. The characters are shown as real people, with human failings, and yet both of them have moral strength and an ethos of honor and responsibility. I liked them and really wanted them to find happiness. The story is well plotted and moves along at an inexorable pace, neither too fast nor too slow to communicate the story. The conflicts the characters face are serious and, unfortunately, all too real in this day and age. If you are tired of marshmallow fluff romances, you need to read this novel. It'll grab you from the very start, and won't let you go until the end." ~Fallen Angel Reviews

5 Roses! "If you have not started the Wounded Warriors Series by Karen Wiesner, you are missing one of the best series I have had the honor to read. Wiesner has taken modern problems that many people are facing daily and is turning them into a fabulous series. Steve has all the wonderful traits women look for. Wiesner has completely captured the feelings of neglect and loneliness children and husbands feel in this type of situation. WAITING FOR AN ECLIPSE is a very powerful novel about a man with strong character who will touch your heart. A word of caution: Once you start this series, you won't want to miss one single novel." ~Escape to Romance

Immense gratitude must be given to the following people for helping lend credibility to the fictitious university in this book:

Christine DeSmet (Director and Teacher, Writers Institute at University of Wisconsin-Madison), for answering endless questions about university life and for going above and beyond the call of duty by agreeing to give this book a critique and advance quote.

Dr. Jamie Henke (Faculty Associate at the University of Wisconsin-Madison; music theory, music history and appreciation courses for the Department of Liberal Studies and the Arts and the School of Music), for sharing specifics about the music department of a university.

Professor Marshall Cook (Journalism and Mass Communication at the University of Wisconsin-Madison), for answering questions about what it takes to be a college professor and the steps to that goal.

Trevor Bothwell, for miscellaneous college information.

Kim Hansen and Kelly Kesery, who live in Milwaukee and helped me immeasurably to put my characters in that setting.

Pam Ford Stutz and Jody Allen, on the WisRWA list, for finding out about community football teams in Milwaukee for me.

One

Sunlight seemed to pull him into its spotlight as he emerged from the DeSmet Building. Steve Thomas did what he'd done for at least half of his life: Stopped, squinted, slipped on his shades and avoided the bright rays. His glance traveled to the building across from the one he'd just left. The Drug Crisis Center shared the parking lot with the DeSmet Building. Right on time, Kristina Ingram pushed open a glass door and came out, searching for and finding him with her gaze. Her welcoming smile, even a hundred yards away, was as bright as the sunlight. He found himself soaking it up gratefully after the day he'd experienced.

For the past five years since she'd come to work at the Center as a counselor, they'd had this same ritual. Somehow, though his schedule was different most days and erratic at best, she left work at the exact same time he did each day.

Steve relaxed, returned her smile as they approached each other. Her hair, the color of cherry wood, was caught up behind her neck in a bun that was rapidly losing form. As the wind caught the loose strands, he remembered what it looked like down and free. *She's got a really nice neck.* He found himself laughing inside at the crazy thought. It felt good to laugh, even to himself.

"You did it!" she exclaimed when they were only a foot apart. "Congratulations! I'm so proud of you, Steve... I mean 'Associate Professor Thomas.'"

Steve didn't bother to wonder how she'd found out. Kristina seemed to know everything going on at Eisner University.

"Thanks. If I had to go through one more committee..." He'd had his share of congratulations today for getting tenure and making Associate Professor status. Also his share, maybe more than his share, of mean-spirited teasing and ridicule wrapped in false sincerity either behind his back or to his face. Some of his peers at the college called him "the scholar," and not fondly. They assumed he was trying to be the pet among the elders. The truth of the matter was, college, getting his master's, his Ph.D., and now tenure as he worked toward full professorship was all that'd kept him sane for the past thirteen years.

Thirteen years--sounded like so little when it felt more like forever. Being here was where he *avoided* stress. Here he could fill the hours of his day, away from the loneliness, the silence, the endless problems. The black hole of emptiness sucked him in whenever he left this place. But his colleagues wouldn't understand because all they saw was that he made them look bad or he took what they thought they deserved. He didn't care to disclose the truth for most of them either.

"What was the reaction?" she asked because she knew about the rivalry he didn't encourage, let alone get involved in.

He shrugged, but she seemed to realize he'd had a tough day because of it. "They're just jealous, you know," she said, a mischievous twinkle in her eye as she brushed a strand of her hair off of her lips. "You wear leather while they wear wool with reinforced plaid sleeves." She touched the sleeve of the light, straight-cut, leather jacket he wore over black jeans and a dark t-shirt.

Steve laughed at the realistic parallel. He'd never fit in with the dress code and never tried. Most of his colleagues followed the rigid ideal of dress because it was an obvious way to get in the good graces of the executive committee.

Surprising him, Kristina stepped forward and hugged him. He almost dropped his briefcase he was so unsure of himself in the position, but then she backed off and smiled at him again. "Have you got time tonight to go out for a celebration glass of champagne? My treat."

They'd never been in a social situation before--outside of a quick lunch or soda at one of the restaurants nearby the campus. She had no way of knowing he didn't drink alcohol, even if she might know *why* he didn't. Why did their professional friendship strike him as unusual? There was no reason he'd see Kristina outside the campus.

He shook his head immediately. "I can't. Too much to do. Thanks for asking though."

Her obvious disappointment almost had him wishing he could say yes. She knew why he couldn't and didn't push it. They left the sidewalk for the parking lot. After she unlocked the door of her car, he opened it for her.

"See you tomorrow," she said softly. "Do something for yourself tonight. All right?"

Steve nodded and got the feeling she understood the impossibility of that from the concerned look in her eyes.

"'Night, Kristina."

She smiled, and he remembered the sunlight when he'd come out of the music building. Her smile was like that. Blinding. Revealing. Only he didn't want to avoid it. Sometimes he wished he could stay where she was, where things weren't complicated or stressful. It wasn't fair to think she was the only sunshine in his life. Not at all. But he thought it anyway.

After shutting her door, he walked toward his car, turning to wave at her as she drove past him out of the lot. Sighing, he got into his car, remembered her comment about the wool sweaters and laughed.

The memory of her hug returned. Just a friendship hug. *Warm* friendship hug. Body to body. The laughter dried up and made his throat feel cramped with emotion. Confusion and straight-out fear gripped him.

No. Hell, he had to think about getting dinner ready. Doing dishes. Helping Val with her homework. Laundry needed to be done. Then getting Val to fall asleep, to stay asleep for a while anyway, just until there were no monsters or nightmares to wake her. Only then would he have time to do the work he brought home every night. None of those tasks applied to his wife because he couldn't predict Jessie.

A few minutes later, he was on the freeway and leaving Brookfield. He lived in Greenfield on the southwest side of Milwaukee. Ironic, he often thought driving home, that his family lived in such suburbia.

The closer he got to home, the more his stomach clenched. He lived in a good neighborhood, in a solid, two-story bungalow. It was about the only thing in his personal life that was good.

As soon as he turned the corner down the street he lived on, he knew something was wrong. Evangeline, the nanny who worked for them, picked up and stayed with the kids after school every day, wasn't there. Her car wasn't in its usual spot--parked on the street in front of the house. That meant Jess had to be home. She'd come home and sent Evangeline away. The fact that no one had paged him didn't make him feel any more relieved.

Every light in the house was on. The front door stood open. Music spilled out into the street as if a live band rehearsed in their garage.

Steve didn't bother pulling into the garage. He didn't take his briefcase. He parked on the garage approach on a slant and jumped out of the car. As soon as he ran up the porch steps, he saw his eight-year-old daughter huddled in the corner crying.

His teeth clenched as he picked Valerie up and held her tight against him. *Now what, Jess? Now what, dammit?*

He didn't want to go inside the house, almost as much as Val didn't, when he took the steps toward the screen door. "Please, Daddy, I don't want to go inside. Let me stay here," begged Val.

If not for the chill in the September air, her thin shirt and alarming frailness, he would have let her stay outside.

"Val, baby, where're your brothers? Is Ronnie still at football practice?"

Her face red, pinched, and miserable, she nodded. "Tom's at Aaron's."

When Steve opened the screen door, Valerie huddled her face into his shoulder and he barely heard her whisper, "I hate her, Daddy."

He increased the pressure of his arms and prayed he hadn't heard her right or that it was the wind. Regardless of whether she'd voiced it, he knew the truth he didn't want to face.

The stereo in the living room was the one blaring, and he slammed the button to get it to shut up. In the silence, he knew Jess wasn't downstairs. She'd come home, told Evangeline to get out, turned on the stereo to block out the silence and had gone to their bedroom. *Left the kids alone again.*

"Go in your room and close the door, baby," Steve said softly on the landing upstairs. Val did it without a moment's hesitation. Then he turned toward the closed door of his bedroom.

From outside, he heard the screech of tires in front of the house. One of Ronnie's much older friends dropping him off. Just in time, too.

Steve shoved open the bedroom door, wondering almost inappropriately why she never locked it. Or didn't she think she had anything to hide? *Hell.*

Inside his bedroom, he saw exactly what he expected to see: his wife lying naked in their bed next to another man. A needle was stuck in her arm, and she wasn't moving. Even when Steve said her name, she didn't stir. All the rage and fear and humiliation crumbled inside his head, yet Steve acted by rote. He checked her pulse and found it slow, erratic, barely there.

Behind him, he heard his son, a twelve-year-old boy with the eyes of an old man, swear. Steve covered Jess before turning to Ronnie and saying with the last vestige of his control, "Call an ambulance."

The long-haired guy next to Jess stirred. Steve didn't wait for him to come to full consciousness in his own good time. He walked around the bed and yanked the bastard straight up before shoving the clothes he'd gathered at him. "What did you two shoot up?" he demanded, and the creep stumbled, incoherently telling him sheet rock--LSD and crack--as he struggled with his pants.

"Get the hell out. Now."

As soon as he fled, falling down the stairs judging from the ruckus, Ronnie picked up the phone next to the bed. Steve watched him punch out the number without taking his eyes off his mother for even a second. He summoned an ambulance as though he'd been doing it forever. And he had. He was twelve years old, and he'd done this more times than he could remember.

Damn you, Jess, how much more? How many times can you put us through this?

He'd known the peace wouldn't last. He'd never believed for a second it would.

"Daddy?" Val's voice drifted into the room from the hall, and Steve glanced at Ronnie. Even Ronnie's glare at him was familiar, and all Steve could think was that this had to end. All this shit. Somehow. Soon.

It had to.

* * * *

"I'm hungry, Daddy," Val said softly. Steve brought his hand to the back of her head, smoothing her pale yellow hair. She eased closer to him on the waiting room chairs, putting her head on his chest.

"I know, baby. It won't be long now. We'll pick up Tom, then go through the drive-thru on the way home. Get anything you guys want."

Small consolation, but their lives were built on small consolations and Steve gave them whenever he could. Maybe it wasn't good for them, maybe he wasn't firm enough, maybe he indulged them too often. He'd never been able to withhold the little joy he could give them. When they looked back at all this when they were older, he hoped they'd remember these things and say it wasn't all bad.

Glancing across the waiting room of the ER, Steve caught his elder son's dark eyes. Ronnie looked away immediately, hostility so fierce that Steve felt it run through him like a hot knife. He couldn't help Ronnie. It was too late. The damage Jessie had done went too deep to ever bring him back.

All of his life, Ronnie had seen his mother's insanity--her drinking, her drugs, her cheating. He saw and heard the fights. He saw the way Jessie remained oblivious to his brother and sister. Occasionally, Jess noticed Ronnie--when she needed him. Then and only then. Not a minute sooner. It'd created a vicious cycle in him. He wanted his mother's love more than anything, so he remained loyal to her, making excuses for her bad behavior, even when she ignored and used him. In order for him to remain loyal, her enemies had to become his enemies. Steve had become his own wife's enemy because he hated the things she did, couldn't accept them anymore. He'd spent years trying to get her to change. He'd spent years *failing*. He'd lost the war for his son as well.

Feeling his continued gaze on him, Ronnie turned to him, his lip curling. "You shouldn't have let her go back to work. You should've let her recover longer."

"*She* made the decision, Ronnie. I didn't say anything one way or another." Steve heard the desperation in his own voice. He wanted his older son to believe him, just once. To assume the best of him instead of the absolute worst.

"When do you ever *need* to say anything to her? She knows what you think of her. She tries so hard to please you, and it's never enough for you."

Swallowing, Steve felt tears sting his tired eyes.

"Stop defending her!" Val said, her voice watery as she turned toward her brother. "She did it to herself. Daddy tries to help her and she just... She'll never change. Why do you defend her? She doesn't care about you. She hates everyone, but she needs us."

"Val..." Steve started, but Ronnie was already on his feet, stalking out of the room.

Steve's attempt to call him back went unheeded, and he sat forward, his head in his hands. He wanted to let the scream building in his throat out. Let it fill the room, the whole world, until he collapsed under its weight.

"I hate her, Daddy. I hate her," Val said on a sob.

"Don't say that, baby. Please don't say that." She was crying again, and he was helpless to her tears. Nothing he did ever mattered. His actions, his words, couldn't change anything. Yet he pulled her into his arms and held her against him.

"I wish she'd die this time," Val whispered, and Steve wanted to scold her and beg her not to voice that ever again. But he understood. God in Heaven, he understood. She wanted this all to end. She didn't want her mom to wake up, leave the hospital saying she'd go to rehab and everything would be all right again soon. A couple weeks later, she'd come home, clean, apologizing and claiming she wouldn't slip up this time. That she'd be a model mother and wife.

None of them believed her, not anymore, but predicting how long before her restlessness, boredom, and depression took over was impossible. Sooner or later, she'd be back on the drug and booze binges, screwing everybody in sight before she landed in the emergency room. Again. It never ended.

Valerie wanted all that to end. Hell, Steve couldn't blame her for that. While the kids knew what had made their mother the person she was, they couldn't understand it. A part of Steve didn't want them to understand. He'd already lost Ronnie. He wouldn't risk losing Val or Tom.

Footsteps came toward the waiting room, and Steve turned to see Dr. Harvey coming in with his arm around Ronnie. Steve stood, lifting Val in his arms at their approach. The doctor greeted Val, handing her a lollipop and asking where Tom was. He gave her an extra lollipop to give to him. He'd been handing out lollipops to the kids since they were babies, all at events similar to this, and he hadn't seemed to notice they weren't two feet high anymore.

"How's my mom?" Ronnie asked, and Steve heard the accusation in his voice as he shot a glare at him. In Ronnie's mind, Steve should have been the first to ask.

"It's touch and go at this point. You know how these things work. Who knows better than you?"

Steve felt his face flush at the humiliation he knew Dr. Harvey hadn't intended to make him feel.

"Wasn't she just in here a month, month and a half ago?"

By sheer chance, Dr. Harvey had been working the emergency room that time as well.

"Rehab didn't take?"

There was nothing to say. Rehabilitation was part of Jessie's cycle. From a doctor's point of view, it had to sound like a damn waste of time and money. There was no such thing as permanent rehab, not for someone like Jess.

"There's nothing more you can do here tonight, Steve. Why don't you take the kids home? We'll call you if there's any change. Get some rest."

"I wanna see my mom," Ronnie said instantly, predictably.

Dr. Harvey nodded, putting his hand on Ronnie's shoulder. "Sure. But not too long."

"I don't want to go in there, Daddy," Val whispered as soon as her brother followed the doctor out of the room.

Tom hadn't wanted to be here either. Steve had called his middle son from the house, after the ambulance came and went and before he followed it to the hospital. Tom had said they didn't need him there, he'd rather stay at Aaron's tonight. Steve promised he'd pick him up from his friend's after they left the hospital. He wanted Tom with them tonight. Besides, he'd had a bad feeling about Aaron from the first time he met him and not just because of his foul mouth and nose rings. Tom had agreed to be ready when they picked him up.

"When can we go home?" Val asked twenty minutes later. Ronnie hadn't come out yet. Steve knew he'd have to go in after him. *I don't want to see Jess either.* If he could get away with it tonight, despite Ronnie's wrath, he would leave without seeing her.

At the admitting desk, he asked the nurse--a familiar face--to watch Val for a few minutes. With a sad, pitying look on her face, she said, "Sure. Why don't you come back here, honey?"

Getting Ronnie to leave the hospital without his mother would be hard. It never got any easier because the boys' determination grew almost in sync with his physical growth. At twelve, he was already five-seven and well-muscled. Steve knew it wouldn't be much longer before he'd be using his physical strength to protect his mother. And then what the hell would Steve do? He wouldn't hit his own son to get him in line.

Ronnie stood by his mother's bedside and stoically refused to look up when Steve came in.

"Ron, Val's tired and hungry. We have to get your brother--"

"I wanna stay with her."

Steve glanced at the wall. He couldn't look at Jess. He knew he wasn't strong enough to see her. If he looked at her, he'd remember she needed him, but he wouldn't remember why. He'd remember being needed to the point where he didn't exist for any other reason. He'd remember he owed her that much.

"No," Steve said softly. "No, Ronnie. But we'll come back here right after dinner tomorrow. Okay?" When he put his hand on the boy's shoulder, his son shoved away and left the room.

Closing his eyes, Steve took a deep breath. His mind filled with the memory of a cherub with chocolate brown eyes, a mass of dark hair, always smiling, drooling and trying to satisfy his every curiosity. Ronnie had been exuberant about life back then. He'd loved everyone and everything. When Steve held him, he'd stayed there in his arms. He'd *wanted* to be there.

Steve left the room without looking back. Ronnie already had Val by the hand, leading her out of the hospital.

As Steve drove out of the parking lot, Ronnie said, "I'm gonna quit football."

Ronnie was in a community football team for kids his age that practiced after school and on weekends. He'd been the first to make the team and probably would be the first to quit as well. Taking care of his mom was his top priority. Besides, sooner or later, Jess would ask him to stop going.

"You need a life outside the house, Ron," Steve said, knowing anything he said wouldn't mean a damn thing to his son.

He'd enjoyed football in high school, purely for the sport of it, not the competition, and Ronnie loved sports.

"Mom needs me. She counts on me."

She's the mother. You're supposed need and count on her. "Don't quit," Steve said simply.

Ronnie didn't answer.

The silence in the car continued after Tom got in. Steve noticed he didn't ask about things. He just said he was hungry. At eleven, his middle child was even more withdrawn than Ronnie. Tom spent most of his time in front of his computer or the TV, headphones on to block out everything else.

Dinner was something Steve could take care of. He could make a meal, set the table, force himself to eat, hoping they'd do the same. Ronnie took his food up to his room, saying he wanted to start his homework. Steve wanted to forbid it, but he had no desire to fight. None of them did.

"You want me to help?" Tom asked after the meal, and Steve shook his head. "Thanks, buddy. I'll take care of it. You got homework?"

Tom shook his head, muttering, "Did it at school."

He never seemed to have homework, always said he did it at school. He appeared to make no effort based on an avid disinterest in school, but Steve couldn't lecture him for it since he got B's easily enough.

Steve kissed the top of Tom's head and noticed the length of his hair. The smell of smoke in it. He didn't mention either. Despite his middle son's seeming obliviousness to most of life, Steve knew Tom was sensitive. Getting on him about his homework would make him withdraw even more. Even saying a haircut was in order might hurt his feelings. Asking him if he'd been smoking would be worse. Maybe Aaron's parents smoked.

Sullen as usual, Tom got up from the table and went to the living room. A minute later, the TV blared.

"Will you help me with my homework?" Val asked. She'd barely eaten anything. From the time she was born, she'd been apathetic about food. She barely ate enough to keep herself alive. She was much smaller and frailer than most of her classmates, so pale that her veins stood out starkly beneath her skin and her lips always looked blue. Her brown eyes looked huge within her tiny face.

Helplessly, Steve looked at her sipping her milk because he'd asked her to drink all of it, and he suddenly wanted to get the kids together, get in the car and go. Anywhere. Never look back. His hands tightened so hard on the back of the chair, he was afraid he wouldn't be able to disconnect from the reckless feeling inside him.

He'd brought his kids to this. *He'd* been the one to go against everything he knew was right because he couldn't say no. He couldn't resist temptation. He'd told himself it was okay because he could be everything Jessie needed. Now Ronnie was caught in the same net he'd been ensnared in. Tom wanted to avoid the world so no one and nothing could hurt him, ever. And Val was afraid of the world. She was helpless in it, and the demons around her tormented her night and day. The only way out for all of them was the one thing he couldn't allow himself. They suffered for that inability as much as he did.

"Daddy?"

He needed to clean the kitchen, get laundry started, or he'd never get any sleep tonight. But he said, "Yeah. Yeah, baby. Whatever you need."

Two

"How will I get through my life without you, Kris?"

Kristina Ingram smiled at Curtis, a college kid on the edge of real manhood. He graduated next summer. Just five months ago, he'd been referred anonymously to the Drug Crisis Center and had come willingly. He'd gotten to the college on a scholarship, but only came because of it. His problems at home had led him to alcohol and drugs. He'd managed to get by most years, despite all his troubles. Now, for the first time in years, he was clean, sober, his GPA was 3.7, and he was headed in a firm direction.

Well in advance of his graduation, Kristina felt it necessary for him to discontinue his frequent visits to her office. Right now, he was relying on *her* for his courage. Every problem he faced sent him here, seeking reassurance and the resolution to go back out and face life all over again. He needed to find his own courage before he went out on his own.

"Curtis, you don't need me. I know you think you do. But you have everything you need to get by inside of yourself."

"No." He shook his head, his bound dreadlocks remaining in place. "I ain't got nothin'."

Kristina walked around her desk and shifted things back so she could lean on the edge. "You don't have *anything*, Curtis? You don't have good grades? You don't have job prospects when you graduate?"

He grimaced. "You know what I mean."

"Are you the moron your mother thinks you are?"

His young face went hard as stone. "No."

"Are you the deadbeat loser who'll never amount to anything, the way your father says?"

On an exhale, he nodded. "Yeah, I see what you're sayin'."

Outside her open door, Kristina saw Steve approach, then back off when he saw she wasn't alone. Suddenly, she couldn't breathe and her mind went blank as she realized he'd come to her. He'd come to see her. Talk to her.

Feeling her hands tremble, she put them behind her back. In a few minutes, he would occupy the small space of her office with her. He would be close enough to... If all she could do was look at him, that would be enough.

With effort, she swallowed against the dryness in her mouth she hadn't noticed before, then turned back to Curtis. "You have everything you need, Curtis. You know these things about yourself. Nothing else matters. No one can take them away from you unless you let them. But right now you need to stand on your own. You don't need me anymore. That's good news. "

"Well, don't you...?"

He glanced away as if embarrassed, and Kristina felt the twinge of betrayal she always did when she had to tell someone she needed to keep a professional distance. He believed he was in love with her, just like many of her male cases had in the past five years she'd worked here. She was one of the few people who took an interest in them, cared about them, and encouraged them to live up to their potential. Curtis would realize on his own, after he'd been away from here for a few months, that his love amounted to gratitude.

He rose suddenly, and Kristina stepped forward and took his hand. "Believe in yourself, and you can do anything. I know it and you know it, too. Good luck."

"Thanks, Kris. For everything."

She nodded, smiling and feeling tears sting behind her eyes. She'd worried all night how this would go down. In the past, it usually hadn't ended well.

As Curtis left, Kristina reached up to feel her hair, make sure it was in place, and to push her over-sized glasses up on her nose.

Steve appeared in her doorway again, and she knew immediately he hadn't slept much and something was very wrong. Her first instinct was to grab hold of him and to try to take as much of his pain inside of herself as she could. The instinct was one she had to tamp down on constantly with this man.

To give herself some distance, she smiled, welcomed him warmly, but pivoted away. "Would you like a cup of coffee?"

A million times, she'd wondered if she was just contradictory as all get-out, or if he was. Never before had she met a man so impossibly attractive who looked like hell so much of the time. He always looked like he'd gone ten rounds with a ruthless opponent. Yet he was so beautiful, so gentle, so sweet and sexy--

Behind her, she heard him sigh. She looked over her shoulder at him.

"Oh, God." She slammed down the coffee carafe, ran to her door, shut and locked it, then flew to him.

He sat on the couch with his hands in his hands, sobbing like she'd never heard a man do before in her life. He held it all. Forever, he'd just held it all until she'd wondered how he could even stand, let alone keep it bottled up.

"Oh, Steve, what happened?"

What was appropriate here? She didn't care, not when he was like this. She'd never seen him fall apart. She knelt before him and put her arms around his shoulders, holding him against her securely.

He'd told her about his wife--her drinking, drugs, infidelity. How she didn't seem to care about her own children one iota, leaving them unattended without a single thought to the consequences. He didn't need to say a word for Kristina to know he'd gone home last night--not to a loving wife who would congratulate him on his achievements--but to his unsupervised children, his *un*blushing bride beside another man in their bed and drugged to the hilt. His wife had no doubt spent the night in the emergency room while Steve spent the night taking care of everyone and everything, trapped in his own personal hell.

The bitch.

Kristina didn't think about the irrationality of hating a woman she'd never met, especially hating her to the extreme level she hated Jessie Nelson-Thomas. The irony was, of course, that she worked with drug addicts, or former drug addicts, on a daily basis. She understood the mind of an addict. Yet she felt not one ounce of sympathy for Steve's wife. No matter how many times she lectured herself for her own illogical attitude, she couldn't rid herself of it in Steve's.

"I can't..." he uttered, his voice hoarse from fatigue and grief. "I can't take this anymore. I can't. But there's nowhere to turn. No way out."

Leave her. Leave the selfish whore! That's the only way out. You know it, but for God only knows what reason you refuse to take it.

She held him, stroked his tangled hair, murmuring comfort that would never be enough--for either of them. He allowed all of her caretaking, and she could only believe he needed it and it eased his pain. She didn't allow herself to believe no one else would comfort him the way she did.

When she couldn't see out of her glasses for her own tears, she squeezed her eyes shut. "I wish I could help you and your children, Steve. I wish I could do something, anything to make the pain go away for you."

When she realized her heart screamed for him to put his arms around her, too, do more than simply allow this support, she hated herself for her selfishness. Steve lived his life in a black hole of misery. He didn't know comfort. He knew cold loneliness, rage, fear, and grief. Whatever got him and his children through. Whatever helped his kids cope without falling apart so completely, he'd never be able to put them back together. He was so lost in his torment right now, he probably didn't feel her at all.

Somewhere in the distance, a bell went off. He drew back from her instantly as if he'd been roused from sleep.

"I've got a class." He stood, wiping his hands over his face, which looked ten years older than it had last night.

Kristina shot to her feet, halting him with her hand on his arm. He refused to look her in the eye, and it made her want to scream, *Never be embarrassed to show me your emotions! You don't have to feel that way with* me. "Come to my apartment. Tonight. Have dinner with me. We can talk," she said.

As if he couldn't breathe, he said, "I can't."

"Then just come over. Anytime. You need to talk to someone, Steve." He knew where she lived, just blocks from here, though he'd never been to her apartment. He knew her home phone number, too. She'd found an excuse to give him all that information long ago.

He shook his head, moving toward the door. "Kids. I have to..." He fiddled with the lock for a second, then turned back, not meeting her gaze again, and said, "Thanks."

Kristina followed him to the doorway, saying quickly, "I'm always here if you need me--"

She wanted to tell him that wherever she was, he could contact her. Whatever time it might be. But he was already walking away, down the hall, holding it all inside again.

Slipping off her glasses, she pressed her fingers against her eyes to stop her tears. Her action didn't help. She closed her door as the first sob slammed into her chest.

"Come to my apartment."

"Have dinner with me."

"Leave your wife."

Why not "I love you; there's nothing I wouldn't do for you, Steve Thomas"? Add that to the list of things I've never said to you and thought I never would.

Kristina had never asked Steve to her apartment or out to dinner because he was married. He and his wife had three children. He would never leave Jessie, regardless of what low-down, horrendous thing she might do--and *had* already done, frequently--to him.

He would have rejected me. He did *reject me.* But she found herself not sorry she'd asked him those things. Maybe someday he'd feel he had nowhere else to turn and come to her again.

When she realized she was about to launch into another private lecture about wanting what she couldn't have and being a friend to Steve was what she *could* have, if she could just keep her own emotions in check, Kristina forced herself to sit at her desk.

She'd come to work for Eisner University's Drug Crisis Center five years ago. She knew Steve had been on the tenure track as an assistant professor in the Music Department since he'd attended this college as a student. They'd met in the parking lot the two buildings shared only days after her first day of work.

She'd never forgotten a moment of their first meeting. It'd solidified her decision to go against her father's wishes for her to become a lawyer. He'd never forgiven her for her major in education and minor in counseling. She'd been offered better positions inside and outside Wisconsin, but she'd never considered them. She'd realized, after many years away, how much she loved her hometown of Milwaukee. Besides, she'd missed her mother.

After rubbing her glasses dry with a microfiber cloth, Kristina told herself she was hopeless.

"What's a head case like you doing counseling other people? Yeesh." The self-accusation sounded loud in the silence of her office. Embarrassment filled her, but when she noticed her shirt was wet with Steve's tears, she nevertheless pressed her hand to those tears and closed her eyes to savor the memory. He'd come to her. Life wasn't fair to him. She would take his pain if only she could. Nevertheless, she couldn't help the tiny bit of happiness she felt. Steve had come to *her*. He trusted *her* with the hurt in his life.

Another sob worked its way up from the depths of her soul into her throat, making her shake at its force and wrap her arms around herself. *Lord, let me love him, even if from afar. That's all I want.*

Then she subjected herself to the old lecture about being content with what she could have of the man who unknowingly owned her heart.

Three

"You guys almost done or what?" Ronnie demanded, as if he'd spent hours waiting impatiently for them. They'd entered the restaurant less than fifteen minutes earlier and their orders had arrived barely two minutes ago.

Steve kept himself in check, just like he had that morning when the school called him to say Ronnie had disappeared after second period. Figuring out where he'd gone didn't take Steve longer than a second. Ronnie had gone to the hospital. Steve left the college in the middle of a lecture to get his son back in school. Neither of them had said more than a dozen words during that episode. They'd been through the same thing enough times that the lectures had been memorized.

Steve had come home a lot earlier than usual to take the kids out to eat, just like he'd promised. Ronnie was more interested in the promise of seeing his mother than in the prospect of eating dinner. Tom ignored his brother, the way he usually did, and Val told him to shut up while she moved her food around her plate without interest.

"Look, I want to tell you guys something," Steve began, too aware of the fact that most people would greet his news with happiness, even gratitude. He didn't know how his kids would react. Hell, maybe he did know after all.

He'd started college after high school more to please his old man than himself. He'd wanted to be in a band, be a rock star and make millions. The summer between high school and college had proved he wasn't ready for that goal. His band's demos had been rejected everywhere. He'd started giving music lessons in college to make money. Until he gave up his dream to be a famous musician and took his sister's advice, he hadn't realized teaching was what he was meant to do.

Getting on the tenure track hadn't been easy when he had three kids before he turned twenty-nine years old. But he'd done it all because it kept him sane. He'd gotten his BA in four years, master's in two and completed his doctoral program five years later. At thirty-seven, he barely remembered most of the time or the work that went into it. He'd done it like it was something that needed to be done and he did what needed to be done, always, end of story. Besides, it paid the bills, ones that piled up constantly because his wife couldn't seem to get her head on straight.

He'd dragged the kids to a lot of recitals, a lot of concerts. He'd worked a lot of hours at the college and after the kids were in bed every night. Getting tenure and making Associate Professor wouldn't mean simply more money. They would know it'd mean working toward full professorship. Between preparing and teaching courses, lectures and seminars or overseeing his assistants for those things, recitals, concerts and productions, his own private research and rehearsing, preparing his application for professorship... Hell no, his home life wouldn't get any easier.

The tension around the table increased as they all looked at him. He wanted to smile, to say, "Hey, don't look like that. It's *good* news," but he wasn't sure they'd agree with him.

"I got tenure. I made Associate Professor."

Looking at each of them, he could see they didn't register the importance, so he kept talking. He couldn't help downplaying the ramifications. The last thing they needed was a major change in their lives right now. Their life had been unstable forever. They wouldn't want to hear it might get worse. "It means more money. Probably the same hours. It probably won't change much. Just my status there."

"Good deal," Tom said softly, surprising Steve and making him want to reach across the table and hug him for all he was worth.

Then Ronnie spoke, bitterness lacing every spit-out word. "Yeah. For *him.* It's all he cares about. His goddamn career. While Mom's in the hospital."

He'd expected Ronnie's reaction, but it didn't make it any easier to hear.

"She put herself in the hospital. She's stupid," Val said.

Ronnie's fist impacted with Val's arm before Steve could stop it. In another second, she burst into tears. "You big jerk! I hate you!" Everyone around them stared. He wanted to take back his news or walk out as fast as he could go.

"Don't hit your sister," he said to Ronnie, more calmly that he felt. "You've got a problem with *me*, deal it out to *me.* I'll take it."

Ronnie didn't say anything, just sat glaring down at his empty plate.

"My job is my job. I don't control your mother." *There's not a person on earth capable of that, not anymore.* "This won't change anything, you guys. I promise." He'd keep that promise if it killed him.

In the silence that followed, Steve forced himself to eat, although he'd long lost his appetite. He had to set a good example for the kids, but mealtimes always seemed to feel like this. Awkward and stressful--like a chore that made him want to go hungry instead of facing it. But they needed stability, and eating was one of the few things they all did together.

"Twelve years old and pussy-whipped by your own mom," Tom said under his breath, choice phrases stolen from his new best friend Aaron, no doubt. Ronnie would have punched him, too, if Steve hadn't grabbed his arm. As Ronnie swore at Tom, Steve wondered what everyone around them was thinking. But he already knew that. They thought, *Bad father; can't even control his own kids.* His private thoughts paralleled--*Bad father; can't even* help *my own kids.*

Valerie cried through the rest of the meal and begged Steve not to make her see her mother. He wondered if not forcing her to would make him an even worse father.

After they arrived at the hospital, they talked to the doctor, then all went into Jess' room together. She was doing well, she was awake, but she didn't want anything to do with them. When Ronnie said, "The doctor says you won't be in here long this time. Just a day or two, and then we can bring you home," she ignored him completely, turning away.

Steve's coldness toward her surprised him. It seemed to grow each time they revisited this scene. He used to forgive her completely, unconditionally because he was so damn glad she was alive. What else mattered? Lately, he talked to her, told her to get better, said all those things he no longer meant, while the anger remained just under the surface.

Now he felt so angry, he didn't want to look at her. He didn't want to talk either. He allowed Ronnie to say all the things *he* used to say. He held Valerie, who kept her face turned to his chest. Tom stood off to the side, wordless and uncomfortable, his blond head down. None of them wanted to be here, none of them except Ronnie.

Steve watched his older son, saw the desperation in his eyes as he tried to get his mom to acknowledge him. She stared blindly at the TV, her thick, auburn hair tangled around her face and spilling carelessly down her back. He recognized her blank expression as one of severe depression. She was so far down, she probably didn't even hear Ronnie's voice.

It didn't change Steve's rage. All she had to do is say one word to her son--*one word*--and he'd feel whole. But she couldn't even give him that.

"Ronnie, we need to go," Steve said gently, sure the sound of his voice would infuriate the boy.

"I wanna stay here."

Tears stung Steve's eyes. *She doesn't want you here. She doesn't want* you. From the very beginning, the moment she realized she was pregnant, she'd hoped to spontaneously abort. She'd felt even less for the last two children. He'd been fully aware she'd bore them simply to hold onto Steve for a little longer. She knew he'd take care of them. He'd never leave her if he had something to keep him occupied.

"You can't stay here, Ronnie. You know that. We can come back tomorrow."

"She needs me."

"She's got doctors and nurses. Come on."

As soon as they got in the house twenty minutes later, Ronnie stalked past them up to his bedroom. Tom followed, and Steve knew he'd play computer games until told it was time for bed. Val asked if she could watch TV after she did her homework, and Steve agreed because he had so much work to do around the house.

He joined her later, not surprised she'd chosen *When Harry Met Sally*. Val always chose romantic movies. He found it hard to believe he used to be the same way, once upon a time.

"Daddy, do you think Aunt Wendy and Uncle Paul make a good couple?" she asked, snuggled against his side. She was talking about Steve's sister and her husband, who'd been a life-long friend of his.

"Yeah."

"I do, too. Were they friends like Harry and Sally were before they got married?"

"Yeah."

"Jack and Rose were friends in *Titanic*, and Kate and Luc were friends in *French Kiss*. Then they fell in love and got married."

"More like uneasy alliances in that one," Steve said softly. He stared down into his daughter's tiny, delicately beautiful face that looked more like her mother's every day. She was leading up to something, he knew, something he wouldn't know how to respond to.

"Do you have any friends that are girls?"

Steve exhaled. "You know I do. Your Aunt Gwen. Brenda."

"Brenda lives too far away. Do you think you and Aunt Gwen could ever fall in love?"

Maybe her words were was silly. The whole conversation was, but he didn't find it ridiculous in the least. He was afraid Val would get hurt again, the way she usually did, because she infallibly reacted with her heart instead of her head.

"You know your aunt is like a sister to me, baby. She was married to your mom's brother."

"But he died."

Steve raised his face to the ceiling, trying to tamp down on the emotions that felt too close to the surface today, where he couldn't control them. When he could get himself to look at his little girl, he said in barely a whisper, "I'm already married."

Val shook her head. "You're in a prison, Daddy. You're not in a marriage."

She left the room, and Steve leaned forward, grabbing his hair in two fists. For a long minute, he couldn't control the laughter that bled through his teeth.

Eight years old. How could she know what his life had felt like for, hell, the past almost half his life?

A prison. A prison of endless nights, waiting for Jess to come to him, knowing she would eventually because he was her safety net. He still remembered the emotion that coiled inside him whenever he saw her in the beginning. It was like a hurricane wrecking havoc on his body, from head to heart to... Yeah, there, too. He'd been as addicted to Jessie Nelson then as she was addicted to her crash-and-burn cycles now.

Maybe the worse part of the situation was that she'd known of his addiction to her. He'd given her all the power because he'd been helpless to resist her, even when he realized she gave everyone else the love he needed. She *expected* to find him waiting, taking care of things, being faithful to her. If he felt empty, lonely, hurt, it was his own problem. After all, he'd known what he was getting into from the very beginning.

He couldn't deny that. But the truth didn't make his loyalty any easier to manage when she finally came back around--no warning, no excuses, no explanations, with that goddamn *how-dare-you* expression or the *please-forgive-me* one. He'd never been able to decide which one was worse. In the end, they both made him feel like his love was worthless until she wanted it, then and only then.

Sometimes he fought it. He wanted to tell her to go to hell. *Fight your own battles. I'm through. I can't do it anymore. We've already lost, a million times over. There's nothing left to fight for.* He was weak. He'd always been that way with her. He'd let her make love to him. He'd listened to her issue a thousand promises, ones he never believed. He'd never been surprised when she left him and broke a thousand and one promises the next time.

A prison. That was exactly what his marriage had become. Only there was no way out of this one.

"Do you have any friends who are girls at the college?" Val asked after her bath, while she had a snack before bed. She picked up the conversation like they'd been having it the whole time, and Steve felt so raw he could barely think.

"What do you want me to do, baby? Tell me. What are you getting at here?"

Her eyes widened with uncertainty before she looked down at the nibbled apple in her hand. "I was just... Me and Tom talked about it. We both said it'd be okay with us if you did. We'd be on your side. I know Ronnie wouldn't--"

Steve reached for her hand, and her gaze shot up to his. "If I did *what*, Val?"

Pursing full lips tinged blue, she said softly, "Don't be mad. Tom said not to tell you what we talked about 'cause you might get mad. But you can get a divorce if you want. You don't have to stay married to her for us."

He'd never talked about his marriage to the kids before. He'd certainly never believed they might have talked about it together. Divorce...

Leaning forward, he pressed his mouth to her cold palm. "It's not that easy, baby." He enclosed her tiny hand between both of us. "I want you guys to be happy. I want you to have a mother. But it's not that simple."

"Then why do you stay with her? Why do you care at all? She only likes you when she needs something. She doesn't care about us, not even Ronnie."

He'd prayed never to have this conversation with his kids. He wanted to just pull her into his arms, hug her and say it'd be okay. He'd take care of things. It was how he'd handled everything up to this point.

"Tell me why you stay. Please."

Steve shrugged. "She's been through a lot. You know she has. Her parents... You know her brother died. He was everything to her. I don't know if she'll ever get over his death. I don't know if I ever will." He'd said the same words at least a billion times over the years. When it came to Jess, they were the only ones he truly believed. Yet they sounded hollow when he handed them to Val.

Apparently she heard the hollowness as well. "But that was like a hundred years ago!"

"Thirteen years. Time doesn't fix some things, baby. It's not that simple."

"I think there's something you're not telling us. Is it that bad?"

Steve stared down into her face, brushing her long, baby-fine hair, already dry, back from her forehead and shoulders. To her mind, everything was simple. Something was confusing, you explained it. Something broke, you got a new one. Something hurt, you hid from future pain. But she knew about demons showing up out of nowhere, finding you no matter where you hid and no matter how you tried to explain them away. She knew about all that. And Steve blamed himself for it. He didn't know how to help her either.

"It's almost nine, Val. School tomorrow. Come on."

He read to her for awhile in her purple and white room loaded with young adult romance books and stuffed animals, then stayed with her until she fell into light sleep. She woke as he tried to slip out the door, and he had to reassure her over and over that if she needed him he'd be right there.

Giving Tom and Ronnie the five-minute knock, he went down to fold a load of laundry. Tom still sat at his computer when he came back. Steve slid the headphones from his ears, saying, "Come on, buddy. Time for bed." Tom grumbled but shut down his computer while Steve put away his laundry.

Once he was in bed, Steve couldn't help thinking his son looked like a little boy--one who faced too many adult things. He kissed his forehead. If he was stronger he could ask Tom about the things Val brought up. He couldn't do it. He just said, "I love you, buddy."

Ronnie's light was off, definitely not like him since he usually required a couple five minute warnings before he finally went to bed. After setting down the laundry basket, Steve turned the dimmer switch up a notch.

He'd used the trick enough times himself as a kid to recognize that the lump under Ronnie's covers wasn't his son. Steve's heart skipped a beat as he whirled, tripping over the basket in the hall. He grabbed the phone in his room a minute later. Somehow Ronnie had called a friend for a ride and sneaked back to the hospital.

Steve's frustration warred with his terror that his son had left here by himself. How the hell had he gotten out of the house without Steve seeing or hearing him? Most of Ronnie's friends were high school seniors, so he always had a ride when he wanted one, but Steve didn't like the idea of him unsupervised in a city like Milwaukee. The hospital was only ten, fifteen minutes away by car. Maybe he'd walked, and that thought was worse.

The hospital confirmed Ronnie's presence and told him to hold on. A few minutes later, Steve's sister-in-law Gwen got on the line. "Hi, Steve. Ronnie is here. I was going to call you in a few minutes. I knew as soon as I saw him here he hadn't told you he was going."

Steve closed his eyes as his heart struggled to return to normal rhythm. "What are you doing there so late?"

"I had a feeling I'd be needed," Gwen said, and he felt her smile through the wires. Gwen believed herself to be psychic. She called it "seeing it in her mirror." While Steve didn't put much stock in stuff like that, he couldn't count the number of times he'd found himself believing she possessed more than mere good intuition. "We'll bring him back to you on our way home."

"Thanks, Gwen."

Short of padlocking all the doors of his house from the *inside*, Steve didn't know how to keep Ronnie from leaving anytime he felt like it. Forbidding it wouldn't work. It never had. What the hell could he do?

An hour later, Gwen brought home Ronnie. Accepting Gwen's hug after Ronnie stalked inside and raced up to his room, Steve thanked her for bringing his son home.

"Don't blame yourself," she said softly, and he could barely get himself to meet her eyes. Instead, he greeted her daughter, Allison, who was the same age as Ronnie, and never failed to amaze him how much she looked like both her mother and father.

"They moved Jessie to a regular room," Gwen told him.

Steve nodded uncomfortably. He felt as though Gwen knew his anger was greater than his forgiveness this time, knew he didn't want to deal with Jess' bullshit this time.

"We'll go so you can talk to him." Gwen hugged him again, saying, "It's all right. What you feel is all right, Steve."

He didn't have a single doubt she did know what he felt. Only it didn't seem all right to him. Jessie was sick. She had some kind of disease or disorder or something that drove her to this point over and over. What kind of person would harbor anger for someone who was sick? Even with the validity of Jessie's illness, so often now Steve came back to the fact that her scars were no excuse. Like he'd told Val, it wasn't that simple.

When he went up to Ronnie's room, his son was already in bed, lights out, turned toward the wall. Steve spoke into the darkness. "I don't want you to leave the house like that again, Ron. I need to know where you are and where you're going. When I came up here and found you gone, I was terrified. Anything can happen out there. I can't protect you if I don't know where you are."

"You knew where I went," Ronnie scoffed without moving. "If you'd just let me stay there, I wouldn't have to sneak out."

"It doesn't matter if I did know where you were. I love you, and I don't want anything to happen to you."

Ronnie chose silence, and Steve bled in it.

In the darkness of his own bedroom, he thought about the irony that Val and Tom claimed they'd be okay if he divorced their mother. And Ronnie would never forgive him for as long as he lived.

* * * *

"Daddy!"

Steve had already left his bedroom before he was fully awake. It was the third time he'd gotten up that night at Val's cry. This time, it took longer to soothe her back to sleep, and he knew he wouldn't be able to sleep anymore that night. He'd gotten used to less than four hours of sleep a night, first waiting for Jess, then taking care of the kids. Valerie had been having nightmares, or whatever it was that woke her so often each night, for as long as he could remember. Recently, she'd admitted that a witch haunted her dreams, but she never wanted to talk about it beyond that.

He went downstairs to the cluttered living room that doubled as his office--a room that might have been spacious if not for all that was expected of it. Crammed inside was an upright piano, entertainment center, his desk and laptop along with a sofa bed, two chairs, a coffee table and two end tables covered with mail and magazines.

Turning on the small piano light, Steve sat before the keys without making any motion to play.

"Come to my apartment. Tonight. Have dinner with me. We can talk."

Steve remembered the words suddenly. The person who'd said them appeared in his mind. He'd spent most of the day trying to avoid. That godawful embarrassing memory this morning, in Kristina's office. Originally, he'd intended to talk to Daniel Cook, the department chair, but somehow his feet had taken him across the parking lot to the Drug Crisis Center.

The only people on the campus who knew about his home life were Daniel and Kristina. Daniel had been his mentor as long as he'd been at the college. Talking to him was natural. Yet he'd gone to Kristina this morning, bawled like a baby in her arms.

He'd confided in her briefly in the past. He'd never fallen apart in front of her. Daniel had never even witnessed that from him. And Daniel certainly wouldn't have reacted the way Kristina had.

His throat felt tight as he remembered the feel of Kristina's arms around him, holding him to her breasts. Deep down in a place inside himself that he didn't know well enough to trust, he understood he'd gone to her because she would comfort him the way she had. He'd *needed* comfort. Her comfort. All his friends, his relatives--they all knew Jessie. They knew what she'd been through. He'd always had to assume that their sympathy for both him and Jessie was equal.

Kristina was the only person in the world who sympathized with him and only him. She'd never met Jessie, never even commented on his wife and the things Steve had told her about their marriage. Yet he knew he could count on Kristina's sympathies resting solely with him.

Steve leaned his head against the wood of the piano and allowed himself to remember her selflessness toward him today. She'd cried with him, *for* him. How could one person be so altruistic?

He understood it because the trait ran in his family. Both he and his sister suffered from Good Samaritan Syndrome often. No, actually he and Wendy were more like *addicted* to helping people who couldn't or wouldn't help themselves. Kristina seemed to want to help everybody. It was one of the things Steve most liked about her. The kids on the campus loved her. Even those without drug and alcohol problems went to her because she was the best to talk to. She really cared about them. People weren't just cases to her.

Kristina Ingram was a good person. In some ways, she reminded him of Jessie's brother, Tommie. Tommie had been the one to fix the problems in their group of friends, to talk them down if they were on the edge, to give them what they needed to believe in themselves. Kristina was like that. But Steve wasn't her patient. Why did she do it for him?

He'd confided in her a number of times, but he'd never felt he had the right to ask her about her life. Her *private* life. He'd wondered about it anyway. She wasn't married, he knew that much. He assumed she dated because she was nice, sweet and beautiful--something she tried and failed to hide from her patients at the Center by putting her hair up, wearing neutral clothes and those over-sized, purple framed glasses that slid down her nose every five minutes. She was just a friend, all he could ever feel for her with his life as crazy as it was. But he wondered about her sometimes.

He'd also wondered what she thought of his life. He'd never asked and she certainly hadn't offered her opinion. She was a counselor, but she was also sensitive enough to help only when someone asked.

I've known her for five years, but I don't know the first thing about her.

"Then just come over. Anytime. I'm always here if you need me."

Ah hell, why am I even thinking about this? About her? Jess is in the goddamn hospital again, and I don't know if I can take her back this time. But I can't leave. You want to think, think about that.

He turned, leaning toward his desk to open his laptop, all the while damning himself for wishing he was free to go to Kristina's, where he was accepted, where someone cared about *him.*

Four

A noise in the living room had Kristina shooting to her feet, yanking off the soiled yellow latex gloves she wore to scrub her oven. Her heart beat wildly as she rushed through the swinging door of her kitchen, into the living room and to the front door. When she used the peephole, she was embarrassed to realize she'd imagined it. She'd wanted it to be true so badly, she'd heard what she wanted to hear.

Just to be certain, she unlocked the door and peered out into the hall. At two-thirty in the morning on a weekday, the quiet in the halls of the apartment build was almost surreal. Disappointed, she relocked her door and leaned against the solid oak with a groan.

Had she considered for one moment Steve might take her up on her offer? He had three kids not even in their teens yet. While she suspected he retained a support group of sitters for them, since he was the only parent who worked and cared for the children, he would never come here this late.

He'll never come here period. *Accept it.*

When her cat, a Maine Coon that looked like a giant yellow tabby, came out of the bathroom, Kristina realized what she'd heard that she'd mistaken for a knock at her door--her cat had flushed the toilet. Katrina chirped softly at her. The director at the Center had given Kristina the feline after concluding she wasn't a cat lover any more than she was a rabbit, fish, or bird lover.

Trina sat staring at Kristina, blinking her green eyes tiredly.

"Did I wake you, princess?" Kristina asked, and Trina chirped again at her before coming to curl around her legs once. Then she walked back to the bedroom, where she'd curl up on the bed lazily until breakfast-time.

Kristina sighed before going back into the kitchen to finish cleaning the oven. *Bet Steve's wife never wakes up at all hours of the night and organizes or cleans her house instead of sleeping. Women like Jessie sleep like the dead because they never sleep alone.*

While Kristina had never met Steve's wife, and had absolutely no desire to, she'd seen the woman in magazines. She'd wanted to hate Jessie thoroughly from the first time she'd heard of her, hate her right down to her looks. Unfortunately, Jessie Nelson-Thomas was a woman few females liked for the sole reason they could never compete. Jessie was nothing short of drop-dead gorgeous, every inch of her. If Steve could be considered purely superficial--and maybe at one time in his life he had been--Kristina understood what attracted him to his wife so irresistibly. Assuming that attraction must have worn off, she couldn't understand why he stayed, even if Jessie's behavior was beside the point.

Steve was a man in a rare class by himself. He loved his children completely and unselfishly. They always came first with him. She'd wondered endlessly what kind of a person he'd been before Jessie scarred him so deeply. She imagined him as romantic, kind, gentle, generous, just a bit dangerous.

Maybe she would never really know him the way she wanted to, but a part of her believed she could see into his soul like no one else ever had or ever would. She'd believed that from the very first time she met him.

As she wrapped a paper towel around her hand and dried the inside of the oven, she wondered if Steve remembered the day they met. She recalled it like it'd happened yesterday instead of five years ago.

She'd just started working at the Center a couple days before and emerged from work late one evening. Freezing rain came down, and the pavement leading to the parking lot was so slippery she'd stepped carefully. Nevertheless, both of her feet went out from under her without warning. Her purse and tote bag had flown from her hands.

She supposed now that she'd looked hilarious, but at the time she'd been so totally disoriented by the fall, she didn't collect her thoughts until she heard a voice that pulled her back to reality.

She'd looked up. Someone stood above her. Tall and muscular--she'd noted his strong physique immediately. His face seemed shadowed and carved from stone.

Staring up at him, she'd become even more disoriented. Her head spun and she couldn't breathe or form a coherent thought to save her life.

He asked if she was all right, and she thought, *No. How can I be? I'll never be all right again. I've fallen...for you.*

He leaned down, and picked up her purse and bag. "You okay, honey?" he'd asked again.

Swallowing with difficulty, she tried to speak something along the lines of 'I'm fine. Thanks for asking.' Instead, she heard the words, "Who are you?" emerge from her mouth.

"Steve Thomas. Assistant Faculty. Music Department. Think you can stand, or do you need help up?"

Steve Thomas. Assistant Faculty. Music Department. Steve Thomas. Assistant Faculty. Music Department. Steve Thomas. Assistant...

"I think I need help."

As if his feet were unaffected by the sheer ice, his arms slipped around her and she came erect beside him with little or no cooperation on her part. Her feet slid again once she stood, but he caught her easily, holding her against him until she found her own footing.

When he smiled teasingly, she almost started crying. She'd never been more attracted to anyone in her life. He had shoulder-length, blondish-brown hair that hung around his face, as if he didn't care how he looked. He had more important things to worry about. Yet the carelessness made him look rakish and sexy. Five o'clock shadow followed the strong line of his jaw while thickly tracing his full lips. His brown eyes were haunted yet kind. They made him look old in a sad way, as though life had been hard on him and he carried the weight of the world, despite how heavy it'd become.

"Maybe I should walk you to your car."

She forced herself to laugh, nodding despite the fact that she never wanted to move from this place. The feel of his arms around her, the hard lines of his body against hers, had to be the most perfect union she'd ever experienced.

He kept his arm around her as they walked slowly to her car.

"I'm Kristina. Kristina Ingram. I'm a counselor at the Center. I just started a couple days ago."

He nodded, but she could tell he wasn't paying that much attention to it because he figured he'd probably never see her again after this.

At her little Toyota, she reluctantly took her bags from him. She thanked him and they laughed a little bit more. She memorized as much of him as she could. His black leather jacket, black jeans, dark green shirt. The lines that bracketed his nose and mouth. The flare of his nostrils. *Steve Thomas. Assistant Faculty. Music Department.*

He'd said goodbye, again with that air of finality, and closed her car door. She breathlessly watched him walk to his car before she started her own and drove away at a snail-pace. She'd stared after him until he disappeared from her rearview mirror. Then she re-lived the feel of his strong arms around her, his body against hers, something her mind went back to so often she might never forget.

He must have seen me fall the second he walked out of DeSmet Building, she'd realized then. Instead of being embarrassed, she'd thanked God profusely for the rest of that nearly sleepless night.

She'd never been the type to go out of her way to meet men, talk to them or get them to notice her. She didn't know how to do those things. With Steve, she didn't feel she had a choice. Her heart had chosen him from the minute she laid eyes on him, since he'd literally blocked the sun out with his presence in her life.

The morning after their meeting, she'd asked Hillary if she could get the schedule of one of the Assistant Faculty members from the Music Department. The Center director hadn't understood then why she wanted it, and Kristina's lie didn't make much more sense, but since instructors' schedules weren't kept secret, Hillary had shown her how to call up each schedule on her computer.

From that day forward, Kristina had merged her life to Steve Thomas' schedule. She got to work at the same time he did each morning, she left at the same time he did each night. When he took breaks in the teacher's lounge, she was there whenever she could be. No one had ever questioned her presence in the DeSmet Building, least of all Steve. She knew about his favorite haunt on the campus--a quaint little restaurant called Tilly's, and she knew exactly when he went there. This semester, he went on Monday, Thursday and Friday each week, at two-thirty in the afternoon. She saw him there each time he went, and he'd never wondered why their schedules merged every semester, every week, every day. He always appeared glad to see her. From the first time they'd run into each other after the meeting on the ice, he'd seemed more than glad. Her presence made him happy.

Little by little, he'd told her about himself. Hearing he was married and had three kids should have turned her off. At the very least, his family should have made her back off. It'd done the opposite. She knew he was unhappy. He shared her unhappiness with her, as well as his few joys--like his new Associate status and tenure. She cherished the knowledge that she was one of the bright spots in his life during the school year.

During the summer, she saw him much less often. That was the hardest time of the year for her, but she might see him here and there, since he frequently taught summer courses. She'd taken at least one of the courses he taught every summer and talked to him after class each night. In five years, it was only during the endless summers she doubted their path to the future lay together.

The slightest encouragement kept her going--and the feeling inside that said there was no way she could live if Steve left her life forever. That was her greatest fear. But then she knew herself--she'd probably follow Steve to China if he ended up going there.

Kristina had been told repeatedly the reason she was such a good counselor stemmed from her tenacity. Her stalwart determination to never give up, not even on the hardest, most hopeless cases was the secret to her success.

It's not as if I have suitors lining up at my door anyway. She closed the oven door and shed her rubber gloves. *There's no reason to give up hope I might someday be able to love Steve the way I want to. He came to me today. Me. He trusted me with his deepest pain. Now all I have to do is make sure he knows he can do that anytime, anywhere. There's reason to hope.*

She cleaned up the paper towel, flipped off the lights and went to bed with the memory of Steve's arms lulling her to sleep.

* * * *

Steve dropped his lecture notes on his desk and checked his voice mail messages. Most were left by students asking questions. One was from the coach of Ronnie's community football team.

Ronnie had quit; was Steve aware of that fact? He sighed and sank into his chair. He was aware now. And he'd let it slide with Ronnie, like usual.

It was almost two-thirty. He usually went to Tilly's on Thursdays, since he had an hour free. He knew Kristina would be there. As much as he wanted to see her, he wasn't sure how he'd get himself to look at her. She was a counselor. She probably saw grown men break down in front of her all the time. That fact didn't make it any easier for him to want to face her after he'd been the one to lose control.

She won't act any different. She'll come in the restaurant with that smile like sunshine, and all the tension will disappear.

"Steve, you wanted to talk to me?"

Professor Daniel Cook ducked into Steve's office as if he was on his way somewhere with only a minute to talk. Steve stood quickly and started tidying his desk. His office looked a lot like his home--cluttered, stuffed with junk, and clean only on the surface.

"Just thought I'd drop in to find out what you're plans are tonight."

"Hey, Dan. About the staff meeting..."

"Five-thirty."

"Yeah. I can't make it."

Daniel pushed open the door further and came into the office frowning. Steve knew exactly what he'd say, and he did: "You just made tenure and moved up to Associate, Steve. Skipping meeting isn't exactly going to show your appreciation. Some might wonder..."

...if I deserve tenure and Associate status…if I'm not a team player. Steve had heard it a million times.

"Jessie's in the hospital again." He knew for a fact Ronnie wouldn't wait past five-thirty to see his mother, and, if Steve didn't take him, he'd find some way to get there on his own.

Daniel's well-lined face creased in astonishment. "*Again?* Didn't she just come out of rehabilitation a couple weeks ago?"

Steve barely inclined his head, unable to face his mentor's too wise eyes and far too knowing expression.

Sighing, Daniel nodded, and Steve felt his unvoiced sympathy. "I'll make the necessary excuses for you, Steve. Medical emergency."

Nothing most of them hadn't heard from him before. He knew the rumors about what exactly constituted medical emergency, ranging from cancer, schizophrenic, and alcoholic or drug addict. He'd never confirmed the gossip, avoided the whole issue when it came up, and Daniel somehow guarded his secret without pissing off the executive committee with his ambiguity.

"If you need to talk, you know where to find me."

Steve thanked him before he left. Daniel was a good friend. He took care of him and had for many years. He didn't push when Steve didn't feel like talking, but he was there whenever he did.

So why don't I want to talk to him this time?

He thought of Kristina, walking into Tilly's the way she had for the past five years, approaching him apologetically. *"Am I disturbing you?"* written on her face. She always seemed happy when he invited her to sit with him.

He used to bring work with him to Tilly's. Now he brought the work, but spent the entire time talking to Kristina.

Ah hell, humiliation or no humiliation, he'd go, just like always. He stuffed work into his briefcase, thinking, *Maybe she'll beat me there for once, and then what the hell do I do?*

Five

Kristina flipped through the pages of the book she held, but didn't look away from her vantage across the street from Tilly's for an instant.

Steve was late. He was never late. Had he decided not to come today? Because of his wife? Because of what happened in her office yesterday?

Her chest tightened, and she bit her lip to keep from sobbing out loud. Then she saw him turn the corner, just like usual, his head down, briefcase in hand. The sidewalk was crowded like always on a weekday. He waded through it toward the restaurant.

That Steve brought work with him to Tilly's had never escaped Kristina's notice. The first couple times she'd joined him there, he'd actually had the work out, but hadn't glanced at it again until he gathered and returned it into his briefcase. He didn't bother taking anything out anymore, as if he was waiting for her to join him and make working unnecessary.

Kristina shoved the book she'd used as a cover for her presence in the store onto a shelf, grabbed her tote, and flew outside. Impatiently, she waited for cars to go past before she hurried across the street.

Tilly's was a casual sit-down restaurant that served everything from sandwiches to spaghetti and every snack and beverage known to man. It wasn't the most popular place on the campus, which was why Kristina assumed Steve frequented it.

Steve sat at his--their--usual table. She noticed the waiter held back from asking him for his order until she approached. That someone saw them as something of...well, an *item*, pleased her, but she worried Steve would shy from the appearance.

"You're running late, too," Steve said after she sat across from him in the back booth and the waiter left with their orders.

A moment of worry froze her mind. He was late. He was never late. She *always* showed up three minutes or less after him. If he was late, she was late as well. Would he realize?

"Look, ah..." He shook his head, glancing down at his hands on the scarred oak of the table as if afraid to face her. "I'm sorry about yesterday morning."

Kristina didn't even consider that she was off the hook about her lateness. She reached across the table and took both of his hands in hers. Her intense gaze must have drawn him because he lifted his gaze to her.

"Don't ever apologize for showing me your feelings, Steve. I care about you. It meant so much to me that you opened up to me like that. I want you to know I wasn't a counselor then. I'm a friend. I'm always here for you."

Only until her rush of words halted did she realize she'd said way too much. The expression on Steve's face showed wariness, confusion, and possibly a hint of pleasure.

Flushing, she smiled and forced herself to let go of his hands and bury them in her lap. If she didn't defuse the tension right now, she risked everything.

They were alone in the restaurant, other than the staff, but she glanced around before saying, softly, "Talking to young kids all the time is hard. That's why I hang out in the DeSmet Building and here. I need interaction with adults to keep me sane."

He had to accept *anything* to explain away her words, she realized. What she'd said did nothing to cover the honesty of her words, the intention behind them, which seemed blindingly obvious to her. He nodded, looking relieved instead of more confused. "I understand that. All day, it's kids. College kids. My own kids. I love them, but sometimes it's nice to just be an adult with another adult."

"You don't get that very often, do you?"

Their drinks arrived. Steve removed the straw from the well-iced cola, per his habit, before drinking and shaking his head at her question.

"Neither do I." She poured her carbonated water over the glass of ice. When she glanced up at him after squeezing and dropping the lime into her glass, she noticed where Steve's gaze held, but he averted his eyes quickly. No, she had to be imagining Steve would look at her chest. Or he'd stopped there unintentionally on his way to looking at something else.

Talking herself out of the obvious didn't help her at all. Her nipples tightened at the mere thought of Steve looking at her breasts. He'd never done anything that could be misconstrued as inappropriate with her. Somehow that fact aroused her even more now. Maybe things were changing.

But how could that be? She couldn't find any logic in it. Steve wasn't the type of man for an affair. Not after putting up with his wife's endless affairs over the years. Was he considering a divorce? She had to know! But she couldn't ask him straight-out. She knew part of the reason he liked to talk to her was because she rarely offered advice, analyzed or psychoanalyzed him.

She listened. No one else did that for him.

"But you're married," Kristina said. "You have someone to talk to at least part of the time."

Steve's half grin was mild. "Jess isn't much of a conversationalist. She avoids communication."

I could bleed for him so easily. In a marriage, the worst kind was the one without communication. He was so truly alone in his.

"Was it always that way, if you don't mind me asking?"

He shrugged. "Yeah. We weren't friends. Not even..." He grimaced. "I've known her since she was born. We were neighbors. Her brother was my best friend. She needed me. And I promised Tommie..."

"Her brother?"

Steve nodded, his hands cupped around his sweating glass. "I promised him I'd never get involved with her, but I think he knew all along that it was going that way. She always knew just how to play me."

Kristina held her breath, feeling a little like his wife at the moment--manipulative. She knew the only way to keep Steve talking was to keep her silence.

"She's, hell, she's gorgeous. I don't know if you've ever seen her, but she was like that since we were kids. She should've been like a sister to me, but..." He laughed, obviously humiliated at his own sexual pull to his wife. "I don't remember a time when I didn't want her. She obsessed me. Worse, she made me respond to her vulnerability, the way my daughter does now. Like I'm the only person in the world who can make her feel right, even if it's only temporary. It's always temporary with Jess."

Kristina wanted to ask why Jessie had been vulnerable, but she accepted that now wasn't the time. Instead, she smiled and asked a little playfully, so he wouldn't withdraw, "What were *you* like back then?"

Again Steve laughed in seeming embarrassment, maybe even awed at the difference in himself. "I loved women. I wasn't exactly looking for a commitment back then. I was in and out of relationships, never had my heart broken seriously. I liked waking up to someone familiar, someone I could make happy. I was romantic. It's hard to believe that, but whenever it had to end, I'd think to myself 'There's another girl, always another girl.'"

I want to see that side of you.

Kristina heard the things he didn't say: That he'd been hurt when a relationship ended, but he healed quickly. He didn't have scars from those encounters. His wife gave him all the wounds he carried.

"But then Jess was in trouble all the time. She'd call me, wanting me to bail her out. And I've got the Thomas curse--I fall hard for the one I want to help most. I told myself I was being faithful to my promise to Tommie because he would want me to take care of her. That didn't last long. Not when--"

He didn't finish, but she understood that he'd broken his promise to his best friend by sleeping with Jessie.

"She'd walk out all the time, even during the slightest disagreement, and say I was trying to cage her. But she always came back to me. Idiot that I was, I assumed that meant I was special."

Kristina's heart almost had her hurdling the table in her fervent need to assure him he *was* special. His wife was the idiot.

"Steve, do you have anything for yourself?"

His haunted, soulful eyes met hers, and she could see he didn't really know what she meant. "My kids."

He was sweet, and it was sad that he considered his kids for himself, not for both him and Jessie. His love for and protectiveness toward his children only made her love him more. "No. I mean, something for you. Something *just* for you."

"My job."

He had to consider his job a relief, a refuge from the hell he lived in at home. But he didn't seem to have a clue what she really asked him. Reaching across the table again, she touched his wrist, imagined yet again that he instinctively wanted to let her take his hand, but the flex of his fingers went to his glass instead of her.

"I mean, something outside of your family, your home, your job. Something that has nothing whatsoever to do with any of them, but has everything to do with *you* and how you keep yourself whole and sane."

He held her gaze, even when she knew he wanted to look away. She allowed herself the momentary thrill of believing he thought exactly what she did: *You. You're what I have just for myself. You're my refuge, the glue that keeps me together.*

But then he broke away and said softly, simply, "No."

God, she bled for him so easily.

* * * *

Kristina passed by the lounge at the Center, but backtracked when she saw the Director, Hillary Young, alone in the room. She decided to get her coffee from the lounge instead of making a fresh pot in her office.

Her life was a lot like Sandra Bullock's character in the movie *While You Were Sleeping*, a favorite of hers. She had very few male interests, very few friends. She *dreamed* more than she *did.* She considered Steve her best friend, though there were so many things they didn't know about each other and many private areas they didn't or couldn't talk about. She couldn't be completely honest with him. Her best female friend was Hillary. Despite that she could talk to Hillary about most of the private areas of her life, her friend was so busy with her career and her own life, with a husband and two kids, she didn't have time to indulge in a lot of intimate conversations. Even in high school, Kristina had been the girl everyone came to with their problems, but she had no one she could stay up with all night, eating junk food, and gabbing about everything and nothing.

She wanted to talk to someone now and dropped the hint with a deep sigh as she went to get a paper cup.

"Hmm, a sigh that big means one thing," Hillary said from behind her, at one of the tables. "Yup, Thursday, three-thirty. You must have been at Tilly's with you-know-who."

Suddenly, Kristina didn't feel like talking. She well knew Hillary's opinion of her relationship--imaginary relationship, Hillary would say--with Steve. She didn't want a lecture. Darn it, she wanted to talk to someone.

Without acknowledging Hillary's penchant for ruthless teasing, Kristina opened the door of the snack cupboard to find a cookie to finish the lunch she'd just had with Steve. The shelves were a mess of boxes, bags, and packages put there with little or no thought. She divided the shelves into sweet snacks and salty ones, intending to ignore Hillary if she decided to pursue her ridicule.

"Have you had a date lately?" Hillary asked, moving to the cabinet with her half-empty coffee cup.

Hillary was barely five-four, with a plump, vivacious body that somehow fit her personality. But the sweet expression on her face didn't always match her actions or words.

Kristina shook her head as if it was no big deal.

"How long has it been?" Hillary demanded.

Kristina knew that unyielding tone and wished to God she'd never come in here.

Since you fixed me up with the moron who kept asking me all the places I'd have sex in. That surely killed my enthusiasm for dating. "I don't get a chance to meet a lot of single men my age--"

Hillary shook her head. "Don't give me that *fossil* again, Kris. There're plenty of places to meet good-looking single guys in this city."

"I don't frequent any of them then, I guess."

Hillary filled her cup. She glanced with disapproval at the purple blouse Kristina wore with black slacks. "Is this what you wear when you leave here?"

Kristina thought about the clothing she wore at home--baggy shorts, cami tops, pajamas, occasionally sweats. Then she answered honestly, "No."

"What do you wear to the grocery store?"

"Clothes."

"Really?" Hillary shook her head. "I met LeVar in the grocery store. He said he noticed how sexy I was right away and followed me around the store, trying to think of an excuse to talk to me."

Kristina eyed her supervisor's clothes. Hillary could never be called thin. Sometimes she seemed to wear clothes one size too small. Kristina's body was somewhere between not big and not small. The clothes she wore fit her the way they were supposed to. And, no, she didn't dress sexy at work. She dressed professionally so the kids who came in could never accuse her of leading them on if they developed an infatuation with her. She'd learned that lesson early in life, from male friends who started out wanting her ear and ending up wanting much more than that.

"Whatever happened to that old boyfriend of yours?" Hillary changed the subject abruptly, as if the option just occurred to her. "When did he last come around?"

"Matt? I haven't seen him for at least a year."

Year and a half. You remember. Summer classes hadn't started yet and you hadn't seen Steve in weeks. You remember because you were weak and you'd begun to doubt.

Kristina returned to sorting the snacks, hoping her lack of emphasis would put Hillary off the bone she'd foolishly thrown her.

"Let's get down to the heart of the matter, honeychild. When's the last time you had any sugar?"

Kristina's head whipped toward Hillary in shock, then she rushed to close the door of the lounge. "That's personal, Hillary. What would you say if I asked you the last time you and LeVar..."

"Last night. We took advantage of this gorgeous Indian summer and had our sugar in the hot tub."

Flushing again, Kristina stared at Hillary in alarm, so that her friend chuckled. "There's no shame in it, Kris. The only shame is if you're not getting your share. I'm sensing strongly here that you're not getting your share. It's been that long, baby girl?"

"I have to get back to work. I don't want to have this conversation."

"Don't tell me--" Hillary stared at her, her dark eyes comically wide. "A year? It's been since you last saw Matt Reimann that you've gone to bed with anybody? Damn, girl, no wonder you're interested in the only good-looking guy about your age around this campus, even if he's got a deadbeat wife and three kids. Let me fix you up with someone, Kris--"

"We are not having this conversation," Kristina insisted, walking out of the lounge.

"You'd like him. He's perfect for you--" Hillary yelled after her.

Kristina increased her pace to her office. *She'd have a cow if I told her Matt's not only the last guy I had sex with, but the* only. *Ever.*

Kristina shut the door of her office with an unlady-like, *so there!* snort, and went to her desk. She'd been somewhat relieved about Matt's longer-than-usual absence. He showed up every once in a while, frequently when he was down on his luck. Somehow, he always seemed to know exactly when she was at her most desperate, too. He convinced her too easily she shouldn't waste the attraction they had, and she was needy for a man's arms. Needy enough to have no self-control at all to resist what Matt offered her, no strings attached. When he left, she always felt mitigated and embarrassed.

Dating--she felt the same way each time once the night ended. That she didn't want to do it again anytime soon. *Hmm, imagine what Hillary would say if I told her I have a better time staying home and reading a book.*

Six

Today was no different than any other day, Steve told himself as he followed Kristina's car out of the parking lot. So why did he feel so *weird* tonight, saying goodnight to her?

He wanted to block the memories out, push them down where he'd never have to face them. He spent a lot of time feeling scared, out of control, but it was usually about something that happened. *Nothing* had happened with Kristina, nothing out of the ordinary, and yet...

Nothing *happened, man? You were looking at her chest. You don't do that ordinarily. Hell no.*

He didn't look at Kristina like a man looked at a woman. He looked at her like a friend. So why did he notice the violet tinge of her blue eyes that contrasted so amazingly with her reddish brown hair? Beautiful eyes with thick lashes like sable. She hadn't been wearing her glasses today. Maybe that was why he'd noticed. But her hair had been up, like usual, and he'd seen how rich the color of it was, how silky and thick it looked, the delicate way the strands framed her pretty face. He'd wondered what she felt like--her skin, her hair, her mouth.

And then he'd looked at her breasts, because he remembered how *they'd* felt against his cheek. Soft, with not a damn thing to bind them. Beneath her cotton shirt yesterday, she'd been naked...

Steve clenched the steering wheel in his hands until it felt like it'd snap in two.

Everything had been appropriate up until now. Appropriate. *You didn't do that part consciously even. No, you've been in a goddamn fog for the last ten years, and you liked it just fine that way. You don't notice a woman, you don't want her. You tell yourself it doesn't matter if she's a man or a woman. You don't want anything from her that complicates things more. Appropriate. Now that was simple.*

Like an accusation, his mind surrendered the one inappropriate moment he'd had up until today with Kristina. The image of Kristina in the teacher's lounge in the DeSmet Building, about a year ago, came to him. He'd been working late. She'd said she'd been working late. They'd been alone in the room. She'd started talking about something, God only knew what. At the same time, she'd reached behind her and started unbinding her hair. Long, thick waves of hair tumbled over her shoulders in masses. Up until that point, Steve had never seen her with her hair down. She told him she dressed plain and wore her hair up, wore glasses to discourage her male cases from being interested in her.

As she'd slipped off her glasses that night, he'd realized he'd been fooled by her disguise as well. She wasn't plain. He'd never thought her get-up really worked because she was obviously attractive, but until that moment he'd never realized she wasn't merely pretty or cute.

That night, he'd seen her as a woman. Beautiful, sexy, capable of satisfying any man she set her sights on. He'd noticed her sleek, softly curved body. He'd noticed her breasts, not big, not small. Perfect.

Her nipples had hardened after she'd noticed him looking at her chest today. The restaurant had been overly warm. She couldn't have claimed cold. Hell, he hadn't wanted an explanation. Not then. Now, just contemplating the possibility that his gaze alone might arouse her, he wanted to push it all back down where he'd never have to face any of his guilt.

His body didn't let him off so easily this time. For the first time in years, he not only got an erection, but he couldn't control his arousal at all. The more he tried to rid his mind of memories of Kristina, the more the image of her today and that night a year ago affected him physically.

"Don't ever apologize for showing me your feelings, Steve. I care about you. It meant so much to me that you opened up to me like that. I want you to know I wasn't a counselor then. I'm a friend. I'm always here for you."

His fear increased with the memory of the words she'd said to him in the restaurant. For one minute of horror, he'd believed she had feelings for him. What other explanation could there be for the things she said? He'd allowed her to talk him out of believing that.

What was her explanation? He couldn't remember now. Something about needing to talk to people her age. But that was no explanation for what she'd said.

Did he really *want to* believe she could be interested in a head-case like him? She knew about him, a lot about him. No single, gorgeous woman in her right mind would be attracted to him. Would a single, gorgeous woman in her *right* mind invite him to her apartment again, or invite him to call her at home if he ever needed to talk? Would she do it out of friendship? Or was he some case she wanted to fix? Steve wasn't sure if he liked that explanation any better than the thought of Kristina being attracted to him.

His life was complicated enough. He didn't need--or want--any more problems. And an attraction to Kristina would be a big, goddamn problem.

He drove into his driveway too soon and had to sit there for a few minutes, filling his mind with the image of Jess in bed with another loser to push away the thoughts of Kristina, down into the dark place where all the things he couldn't allow himself to want got crammed.

Inside the house, he found Evangeline in the living room, helping Val with her homework. Valerie came to hug and kiss him immediately. Then he asked Evangeline if Ronnie was home. Even with her assurance that he was upstairs, Steve couldn't get himself to trust it. He went up, knocked on his son's door, then entered. Ronnie looked up from his desk, where he did his homework. He was eager to see his mother and didn't want anything to get in the way of that goal.

"Hey," Steve said in greeting.

Ronnie didn't say anything, just went back to his work. There'd been a time when the kid greeted his appearance with happiness, too, just like Val still did.

"We'll go see your mom right after dinner," Steve gave him exactly what he wanted, softly.

Ronnie bestowed him with his gaze once more, nodding in reluctant gratitude.

Steve pulled the door closed and went down to the kitchen. Tom was there, and Steve couldn't help smiling at the mess he'd made. A recipe book sat open, a box of spaghetti noodles and a jar of sauce next to it, and Tom carefully rolled meatballs that he put in a skillet.

"What's going on here, buddy?" Steve said, moving up behind him and giving his shoulders a squeeze. He smelled cigarette smoke again. Did Tom's new friend Aaron smoke around him? At school? Evangeline picked the kids up from school most days, so he couldn't have been smoking in the car.

"I'm making dinner." His tone sounded unsure.

"You didn't have to do that. Looks like you're doing a great job though."

A rare smile came to Tom's face, and Steve basked in it. "Let me put my stuff on my desk, and I'll finish this up."

Tom shook his head, picking up the skillet and bringing it to the stove. "No. I can do it."

"I appreciate it, Tom, but I don't think you're old enough to use the stove."

"Sure I am. I'll be careful."

Gently, knowing how sensitive Tom could be, Steve said, "I know you would be, buddy, but it's not safe. I don't want you to get hurt."

Just as rare as that smile had been, so was the unguarded look of dejection, *re*jection that crossed Tom's face for only an instant. Then the hurt was gone, and he returned to lock-up mode. He muttered "Whatever" as he left the room.

"Tom--" Steve followed him, already aware it was too late. "You did a great job. Thanks for helping."

Ah, hell. Do you ever do anything right?

Steve slapped his fist against an open cupboard door and it flew back open toward his face. He caught it before it hit him.

"Do you need me any more tonight?" Evangeline asked from the kitchen archway. Evangeline was about five years older than him, unmarried, and everything else he knew about her were the things she'd put on her résumé and he'd found out while checking her references. She was good with the kids, they trusted her and, after a few years with no problems, he trusted her.

Shaking his head, Steve moved over to her, taking money out of his wallet. "Thanks, Evangeline. See you tomorrow."

He finished making dinner, regretting whatever it was he'd done to hurt Tom and unsure how to fix it. His son had heard only that he didn't trust him, not the truth that he wanted to protect him.

Maybe if he could understand more about the human psyche, like Kristina did, he'd be able to help his kids. Instead, all he seemed to do was disappoint them.

"Can I stay overnight at Aaron's after school tomorrow?" Tom asked during a quieter than usual meal. No one seemed to want to talk. Steve's attempts at conversations met dead-ends.

Aaron was new at Tom's school. He'd just started that year. Tom's best friend had always been Timothy Rushing. While the Rushing clan was one Steve avoided for personal reasons, Timothy was a good kid and Steve approved of him. He realized now that Timothy hadn't been around in a while.

If he made another excuse about why Tom couldn't stay at Aaron's, Steve knew it wouldn't be accepted. "I'm not sure about him. I know he's your friend, but I just have a bad feeling about him."

"Why? Because he's got nose rings and hair down to his ass?"

And a foul mouth, don't forget that. 'Ass' was just a word, but Steve found himself lecturing Tom instinctively about swearing.

"You swear when you're mad. Mom does all the time," Tom pointed out, always logical.

What could Steve say? Even though he asked the kids to go in their rooms or outside when he and Jess fought, he never doubted they heard every vicious word anyway.

"Look, I don't think he's good for you. I want you here."

"Why? You don't need me anyway," Tom muttered without looking up from his plate.

Steve's frustration grew, with himself, with his seeming inability to keep his own kids on his good side. Bad enough he was always at odds with his older son. The last thing he wanted was Tom to hate him for some reason or *no* reason. "I said I was afraid you'd burn yourself if you cooked dinner, Tom. I didn't say I don't need you or appreciate what you did. What you do. I didn't mean that at all."

"Whatever," Tom threw out coolly once more.

By the time they left for the hospital, Steve felt like he had nothing left to hold onto. Tom was pissed at him. Ronnie was only complacent because he was getting what he wanted. Val complained again about not wanting to see her mother.

It wasn't until they entered Jessie's room that Steve wondered why the hell he put them through it. Why force the kids to see their mother? Why coerce them into the ordeal?

Instead of alienating everyone tonight, Jessie was needy and acted like her kids were her whole life. Valerie and Tom allowed her hugs and kisses but moved into the corner of the room as soon as she let them go and turned her fickle attention on her older son.

Steve watched her, and his anger grew because he knew what was next. As soon as she got what she needed from Ronnie, she'd turned her attention to begging Steve for his forgiveness. And, goddamn it all, he didn't want to give it to her. He wanted to hold it out to her like a prize, then take it from her every single time she got close enough to reach. He wanted to be cruel, as cruel as she'd been to him, in word and in deed.

Because he didn't have that ruthlessness in him, he avoided her every attempt to catch his gaze. Even when she asked the kids to leave them alone for a minute, he refused to turn in her direction.

"I'm sorry," she said as soon as the door closed them alone in the room together. Her throat sounded hoarse and, for once inadvertently, sexy. "Don't be mad at me, Steve. I'll do whatever you want."

He couldn't help his snort at her temporary pacification.

"Say something, dammit," she begged finally, as if his silence drove her to insanity.

Steve glanced at her in disbelief. She sat up on the bed, her wide, full mouth pouting at his anger. It didn't affect him at all anymore.

"What the hell do you want me to say? I found you in bed, in *our* bed, with another guy. Our son saw you. You had a goddamn needle sticking out of your arm and you could have been dead for all he knew. But you weren't thinking about any of us then, were you? You know damn well that this was far from the first time. How many times do you think you can do this to me? To us? How many times do you think we should forgive you?"

"*They* forgave me."

"Ronnie did."

"Pussy-whipped by your own mother." Steve cringed at the memory of Tom's words.

"Come here," she said softly, and Steve met her eyes. He knew exactly what would happen if he went to her. Not for one minute did he consider going either. He shook his head.

"I just...shit, I was back there, at Nelson Industries. I was fucking *there* and all this crap came down on me."

Her parents owned a multi-million dollar company, something that had taken up all their time when Jessie and Tommie were kids. Servants had raised the two of them. After Tommie's death, their parents realized the error of their ways and asked Jessie to take over the company. They saw her acceptance of the family business as her forgiveness of them. Jessie went to work for them whenever she was clean, but she'd never taken over the reins of the company. She had a deep-seated need to punish them forever.

"Dammit, Steve, I'll make it up to you. I promise. That'll never happen again. Just don't...please don't leave me. Not now."

He couldn't take her promises or her tears, the ones she turned on so easily. The betrayal he felt pushed up from under his skin like sharp blades. He looked away from her, knowing he had to leave the room. "Just worry about getting clean again," he said under his breath, walking out even though--hell, *because*--she was weeping.

Ronnie waited right outside the door and darted into the room when Steve emerged. He saw Tom and Val slumped in chairs in the waiting room and decided he wouldn't drag them here anymore. If they didn't want to come, he'd drop them off with Gwen. Since Allison was Val's best friend, despite the four-year age difference between them, she'd agree in a heartbeat. Tom would agree just so he wouldn't have to come here.

At that decision, he felt his anger lessen. Part of his fury came down to shame--shame about his feelings for Kristina earlier. The anger came from wondering why he had to feel ashamed. For anything. He hadn't done anything about those feelings he'd had. He'd let them go. And his friendship with Kristina wasn't inappropriate in any sense of the word. His friendship with her was a good thing.

He hadn't voiced his thoughts then, pushed them forcefully out of his own mind instead, but when Kristina asked him if he had something just for himself, his first realization was, *This. You.*

The time we spend together is just for me. You don't side with Jess at all. You're mine.

Because he'd been afraid she'd misconstrue his meaning, especially after those things she'd said about caring for him, he'd said he didn't have anything just for himself. But *she* was his refuge. When it all came down on him, he went to her for comfort. He went for himself.

Instead of going into the waiting room, Steve found himself heading for a payphone. A minute later, Gwen got on the line. He asked her if she'd mind coming over tonight and staying with the kids for a couple hours.

Even as he did it, Steve tried not to think about why he was doing it. The guilt came when Val asked him and he heard himself offering what he had a thousand times before--legitimately. He told her he had a recital, and all the kids accepted it.

By the time they got home, Gwen had arrived with Allison and told him he didn't have to hurry back. He found himself walking to his car, wondering if he could really do what he'd set out to do or if he'd end up in his office, experiencing equal amounts of relief and regret for his own cowardice.

* * * *

"I'm fine, Mom. You're not hearing anything in my voice," Kristina insisted, regretting that she'd allowed her loneliness to slip through her tone when she'd answered the phone.

"Are you sure, darling? Because if you prefer not to live alone, or if you just can't afford to, your room is still exactly the same as when you left."

Kristina tried not to laugh at the mere idea of moving back to her parents' home in Elm Grove. Despite her mother's pleas to continue her education closer to home, she'd moved out the year she started college in Chicago.

"Mom, I'm thirty years old. I enjoy my independence. And I can certainly afford my rent."

Her mother wouldn't say what her father would in a heartbeat: if she'd finished law school and passed the bar, she could have had a ritzy condo or a two-story, marble and hardwood floored home with five bedrooms, a breakfast terrace, and an acre of property to spare.

She liked her apartment, be it ever so humble. It was located in a good neighborhood in Brookfield, not too far from the university. Her landlord had allowed her to have some professional renovation done, at her own expense, to her tastes. The living room that opened onto a third-story balcony had floor to ceiling, built-in bookshelves, and a ventless fireplace with a mantel. In the past five years, this comfortably-sized space had become a home to her and her many adopted pets.

"How is Dad?" Kristina asked, mostly out of politeness. She didn't want to tell her own mother she couldn't bear to be in the same room as her father, let alone have a conversation with him. Her mother knew that was the case anyway, without the words. After having spent so much time being at odds with him, Kristina had accepted that her father's love for her rested entirely on whether or not she did what he wanted her to do. He'd been perfectly happy to never see her again during her years of college.

She'd only come back to live here and work because her mother had been diagnosed with Parkinson's Disease and because she'd missed the city she'd lived in all her life save her college years. Eisner University had hired her out of hundreds of applicants, and she loved her job. She couldn't imagine ever moving again. Here, she had a life she loved and she could be close to the people she loved.

"You know your father. He never changes, darling."

Translation: *He's been grousing about your job again--an obvious dead-end--and about you, the non-lawyer, who threw it all away for nothing.*

"I'm calling because our anniversary is in a couple weeks and we'll be having a party. Please tell me you can make it."

Legitimate as the announcement was, Kristina didn't doubt the invitation was a pretense for her call. She'd be seeing her mother in the morning for an early breakfast. She could have told her then. Kristina accepted that her mother was worried about her because she didn't date, had few friends, and didn't have a life in the single, fancy-free sense.

The anniversary would be another no-way-out-of-it occasion. Kristina sighed, playing with the string on her loose jogging pants. At some point during the party, her father would pull her aside and try to talk her into leaving her job to go back to law school. She couldn't avoid it.

"All right, Mom. Will you be sending an invitation so I can put it on my calendar?"

"They'll go out next week. I'll try to talk to your father--"

"You said it yourself, Mom. He'll never change."

"I'm sorry, Kristina darling."

"I know. How are you?"

"Good days and bad days. You know how it goes. Elise helps me though. I'm not sure what I would do without her."

As soon as her mother had been diagnosed, her father had hired a full-time nurse who lived in the house with them and took care of her mother. *Like him or not, there's no doubt Dad loves Mom,* Kristina conceded. He'd fallen in love with her right out of law school. She'd been a paralegal. He'd married her, provided everything she could ever want and need, and he always made time for her, regardless of how hectic his schedule was. Even in public he adored her. Their relationship had set the groundwork for Kristina's ideal of marriage.

"You know you can call me if you need anything."

"I know, Mom. See you at the house in the morning."

"Yes, see you then. I love you, Kristina."

"I love you, too, Mom. 'Night."

Kristina hung up, barely having a moment to reflect on the conversation before she heard a knock on her door.

Hillary. She'd expected Hillary to come to her office or waylay her in the parking lot with that insufferable address book of hers. Kristina had dated most of the young, single men Hillary knew. She'd learned her lesson.

Standing, Kristina inched her ruffle-edged cami top down and went to the door. As soon as she put her eye to the peephole, she let out an instinctive squeak of shock. *Steve. Steve Thomas. At my door. Right this minute. Looking like he wants to run!*

That made her yank the door open, only the chain lock had been pulled earlier, and she didn't get far. Blushing, she murmured, "Sorry! Hold on." She closed the door again and unlocked it.

Her entire body felt as though it was made of tiny firecrackers. Every nerve jumped under her skin, and she became afraid she couldn't control herself.

"I have no idea why I'm here," he said softly, looking at least as embarrassed as she felt.

Her mouth dry, she asked, "You don't know?"

He shrugged. "To talk. Take you up on your offer."

"Come in."

He pushed himself off the wall he leaned on next to the door and came in. Kristina watched his rigid back, then carefully closed her door. *No, I shouldn't even think it, but there's no way I* can't *think it. What if he's here for...for an affair? Worse, a one-night stand?*

Never once had she considered an affair, let alone a one-time experience. She'd considered being Steve's best friend for as long as it took. She'd considered him leaving his wife and pledging his life to her instead.

He's never been anything but...yeah, it fits--appropriate to me. To our "colleague friendship." He doesn't seem like he came here for sex. He's staring around my apartment like he's as uptight as I am.

Kristina accepted shamefully that she couldn't refuse him. If he reached for her, touched her in any way, she would be helpless to resist him. But she'd lose respect for herself as well as for him if that happened.

Sex for the sake of sex or for revenge would leave him humiliated. He'd regret it tomorrow. He'd never be able to face her again. She couldn't take a risk that pivotal.

Even if he'd had some crazy notion of coming here for sexual comfort, she would steer him away from thoughts like that. It just might kill her, but she'd give him all the emotional comfort he could handle. She'd be true to the trust he put in her by being strong enough to refuse, if it came to that.

"You've got a lot of pets," he said, looking from her two fish tanks--one saltwater, one fresh--to the powder-blue parakeet perched on the bar of the balcony blinds, to Trina curled up comfortably on the sofa.

"I also have a rabbit. Hillary, the director at the Center, says she's looking for the perfect companion. So far, the fish, rabbit, parakeet, and cat aren't it, and her husband doesn't like dogs. I've been adopting them. I'm just glad she hasn't thought of a snake yet."

Steve laughed, and it took Kristina a minute to realize she'd said anything funny. *Relax. He's here. He's finally here. He trusts you that much. He wants to talk to you and share his heart. All you have to do is relax and make good on that trust.*

Yeah, that was all. Easier said than done.

Seven

He shouldn't have come here. He should have been a coward. Seeing Kristina in those purple sweat pants that dipped so low, he knew she couldn't be wearing anything under them told him that first thing. The short, tight shirt that showed off her concave, well-tanned stomach finished the job.

Shows off more than her belly-button earring.

Something Steve hadn't thought about for over a decade, maybe more, came to him: His bedroom as a teenager. Clean only on the surface. Clothes, records, sheet music, and instruments everywhere. On the inside of his closet door, he'd had a poster that'd been his ultimate fantasy back then and throughout college. A naked brunette on skis. She'd had not-big-not-small breasts that curved upward in a horn of plenty shape, ending with rosy red nipples. He'd never met a real-life woman shaped like that. *Before now.*

Kristina's tiny top was thin, white, ribbed, but she couldn't hide the fact that she wasn't wearing a bra. Why should she? She'd been relaxing for the night until he arrived. She could dress any damn well she pleased. She'd asked him here, but she'd never expected him to come. The last thing she deserved was him ogling her now that he had accepted the invitation.

She blushed, adorably nervous. He had a strong feeling she thought maybe he'd come here for sex--something that'd never crossed his mind until she opened the door. He'd thought about it then, dammit. Hell yeah, he had.

He turned away and looked around her apartment. She had hardwood floors, covered with fringed rugs of all shapes and colors, mostly shades of purple. Every wall except the fireplace/balcony one had floor-to-ceiling bookshelves, neat as a library. The shelves bracketing the fireplace held a TV, a deluxe stereo, and a CD collection that could rival his own. Because he was afraid to look at her, afraid his body would respond the way he'd thought it'd forgotten to long ago, he made a half circle around the sofa and looked at her CDs. Classical. Mostly classical. Some soft rock...

He felt, more than saw, her come to stand beside him by the fireplace. "Can an Associate Professor of music studies tell something about a person by their music collection?" Kristina said.

"Yeah. You're organized. Noticed that right away." All her classical CDs were organized alphabetically by the composer's last name.

Kristina laughed as though embarrassed by her extreme tidiness.

"You like Classical. You've got refined tastes." He pointed to the mid- to lower shelf levels. "But here we start to see you're not all uptight sophistication. You like some emotional music. Soft rock ballads--" He pulled a compilation CD out halfway. "You're a romantic. Hmm, these are out of place."

"Something is out of place?" She darted closer, a look of disbelief on her face. He pointed to her Gregg Stevens' CDs. "Oh. You said you were a friend of Gregg's, so I thought I'd try them out. I've never known a world-famous musician before. I guess I don't know Gregg either, but it's as close as I'll ever come."

"What do you think?"

"Of his music?" She pushed her glasses back up on her nose. A second later, they slipped back to the end of her small nose. "Most of it is really good. The lyrics are wonderful. But I think he's more guitar-driven than I am. My mom used to call that 'long-haired music'."

Steve chuckled at her mild understatement.

"Were the two of you in a band together at one time? I thought you told me that."

"Yeah. When I was in college. I had to give it up."

She looked like she wanted him to go on, but he wasn't sure he wanted to talk about what remained something of a sore subject with him.

"Imagine if you'd stayed in the band," she said. "You would be as famous as he is now."

No, that wouldn't have happened. Steve had accepted the truth long ago, but he'd never liked it. He nodded at Kristina anyway, shrugging. "Maybe."

He glanced at the bottom of her CD shelves, then squatted down by them to pull out the CDs there. "Bottom of your shelves is always where your least favorites go." The CDs at the bottom of her collection were the ones she'd bought in connection with the course he'd taught last summer, Introduction to Cool Jazz. "Decided you weren't a fan?"

Blushing, she stumbled to make an excuse about why she'd taken the class, but he just shook his head. "I'm not much a jazz fan either. I've studied it. I listen to it occasionally, but it's not really my thing. At least you learned something from the class."

He forced himself to stand because he was eye-to-earring with the gold hoop in her outie belly-button. He found the nose rings Tom's friend Aaron wore disgusting. Kristina's wasn't. Not by a long shot.

"Do you want to sit down?"

Hell, he couldn't stand here and comment on her CDs all day. They walked around the couch from opposite sides, sat at opposite ends. She tucked her legs under her, facing him, her breasts bouncing lightly. Steve clenched his hands to keep himself from reacting to the thought, *She's not wearing a bra. That tiny top slips up another millimeter, and I'm a candidate for the loony bin.*

"I didn't expect you to be here," he said the first thing that came into his head. Her mega-cat stood between them, stretched, then stepped into Kristina's lap and covered her chest and belly almost completely. Steve breathed a mental sigh of relief.

"Where did you expect me to be?" Kristina asked, easing off her glasses and setting them on the coffee table. When she put her face against the cat's and stroked it with her cheek, Steve saw the color of her eyes clearly. Blue. Violet. A little of both, thickly fringed with those cherry-wood, rich lashes. Even her silky brows qualified as beautiful, arching slightly over her beautiful eyes. Her hair hung loose for once, spilling over her shoulders in exuberantly free waves.

You don't give yourself enough credit, honey. You think if you bind your hair up and put those big glasses on no one can tell how attractive you are. You think they conceal your beauty when all they really do is intrigue everyone who looks at you. Even the professional wardrobe just adds to the intrigue.

Steve looked past her, shrugging though he felt anything but casual. "I don't know. You're single. You're young. You're beautiful." He didn't want to say that last part. He couldn't stop himself from it and kicked himself immediately after, especially when her expression blended two completely different emotions: pleasure and wariness. Maybe she liked hearing she was beautiful, but she'd begun to think he'd come here for sex. For some reason, he knew she believed it.

"I don't usually date on weekdays," she said in barely a whisper. "Actually, I don't date much at all. I'm not comfortable *out there.* It all seems too fast to me. Whatever happened to dating for long periods of time and just enjoying each other's company? Now it's all sleeping together to find out if you're compatible that way *first*, instead of getting to know each other and then jumping into the physical aspects. Nothing seems to last anyway." She buried her face in her cat's thick white bib.

Steve had looked at her, long before he'd allowed himself to really see her. Now that he had, he realized looking didn't seem like enough. He didn't want to, but the urge to touch her came over him as he watched her. He wanted to cup her face in his hand, explore her face with his fingertips, trace her eyebrows, the lines bracketing her smile and her soft, sweet lips.

"So what's happening?" she asked gently. "Is your wife out of the hospital?"

Ice water. All over him. He didn't want to talk about Jess. Not tonight. Somehow, that felt like giving her exactly what she wanted. "No. Kids are with Jessie's sister-in-law at the house." He sat forward, suddenly feeling so tired he could barely keep his eyes open. He rubbed his face with his hands. "I've put them to bed almost every night of their life. I can't stay long." Val would wake up, more than once, and he had to be there when she did to push back the darkness for her.

"I'm sorry," he started, before Kristina scooted over closer to him. He felt so locked up, he was convinced his spirit had left his old body and taken this one instead--one he didn't recognize, didn't understand, and couldn't control. "I'm sorry I came here 'cause you're the only person..." He shook his head, glancing at her.

She sat so close, her skin smelled like flowers. A whole meadow of them blooming in the sunshine. He closed his eyes and thought, *Sex. Even if I came for that and Kristina agreed, I don't know what the hell to do anymore. And I'll never give Jess the satisfaction of thinking I'm just like her.*

"I'm the only person who *what*?" Kristina prompted.

"All my friends, all the ones I grew up with, the ones who've always been there and always will be...they understand what I've been through. They understand what Jess has been through. You've never met Jess, and maybe you don't feel anything about her one way or the other--"

"I despise her."

Steve turned again, this time with his whole body, and she seemed close enough to kiss. "What?"

A dull red settled hard into her cheeks. "I despise your wife. I don't know her. I don't know her side of it. But I know she's hurt you. She's hurt your children. She doesn't give you or your kids the respect, love, or loyalty you deserve. I despise her for the scars she's given all of you."

He couldn't move when Kristina's warm, smooth fingers touched his jaw, cupping one side of his face in a tenderness he couldn't remember feeling for so long it might as well have been forever. He wanted to put himself in her hand, ask her to touch him and heal him with her balm.

He couldn't need this woman, let alone want her. He couldn't move away.

"You're the only person on my side. My side alone. Even Dan at the college. I've known him for so long, and he knows Jess. I know it's not fair, but you don't know how damn good it feels to have another adult on my side. And I know it's not fair to put it on you--why should you even want it? But right now I don't have much. I don't have anything for myself. Anything but you. I don't even know what that means, but you've been a friend to me. I'll never be able to thank you enough for that."

Tears hung at the edges of her lashes, but she tried to hold them back, smiling as she said, "You were the first person I met when I came to work at the university. Your friendship is important to me, Steve. It means so much to me that you trust me. I don't have a lot of friendships, but the ones I have last a lifetime."

He shook his head, disgusted with himself. "It's one-sided."

"What is?" she asked, reaching for a tissue from the purple box on the coffee table.

"This friendship. I'm always loading you down with my problems. You probably feel like you can't say anything to me about your life. Straw that broke the camel's back." He said it lightly.

She smiled sadly, dabbing at her eyes. She'd drawn back enough that he could breathe again without wanting.

"My life is an open book. And it's a boring one," she told him. "I work, I buy stuff for my apartment, I eat dinner alone almost every night. The people who might be considered friends of mine have their own lives. When they go home for the night, well, why should they give me a thought? I certainly don't expect them to."

It didn't sound fair or believable. A person like Kristina, warm, caring and nice, should have more of a life than that. She shouldn't be lonely.

She shrugged, making her loneliness count less than he sensed it really did. "You've already figured out that I love classical music and soft rock. Not a fan of jazz. I'm sure you noticed I love purple--anything purple."

He didn't want to know what her favorite food or color was. He didn't even want to know where she ate dinner every night, alone. He wanted to know why she adopted her bosses' pets instead of letting them be put in a homeless animal shelter or sold off. He wanted to know why she had few friends who didn't spare her a thought at the end of the day. He wanted to know why she cared about him so much and considered his friendship meaningful. He wanted to know. Yet he didn't.

"Where are my manners? Let me get you something to drink," she said suddenly in his pause. "I have just about everything, so name it and I'll get it for you. Diet cola? You drink that at Tilly's all the time."

He needed a minute alone, so he nodded. Keeping himself from watching her go into her kitchen wasn't possible, but he pushed the heels of his hands against his eyes when she disappeared behind the swinging door.

What are you doing here? You've got friends. Plenty of friends. And you're not attracted to even one of them. They're safe. You don't need this. Walk away now, before something happens you'll never forgive yourself for.

Steve leaned back on the couch, closing his eyes to stop the lecture. He was exhausted. He hadn't slept much the night before, between Val and the things he'd had to do. Now he just wanted to shut it all off. He had to go home. Be there for Val. Be there when the kids got up for school tomorrow. He had too much to do.

* * * *

Steve hadn't awakened by the time Kristina showered and dressed for work. As she hadn't been able to the night before, she couldn't get herself to wake him now either. For years she'd had a strong suspicion he slept very little--and not simply because she knew all his responsibilities with his kids, work, the house. *His wife.* He always looked exhausted. His eyes were ringed by shadows, and he had the look of someone who hadn't had eight hours sleep in a row for so long he'd forgotten how refreshing it could be.

She'd come out of the kitchen last night to find him asleep, as if in mid-thought. Helplessly, she'd looked at him and smiled, murmuring under her breath a line from one of her favorite romantic movies--"He sleeps."

After a few minutes of watching him, wondering if he'd wake, she'd taken the cold drinks back into the kitchen. He hadn't even stirred a half-hour later, when she'd put a blanket over him. She'd wanted to look at him forever, look at him *at peace* for the first time in all the time she'd known him.

Instead, she'd dimmed the lights, locked the door, and went to bed herself. A sleepless hour later, she'd come back. He'd only moved to put his feet up with him on the sofa, probably without regaining consciousness. She knew if he woke, he'd be horrified and leave. Kristina had wondered if she shouldn't ask him if he needed to call home, but then she'd reminded herself what she knew of Steve. Whoever he put in charge of his kids was utterly trustworthy. They knew where he was or could page him if they needed him. No one had called.

In the shadows of her living room, she'd looked at him, thinking, *Even in sleep, probably the deepest sleep he's had in a long while, his expression is tense. He looks like he's waiting to bolt upright for any reason.*

Yet he slept on, regaining partial consciousness only twice during the night. The first time he'd muttered, "It's okay, baby, Daddy's coming." The next time, he'd said, "I'm here, Val. I'm here, baby. Go back to sleep." Both times, Kristina had soothed him with a whisper and light touch to his brow.

He'd spoken to his daughter, his youngest child, Valerie. Kristina's training as a psychologist had forced her to wonder about what he said. Did his daughter wake often during the night and need consolation from him? Why? What had traumatized her so much? Whatever it was, she knew Steve had done everything in his power to reassure Valerie. He wasn't the cause of her trauma. Kristina would stake her life on that.

However unbelievable, many parents couldn't conceive of the scars they caused their children with their fighting, be it verbal, mental, or physical. Most of Kristina's patients had experienced some degree of childhood trauma that led them to deal with their problems by using drugs and alcohol. Because Steve had said the words in his sleep and hadn't asked her for advice about the situation that caused it, Kristina couldn't talk to him about it. She'd have to wait for him to bring it up, if he ever did.

Kristina got her purse, uncertain whether to allow him to continue the sleep he desperately needed or to wake him. At the last minute, she wrote a note, which she propped on the coffee table in front of the sofa. She would be late for breakfast with her mother, she reminded herself as she continued to look at him.

Last night had been a dream come true for her. Steve had come to her. He'd been uneasy about it, but he'd opened up to her, admitted that her friendship was important to him. She didn't want this new forging to end. But it wouldn't, would it? Yet he'd said he didn't want their relationship to be one-sided.

Crouching in front of him, she smiled sadly as, only in her mind, she traced the lines on his face. What she wouldn't give to soothe every worry from his life.

Soft as a butterfly wing, she pressed her lips to the corner of his eyebrow.

He stirred. She backed away and had to convince herself on the way out of her apartment that the lines in his face hadn't eased with her kiss.

As she started her car, she wondered what he would feel when he woke up and found himself still on her couch. Barely six o'clock, still early, not having her there might provide him with less stress over where he'd spent the night.

As she drove to Elm Grove, she re-played the night over and over in her mind. *"You're single. You're young. You're beautiful."* Steve thought she was beautiful. He was attracted to her, even though she knew with certainty he didn't want to be. She'd seen the way he looked at her. The way he avoided looking at her was just as obvious.

Instead of being disappointed by his reluctance, her estimation of him as a man had increased. Steve was well aware he was married. His marriage wasn't a good one, yet he'd made promises he kept valiantly. He didn't forget his vows or principles out of desire or even anger. She'd never respected him more.

While her mind screamed, *"She's making you and your children miserable, she'll obviously never change--she's proved that at least a hundred times over, why don't you divorce her?"*, she knew Steve must have good reasons for staying in the marriage. Someday, maybe he'd trust her enough to share those reasons with her.

Eight

Steve sat up straight when something big landed on him and chirped loudly in his face. For a second, he could only stare at the giant cat and wonder if he was having a nightmare. He'd never heard a cat make such a strange noise before. Then he looked around. *Kristina's apartment.*

It was a nightmare, but it was also reality.

Steve gently pushed the cat off him, along with the blanket, and forced himself to his feet. It was quarter after six in the morning. If he left here now, he could be home before his kids woke up. The last thing he wanted was to face Ronnie right now. What the hell could he say that wouldn't be twisted into a crime he hadn't committed?

Where was Kristina? She usually got to work around seven, the same time he did. Was she still asleep?

Then he saw the note card propped up on the coffee table. His name was written on it. A little wary, he picked it up, opened it and read: *Good morning. I didn't have the heart to wake you, you seemed so tired. I was sure if there was a problem at home, someone would know how to contact you. I had to leave early to meet my mother for breakfast. Make yourself at home, though I have no doubt you'll leave as soon as you wake. Last night meant a lot to me. I'll see you later today. Kristina*

Steve set the note on the coffee table, flat, so she'd know he read it. He couldn't keep it. If Ronnie saw it, he'd assume "Last night meant a lot to me" meant more, or less, depending on the point of view, than it really did.

He had to get out of here. He folded the blanket and punched up the pillows on the sofa, embarrassed about his inability to keep awake last night. He hadn't slept much the night before or the night before that. Kristina must have wondered what was wrong with him. First he showed up out of nowhere, tense as hell, then she couldn't help but wonder if he'd come for sex. Finally, he'd fallen dead-asleep on her couch.

Later, she'd wonder what was wrong with him, too. He was selfish. Her friendship had been easier to accept when it required nothing of him. How could he continue this relationship with her? If he allowed it to grow, if he got to know her outside of the unselfish shoulder he cried on when all the shit came down on him, he'd start to like her. He'd *really* like her. It was a risk he couldn't take. His life had enough complications.

Turning the lock on the knob and closing the apartment door behind him, he walked down to his car. *She let me sleep because she "didn't have the heart" to wake me. She covered me with a blanket while I slept on her couch. She left a note, a nice, sweet note that tried to erase how mortifying it was for me to wake up in her apartment.*

He remembered something else as well. A kiss. On his forehead. *Or maybe her cat was getting friendly.*

What the hell would he tell Gwen? He fell asleep in his office after the recital? She was a light sleeper. She'd know he hadn't come home last night, even if he did manage to slip in without waking her, shower and get into fresh clothes.

When he walked in the house, just like he thought, Gwen was awake, showered, and poking around the cupboards for something to feed the kids. He could barely look at her. Her gaze was nowhere near accusing, yet he couldn't face her smile. He started to say something, some half-assed excuse that would convict him even as he said it, but she waved it away. "It was no problem. We had a good time. I love spending time with your kids. So does Ally."

"Are they still sleeping?"

She nodded. "Go ahead and get showered. I'll start breakfast. Then you can get them up for school."

She knows. Steve went up to his bedroom. *She might not know who, but she knows I was with a woman last night. She might even know it was platonic. I think it was anyway.*

"Thanks," he said when he came down later. "Nothing happened. I just fell asleep."

"I know, Steve. Don't feel like you have to explain yourself to me. I know you." She turned from him to pour his coffee. "I know Jessie," she said softly, her eyes expressive when she looked at him again.

Even with Gwen's pardon, Steve couldn't get himself to go to Tilly's that day. The time he usually went passed like alarms going berserk. Ignoring them only seemed to make them worse. He imagined disappointing Kristina after all she'd done for him, and it made him feel like he might lose his mind. He didn't deserve her friendship or her genuine concern.

His gofer, Garret, walked into his office without knocking, as usual. Garret was a student working toward his masters. He was young, wiry and, in Steve's day, he would have looked like a geek to the girls. In his own generation, Garret was a heartbreaker.

Steve dragged his gaze away from the clock to greet him.

"Handouts you wanted. And I set up the music stands," Garret said, unloading a stack on Steve's desk.

"Thanks."

"You look like hell. Worse than usual," Garret said with his usual lack of tact. "What are you doing here anyway? It's Friday. You go to lunch at Tilly's at two-thirty."

Steve shrugged, offering the lame excuse of, "Things to do."

"I know your schedule, at least the one in your daykeeper. You don't have anything to do that you're not making yourself do. What's up?"

"Nothing. I'm tired." *Not too ironic, since you actually slept your forbidden eight hours last night.*

"You know what you need?"

Steve grinned at the cocky kid who reminded him of himself in college. "In your estimation? I can guess. Garret's answer to everything that ails you."

"You need to--"

"--get laid," Steve said with him.

Garret pointed at him like he was saying Bingo. "Re-focuses your mind inward. Relaxes you. Puts you to sleep like a baby after. You can't lose. I'm telling you, dude."

You *can't lose.* I *can.*

A tap on his door was followed by Kristina putting her head in. She apologized, her expression more chagrined than it needed to be as soon as she saw he wasn't alone. Garret sweet-talked her out of coming back later.

Embarrassed, Steve glanced at the clock. It was three o'clock. Had she gone to Tilly's, waited for a half-hour, then came here?

After eyeing Kristina from every interesting angle, Garret abandoned Steve to his own weakness. She smiled uncertainly as the door closed behind Garret. "I'm sorry for interrupting."

"I'm sorry for falling asleep on your couch."

She shook her head. "Don't be. You looked like you could use some rest. It wasn't an imposition at all." Her smile wavered. He understood she didn't seem aware why he didn't know how to face her.

"Are you regretting it? Coming to my apartment last night?"

Steve heard the tension in her voice, almost fear, and those things made everything worse. Why the hell did she need him as a friend? She *didn't.* Whatever she wanted or expected, he couldn't give her.

"Look, Steve, I know you think this friendship is all one-sided, but don't feel that way. I don't want anything from you. I'm not even asking for anything except friendship. Nothing more."

"I don't know if I'm capable of that," he said because he had to say it. She deserved that much at least.

"That's all right."

Why? Why is it all right? he wanted to demand. But he couldn't take that last step to drive her away.

"I can see you're busy this afternoon, but maybe you'd like to join me for dinner tonight? There's this place only a block from where I live, Feng Shui. Trendy name, but good food. Around six o'clock?"

Her glasses had slipped down her nose again, and he fought the urge to stand up, push them back where they belonged or fling them off altogether. And, while he was in the grip of insanity, tell her he'd be there at six sharp.

"I'm sorry, Kristina. I don't want to hurt you, but I can't. I've got too much stuff--"

"No problem. I'll see you. Take care."

In less than a second, she flew out the door with her pasted-on, I'm-not-offended smile. Steve didn't have a single doubt he'd done what he'd never wanted to. He'd hurt her. He might have made her cry.

Hell, maybe it was for the best. As much as he wanted to go after her, making up would complicate everything further. If he had to *see* her cry--

"Who was that?" Garret ducked back in to ask. "Is she a student? Or does she work on the campus?"

Steve found his protective instincts rising. He shook his head. "She's too nice for you, Garret, that's what she is."

"That's what they all say. Next thing you know, they're handcuffing you to the bed."

"Seriously. Stay away from her."

Garret raised a busy eyebrow. "Saving her for yourself?"

"Go. Now."

Steve knew for a fact Garret would discover all about Kristina before the day was out. And it bothered him more than he wanted to admit to himself.

* * * *

Gwen's car, not Evangeline's, was parked in front of the house when Steve got home that night. He knew she'd left that morning, taking all the kids to school on her way.

She was talking on her cell phone when he came in the front door. When she indicated to him she'd be one minute, he glanced in the living room to see the four kids playing a game. In the kitchen, he set down his briefcase. Why was Gwen here? Did they have plans he couldn't remember?

He could tell from her words she was talking to her agent. During the years she'd been married to Jessie's brother, who'd been a popular race car driver, Gwen had gotten noticed as Tommie's most valuable trophy. Modeling jobs had come from all over the world. After Tommie's death, she'd given up modeling altogether, between grief and caring for her daughter. She was thirty-seven, but she could still pass for twenty easily. Her face was in demand as much now as it'd been back then, maybe more so because she said no so often.

Steve looked at her and wondered how long she'd grieve. In some ways, he thought she was more beautiful than she'd been when she was younger. Her parents had been an interracial couple and passed on all of their most attractive traits to Gwen. Long, silky black hair that tumbled well past her shoulders, a heart-shaped face and a petite frailty that concealed a rock-solid inner core. He remembered, vaguely surprised he'd forgotten, that he'd dated her for a short time when he was a teenager, before Tommie admitted he was in love with her.

"Sorry about that," she said when she hung up and flipped her cell phone shut. She hugged him.

"What's going on?" he asked warily.

"Nothing." She gave him her multi-million dollar smile. "I just got to thinking after I left here this morning: You don't get a lot of time to yourself. It's a Friday. You should take some time for yourself. I'm going to take the kids to see their mother. Then we'll eat and see a movie or whatever we decide to do."

Steve said, "You don't have to do that."

"I know I don't. I want to. You don't have anything for yourself, Steve. You spend all your time with the kids, work, Jess. You need something that has nothing whatsoever to do with any of them. Something just for you."

Steve stared at her in shock. She'd said almost exactly what Kristina had on Thursday, at Tilly's.

Easing her across the kitchen to the far side, where the kids wouldn't hear them, Steve asked quietly, "What do you know?"

"What do you mean?" Gwen's exotic eyes went wide with surprise.

Had she seen him with Kristina? Had she assumed the worst? She didn't seem to be blackmailing him, and he knew she'd never do that even if she had something on him. She seemed to be trying to genuinely help him. He couldn't say anything, just looked at her and felt guilty as hell. He didn't even know for what.

"Steve, I don't know what you're talking about, but, yes, I did see you in my mirror. I saw you and flashes of purple. There was a healing peace in that purple. And I thought you deserved some time to yourself. Whatever I can do to help, I'll do. We've both been through so much."

Purple. Kristina wore purple all the time. Her office was decorated in purple. Her apartment was wall-to-wall purple.

Gwen put her hand on his arm, her voice low. "I know Jess is putting you through a lot, Steve. I know Ronnie doesn't make it any easier. I don't think you can take much more of it, not without losing your mind completely. Take something for yourself and don't feel guilty for it. *You deserve it.* You really do. Maybe it'll help you decide what you should do about things."

Had he been that obvious about his grip on his own sanity, or had she seen it all in her magic mirror? He wasn't sure, but he took his escape with a guilty nod.

"Should I bring them back here when we're done?"

"Okay."

"Good. Don't worry about how late it is either. Have fun, if you can get yourself to."

She hugged him again, and he wondered when she'd do something for herself, too. Right now, everything she did was for her daughter and for Steve's family. He understood a part of Gwen didn't believe she could ever get over Tommie. But she deserved to have someone love and take care of her.

While she rounded up the kids, Steve wondered what he'd do with himself tonight.

Maybe you'd like to join me for dinner tonight. Around six o'clock?

Val came to hug him once she put on her coat. Tom asked what he would do. Before Steve could say anything, Ronnie injected, "You're gonna see Mom. Aren't you?"

The accusation in his tone didn't allow Steve to say what he really wanted to--*I can't.* Instead, he shrugged. "Probably."

Ronnie's glare told him he'd better. Gwen caught Steve's gaze in sympathy.

As the five of them piled into Gwen's car, Steve watched them, feeling lost. He wasn't used to having time for himself. Every day was jam-packed with things needed had to do and not enough hours to do it all in. He did have things to do--he'd brought work home. There was always research, preparing lectures, going through the e-mail Garret weeded out for him, the bills, cleaning the house.

None of it appealed to him. To stall a decision, he went upstairs and took a long, hot shower.

It's not a date. It wouldn't be a date. It'd be an apology for hurting her. And two colleagues who happen to be friends spending time together. I don't even know what the hell a date is anymore anyway.

As he swiped the steam from the mirror, he told himself if he didn't shave, it wasn't a date. He looked at himself in the mirror and realized he wasn't much to look at anymore. He barely had time to shower and shave before he had to make breakfast, get the kids ready and drive them to school. Then he had to take himself on to work.

He used to be good looking. He remembered it, but the realization was like someone else's memory. The guy staring back at him now could have passed for a hundred years old. While he wasn't fat, he wasn't muscular either. He didn't work out anymore, didn't have time. Hell, he barely combed his hair once a day. He used to care about his appearance. He used to care what the opposite sex thought of him.

Date? Who was he kidding? Maybe the reason Jessie cheated was because of him. But, no, he knew it wasn't that. She'd done it *long* before he stopped caring how he looked to women.

He left the bathroom, telling himself the female students at the college came on to him as much now as they had when he was a student himself. Somehow, it didn't make him feel any better.

Working didn't appeal to him any more now than it had before his shower, and he left the house telling himself to go see his wife. The anger he felt at the thought had him turning in the opposite direction. Later. He didn't want to face her. If he did, he'd have a stronger desire to see Kristina. That would confuse why he went to her. If he went now, he could say he wasn't doing anything wrong.

They arrived at the restaurant she'd specified at almost the exact same moment. He'd parked his car, and she came toward him on the sidewalk. She wore not-tight, not-loose shorts with a V-necked cotton shirt tucked into it, emphasizing her curves and her long, shapely legs. Her expression told him more than she might have intended. His presence made her happy, embarrassed, surprised and unsure--all at the same time.

Saving her for yourself? Garret had said teasingly, and Steve wondered now if that wasn't the truth. He'd been thrilled when Garret reported he'd found out all the information Steve withheld about Kristina on his own, but that she'd left work early. Given the fact that it was almost six-thirty, Steve would bet his next paycheck she'd thought seriously about not coming tonight. Either because she'd believed he'd never come or because he'd hurt her that bad.

"I'm sorry," he said as soon as they stood in front of each other before the glass doors of the restaurant. "I don't know what I'm doing here, but I'm sorry I went from telling you your friendship means a lot to me to dropping it like that. I don't think I know how to be anybody's friend."

"You're afraid. So am I," Kristina offered.

Sounded simple, but why would she be afraid? She had nothing to gain or to lose.

"Then why are we here?"

She swallowed, averting her eyes toward a couple going into the restaurant. "I don't make friends very easily. I never have. I have so few people in my life I feel comfortable with. So few, I really can't think of anyone off-hand. Anyone except you. I'm not even really comfortable with Hillary, and she's the closest thing I have to a girl friend. I feel like I don't understand anyone and they don't understand me. With you, I don't feel like that. Maybe it doesn't make sense, but I believe what we have is rare and I don't want to let it go. You don't have to feel obligated to me because I feel like this, if that's why you came here tonight."

He'd never wanted to hurt her feelings or make her cry. An apology wouldn't have made her feel any better. Maybe it would have made it worse. But he hadn't come here tonight out of obligation. *More like I can't help it. I want to talk to you. See you. And you're right--it doesn't make sense, it's not safe, but I don't want to let it go either.*

"Maybe you feel comfortable with me because you know I've got so many more problems than you do."

"Maybe," she conceded, then laughed with so much flourish and appreciation, he found himself smiling, too. Her eyes sparkled brightly, free of those silly glasses, he wondered if she had any idea how attractive she was.

They went inside the restaurant. They got a table immediately and ordered drinks. The restaurant looked like a popular place for couples. Every one of the black bistro tables had one man and one woman, similar in ages to each other, and Steve suddenly felt uncomfortable with the thought that everyone around them might think he and Kristina were a couple. What if he saw someone he knew? *I'll introduce her as a colleague from the college. And then they'll ask me on Monday if I'm having an affair. Shit.*

"You know, it's been five years since you've shown me pictures of your children," she said in the silence.

She couldn't have said anything more perfect. Steve pulled his wallet out and handed her a recent picture.

"This is Valerie. She must be eight, right? She's so beautiful. So *delicate*," Kristina said, her eyes shining. She turned the photo and read: "Valerie Suzanna Thomas."

When she took the picture of Tom from him, she sighed sentimentally upon viewing it. "Oh, Steve, you two look so much alike. He's like a smaller version of you." She looked up again, teasing as she said, "Now I know what you looked like when you were eleven."

Steve smiled in uncontrollable pride at her response to his kids.

"Thomas Nathan Thomas," she read from the back. She glanced at him. "Wow, who named this one?"

Steve grinned. "Jess did. Ronnie's middle name is Tommie. Ronald Tommie Thomas. She wanted Val's middle name to be Tommie, too, but I couldn't let her do it."

Kristina laughed.

She took the picture of Ronnie he handed her, and her eyes widened. "Are you sure he's twelve? He looks like he's eighteen. I bet he's already got girlfriends."

He would if his mom didn't require so much of him. "He's twelve, but he's always been a big kid."

"He doesn't look much like you." Kristina was studying the picture too closely. "He's so dark. Your wife has auburn hair, doesn't she? That's like strawberry blond. Let me see if I can remember my genetics: You have a little b phenome. Your wife has a little b phenome--"

The confession came before Steve could stop it: "Ronnie isn't my son. Biologically anyway."

Kristina's face flushed in mute astonishment.

Steve took a deep breath. "He doesn't know, and I'll never tell him."

"When did you find out?"

"I always knew. But, if I hadn't stayed with Jess, she would've had an abortion. I couldn't let her do that. We got married, and he's mine and nothing will ever change that. I loved him from the minute they put him in my arms." He put the pictures back in his wallet.

He could see she had a million questions bursting to be set free. The waitress brought their drinks, took their orders, and Kristina didn't say anything after she'd gone. She crossed her arms, one on top of the other, in front of her. When she leaned forward, the V of her shirt seemed to widen just like his anticipation of it did. He lifted his gaze.

"How did you know Jess has auburn hair?"

"I've seen her." She picked up her glass of wine, avoiding his eyes as she murmured, "In magazines."

Magazines? The majority of the magazines his wife had been in were the porn kind.

"Don't think I go around looking at girlie magazines or that I'm a lesbian," Kristina cried softly, her mortification in both tone and expression. "I was just curious about her after I met you. I wanted to see what she looked like, and an old boyfriend of mine told me she was kind of famous. In pornographic circles anyway. He showed me the magazines."

Yeah, his private life had been fodder for the rumor mill at the college for years. Finding out Kristina knew about Jessie's sordid past brought back the humiliation he'd gotten used to over the years.

"I can see why you two had beautiful children together," Kristina said.

"Jess is beautiful."

"So are you."

Steve faced her, and she said defensively, "Well, you are. You can't doubt that when our waitress did everything short of throw herself in your lap."

He hadn't noticed the waitress doing anything except serving them. He hadn't noticed any woman here except Kristina. Why did it feel so good to know she found him attractive? *Obviously something wrong with her for thinking it, but I like it.*

"We're talking about me again. What about you? How come you're not married with kids? I know you like kids."

"I do. I love them. Any age." She set down her glass, shaking her head when a waiter offered her more wine. "One glass is my absolute limit," she told Steve after he left. "Have you ever seen the movie *While You Were Sleeping*?"

"It's one of Val's favorite. I've seen it more times than I cared to."

Kristina smiled. "Her life--Lucy's--that's mine. I have some work friends. My family life is strained--with my dad anyway. I rent an apartment when I really want a big house, one big enough to hold all my pets and maybe a family someday. I date occasionally--when I can't talk Hillary out of setting me up with her peculiar friends. I spend more time dreaming about the life I want than doing anything to make it come true. But then I don't even really know what I want. I mean, some things I do. The house. My job, definitely. Mostly, I'm just waiting for life to come knocking on my door. I hope it's good when it finally shows up."

They laughed together, but Steve felt sadness when he thought about Kristina alone, waiting on life instead of living it.

"My dad wanted me to be a lawyer. I actually started college, thinking that was what I was going to do, but I knew almost immediately it wasn't for me. I changed my major, and he hasn't forgiven me since."

"Then he doesn't understand what you do or the impact on the lives of the kids you help. You help them put their lives together, sometimes for the first time. They love you."

She smiled shyly, obviously pleased with the compliment. "My mom understands me. I think she's proud, so it makes up for a lot, and I don't want my parents to be at odds with each other over me. I don't think they are. Before my mom was diagnosed with Parkinson's Disease six years ago, she did everything she wanted to do. She wasn't like me--she was never one to sit around, waiting for something to happen to her. My life is almost half over and it feels like it's barely begun."

They stared at each other for a long, silent minute, then Steve said, "My life is half over and I couldn't start over again if I tried."

"Do you really believe that?"

He'd believed it for most of his life, particularly the last thirteen years. He'd made a decision, a really bad one, based on lust, anger and stupid obsession, and it wasn't a decision he could go back on. Not when he'd made a promise to someone who wasn't around to relieve him of it or even hold him to it. No, he couldn't go back and start over.

Their meals arrived, and he turned the topic as far from his mistakes as he could. He listened to Kristina tell him about her years in Chicago, where she attended college, and about the work she did at the Drug Crisis Center. He told himself a dozen times to keep his eyes on her face, not her mouth or any lower, and he told himself two dozen times that this wasn't a date. They weren't doing anything wrong. He'd leave here alone, go home, get some work done. No big deal.

"I'll walk you to your car," he said outside the restaurant.

"I walked. My apartment is only a block or so from here."

He couldn't let her walk alone, even if this was a decent neighborhood.

"I'll walk you home," he found himself saying.

It's not a date. But her soft smile of thanks, coupled with the arm she slipped through his, insisted he was fooling himself if he really believed that. He needed a shrink, that was for sure.

Nine

"What do you think?"

Kristina turned to Steve. She'd spent the night telling herself she must be dreaming. After leaving the DeSmet Building in humiliating tears, she'd avoided all contact with anyone else, locked up her office and went home. She didn't have any appointments that afternoon anyway. Fool that she was, even when she'd convinced herself Steve would never show up at Feng Shui, she'd gone. The fact that he had come couldn't be reality. If it was reality, he must have come only because he knew he'd hurt her by trying to avoid her and abandon their friendship.

"Think of what?"

When she glanced up, she found him looking away, down the sidewalk stretched before them.

"You said you despise my wife. So what do you think of my marriage? You're a counselor, right? A psychologist. What's your professional opinion?"

Shocked, she shook her head. "Oh, Steve, I can't! It's none of my business. I can't pry into something so personal--"

He faced her, meeting her eyes. "You're not prying. I'm asking you for your opinion. Believe me, honey, I know it can't be good."

Kristina almost laughed, but she couldn't. "I've had some bad experiences in this area, Steve. Can you understand? When I tell people I'm a counselor, they always end up asking my opinion about some area of their life and they won't back off until I give it. Then they never forgive me, and they think I'm psychoanalyzing their every move when I'm not and never wanted to in the first place. I've made it my policy not to offer advice, even solicited." She couldn't risk losing Steve over a truth they both knew without voicing.

"I won't hold it against you. I promise. I trust your opinion. I feel like I've been over this damn thing so many times, I can't see straight anymore. I know my own limitations. It'd be nice to hear what it looks like to an outsider."

Again, Kristina shook her head, unwilling to offer anything by way of advice. Anything she said would come back and bite her in the butt eventually. She couldn't take the chance in this case. "I don't know the whole situation. I only know part of your side and none of your wife's. My opinion would be worthless."

"Okay. It'd be worthless. We both accept that. I still want to hear it."

Sighing, Kristina recognized all the signs of the beginning of a bad situation. Yet she couldn't refuse him. "All I can offer is a very general assessment. You understand that?"

He nodded, shifting to the edge when the sidewalk became crowded. Since they were arm-in-arm, she automatically went with him.

"It seems like your wife could be--*could be*, not necessarily *is*--punishing both of you, and inadvertently your children, by forcing you to stay together in constant misery. She won't let you go, not without heaping on the guilt or playing on the guilt you already harbor. And she tortures and pushes you away with the things she does--the drug binges, the affairs."

They reached her building, and she glanced at Steve as they entered, almost afraid to see his reaction. His expression made her cry out. She'd hit the mark bull's-eye and wasn't sure whether to cry or feel secretly, guiltily, glad she knew him better than she thought.

"Oh, Steve, I'm so sorry. I didn't mean--"

He'd leaned back against the wall in the foyer, and she saw he smiled weakly. "You think everyone sees that, or you're just good at what you do?"

"Have you ever told anyone else the things you've told me?" Kristina asked in regret. She'd wounded him, embarrassed him maybe, at the thought that other people could see what a fool he was for letting his wife play him the consummate, cruel way she did.

He shook his head.

"Then I'm just good."

His laughter was hoarse and choked. *Please don't cry. I'll cry, too, and then you'll know I love you.*

Taking a shaky breath, she turned and leaned against the wall, shoulder to shoulder with him. "Steve?"

He glanced at her.

"Are you happy? Are you *really* happy with her? I just can't understand why you do it, why you take it all as selflessly as you do. Is she your best friend and you can't hold anything against her because of that? Do you love her so much she's your soul and leaving her would mean leaving your soul?" Kristina swallowed, unable to stop herself from continuing, even when she saw the pain in his eyes. "Do you stay because when you make love, you know she's the only one you could ever be with?"

He started laughing again, this time so hard and so long and so unwilling to share with her what was funny. Kristina knew he bled inside deeply enough that he'd lost all control. Tears stung her eyes as she pivoted toward him. He wouldn't answer, and he had no obligation to. Yet she needed to know.

Tears had filled his eyes and were running down his face when he straightened. He stared at the wall across from them, his laughter becoming short and bitter. "I have to ask my wife if she used a condom with all the guys she fucked when she wasn't with me. When she comes back, I'm so pissed off that she touches me and I feel nothing.

"I don't want to drink, I don't want to smoke, I don't want to cheat on her because I know what it feels like to know what you give each other means so little. I haven't made love to anyone who gives a damn about me since before I threw everything away and got involved with her. But I did get involved with her, and that means I have to take everything that goes with her. If I leave, I'll kill myself because I can't live with the guilt of breaking my promises. I made her what she is..."

Steve pressed the bridge of his nose between his thumb and index finger ruthlessly, muttering, "...or I made whatever and *whyever* the hell she is *worse.*"

Kristina heard everything he said and she heard everything he didn't. He wanted to leave his wife more than anything in the world, but for some unvoiced reason locked inside of himself, he couldn't or wouldn't.

She lifted her hand to his face, urging him to look at her. Her tears clearly startled him, but he didn't look away. It meant everything to her that he wasn't even thinking about running away. "Steve, I know you believe that. And I know you must have damn good reasons for why you believe what you believe. And I know you love your children more than anything else in the world. You do everything in your power to protect them from pain. Maybe the debt you've been paying *has* been paid. Maybe you've been paying so long, you haven't realized that. Your children are paying, too, though. I don't want to remind you of that because I know how much you've already suffered. But what you do won't have to be simply for you. You might be doing the best thing for them as well. It might even be the best thing for your wife, if you think about it in the long-term."

"I know," he said softly.

"I know you know, Steve. I never had any doubt."

"Tell me what to do," he said desperately, his eyes locked on hers and his face only an inch away.

"I can't." *I wish I could. I wish I could make it all better by telling you. But I'd never forgive myself for it because I would never really know why I told you.*

He closed his eyes, arcing his mouth toward her palm when she caressed his face. Kristina felt the touch dart through her hand, her arm, throughout her whole body. When he faced her again, he still didn't open his eyes. His lips came to hers, barely meeting. He held there, and Kristina stopped breathing for an instant. But then he breathed, sighed and she sighed shakily, feeling like she might die. Or come to life for the very first time. They held suspended together for both a heartbeat and a lifetime. God, so close, but never close enough to satisfy her desperate love.

"I'm sorry, honey. Dammit, I'm sorry. I can't do this."

His harshly whispered words shattered the spell, and he disappeared in the silence punctuated only by her sob.

You're my best friend, Steve--I can't hold anything against you. I love you so much, you're my soul and leaving you would mean leaving my soul. You're the only one I could ever be with.

And now it was over.

* * * *

His head whirled like a hurricane as he stalked down the sidewalk blindly. He couldn't think. All he could do was move. Fight *it*--the trouble he'd told himself he wouldn't come looking for. He'd found it. Hell yeah, he'd found trouble in a perfect package. He'd depended on Kristina for a long time, probably longer than he'd ever considered the fact. Now he wanted her.

He couldn't go home like this. He sure as hell couldn't see Jess. With her overdeveloped, hypocritical jealousy, she'd smell Kristina's perfume in a heartbeat.

Getting to his car required more luck than skill. He spent a full minute trying to fit his key into the ignition before he gave up and slammed his fists on the steering wheel.

"I got into this whole damn thing without thinking, Tommie. I wanted Jess and goddamn the consequences. Now what do I do, man? Break another vow?"

Steve caught his own eyes in the rearview mirror and had to look away at the shame he felt. He hadn't kissed Kristina, dammit. He hadn't. But he hadn't not kissed her either. *I breathed in a part of her soul. She breathed in a part of mine. Ah, hell.*

He realized suddenly he didn't need to do anything. He didn't need to accept it was all over. All he had to do was never see Kristina again. That would make it right.

"I can't do that," he whispered.

Could he? Could he avoid her forever on the campus? Elsewhere? Could he keep himself from going to her?

The image of her tears, the way she'd cried for him, touched his face like she wanted to heal him or take his pain, came to him and he knew he couldn't go through with never seeing her again.

That almost kiss had happened so fast. It was possible she hadn't wanted it but hadn't had time to refuse it. She cared about him, God only knew why. She thought he should divorce his wife, but it didn't mean so the two of them could be together. And even her comment about finding him attractive... No, no way this woman wanted to share his sick, screwed-up life.

"Maybe the debt you've been paying has been paid. Maybe you've been paying so long, you haven't realized it."

Steve shook his head. Even if Kristina's words were true, he'd never know it. Tommie was dead. Steve's debt would only be paid upon his own death. *Remember that, and maybe you'll get through this...this trouble.*

As he drove home, he told himself a weekend away from Kristina would increase the distance.

His house was quiet, dark except for the foyer light. Gwen's car was still outside. He shed his coat as he walked past the kitchen. Out of the darkness on the stairs came Ronnie's voice: "Where were you?"

Steve heard the fury in his tone. Shit. He didn't doubt for a second that Ronnie had checked up on him, too. He'd called his mom at the hospital and asked her if Steve had been by.

For a minute, Steve couldn't say anything to his son. He felt the accusation's full weight. Then he realized in Ronnie's mind, it didn't matter if his mom had cheated on him a thousand times. If Steve cheated on her even once, he was branded a criminal for life. He *hadn't* cheated either. Barely a kiss didn't qualify as cheating on a spouse, especially since he'd walked away from it.

"Ron, you assume the worst of me in every scenario," Steve said in an exhausted voice. "Assume you're assuming the worst this time, too. Go to bed."

He walked past his son on the steps. Val's door stood open and, in the glow of the nightlight, he saw Gwen soothing her. Val couldn't have been asleep longer than a half-hour and already she'd had a nightmare.

Gwen glanced up at him as he entered the room.

"Daddy," Val said tearfully.

"It's okay, baby. I'm here."

Gwen got up, and Steve lay down next to his little girl. She cried in his arms for a long time and he couldn't make her tell him why. Clenching his teeth against a desperate need to scream, he closed his eyes. *I can't do anything for Val. I can't make Ron stop hating me. Tom tries to help out, and I break his spirit without knowing I'm doing it. Nothing I do for Jess makes any difference at all. I can't even save myself.*

He was surprised to find Gwen still downstairs when he finally got Val to sleep again.

"How long has she had these nightmares?" Gwen asked softly in the kitchen.

Steve wiped his eyes, shaking his head at her question. "Years."

His own guilty conscience told him Gwen would call him out for where he'd been and what he'd done, just like Ron had, but she didn't bring it up. Looking concerned, she stood, getting her jacket.

"Would you mind carrying Ally out to my car? She's asleep on the sofa."

"Thanks for taking the kids," he said once he gently placed Allison in the backseat of Gwen's car.

Gwen hugged him, whispering, "Please tell me if there's anything I can ever do for you and the kids."

"Thanks."

He watched her drive away before going in the house. After locking up, he checked on Tom and Ronnie, then went to his bedroom. Sitting on the edge of his bed, he let himself admit the truth. *I'm not happy. I stay with Jess out of guilt and obligation that are bigger than anything. Bigger even than my need to protect my kids. But this can't go on. We can't keep doing this. If we do, the thing that snaps could be one of the kids. I can't risk that. But how the hell can I leave? Ronnie will never leave with me. I can't lose him. And if I don't take care of Jess, I'll never forgive myself.*

Steve stripped off his clothes, pulled on sweats. In the darkness, he closed his mind off to the no-win situation bombarding his brain ruthlessly. The only thing that gave him peace was the thought of Kristina.

She'd stared at him as if everything inside her was bleeding for him--too much of a mirror. He was bleeding and sometimes he thought he'd never stop. He'd closed his eyes, turned his mouth toward her palm when she touched his face. Her hand felt so good. Her touch, like a gift from heaven. He hadn't felt anything for so damn long. When Jess touched him, when they made love, he felt dirty. Ashamed.

I wouldn't feel that with Kristina. I know that. I wouldn't lose my erection thinking about all the other men, the ones Jess has been with. The ones she brought to our bed. A single kiss with Kristina, and I'd feel whole again, even if it's only for a minute.

Without opening his eyes, he'd shifted toward her, touched her lips with his own. Everything inside him fell apart and came back together, whole. He'd felt like he could reach down inside of her and know her just by being close to her. She'd given him everything she possessed. And he had absolutely nothing to give her in return.

Ten

Kristina stood back and viewed the collection of books filling the shelves in her living room. She'd spent the night arranging them alphabetically, while drowning the room in a symphony of music. At least until her neighbor knocked on her door and complained about the noise.

She hadn't wanted to think. She'd wanted to shut her mind off completely. This job had done it. Now, thank God, she felt exhausted. She could spend the next few hours locked in hopefully dreamless sleep.

After a quick shower, she slipped into a t-shirt and panties, then sank under the covers with her sleep mask in place. As soon as she closed her eyes, she saw Steve's face, felt the subtle pressure of his soft, firm lips, and a sob worked its way up from her chest. It was over. Whatever it was. Steve would never want to see her again, even in passing. She'd heard the finality in his voice when he'd said, "I can't do this." He'd breathed in her soul and left her hollow.

Trina's warm, furry body curled up near her, and Kristina pulled her closer. "Why don't cats seem to need other cats? How do you manage that? Tell me your secret, Trina."

Trina purred like a vibrating motor, so loudly Kristina almost didn't hear her doorbell ring. In shock, she turned over, flipped her mask up and glanced at the clock. It was six-thirty in the morning. Who would come here so early?

Steve. If it's Steve, I have no willpower, no pride. I'll take anything or nothing.

She got up, tearing off the mask and running like she was in shock to the door. When she peering through the peephole, all she saw were a dozen pink roses. The bell rang again, and she thought, *Steve wouldn't be so insistent* even as she unlocked the door.

"Did I wake you?"

He pushed inside. It wasn't until he was fully in, turning to her, that she realized he wasn't Steve.

"Matt?"

"You're a sight for sore eyes," he said, grinning lewdly as he looked at the little she wore. He dropped a kiss on her mouth and headed for the kitchen with the flowers and grocery bags.

Her mind tried to process the fact that, after a year and a half away, Matt was here again. Matt Reimann had been her first boyfriend. She'd met him in her freshman year of college and grown to love him. Later, she'd realized her love for him qualified strictly as friendship love. He'd had a terrible relationship with his father, who'd spent a lifetime physically and verbally abusing him and his mother. He'd come to her one night--she'd never seen him like it before or since--wild-eyed, dazed, completely lost and confused. His father had killed his mother in a fit of rage.

Kristina had felt completely out of her element to help him. Her comfort seemed so little compared to what he really needed. He'd started kissing her desperately, and she'd allowed it because she knew why he wanted to lose himself. But when he'd gone further, when he'd stopped thinking altogether, she'd asked him to stop. He hadn't and couldn't seem to even hear her pleas. Kristina had been too inexperienced and unsure of herself to take action. All she'd known was she hadn't wanted it to be violent. She'd considered sleeping with him before that, albeit decided against doing so. She'd convinced herself that night his actions were all right.

Only in the last few years had she come to understand what happened that night could be considered rape. Her professional opinion told her that. Since he'd cried, said he loved her, and apologized so many times after the act, she hadn't been able to hold it against him then.

She'd continued the relationship, both monogamously and sexually, even when she realized she would never love him the way she wanted to and he would never love her the way she needed. When he'd taken a job in California the year they graduated, she'd been relieved. The distance would provide them with the friendship she enjoyed, but prevent the rest of what she didn't really want.

Only a year after she'd moved back to Milwaukee, he'd come to visit after quitting his job. He'd stayed for months, and Kristina had found herself back in the groove of a relationship that had more dimensions than she desired. Thankfully, he'd gotten a job and traveled extensively. He dropped in occasionally and their relationship resumed as though it'd never ended. She'd never fully lived down the shame of the things she did with him, out of need, loneliness, not love, before he showed up again and her weakness reared its ugly head once more. It didn't help that Matt always came to her when he'd hit a low point. He needed her to help him get back on his feet, and she did that compulsively because she needed him to ease her loneliness.

Kristina walked into the kitchen and stood in the doorway, watching him put the flowers in a vase, then unload the groceries.

"Do you want me to make you an omelet? You haven't had breakfast yet, have you?" He was handsome as always, with carefully feathered, dark brown hair and a strong face. His body remained honed to perfection. In all the time she'd known him, he worked out every day. She knew he did it to ensure he'd never be a victim again.

Swallowing, Kristina willed herself to have the courage to turn him away for once. "Matt, this really isn't a good time--"

He turned from the open fridge as if he'd suddenly realized something. "Are you alone here?" he asked in surprise. Too much surprise.

Did he think she waited around for him to drop into her life and bless her with his presence? No, she couldn't imagine him being that cocky. He had a cruel streak, very much like Hillary's, but Kristina couldn't imagine he really considered himself her true love.

"No, but--"

He smiled, a charming, irresistible smile that deepened the dimples on each side of his mouth. He looked like he'd come from a hot climate. His skin was impossibly tan under the white, sleeveless sweatshirt he wore. Kristina felt a wave a shame pour over her before Matt even closed in on her. She couldn't resist him. Not now. It was true she was sexually attracted to him. He took good care of himself.

"Good. Because I've missed you, Kristie."

His strong, familiar arms slipped around her, and she felt tears sting her eyes. *I wanted this to be Steve. What is wrong with me? It'll never be Steve. Steve is a fantasy that gets more impossible every day. Matt is real. He's possible, even if it won't last. I don't want it to last. I just want to be in a man's arms again, safe, warm, desired.*

As his hard lips closed over hers, Kristina closed her eyes and gave in, too easily, as usual. She felt his hands snake down past her hips to cradle her bottom, then he held her against his erection. There was no detour on the way to the bedroom, no protest as she took what she could get. She gave what she hadn't been able to bestow on the man she loved. And, as soon as her body reached fulfillment, the tears rose to convict her for her weakness.

Only after Matt took his own release did he mutter hoarsely, "Kristie?" He seemed surprised by her reaction, and why wouldn't he be? The last time she'd cried after sex was that first time.

"I'm all right. I'm just..."

"Does this have anything to do with that guy? The one you've got the hots for? The one married to Jessie Nelson-Thomas?"

He'd ridicule her, and she deserved it. She just didn't want him to. Not this time.

Matt shook his head, rolling off her with a chuckle. "Don't get me wrong, Kristie, I think you're a pretty girl. But how do you compete with a woman like that? No man in his right mind would leave her, even if she does treat him like crap."

Kristina sat up angrily at the edge of the bed, clutching the sheet to her front. She knew Matt had seen every one of Jessie's centerfolds. He'd asked Kristina to introduce them once--as if she'd find it funny. Worse, as if he'd been serious.

"Come on, Kristie. Be realistic. He's not gonna leave her. He might screw you for the fun of it, but he's not gonna leave her for you. Why are you so hung up on it? Why don't you just enjoy what you can have?"

His arms slid around her from the back, one hand cupping her breast beneath the cotton. "Come back here. You can have me anytime."

Kristina stopped his fingers from fondling her nipple. Was he right? She knew she was stupid for holding out for something that probably would never happen. It wasn't as if she hadn't known it would be impossible from the first time she heard Steve was married. But the closer Steve got to her, the further he wanted to run. The more involved she got with him, the more his withdrawal hurt her. They *couldn't* do this, just as Steve had said.

That left her with two choices: She could tell him she loved him and risk the very strong possibility that he would reject her, or she could end it. All of it. The friendship, her need to see him and talk to him in any way, for any reason. End it. And get on with her life without the reality or fantasy of him she'd immersed herself in.

She looked down at Matt, who watched her with an it's-your-call expression.

"You're right," she said softly.

He sat up, holding her with one arm and stroking her cheek with the other. "I'll make the break easier on you, for the first couple days anyway."

Kristina swallowed the pain, took Matt's balm, and closed her eyes to the guilt and fear that would consume her if she let it.

* * * *

Steve let his son win because he couldn't bear to see him lose. Jess called Saturday morning, asking to see Ronnie, and Steve couldn't refuse. He dropped Val and Tom off with Gwen and drove Ronnie to the hospital. He knew exactly what would happen, too, another reason he should have refused. His own guilt hadn't allowed that either.

He watched Jessie beg her son to forgive her, asking him for his help--she'd never get better without it. He watched Ronnie transform from an angry young man to a prideless little boy who would do anything to gain his mother's love.

"I'll get better, Ronnie, and then everything'll be great. I'll be a good mother to you. You'll see. Just trust me."

"Whatever you need, Mom."

Steve's anger rose at what Jessie had done. She put too much on Ronnie's shoulders. At twelve, he already felt like he had to take care of her, like *he* was the only one who could and would. the boy had the maturity and bitterness of a forty-year-old. Jessie's bid for Ronnie's total love made Steve his own son's enemy. She needed an ally, and she knew Steve would never risk losing his child.

"You know what I'd like now?"

Ronnie stared up at his mother, tears running down his face.

"Flowers. I've got all these daisies and carnations, but no one has brought me roses. Will you go down to the gift shop and get me some roses?"

Steve understood she was trying to get him out of the room now, but Ronnie wouldn't believe that. He'd spend every last penny he had on roses for her. She'd fawn over at them once, then never look at them again.

"I get out on Monday," she said as soon as Ronnie left the room. He'd refused the money Steve offered him. "God, what I wouldn't do for a cigarette before then."

"What about rehab?"

"I'm not gonna take any more shit."

Steve stayed on his side of the room as he shook his head. "Are you going to try killing yourself anymore? Because that's what you're trying to do, isn't it? Intentionally or unintentionally, that's what you're doing."

"Why don't you come over here?" she invited softly.

Steve shook his head.

"Then I'll come to you--"

She was hooked to an IV, made a feint to remove it, and Steve forced himself to go to her before she upset the stand.

Her eyes were dark, hollow, but the emotion in them was fierce. He'd seen it all before though. This was her please-forgive-me expression. He knew exactly what she'd say and how she'd say it. He knew every promise. Every promise she'd break.

"I know I've made you a million promises, Steve, and I know I'm not very good at keeping them. But I slipped. I was at work and my mom started talking about some bullshit. I got so mad, I couldn't see straight. I know I should've called you, let you talk me down."

Steve almost laughed. She'd never called him *during* a crisis. She didn't recognize a crisis when it stared her point-blank in the face. She only called or came to him once the avalanche buried her.

"Please give me another chance, baby. I'm really gonna try this time. I'll be so damn good to you, you won't even recognize me."

He expected the arms she snaked around him, the eyes that looked up at him with every bit of truth she believed she had in her, the kiss that could have seduced him so easily in the past. He didn't respond to any of it, not even when she backed up and eased the gown off her shoulders. Instead, he caught it, put it back over her breasts and walked away from the bed with his jaw so tight, he wondered if it'd snap.

Sex. If her promises failed, she thought sex would heal a hundred wrongs. At one time, he'd allowed himself to believe it could, too.

"God, I'm fucking trying, Steve. Please don't do this to me. I need you. I can't live without you, even if you can live without me--"

He left the room because he couldn't listen to her beg even one more time.

"Your wife is punishing both of you by forcing you to stay together in constant misery. She won't let you go, not without heaping on the guilt or playing on the guilt you already harbor."

He couldn't face Ronnie either. Not now. Steve asked the nurse to tell his son he was out in the car before he stumbled to the parking lot, his head full of condemnation. *"I asked you to stay the fuck away from her. You remember that, man? I begged you not to go near her. Now she's yours. You understand that? And you're no friend of mine. You hurt her, you leave her, you fuck her over and I'll be there. I'll be the last thing you ever see."*

And I was. Steve cradled his head in his hands as if he could shut it all off. Tommie had promised to haunt him thirteen years ago and he'd damn-sure made good on his threat.

Eleven

Kristina had tried to be late. She couldn't see Steve, and changing her schedule to avoid him would be no hardship. After all, she'd changed her schedule to include every glimpse she could get of him. This would be easier. But he pulled into his space as soon as she got out of her car. She could have rushed into the Center, but she found her legs paralyzed unwilling to move until she saw him.

He stepped out of his car, and their eyes locked. There was no joy at all in the gaze, the way there used to be. Steve had withdrawn into a protective place inside himself.

Guilt for having spent a weekend making love to another man, one she didn't love, one who'd left this morning with a cheery, "Catch you some other time" poured over her. She felt as if she'd betrayed Steve. As if her vow to herself to let this thing she had with Steve go was a betrayal of the friendship she'd promised him.

She found herself bumbling out words, asking how his kids were.

"Jess is coming home tonight," he said softly, looking away for an instant.

Tears slammed into her eyes, tears she couldn't control at all.

His expression softened when he looked back. "I'm sorry, Kristina. I can't see you anymore. I can't come to your apartment." He averted his gaze as if he felt ineffectual to finish what he'd started. "I'm sorry I've relied on you so much."

She shook her head, dislodging the tears. "It's no trouble. Never was. Never will be."

"Thanks," he said faintly.

If she had an ounce of faith left she would have believed he was falling apart just the way she was.

But he walked away, kept his vows. Fool that she was, she loved him even more for it, too.

* * * *

Ronnie talked almost incessantly on the ride home. Steve wanted to block out the desperation in his son's voice. Wanted to block out the fact that his wife was coming home like everything was fine, everything was normal, and the anger that sat in his chest wasn't burning a hole in him.

They had dinner out, but none of them ate much. As soon as they got in the house, Jess said she was tired. Steve ignored the look she gave him before she went up. He tried to forget the invitation by doing laundry, helping Val with her homework, preparing lectures for the next week, checking his e-mail.

He saw one from his TA, Garret, and clicked on it. When it opened on the screen, he read, "Asked the gorgeous counselor out today. She turned me down flat. I plan to try again later. G"

Steve couldn't imagine why she'd turned the kid down, despite the age difference. Garret was popular, charming. He didn't have a shitload of problems facing him.

I hurt her today. Hurt her badly. I'll never forgive myself for the pain in her eyes. God only knows why I mean anything to her at all. She should be glad to get rid of the burden of being my friendship.

It still wasn't clear in Steve's mind why he'd done what he had today. He'd spent the weekend with his kids, facing the fact that Jess was coming home. An icicle had formed inside him for his wife, one that damned the guilt he felt. What could he do? He had no idea. But it was clear to him that spending any time at all with Kristina would increase his temptation to take his pain to her, in every way. And that wouldn't be fair to her, even if there was a remote chance she wanted him, too.

After he got the kids in bed, he went back to his upcoming lectures, but kept remembering what Kristina had said: Jess punished them. Why? What had happened to her that she felt she had to punish them for her misery?

Steve shook his head, hitting save automatically on his notes. He needed to get some work done, not simply to avoid going upstairs to face his wife's seduction. There was no way he'd allow her to cajole him into forgiving her with sex. She tried it every time but didn't seem to notice it hadn't worked in years.

The third time he had to go to Val, he realized he felt too tired to push himself to work any more tonight. He stared at his bedroom door. *I'll sleep on the sofa--*

The door opened, and Jess stood there in a few scraps of purple. Why did she have to wear *purple*? Her expression wasn't seductive. She stared at him in a plea he had no doubt she believed was genuine. It didn't feel that way to him. He'd seen her falsehoods too many times. "Come to bed," she whispered. "Please."

He didn't follow her for any more reason than that he wanted to know the truth.

"Did something happen to you to make you like this?" he asked as she closed the door behind them. He sat on the edge of the bed.

Jessie pursed full lips, looking like she wanted to pretend she hadn't heard him say anything. She leaned against the door, her hands behind her. The position displayed her heavy breasts, nipples hard and visible through the lace, to perfection. Steve was he unaffected by the sight of what would have had him rock-hard with desire years ago.

"I need to know, dammit. It's the least you owe me."

"Tommie died. You know why the fuck I am the way I am."

Steve shook his head at her. "You were like this before Tommie died, and you know it. You've been like this for a long time. Something happened. When you were a kid or a teenager. I know your parents ignored you and Tommie by working all the time. You had a new babysitter every week. I know that's part of it. But it's a lot more than that. Tell me, goddammit."

Her jaw tightened. Her eyes darkened. "Don't ask me that," she said in a low voice that revealed anger, fear. "Don't ever ask me again."

In the silence that followed, they stared at each other, neither yielding. *What if she actually tells me something? What if it's bad? It has to be bad. And then I can't just walk away. Would it make up for everything she's put us through? Maybe I don't want to know.*

Steve looked away, feeling like he might collapse from the weight of everything coming down on him

"I can't help what I am. I know it's not fair to you or them--" She indicated the kids with a jerk of her shoulder. "I get depressed and I stop thinking. It doesn't mean anything happened. It just means I need to avoid getting depressed."

Her voice came from closer, and he glanced up at her sleek, sinfully curvaceous body. He saw the tattoo, just above her hip--a sword covered with tangled, thorny rose vines and spotted with ink-blood. "I know what'll make us both happy," she said, soft and captivating. "Don't think, just feel, baby. I promise you'll forget everything."

It wasn't true. He knew it wasn't true. He *wanted* it to be true because it might get rid of the chilly anger inside him.

Closing his eyes, he let her ease him back. He let her undress him, crawl up beside him and kiss him skillfully. When he looked at her over him, so damn sexy, his too-often-betrayed body stopped responding, but she kept going down his body with her hot, wet mouth slithering over his skin.

Don't think, just feel. Remember the first time you took her. Remember how insane with lust you were, watching her alone in your bed, touching herself. By the time you entered the room, both of you could have died from need. Instead, you lived--like you only dreamed of for so many years. Every fantasy became flesh and blood because there was nothing she wouldn't do or give.

Remember another man was in this bed with her not more than a week ago.

Steve's eyes opened abruptly.

Her hands cradled his soft manhood and she worked her lips, tongue and teeth over him from tip to balls.

That guy wasn't the first one in this bed with her. Not by a long shot. She'll never change. You give her another chance, she betrays you. You give her another chance, she betrays you one more time. It'll never end.

"What's the matter?" she asked at his lack of response.

Steve's teeth clenched hard, holding back a scream. Dragging his hands through his hair until he clutched it painfully, he closed his eyes again.

Tiny white, thin top that didn't hide the fact she wasn't wearing a bra... Reaching behind her, unbinding her hair. Long, thick waves tumbling over her shoulders in silken masses. Belly button earring he wanted to touch, tug gently, put his mouth on...

"I wish I could do something, anything to make it all go away for you, Steve."

Breasts curved upward in a shape like twin horns of plenty, ending with rosy red nipples. Kristina's shape...

"That's more like it."

At Jessie's purr, Steve sat up while forcing her away from him. *Ah hell, I knew it. I knew this would happen. I spent the whole goddamn weekend waking up with a hard-on like when I was a teenager--for Kristina.*

His shame increased when he pulled on his jeans and couldn't get the zipper to close. *Can't do this. Can't do it anymore.* The weight of his responsibilities made him feel like his chest would fold up and crush him.

He leaned his forearms against the door. Jessie came up behind him. He felt her distended nipples against his back, her cradling hips, her fingers snaking into his open pants again like a monkey that couldn't let go of a withdrawn banana. "Whatever you want, any way you want it," she whispered. "I want you. I know you want me."

Can I do this? Can I close my eyes, think about Kristina and let Jess do what she does best on me?

The mere thought had him shoving her away again, yanking open the door and getting out of there as fast as he could.

I don't want Jess. But I can't cheat on her either--in my mind or in reality. I can't do this. Never again.

Twelve

No rest for the wicked. Steve pulled into his parking space on campus and immediately looked for Kristina's car. She hadn't arrived yet. She hadn't pulled in by the time he got to the doors of the DeSmet Building.

You can't see her anyway didn't console him anymore than waking up that morning on the couch, avoiding Jess as he got the kids ready for school. She'd said she'd drive them to school, and he'd allowed it because he hadn't wanted to fight with Ronnie. Jess had already confided something to their older son, drawing her ally--the only one in the house--in her corner. Ronnie was so protective, he'd follow his mom into the mouth of a volcano if she asked it of him. Hell, he'd follow her regardless of whether or not she asked.

His pager went off as he walked upstairs to his office. Pulling it out of the pocket of his coat, he saw his own phone number in the display window. *Jess, needing the consolation I didn't give her last night?* He thought about ignoring it, but his experiences in the past wouldn't allow him to.

Once in his office, he dialed and Ronnie answered on the first ring.

"What are you doing home? You're supposed to be at school."

"Mom took something."

Steve closed his eyes as blackness rushed at him and threatened to swallow him whole.

"Is she conscious?" he asked numbly.

"Yeah. She's okay. She didn't OD. She's just high. I don't wanna leave her alone."

"Where are Tom and Val?"

"School. She dropped 'em off, and we came back here--"

And you watched your own goddamn mother shoot up her poison. All part of her fucking plan to make me feel guilty for rejecting her last night.

"What did you do to her?" Ronnie demanded.

"I'll be there in ten minutes."

Steve hung up just as Garret came into his office. He got out his notes for the lecture he was supposed to give in fifteen minutes. "Tell Janice to give the lecture."

"No problem. What's going on?"

"If she can't, get another TA to do it."

Garret nodded. Then Steve stalked out of his office, back out to his car. Before he streaked out of the parking lot, he saw Kristina's car.

Why should I feel guilty? Steve's head felt like it was on fire as he raced toward home. *Jess cheated on me. A million times. Why should I feel guilty because I didn't want to be the next guy in line to fuck her? The next notch in her bedpost? Why should I feel guilty for her reaction to getting what she deserves? Her depression?*

He grabbed his cell phone and punched in the code for Gwen's phone number. She answered just when he thought she wouldn't. "Can you pick Ronnie up at my house and take him to school?"

Whatever question came to her mind in the slight pause answered itself from experience. "I'll be there in a few minutes."

She lived in Oak Creek, not far from his house. She arrived almost at the same time he did.

"Didn't she come home last night from the hospital?" Gwen asked when they met on the sidewalk.

"Yes, but why are you surprised?"

"Do you want me to talk to her?"

Steve snorted. "Talk doesn't go anywhere with her."

Gwen nodded and followed him inside.

"Go to school," Steve said when he saw Ronnie sitting beside Jess, in their bed, upstairs.

"I wanna stay with her. What the hell did you do to her this time, you bastard?" Ronnie's face looked hard as granite.

"Go to school!" Steve shouted.

Gwen's voice was placating. "Come on, sweetie."

Glaring at Steve, Ronnie allowed his aunt to lead him out of the room.

Jess opened her eyes, murmuring, "Couldn't help it. I'm sorry."

Her gaze was drugged. She brought her cigarette to her mouth, and Steve wanted to scream at her for that, too. He never allowed her to smoke in the house when the kids were in it. He knew she did when he left.

"I don't want to hear any more of your apologies and excuses. How dare you do this shit in front of Ronnie?" He swept a stash of coke from the nightstand. He'd checked the house from top to bottom this weekend and hadn't found any drugs. Where the hell did she get it? Did she buy the shit with their son in the car?

His head felt like it might fly off as he tried not to look at her. "I can't do this anymore. You understand that? I can't put up with another minute of your bullshit. You think your apologies mean anything to me? You think I believe a word you say? But Ronnie does and you use him. You use your own damn son. What the hell is wrong with you?"

"I need him. I don't use him. He's the only one who really cares about me," she insisted, like a child sobbing her hurt.

"And you don't give a shit about him."

"I love him."

"Yeah. You love him. This is how you love him."

After stubbing out her cigarette, she sat up, holding her head. "What do want me to do?" she barely asked in a whisper.

"'Cause you'll do anything, right?"

Wordlessly doped, she stared at him.

"You don't need me, babe. You think you do, but you need a fucking, twenty-four-hour shrink."

Her tears came on like a faucet. "You don't love me at all. You promised Tommie you would, but you don't."

"Do you love me when you fuck every other guy on the planet?"

"They don't mean shit to me," she said softly.

Steve slammed out of the room, ignoring her sobs that seemed to follow him.

"Take care of Jess or I'll come back and haunt you."

What if I don't? What if I leave Jess to take care of herself*? Would you really haunt me for the rest of my life, Tommie?*

She'd snorted cocaine right in front of Ronnie. She might have bought the shit with him in the car. He couldn't allow either to happen ever again. Even if Tommie did haunt him for the rest of his life and Jessie killed herself, he had to think of what affect her bullshit had on his kids.

More calmly than he could have imagined himself, he went back upstairs to face her. He threw a brochure on the bed. "We talked about this before, but you kept insisting you wanted the quick-fix rehab. This time you'll do this program. You'll do it or--"

She'd been rehabilitated at the same place for years. In two weeks, she was supposedly drug and alcohol free. She rarely attended the follow-up meetings that went with it. Less than two months later, she ended up back where she started.

The program he wanted her to submit to was a four-week one that didn't consist of mere drug and alcohol rehabilitation. It was supposed to help uncover the reason for the drugs and alcohol and teach the patient how to live without them. Everything he'd heard about the place claimed it was hell on the person going through the program, but the results made it worthwhile.

"Okay. Okay."

Steve went to the closet and got out a suitcase.

"What? *Now?*"

"Yeah. Now. Or never."

He knew she only agreed to go because she thought he'd stay with her if she did what he asked. Maybe it wasn't fair for him to allow her to believe it.

"I didn't buy the shit with Ronnie in the car. I called a friend. He brought it here. Ronnie stayed outside the bedroom 'til I snorted it."

Small consolation. It didn't change Steve's resolve. The way he felt... He had to end this. Now or never.

* * * *

As soon as Steve got back to his office, he called the school to make sure Ronnie had arrived. Relieved at the news that he was there, Steve sank into his chair. *Still have to tell him tonight where his mom is and how long before she comes back. It ain't over.*

He wanted to talk to Kristina, crazy and stupid as that urge was. He couldn't go there again.

I don't care. Dammit, she was the one person in my life I could really trust not to feel sympathy for my wife. She's the one person who could make me feel human again. She cared about me like no one else does or even could. And I screwed it up with my own feelings.

"Steve? Got a minute?"

Looking up, Steve saw Daniel Cook. He stood as his mentor closed the door, obviously about to say something he didn't want overheard. Steve had always invited the man's advice. He wasn't sure why, but this time he felt afraid to hear it.

"My son called. I had to go," Steve said as Daniel took a seat where he'd been a minute ago.

Daniel folded his hands over his paunch. "Your wife?" He somehow managed to say it in a sympathetic, *again?* tone that made Steve flush despite knowing the frustration wasn't directed at him.

"Steve, what have I said to you since your first year at this college?"

Steve quoted the words automatically, "Everyone has their niche."

"Exactly," Daniel nodded, lifting his gaze to meet Steve's. "Are you sure you're in the right niche?"

"Are you firing me, Dan?"

"You have tenure," Daniel said simply, getting to his feet. He clapped a hand on Steve's shoulder. "You know what you have to do. I can't keep covering for you, regardless of how I feel about you--and your family--personally. You know what's best for you, even if it's damn scary to consider it. What more can you do where you are?"

Daniel left the room as abruptly as he'd appeared, and Steve found himself annoyed the way he always was--at first--when his mentor gave him advice. Daniel wanted him to figure it out himself.

He wouldn't be fired, especially over asking a teaching assistant to give a lecture. So the niche didn't refer to his career. Home--his kids needed him. But, just like Steve had told her that morning, Jess didn't need him. He didn't and couldn't help her. She didn't help him, let alone their kids.

Jessie wasn't the niche he should be in. He knew that. Getting out was the best thing for all of them, a scary-as-hell decision, but he'd done everything he could do to keep them all together. He'd given everything. His all would never be enough, regardless of whether he stayed or left with the kids. Daniel had essentially given him the permission he couldn't seem to give himself to separate himself from Jessie.

Ah hell, he was tired of thinking about all this. He knew what niche he wanted to be in. The one that built him up instead of tore him down. The one that believed he was a good person and had no idea he was guilty of so many sins.

Kristina believed he'd paid for his sins long ago. Whether or not it was true, he wanted to be with her. *To hell with the consequences. I deserve something for myself.*

If only she'd forgive him.

Thirteen

"Do you hate me?"

I love you.

Kristina had her chair half turned away from her desk, watching foolishly for Steve to emerge from the DeSmet Building. It would be two-thirty in a few minutes. He would go to Tilly's. She wouldn't.

She swiveled back to her desk and was stunned to see him standing in the doorway of her office. Steve's voice had drifted to her so softly, she'd believed her mind had conjured him up yet again.

"Steve," she said, feeling joy work its familiar way up her throat.

"Do you hate me?" he asked again.

She swallowed. "*You* said you couldn't see me. I didn't say it to you. I understand your reasons for believing you had to."

"That makes one of us. I don't understand why I said it."

"Yes, you do. You're a good man. You had to say it."

He'd come back. There'd been a little absence, but she'd felt every second of it like fire. *Remember your vow? End it or tell him your feelings.* But Kristina knew she wouldn't be able to. Either it would mean sure rejection today. She couldn't take any more of that from him.

"Do you want to go to Tilly's? With me?"

She rose before he'd even finished speaking, got her jacket, and went to him. *With him.*

"What's happening?" She hadn't dared ask until they'd made it out of the Center and headed toward the restaurant. She glanced at him when his arm brushed hers.

"You remember the place you recommended when I asked you about good rehabs?"

Kristina nodded. About a year ago, Steve had asked her, and she'd told him about a place an hour south of Milwaukee. His wife had refused to go because the program was rumored to be intense. The patient--and the patient alone, not a family member--had to commit to a full four weeks before the clinic would accept him or her. The patient wasn't allowed visitors in all that time. Phone calls were only accepted after two weeks and only on a specified day and time. Family members could call and request information about how their loved one was doing, but that was the extent of the communication between the patient and the outside world.

"She agreed to go."

Keeping her own feelings locked down, Kristina said calmly, "They're tough there. They'll teach her to be tough on herself, so maybe she won't fall back into old habits."

"You think it'll help her?" Steve asked.

"They've got a low recurrence rate."

"Yeah. But they've never met Jess before."

"You don't think it'll work?"

He glanced across the street as they walked, and his silence said what he couldn't say out loud for a long minute. "No."

What is this? What does it mean that he's here, that he asked me here? She couldn't begin to guess and knew she didn't have the courage to bring it up. In the whole scheme of things, the reasons wouldn't make any difference anyway. She wanted to be with him, even if he unthinkably used her for his own needs.

Steve held open the door for her. She entered Tilly's considering the usual way she got here. Waiting inside the bookstore, then popping over here as if she'd just happened by.

The restaurant was more crowded than usual, but they got a table instead of their usual booth and ordered drinks. Steve kept looking around, avoiding her eyes. She could tell he wanted to tell her something.

She asked, "Did you want to talk about anything in particular?"

"I treat you like you're my personal shrink, don't I?"

He seemed embarrassed, and her need to reach out to him was strong. "No. You treat me like a friend you need. I'm glad you came to me." *Liar. You're not merely* glad. *You've spent the past four days crying your eyes out every time you're alone.*

He started to take a deep breath, but the words rushed out before he'd completed that necessity. "I don't think I can do it anymore. She'll never change. We're all miserable, and it won't change by holding it together. Val cries all the time, has nightmares. Tom is withdrawn, and I don't think I'll ever be able to bring him out again. He's hanging around with this kid that..."

He shook his head. "I don't know, but he's trouble. And Ronnie--he hates me. He hates me because hating me is loving his mother in his mind. Today, she--" He grasped for air and inhaled. "I think if I don't get them away from her, she'll destroy them. I have to think of them, right? Leaving, asking her to leave, is the best thing for all of us."

"For you?"

He nodded. "I can't take it anymore. I can't play her games. I'll lose my mind or kill myself if I have to do it even one more time. But, hell, Ronnie will never forgive me."

"How do you think your other children will react?"

Steve laughed, but he obviously didn't find his reason amusing. "Not long ago, Val told me she and Tom have talked about it and they think I should get a divorce."

Kristina stared at him in astonishment. In all her years of counseling, she had yet to hear a kid say they *wanted* their parents to get a divorce. No matter how bad things got between the parents, kids always seemed to want to retain the family unit they were familiar with. "My God," she said softly.

"That's bad?" Steve said, obviously already suspecting but seeking her professional opinion.

"That's very bad, Steve. Especially coming from such young children."

When he wrapped his hands around the back of his head and leaned forward, as if the pronouncement placed another huge weight on him, she reached toward him. At the last moment, she held back to keep him from rejecting her. "Don't blame yourself, Steve. You've been trying to hold everything together. Valerie and Tom want to stay with you, don't they? That speaks highly in your favor. You've done right by them and they know it. But they also realize a divorce is probably the best thing for all of you."

"How the hell can I do it? How'll I *ever* do it?"

Some guilt still prevented him from being unequivocal in his decision. Kristina's curiosity about the reasons reached overwhelming proportions, but she knew she couldn't ask him that. He would have to volunteer the information himself.

"I don't want to think about it anymore," he said in exhaustion as their drinks arrived.

Kristina watched him try to clear his thoughts.

He stared at the checkered tablecloth. "So how come you didn't go out with Garret?"

"Who?"

"One of my assistants. Student assistant. He asked you out on Tuesday."

Kristina nodded. "Oh. I'd forgotten. I just, well, he's a little young for me."

"Doesn't seem to bother most of the women he asks out."

Steve's expression seemed strange--not teasing, the way it should have been. It looked serious, but reluctantly so. Was he...? No, Steve couldn't possibly be *jealous*. He certainly had no reason to be. That rationalization didn't quell the burning in her chest at the thought that he might be.

"He seemed nice. I just don't think we'd be right for each other."

Steve looked at her again and she saw so much there in his expression, she knew she had to be imagining it all. He wasn't jealous. He wasn't relieved. He certainly couldn't want her for himself. Frantically, she tried to bury the flare of hope resurrected inside her.

* * * *

Kristina reached for another tissue as her doorbell rang and she sneezed simultaneously. Steve stood before her when she opened the door.

Truthfully, a part of her had waited for him to drop by every night since they'd reconciled. He hadn't until tonight. He'd been very careful to keep everything on the level of friendship. Over the last few weeks, they'd met often on the campus and at Tilly's. She hadn't even needed to follow his schedule to see him.

He'd avoided all discussion of his possible divorce. Kristina knew he believed that, by ignoring it in his mind and in conversation, he might never have to face facts. He'd told his children where their mother was. His daughter's nightmares and crying had decreased. His middle son had accepted the situation wordlessly. Ronnie had blown up at him, but Steve said he'd forced him to face it could be the best thing for all of them. Maybe deep down his older son realized more was going on than strict rehabilitation, and that was why he'd kept to himself and didn't talk to the rest of the family at all.

"How did the concert go?" Kristina asked, waving Steve in with her tissue box. She knew he'd been working late every night in preparation for the concert that had taken place tonight. If she hadn't felt so rotten, she would have gone.

"Good. What's the matter?" He indicated the balled tissues in her hand and the box at the ready.

"I don't know. I think I'm developing an allergy to all of Hillary's castaways. I've never been allergic to animals before, but I've never had this many before."

"Now what did she give you?" Steve said, as he took off his jacket and draped it over the armchair. She'd never before seen him without it. He wore it like protective armor. Kristina tried not to look at his muscular arms, the way his t-shirt, tucked into his jeans, pulled taut against his stomach and chest.

"Guinea pigs. I brought them home and cleaned their cage. I've been sneezing ever since."

Steve smiled. "And you keep them all because--?"

"They need a good home where someone will care for them."

"What if you are allergic to them?"

"Then I guess I'm in trouble." Kristina dumped the used tissues into the trash. "Do you want something to drink?"

"Thanks. But maybe I should go along with you so I don't fall asleep on your couch."

Kristina smiled, then laughed, leading the way into her kitchen. "Are the kids with your sister-in-law?"

He shook his head. "Evangeline stayed late again. Gwen's on assignment in Cancun."

Steve had told her all about his friends--the ones he'd known almost all his life and were like family to him, about his actual family, including a younger sister he was very close to. He and the kids went to San Bernardino during the last part of the summer each year for a couple weeks to visit his sister and her husband. His wife stayed home because of an aversion to California, as she called it, so the time he had with his children there was a time of happiness for all of them. His sister-in-law, Gwen, was a model and took her twelve-year-old daughter with her when she worked, along with her daughter's personal tutor.

Steve had also revealed more to Kristina about the lighter side of his past instead of just the darkness that had somehow seemed to swallow almost everything else.

"I can't stay long."

"I'm glad you stopped by anyway," Kristina said without looking at him. After she filled glasses with ice, then soda. They sat together at her small kitchen table.

"So how come you don't have a date? It's Friday night."

"I almost had one. If Hillary had had her way, I would have. She tried to fix me up again."

Hillary had noticed the change in Steve's behavior because he came to Kristina's office, or left with her, often. She'd seen it as a sign of trouble. Hillary seemed to believe there was no possible way a married man would ever leave his wife, even a man as unhappy as Steve, and she'd tried to save Kristina from herself by fixing her up.

"She does that a lot, doesn't she?"

Kristina nodded. "I could tell you some stories."

"Okay."

"Okay?" Smiling in surprise, she said, "This past summer she fixed me up with this guy named Wendell Wiggins."

Steve laughed just the way she had when Hillary thrust the blind date on her.

"With a name like that, I expected him to be a total geek. Instead, he was this huge muscle-man type. He spent the entire night talking about his beloved car. There were even some tears shed at one point. His, not mine."

Steve chuckled again, and Kristina tried to control the pounding of her heart at the sound. The beautiful sound of Steve happy. Hillary had every reason to worry about her.

Unbelievably, Kristina had discovered that it was possible to fall even more in love with a person you might never be with. The last few weeks had been like a dream she never wanted to wake up from.

"I've never had anyone special in my life," she said suddenly, trying to sound uncaring about the fact because the opposite would reveal too much. Every day she promised herself she'd tell Steve the truth, but every day she chickened out for fear he'd end the fragile relationship they enjoyed. "Not even Matt."

"Matt?"

"He's this guy I met in college. He had this horrendous home life. His father was so cruel to him and his mother. I considered him just a friend until he came to me one night, the night his father murdered his mother in jealous anger, and things got out of hand. Matt was reacting to the grief." Cheeks burning, she tried not to make a big deal out of it. "But our relationship took on a new aspect after that, and he never stays around for long. Part of me really doesn't mind. I know that sounds horrible."

Kristina ventured a look across the table and saw the muted expression troubling Steve's face and eyes. What she told him affected him, but he didn't speak.

"We have a sexual chemistry. That's all. He always seems to show up when I'm feeling most lonely, and he's at a low point in either his career or personal life."

"When's the last time you saw him?" Steve asked hoarsely, for a reason Kristina wished he would reveal.

"Recently. The weekend before you told me we couldn't see each other anymore. Thankfully he didn't stay any longer than that. I don't think I could have coped with it that time.

"Summers are hard. The hardest." *When you're not on the campus, but I am.* "I let Hillary fix me up a lot in the summer, but it never works out. Sometimes I think men just want to get a woman into bed and it ends there for them. But--I know you won't believe it after I told you about Matt--but I think sex should be something that happens after you know someone for a long time. So these guys think I'm both clingy and a tease, or they freak out when I tell them I'm a counselor, like I'm suddenly going to tear into their life and reveal their deepest, darkest secrets."

"You'd never do that. You don't lecture and find flaws. You listen. You're there," Steve insisted, surprising her because she'd expected him to be disgusted by her superficial relationship with Matt.

"Thanks. That means a lot to me."

"You must get lonely a lot."

She nodded. "I miss... I miss being in a man's arms. I think that's the hardest part of being alone. There's something about being in a man's arms that's like nothing else in the world. Waking up there. Having them open to you, take you in, hold you to that hard chest. So you know someone in the world cares about you. I don't expect anyone to understand, but that's why I sleep with Matt. I'm ashamed of it, but it makes me feel wanted and alive for a short while. And that's something."

"I understand loneliness like that."

Kristina swallowed as she met his eyes. "I bet you do," she said. "And I'm sorry you have to feel it, too. You shouldn't have to."

"Neither should you."

Their gazes locked, and it was almost as if she felt his pain and his healing, as if she gave him the same. But then he seemed embarrassed about it.

"I really should go."

As he stood, her mind raced to find some reason to keep him there longer. Some reason to see him again soon. Tomorrow was Saturday. She wouldn't see him until Monday, and that seemed like forever away right now.

"There's an art show at Brady Street district tomorrow afternoon. Do you like art?" she asked, trying to sound casual while she followed him into the living room, where he put on his jacket.

"I can't. I have to get groceries. I shop once a month and, when I do, it takes all day. I have to bring the kids along."

"Really? I've always wanted to shop once a month. Then I wouldn't be running out every few days to get things here and there. Where do you shop?"

"Sentry."

Kristina found herself lying as she set the groundwork for seeing him this weekend, somewhere, any way. "Oh, so do I. In Brookfield anyway. What a coincidence."

Steve smiled in distraction and said again, "I better go."

"Thanks for coming." She followed him to the door, but he didn't open it and she didn't want to be the first.

He turned to her, looking mortified, compelled, uncontrolled. "Thanks for telling me. What you told me. Don't feel bad. We all do what we have to, to get through the night, you know? We're all human."

Now. Now or never. Kristina stepped forward and slipped her arms around him in what could be construed as a hug. Or more. "Thanks," she murmured, smiling though he couldn't see it any more than he could see the tears filling her eyes. "Thanks for listening to the ramblings of a lonely woman."

For an instant, he stood rigidly, as if he was made of glass and she could break him. Then his arms went around her and he held her as close as she'd always dreamed, even closer than the time he'd picked her up off the ice.

"No problem. You're always there for me." His mouth came near her ear, his tone throaty with emotion.

She turned her head so her ear rested against his heart. His heartbeat sounded as erratic as hers must.

"Haven't you ever wondered why I know your schedule by heart each semester, Steve?" Was she actually speaking, or was all of this simply a fantasy she'd be relieved later wasn't reality? "I time my breaks with yours. I use the lounge in the DeSmet Building even though there's one in the Center. I meet you in the parking lot at exactly the same time you come out each morning and each night. I go to Tilly's whenever you're there. Haven't you ever wondered?"

The words "*Because I love you. That's why* everything" hovered on the tip of her tongue, but when she lifted her head and saw his dark, startled eyes she knew she wouldn't be able to say them and finish this.

Stupid, stupid, stupid! As usual, your timing is off. Yet Steve didn't run out, throwing the words "I can't see you ever again" at her as he went. He didn't even slink out. All he said in response was, "No. I never wondered."

He reached for the doorknob. But instead of adding "I never wanted to wonder and I certainly don't now," or ending their friendship, he said, "See you" like he really meant it.

After he'd gone, her mind wouldn't shut off as she tried to imagine what he thought of the things she'd said. What other conclusion could he come to, other than the fact that she was in love with him and had been for years? He might try to convince himself she hadn't meant anything of the kind, yet his mind would return to that conclusion every time.

She was there for him because she was crazy about him. That was why she'd been devastated when he broke off their friendship and why she'd been so happy when he came back to her. Once he accepted the only logical explanation, what would he do? Run from it? Ignore it? Something in-between?

Tomorrow she would find out, whether she wanted to or not.

Fourteen

Did Kristina have feelings for him? More than friendship feelings?

Steve didn't even want to consider the possibility as he drove home that night. Had he encouraged more than friendship feelings? What if he had more than friendship feelings for *her*?

Don't think about that. Don't even admit it in your own head. And damn straight don't think about how it felt to have her in your arms, the way she sighed against your chest like she'd waited forever to be there.

He'd been very careful not to cross the line, the friendship line, these past few weeks. He'd been a good friend, nothing more. That hug qualified as just one good friend being there for another.

After he paid and thanked Evangeline, he checked on the kids. All accounted for. All fine. Asleep. The past couple weeks had been like a fresh start for them. Even Ronnie, unwilling to give Steve an inch, had silently conceded that maybe going to rehab this was the best thing for his mother. Maybe she'd really get better this time. But Steve was afraid he'd inadvertently made a promise he couldn't keep. Ronnie expected his mom to leave that rehab all better and everything would be healed and mended.

Ronnie had been withdrawn since Steve told all of them where their mom was. He agreed he wanted his mom to get better, and maybe this would help. But he still watched Steve with an eagle eye. More than once, Steve had felt like he was trying to pull the wool over his own son's eyes. In one breath, he told Ronnie his mom would get better. In the next, he might take him from his mother for good.

What does it matter? Whatever he did, Ronnie would be mad at him. He'd think the worst. Since Steve couldn't win, why bother trying? He hadn't done anything wrong. So why did he feel guilty anyway?

I don't want to think about that either. Steve pulled his shirt over his head. He'd been avoiding reality, avoiding the decisions that needed to come with it. Anything to feel relief since he'd dropped off Jess. He'd let Ronnie talk to her yesterday during her one phone call, and she hadn't asked to talk to anyone else, though she'd questioned Ron in depth about everyone.

I want this friendship with Kristina. I don't want to give it up, now or later.

He wandered downstairs, into the living room. Clean. Work. He had a dozen things he could do. Instead, he picked up his guitar. He hadn't played for personal enjoyment for years. It'd become his job, no longer his passion. But he played now, closing his eyes because the act felt like pain.

Haven't you ever wondered...?

He'd never wondered about Kristina's schedule matching his, semester after semester. Never noticed she came and went with him. What they shared wasn't regular friendship. It wasn't like what he had with Daniel. With Garret. She'd become special to him in a way they could never be.

Haven't you ever wondered...?

If he'd wondered why her schedule coincided with his all the time, he would have had to wonder if she had a thing for him. No way would he let himself considered that. She was young, beautiful. He was a head-case...

But then she's a counselor--she thrives on helping people. Can't turn down all the crazy pets her boss gives her and she can't give them away. And that relationship she has with the bastard who raped her--what the hell is that, other than plain stupid and desperate? Kristina isn't stupid or desperate. She's level-headed. But she needs to be there for people the same way I do. Loneliness aside, maybe she needs *to help this guy. Maybe she can't help herself. And maybe that's all I am to her--a head-case she needs to help.*

Steve thrust his guitar away from him at the unpalatable thought.

You prefer the idea that she's in love with you and might have been for years?

Knowing he couldn't sleep, Steve worked, pushing away the thoughts of Kristina's feelings, his feelings for her, facing Jess, losing his son. In the end, he satisfied himself by deciding to forget everything for awhile. And he definitely wouldn't ask Kristina what she'd meant by *Haven't you ever wondered...?*

* * * *

"Remember, we're going to the mall later, so don't spend it all here," Steve called after his kids, once they had their weekly allowance and tore off into Sentry like the money was burning a hole in their pockets. "One of you watch Val," he added even though he knew at least one of them would do so automatically.

Shoving his wallet into his back pocket, he turned toward the shopping carts.

"Hi."

For a few seconds, Steve didn't place her face simply because it'd never occurred to him Kristina might come here. Her voice brought recognition, and the way she stood near the carts... She'd been waiting for him. *"Haven't you ever wondered why I know your schedule by heart?"*

"You're shopping in Greenfield today," he said softly when he approached her. Much as he would have liked to be, he couldn't get annoyed at her. She'd told him she shopped at Sentry in Brookfield, but there was a good chance she'd just said it so he wouldn't wonder about it if they ever bumped into each other here.

"I thought I'd try this Sentry today. I hope you don't mind."

Mind? She stood there looking like the only sunshine that would ever warm him. Her hair was pulled up high in an adorable ponytail that professed a carefreeness her expression didn't share. The only thing Steve minded at the moment was that he couldn't acknowledge the truth. He *wanted* to see her.

But his kids were here. Ronnie. How the hell would he explain her presence? Explain it so it didn't raise any red flags?

He shrugged at Kristina, feeling like he couldn't bear it if he didn't let her off the hook. He smiled as much as he could with the tension between them. "Why would I mind?"

Slowly, her lips curved upward in relief that shocked a sting behind his eyes. *I can't remember the last time a woman--and not the college girls in my classes--had a crush on* me. *Why can't I enjoy it instead of feeling guilty?*

Because she's not a girl in college with an innocent infatuation on an older guy. Because it goes both ways with Kristina. And that's not just enjoying--that's damn dangerous.

She matched stride with him, and he glanced at her well-shaped legs encased in comfortable jeans.

"So those are your kids?" Kristina said softly, in a kind of awe.

When he glanced at her, he nodded.

"I'd love to meet them."

Steve glanced at his watch. "They'll be heading back my way in another fifteen minutes or so."

They walked through a couple aisles together. He threw things in his cart, acutely aware her basket remained empty. Any minute now, his kids would arrive and he couldn't think of any way to introduce Kristina without provoking their suspicion.

He caught Kristina's gaze, and she smiled shyly. The silence between them begged for some conversation, but neither of them could seem to find anything to say. He'd promised himself he'd keep his friendship with her separate from his home life. Not once did he imagine he wouldn't want to when the two merged. He wanted Tom and Val to meet her. Knowing her would help them. Kristina was a good person to know. And maybe he'd feel less guilty when he saw her if at least two of his kids liked her.

His cart was half full when Val and Tom wandered back. Val looked surprised, but Tom didn't show any reaction, not even when Steve introduced her as a counselor at the college.

"You work with my dad?" Val asked, smiling as she stared up at Kristina.

Kristina grinned at her. "We both work at Eisner University. I'm very happy to meet you, Valerie."

"You're pretty."

"Thank you. I think you are, too, sweetheart."

Val beamed at her.

Kristina glanced at Tom. "I'm glad to meet you, too, Tom."

"How do you know us?" Tom asked, in his usual not friendly, not unfriendly way.

Pursing her lips, Kristina met Steve's eyes for an instant as if she wasn't sure what to say. What he would want her to say. "Your father has told me about all of you."

"You're his shrink?"

Ronnie's voice came from behind them, and Steve knew without a doubt as soon as he saw Ron's hard expression that he'd heard everything.

"No," Kristina said, trying to sound easygoing. No matter what she did, Ronnie would brand her the enemy along with Steve. "We're friends."

"Yeah," Ronnie muttered, his lip curled viciously. "I bet."

He turned around and walked down the aisle.

"Come back in fifteen minutes," Steve called after him, adding, though his older son probably didn't hear it, "We'll be ready to go by then."

Kristina met his gaze helplessly.

"Don't worry about it," he told her. He'd be the one to worry about it.

"He's like that with everybody," Val said, slipping beneath Kristina's arm, to her side. "So how far is your office from my dad's?"

Val asked her at least a hundred questions in the next ten minutes, as they walked through the aisles, but Kristina was good with her. Steve could tell his daughter soaked in all her good qualities in that time. Tom walked along beside them mutely.

"You didn't get anything." Steve inclined his head toward her basket when they headed toward the cash registers.

"I guess I got side-tracked," Kristina said with a friendly smile at Val. It was a good excuse. Ronnie muttered under his breath behind them like he didn't believe a word.

Ignoring him, Steve said, "We have to go the mall and get some stuff. You want to have lunch with us there?"

Kristina seemed shocked by the invitation, almost as surprised as Steve was at his own boldness.

"Please. Come with us," Val begged, putting her arms around Kristina and looking up at her with angelic fawn eyes.

"I'd love to. Thank you for inviting me."

"We need to stop at home and unload these groceries first."

"I can help you. I didn't end up getting anything on my list this time anyway."

On the way out to the parking lot, Steve threw all caution to the wind. He couldn't win, so what difference did it make? "Why don't you ride with us? I'll drop you off here when we're done at the mall."

Again, Val added her whole-hearted two cents' worth, and Kristina agreed, good idea or not, her gaze locked with his.

What are we doing here? he wondered as they unloaded the groceries from the car and started filling the fridge and cupboards in his kitchen with them. *What am* I *doing? She's in my house. Kristina's in my house, where only my thoughts have allowed her to dwell for any length of time.*

During lunch, Val focused all her attention on Kristina, and Steve couldn't help noting the differences between Kristina and Jess. Kristina treated every word Val said to her as if it was important. She was sweet and caring with her, making Val glow under the attention. The boys were both sullen and got up as soon as they finished eating to play the video games in the restaurant.

Val asked Kristina to go to the restroom with her, and Steve watched the two of them walking hand-in-hand with a lump in his throat. He was scared, but at the same time it felt all right. It couldn't be in the long run, but he didn't care.

Kristina returned, saying Val had stayed with her brothers, as she slid in across from him in the secluded booth.

"She let you go?"

Kristina chuckled. "Only when I said I'd be right here when she got back."

Steve grinned. He couldn't see the kids from the table, but that was all right.

"It would be so easy to fall in love with them," she said softly.

"Val. Yeah." She was like a defenseless puppy. His sons pushed people away, whether they meant to or not.

"All of them," she insisted. "Tom is withdrawn, just like you told me he was, but I also sense a very strong core in him, along with intelligence and loyalty. And Ronnie, he's hurting so much. How could anyone not love him?"

Helpless to his own needs, Steve reached across the table and drew her hand toward him. He held it in both of his, against his chest, and didn't allow himself to look away or shrink from what he did. Most people without kids of their own wouldn't feel sympathy for Steve's, let alone love for them. He'd known she would.

"Thank you so much for today, Steve. I'll never forget it. As long as I live, I won't."

He could no longer convince himself Kristina didn't have feelings for him, the same kind of feelings he'd developed for her. Not when tears shone in her eyes as she looked at him. Not when her unwillingness to make a wrong move just barely kept her where she sat across the table as he lifted her hand to his mouth and kissed the back of it, then the palm she exposed to him.

He wanted to kiss her mouth, more than their breaths mingling and their souls entwining. He wanted to feel the softness of her lips beneath his, taste her sweetness. Her need for him.

As if she'd read his mind, Kristina drew his hand back to her and kissed it the same way he had hers. Every nerve ending in his arm responded to her. Then she brought his hand down, pressing it against her heart, just above her beautiful breast. He felt the wild beat against his palm, and his body pulsed recklessly the way it hadn't in a lifetime.

Ah hell, he couldn't breathe, let alone look away from her compelling gaze. She loved him. He didn't have a single doubt about it. He wouldn't be able to convince himself otherwise later either. She'd branded it into every cell of his body.

When he pulled back, he was shaking. He was aroused.

She was aroused--he could see it in her eyes, the soft pout of her lips and her nipples pushing insistently against her shirt. He'd felt the curve of her breast against his hand a minute ago. He'd never forget it. The darkness would remind him.

Once they left the restaurant, he shopped for the kids in a daze. He dropped Kristina off at her car. He listened to Val sing her virtues until Ronnie told her to shut up. And he wondered, *What the hell are we doing here?*

Scared as he was, he thought he might be ready to know the answer.

Fifteen

Even the next day, Steve couldn't get Kristina off of his mind. He'd spent an endless night alone with the memories of Kristina sitting across from him. He'd gotten an earful from Ronnie as soon as they got home, too--an earful he'd barely acknowledged. Val had asked him a thousand questions he'd fielded almost too easily. He'd given nothing away, and yet...

The need to see her overwhelmed him. What would she do if he showed up there? He couldn't go alone. *Hell no.*

Besides, he already had plans. His mom, Felicia, was expecting them. His parents had divorced just after he'd finished college, something that had come out of nowhere for him. He'd never spent much time wondering about their marriage, except when he was pissed off at his old man and wondering how his mother could stand the bastard's overbearing need for control of everything. His mom had gotten the two-story, modernized Georgian style house in Mequon, the one he'd grown up in, following the divorce.

He was surprised to find Jessie's parents, who were Felicia's neighbors, also at the house. He'd kept in touch with them more than Jess ever did, mostly for the kids. Surprisingly, Jessie had never tried to turn Ronnie against her parents.

"Sorry I haven't called," Steve offered lamely to Clarice and Perry Nelson. Since they knew the rules of the rehab Jess was in, he hadn't figured he needed to call them.

As sophisticated as Jessie's parents were, Steve thought they aged each time he saw them. Jess took after her mom, who was petite yet curvaceous, with dyed-to-keep-it-youthful, auburn hair. Perry was tall and lean, like Tommie had been, with bluish-black hair that'd turned white long ago.

"Felicia told us you were coming with the children today. We're going to drive down to that place and demand they allow us to visit our daughter. What right do they have to keep out family?"

"They won't let you," Steve said as the kids sat down on the sofa in the museum-sized living room. "Jess signed the waiver. She agreed to it."

"We'll see about that," Clarice said stubbornly. Not too many people thwarted her. Jess had told Steve her employees called her the pit bull. When she decided something, she rarely backed down.

While Jess and Tommie were growing up, their parents hadn't paid them attention. They hired servants to do that, maybe believing if kids had all they needed materially, they'd turn out fine. Since Tommie's death, guilt over their failure as parents had kept them begging Jessie for forgiveness. There was nothing they wouldn't do to win points with her. They obviously thought breaking down the door of the rehab she was in would do just that.

"I wanna go along," Ronnie said, and Steve suddenly thought, *Let them. Let them all go. They won't be able to get in, but it'll make them feel better if they try.* Ronnie glanced at Steve. "I'm gonna go."

"Okay," Steve said, feeling ashamed for what he was considering. Ron would go. *If Jess' parents take Ronnie, drop him back here with my mom when they get back tonight, then we can see Kristina. Without censure.*

Steve couldn't talk himself out of it, no matter how good the arguments he came up with against the idea.

* * * *

Kristina could scarcely breathe as she hung up the phone. Steve was coming. He was bringing his two youngest children. They were bringing dinner to her apartment. Somehow, she'd felt strongly she'd be seeing Steve today, especially after yesterday.

She picked up Trina and danced her around the room. "He's coming. He's really coming, Trina, my sweet blooming lass, plump as a partridge, ripe as a peach! Can you believe that? I wasn't just imagining yesterday. It really happened. Steve accepted my feelings. Maybe he even shares them."

She started to laugh at the mere idea, but it caught in her throat. Saying she knew exactly what she was doing would have been a relief. At least there would be some direction here. Steve didn't seem to be planning anything. She certainly wasn't. Everything was just happening. That was scary because it meant they could get hurt. They could be seriously unprepared and let something slip between their fingers because of it. What if she was his transitional fling? She couldn't imagine Steve being so careless and thoughtless, but the fact remained. Something was happening between them, and she couldn't eat, sleep, or think about anything except Steve and the possibilities of them together.

He'd looked at her differently yesterday at the grocery store she so obviously wasn't there to shop in. At first he'd been withdrawn, enough that she'd thought for sure he would tell her to leave. His older son's fury at their relationship seemed to have an effect on him that, well, *freed* him. It was as if he said by his actions *I'm not doing anything wrong here.*

After setting Trina on the sofa, Kristina ran to her bedroom and refreshed her make-up. She'd spent the whole day planning for Steve's drop-in. It didn't take much.

Am I the other woman? The mistress?

Kristina's reflection paled before her very own eyes. Mistress was such an ugly word for one of the most shameful positions a woman could put herself in. Yet she found it difficult to think of what she and Steve shared as something sinful and wrong.

He's married. He has a wife. He's not divorced and hasn't mentioned divorce in weeks. Anything that happens here puts you in the position of being the other woman. He's cheating and you're cheating with him.

Thinking *But I love him. He's my soulmate!* didn't erase the dirty feeling. If he was serious about divorcing his wife, that would be a different story. However, facts were facts: right now any involvement between them was incontrovertibly wrong.

"I can't refuse him," Kristina whispered honestly to her reflection. "I can't pull back now. I can't. I'd never forgive myself if I did. And he'll never forgive himself if something happens before he's untangled himself from *her.*"

The doorbell rang, and she glanced at the clock in surprise. Had he called her from the road? Knowing she'd be eager to see him and would never refuse? Instead of cringing at her too blatant feelings for him, ones he saw, she was glad he knew her so well.

She opened the door to Steve. His children stood in front of him. Kristina smiled at them. Tom moved inside first at her invitation, but Val threw her arms around her. The little girl's clear need for a proper mother figure struck Kristina as both sad and sweet.

She'd fallen in love with Steve's children immediately, the way she'd always imagined she would. They carried battles scars from facing too much of life's harshness too soon. Kids were nothing if not resilient, though. They believed their father loved them more than anything. He would help them heal.

Once Val stepped inside, Kristina met Steve's eyes. It stole her breath again to realize he looked at her differently. A little more openly. A little more honestly. He was glad to see her.

"Hi," he said softly.

"Hi. I'm so glad you called." She hugged him briefly, lightly, wondering if he felt the electricity she did at being so close to him.

"Where's Ronnie?"

"With his grandparents. You didn't eat, did you?"

It was almost seven in the evening. She hadn't been hungry all day.

"No. What did you get?" she asked as she closed the door behind them.

"Chinese."

"Smells great. I'll get us some plates."

"I'll help you," Val offered, her arms very full of Trina.

"Thank you, Valerie."

When Kristina took the bags from Steve, their hands touched and their gazes locked. Unexpectedly, she remembered the feeling of his hand against the upper curve of her breast yesterday. Heat washed over her. *No, I can't refuse him anything, not even to keep my own self-respect. He's all I've ever wanted.*

Even as she went with Valerie to the kitchen, she felt Steve watching her, rearranging everything inside her with the intimacy of his lingering gaze.

A man who wants to make love doesn't invite his children along, Kristina reminded herself sternly. Maybe Steve wanted her, but he wouldn't allow them to get swept away. That was probably why he'd brought Valerie and Tom. They needed a protective barrier between them.

"I like your apartment," Val said as she set the table with the dishes Kristina brought out.

"Thanks. After we eat, I'll show you my other pets. Do you have a pet?"

Valerie shook her head, looking more delicate than ever. "Dad takes care of us by himself, except when Gwen and Evangeline are there after school. There's too much to do as it is."

The words sounded so grown-up, Kristina felt a wave of compassion and couldn't help herself from hugging Valerie. "He does a lot, doesn't he?"

Val nodded, not pulling away from the embrace the way Kristina expected her to. Looking down at her, Kristina brushed her fingers over Valerie's wispy bangs. Her hair, which looked both thick and silky, was gathered at the top of her head with a clasp and spilled over her shoulders in waves.

Kristina's experience with girls who were traumatized by their own mothers was that the girls avoided other women and saw them as the enemy. They felt most comfortable with male figures in their lives and tended to have more male friends in school than female. Valerie seemed very open, maybe because she had female caregivers who genuinely loved her.

Valerie talked throughout the meal, asking Kristina an endless string of questions about herself. Tom ate silently, and Steve watched, quietly contemplative, as she interacted with his daughter. Right after dinner, Valerie dragged her off to the bedroom to see the rest of her pets.

While sitting with the rabbit in her lap, Valerie asked Kristina the question she'd expected sooner or later: "Do you like my dad?" She didn't look up as she stroked the soft white fur.

"Of course. He's one of my closest friends."

"Do you think he's cute?"

Kristina grinned, chucking Valerie under her lightly clefted chin. "I don't think anyone can dispute that your father is *very* good looking."

"Do you have a boyfriend?"

"No."

She's going to be gorgeous when she grows up, Kristina decided conclusively as she looked at the little girl's delicate face.

"Do you want one?"

"Most single women do," Kristina told her, "even if they don't want to admit it."

"Do you want my dad to be your boyfriend?"

Even if they had a romantic relationship they'd spoken of themselves, Steve wouldn't want her to say anything about it. It wasn't her place anyway. "Your father is married, Valerie. To your mother."

"She doesn't love him. Mom doesn't care about any of us. I know you like my dad. I know he likes you. And I like you."

Kristina kneeled closer to her and laced her fingers with Valerie's tiny, cold ones. "Then let's all be friends, all right? I'd love to have you for a friend."

Valerie clearly wasn't happy with the outcome because she'd had bigger goals, but she accepted the compromise for the time being.

When they went back out to the living room, Steve was saying to his son, "Don't mess up Kristina's desk."

Tom stood by her computer desk. He'd pulled out the box for the Journeyman Trilogy computer game.

"It's no problem," Kristina said. "I've never been able to finish that trilogy. It took me a couple months to finish the first one. The second one, I can't get through the space station or DaVinci's studio. So I'll probably never be able to complete the trilogy."

Tom shrugged. "I could show you the ropes."

"You've finished it?"

"Well, yeah. When I was, like, eight."

Kristina grinned. "I am not very good on computers, but I loved the first game." She turned to Steve. "Would you mind if we played for awhile?" He shook his head, the corners of his mouth turned up slightly

She dragged in a chair from the kitchen. In that short time, Tom had her computer up and running. Kristina placed herself entirely in his hands, and he proceeded to amaze her. He also opened up in a way she hadn't anticipated at all. He talked. He laughed. Valerie sat with them for a time, but grew bored and drifted back to the animals.

By the time Kristina looked up again, the room had become dark around them. She glanced back to see Valerie asleep in her father's arms. Steve was watching her and Tom.

"Do you want something to drink?" she asked Tom in a quiet voice.

He asked his father if he could have a soda. Steve nodded his permission

She got up. "Do you want anything, Steve?"

"I'll come with you."

"It's all right. Don't move. You two look so comfortable together."

But he'd already extricated himself from his daughter. Kristina wondered suddenly what he'd done for the last hour or more. What he'd thought about, watching her with his son. She wondered why he followed her into the semi-privacy of her kitchen, where they would be alone together for the first time since unspoken feelings had been exchanged.

Sixteen

Kristina was good with his kids--two of them anyway. Steve hadn't seen Tom open up to anyone, including him, for many years. Sometimes he forgot what the boy was like when he did. And Val had fallen for her immediately, probably because she presented such a contrast to her mother.

Steve wouldn't let himself admit why it affected him so profoundly to see his kids warming to Kristina. She'd made Tom laugh. That alone was worth anything.

He knew damn well why he was following her into the kitchen, though, and he couldn't seem to stop himself. He couldn't kiss her. But he wanted to.

"Your kids are great," she said warily, as she got glasses out of the cupboard.

"You're great with them."

She smiled happily, looking at him for an instant. He saw it--what he'd seen all night and was afraid to accept. Every time she looked at him, her heart was in her eyes. Why was it so familiar? He'd never recognized it before, but, yeah, it'd been there. He knew that now.

"What did you mean?" he blurted out before he lost his nerve. The living room was so quiet he felt he had to whisper. "When you said you know my schedule every semester, you time your breaks with mine?"

She met his gaze despite the flush in her cheeks. "Do you remember the day we met? It was really icy--"

Steve nodded. "You fell."

Kristina swallowed, then took a deep breath before she said, "In more ways than one."

He could tell she wanted desperately to look away, but her eyes remained locked on his steadily, as if she needed to know his reaction. He couldn't decide how to react, what to say. He wished he hadn't asked but accepted he couldn't have stopped himself from it to save his life.

After setting the cups on the table, Kristina rounded the table to stand in front of him. "I've never forgotten the feel of your arms around me, Steve. I know you were just helping me up.

Just you, being you. Being kind. It wasn't supposed to mean anything more than that. But I've never forgotten it. I try to. I can't. You mean too much to me. The first time I met you, I knew you were going to mean everything to me."

Tears hung in the corners of her lashes. Why didn't he gather up his kids and get the hell out of here? This couldn't happen. But his reaction wasn't to flee, like it should have been. He wanted to kiss her. He wanted to hold her.

"I'm married, Kristina," he said quietly. "You know that."

She laughed without amusement. "Do you think I could ever forget it? I wish I could. I wish that could make a difference to my heart. I can't change the way I feel. Sometimes I wish I could, but I love you. I've loved you for so long, I can't remember a time I didn't."

Her words pierced like tiny darts that brought both pleasure and pain when they penetrated his armor. With everything inside him, he wanted to tell her to stop and to never stop.

"When I told you my life is standing still, it's because I feel like I'm alive--really, truly alive--only when I'm with you. Unless we're together someday or it's completely over, my life will stand still."

"Oh, shit," he muttered, closing his eyes. He held onto the back of the chair as hard as he could.

"I'm sorry."

As soon as her fingers tentatively touched his arm, he knew he couldn't hide from any of this anymore. Blindly, he shifted away from the chair, then she was where he needed her to be--in his arms.

This was different than the hugs they'd shared in the past. He felt completely whole with her so close to him, and he couldn't breathe at all.

When he looked down at her, he saw tears running down her face. He brushed them away, lingering at her bottom lip.

"I'm sorry, Steve. It's not fair, but I had to tell you. I don't know where I'm going anymore. Tell me what to do."

He remembered asking the same thing of her, the night he'd almost kissed her, and he couldn't give her an answer now any more than she'd been able to give him one then.

"My life is a mess right now, honey. But you know that. I can't make you any promises. I don't want to lose you. I don't even know what the hell that means. It just... It's the way it is."

She wanted more. Hell, *he* wanted more. Yet she wiped the tears from her face, nodding as she said, "All right." As if he'd given her any reason at all to hope. As if it didn't matter whether or not he'd given her hope. She would wait regardless. He didn't like that, not one damn bit. He had absolutely nothing to give to this incredible woman.

For the moment, they seemed to be in the same place--no reason to hope it could ever work out, yet willing to keep on the way they were because it was better than nothing.

****

"They weren't allowed to see her," Steve's mom told him quietly, her fragile features showing her worry. She opened the door wider. "They were back here within a couple hours."

Ah hell. It was past ten o'clock. Ronnie would want to hear where they'd been, since he knew they hadn't been at his grandmother's. He'd assume the worst, and Steve didn't have the defenses to argue with him tonight. His mind battled total chaos as it was. "Has he eaten?"

"He said he wasn't hungry. I asked him repeatedly."

"How is he?" He didn't really want to know Ronnie was furious with him.

Felicia shook her head. "He's spoken less than a dozen words since they got back. He hasn't moved from that chair either. He demanded to know where you were. What could I tell him? I had no idea."

Her curiosity was obviously aroused, but she didn't ask, thank God. "You've got my pager number. So does he."

She shrugged her frail shoulders. "He said he didn't want to page you."

Steve swore under his breath, glancing to the car where Val slept and Tom hovered halfway there himself. Steve stepped inside the house. The best thing to do was avoid any conversation tonight.

"Come on, Ron, let's get home."

"Where were you?"

"We'll talk about it tomorrow. Val and Tom are asleep in the car. Come on."

"I wanna talk about it now."

Steve didn't hesitate. "You can spend the night here or you can come home with me now. What do you want to do?" Tomorrow they had school, but right now Steve didn't care. Whatever he had to do to avoid this conversation, he'd do.

Ronnie stood reluctantly and went out to the car. Steve thanked his mother without looking at her. She'd never asked him to confide in her before. She certainly wouldn't ask now. He had no intention of answering, whether or not she asked.

The only person he could talk to about this was Kristina, and he couldn't talk to her right now. His sister... But, hell, he didn't want anyone else to know. He didn't have a clue how he'd explain any of this mess outside of his own head, where it was utter confusion anyway.

"You were at that bitch's house, weren't you? And you took Val and Tom there with you," Ronnie said in an ugly tone the second Steve slid in the car.

His son's cruelty made Steve's anger break free. "I don't want you to talk about Kristina like that ever again, dammit. We'll talk about it tomorrow."

"You're fuckin' her, aren't you?"

Steve couldn't speak. He pulled out of the driveway and drove with his teeth clenched hard enough to cause pain.

"Even if he did..." Tom spoke in sleepy voice, always the logical one, in the backseat. "...Mom's fucked around on him a million times. Maybe he deserves revenge."

"I don't want revenge," Steve said on automatic. *I want to be free. That's all. My feelings for Kristina have nothing to do with revenge anyway. Not at all.*

"Don't expect me to cover for you," Ronnie muttered.

"There's nothing *to* cover up. I haven't done anything."

Ronnie snorted, but he fell silent for the rest of the drive.

Sorting through the insanity in his head started to come to Steve slowly. His feelings for Kristina crossed the line--whatever they were, and he couldn't and wouldn't define them right now. They weren't merely a reaction to having someone interested in him, attracted to him, again. Someone who cared about him for the first time in forever. That explanation was too simple because it didn't explain why *he* wanted *her.* He wanted to touch her, kiss her, lose himself completely in her. He wanted to take his kids and run with her, never looking back.

What about Jess? He didn't know, but he had to figure it out. He couldn't let Val and Tom get attached to Kristina until he knew. He'd lose Ronnie completely if he left the boy's mother. *I can't lose Kristina either, but how can I continue with her if I stay in this insane marriage? That wouldn't be fair to her. I don't ever want to hurt her.*

He'd made no promises, yet he felt obligations because she loved him and she'd wait for him even if he didn't ask her to. Whether he wanted to or not, he wanted to be with her. He wanted to be free. There was just no easy way out.

When they got home, Steve set Val on the chair beside the door to take off her shoes and coat. Next to him, Tom pulled off his jacket and tossed it toward the coat tree. It fell short, dropping to the floor. When Steve straightened with Val's coat, picking up Tom's on the way, a package fell out of the pocket.

He saw it as Tom grabbed it, grabbed for his jacket and tried to shove the pack in his pocket. Steve dug it out. He knew what they were before he had them out in his hand.

"Cigarettes? You've been smoking?" He didn't feel anger. He felt shock, like he should have known or should have done something about his suspicions.

"No wonder Timothy quit hangin' around you, dork. Never mind that deadbeat Aaron," Ronnie muttered.

"Are you doing anything else, Tom?" Steve asked. "Are you taking drugs?"

Tom's expression filled with defensive anger. "Why the hell would I ever do that? You think I want to be as fucked up as Mom? They're just cigarettes."

Ronnie already stalked back from the stairs. "You've said your last insult about Mom, you little shit."

The two of them locked together in an instant, both shouting. Val was sobbing, huddled in the chair, by the time Steve got them apart.

"That's enough, dammit," he shouted, holding them both by the shoulder, not as easily as he used to. "We're falling apart here. Don't you guys see that? We can't do this anymore or we'll lose our minds."

Steve let them go, away from each other. He couldn't stop what was happening. There were two sides and they were all separated between them. He felt completely powerless to bring them together.

"You can't divorce Mom. You'll kill her if you do," Ronnie said, breathless from the fight.

"*She's* killing *him*, but you don't give a damn about that, do you?" Tom sneered. "Just as long as Mom crooks her finger your way. But she'll screw you over just like she always does to everybody. She doesn't give a damn about any of us unless she needs something."

Steve couldn't take it anymore as they jumped at each other again. He took the stairs two at a time and shut himself behind his bedroom door.

"Don't be mad at me. I'll do anything you want. I'll make it up to you, Steve. I promise. It'll never happen again. Just don't...please don't leave me. Not now."

"I've loved you for so long, I can't remember a time I didn't. When I told you my life is standing still, it's because I feel like I'm only really, truly alive when I'm with you. Unless we're together someday. Or it's completely over, my life will stand still."

"Me and Tom talked about it. We both said it'd be okay with us if you divorced. We'd be on your side. You don't have to stay married to her for us."

"Tommie died. You know why I am the way I am."

"Take care of Jess or I'll come back and haunt you."

As Steve clutched his head, trying to keep it all in, wanting to avoid it, he shut down the way he only allowed himself to after the kids were in bed, the only time they didn't need him to be whole. He couldn't pick up the pieces for anybody right now, even knowing they could kill each other down there with Val watching the whole thing.

* * * *

In that place between asleep and not quite awake, where he couldn't feel anything because he'd become numb to it, his mind replayed the memory he'd pushed into the darkest corner of himself.

Tommie was back. He and Gwen had just left for their honeymoon a week ago. Why was Tommie back here instead of cloistered in a bed with the love of his life?

It was all Steve could think as he stared at Tommie and Gwen outside his apartment door.

"Where is she?" Tommie demanded.

Steve didn't have to wonder who he meant. Gwen's expression told Steve she'd stupidly told Tommie some part of what he didn't need to know.

Tommie shoved past him into the apartment they used to share. He'd find Jess in Steve's bedroom. He'd find her, naked, in his bed.

"I'm sorry," Gwen whispered. "I'm so sorry. I couldn't change his mind about coming back when he found out Jessie was pregnant."

Gwen couldn't have told Tommie that Steve hadn't made her pregnant. She didn't know the truth herself. Wendy wouldn't have told her, and his sister was the only one who knew the truth. As soon as Tommie found Jessie in his bed, he'd assume the baby was Steve's. It didn't matter one damn bit right now that Steve had never intended anyone to discover he wasn't the father of Jessie's baby. If he'd been able to convince Jess to marry him, no one would have had to know. The only thing he'd succeeded at was stopping her from having an abortion.

He heard Jess and Tommie's heated argument from the bedroom but didn't have the courage to intervene. Tommie would deal with him soon enough. And he'd be ruthless about it.

Tommie appeared a minute later, Jessie chasing after him trying to get him to listen to her. But Tommie looked only at Steve, with every bit of fury he'd expected of him when he found out the truth.

"You're coming with me. Now."

Tommie didn't stop, didn't listen to anyone as he left the apartment. Gwen sobbed out of guilt or something more. It wasn't until later that she'd admitted she spent years seeing this very moment in her magic mirror. The moment Tommie was taken away from her for the rest of her life.

"Are you gonna tell him?" Jess asked Steve fearfully, her eyes wide as a child's. The only thing in the world she feared was her brother's disapproval.

Steve knew the feeling. All his life, he'd wanted Tommie's approval. That dream had shattered long ago. Tommie would disapprove the hell out of this truth.

"If you marry me, I won't."

She swallowed, but didn't hesitate. "Then I'll marry you whenever you want."

Steve shook his head, grabbing his jacket as he left the apartment with the person who used to be his best friend.

The silence in the car as Tommie pulled out of the parking space and squealed out of the lot was enough to make Steve lose his mind.

"You promised me," Tommie said at last, in that deadly quietness Steve feared.

"I plan to marry her, man."

Tommie didn't seem to hear him. "I asked you to stay the fuck away from her. You remember that, man? I begged you not to go near her. You promised me you'd never touch her. You'd never even look at her like that. You remember that?"

Steve turned away, wanting to ask, 'Why is it so bad if I get involved with your sister? You act like I'm the worst possible choice for her when I've spent most of my life taking care of her--the way you wanted me to.'

"You just couldn't help it, is that it? You wanted her and you couldn't say no. Not even for me. For our friendship."

"What friendship?" Steve said on a snort.

"What do you mean, what friendship?" Tommie asked like he was surprised at his response. "We've been friends all our lives. Apparently it didn't mean anything to you."

"No more than it's meant to you," Steve returned softly.

"What the hell is that supposed to mean?" His dark eyes had narrowed in disbelief.

Steve wouldn't tell him. He'd been embarrassed about his own jealousy over Tommie and Gregg's instant friendship since Gregg moved to Milwaukee. Maybe that made it easier to get involved with Jessie despite the promise he'd made to Tommie when they were kids.

"Did it ever occur to you maybe me and Jess love each other?" Steve muttered, feeling the hollowness of his own words.

Tommie pulled the car over to the side of the highway. His chiseled face stared right into Steve like a judgment, like a dagger.

"You damn well better love her. Now she's yours. You understand that? And you're no friend of mine. You hurt her, you leave her, you fuck her over and I'll be there. I'll be the last thing you ever see."

"You think I'm some fucked-up asshole, don't you? You think any other guy in the world is better than me. You got a pact with any of your other friends? No? Just me, right?" Steve's anger overrode his fear of Tommie's disapproval for the first time in his life. "Forget this shit, man. It's none of your goddamn business what I do. What Jess does. You'll assume the worst of me no matter what I do anyway."

Steve shoved open the car door and got out, slamming the door as hard as he could before he walked away. Seconds later, Tommie pulled up beside him in the car. "Get in," he shouted.

"Fuck you."

Tommie kept the car moving alongside him. "Get in, man." His tone was softer, pleading.

Steve kept walking without acknowledging him.

Impatiently, Tommie asked, "Is it yours? Is the baby even yours?"

"I'm a complete bastard. What do you think?" Steve turned around and started walking the other way. A minute later, from behind him, he heard the car squealing around to follow him but he refused to turn around to see what Tommie was doing...

* * * *

Steve sat up suddenly when he realized the house was utterly quiet. It was after eleven. Where were the kids? He stood, rubbing his eyes, and went to check on all of them, Val first. She was in her pajamas and asleep with tears dried to her cheeks. She hiccupped softly in her sleep. Feeling guilty, Steve wondered who'd put her to bed--Tom or Ronnie?

Tom was asleep, too.

He defended me today, ever rational about any and all situations. Even if he thinks I'm doing something wrong, he defended me.

Steve kissed the side of his head, thinking, *I don't want to do anything wrong to make any of you think less of me, buddy.* He remembered the cigarettes when he brushed back Tom's long blond hair. He'd have to have a talk with him in the morning.

Ronnie was asleep, still in his clothes, and Steve knew he'd spend another sleeplessness night on guard in case the boy decided to sneak out.

"I love you, son," he whispered. "I'm sorry."

Ronnie didn't stir.

Downstairs, he found the pack of cigarettes in the garbage. Steve had no idea how he knew, but Tom had put them there. Why? Because he didn't want to cause his old man any more grief? Steve could only wish.

Seventeen

Kristina would have called in sick the next morning if she hadn't had a compelling reason to go to work: Steve. She was tired and she felt like she'd gone twenty rounds with a demon.

A part of her was afraid to see him. A better than average chance existed he would end this, this thing, between them again, possibly for good. But she had to see him.

I have more to lose this time, she thought as she arrived on DeSmet Street. *I love his children. I love him more than ever before. They're all so scarred.* It was silly, maybe, but she wanted to help them heal whether or not she and Steve could ever be together.

Steve was standing by his car as she drove into the parking lot. Waiting for her? *No.*

Yet he came to her, helping her out of her car. Her eyes welled up with tears at the sight of him. He looked exhausted, drained of any emotion or energy to rid himself of the emptiness he obviously felt. She'd spent most of the night after he left crying, terrified that she'd chosen the exact wrong time to admit her feelings for him.

"How are you?" he asked.

"How are *you*?"

He shook his head. "I have to make a decision. About my marriage. I have to do it before she comes home in two weeks."

Kristina's every nerve ending stood in panicked anticipation.

"God, don't look at me like that, honey," Steve said softly, as if she'd hurt him with her inability to conceal her emotions.

She hated herself for the tears she couldn't control. The last thing she wanted to do was make this harder on him. She couldn't speak, not even to apologize, around the determined sob blocking her throat.

Steve reached for her hand, closing both of his around it. He wanted to hold her, she realized when her eyes met his. The parking lot was too public, but he told her what he felt in a mere glance and the pressure of his hands holding her in agony.

"Tilly's? Two-thirty?"

Kristina's heart soared at the tiny flare of hope he gave her.

She nodded. He squeezed her hand again and wiped a tear from her cheek before he quickly walked away.

Until he made a decision, a final decision about his marriage, their relationship would be like this. Desperate creature that Kristina was, she accepted the bone eagerly. She'd take whatever she could because it was all she had.

* * * *

After weeks of talking to Kristina about every single angle of his life with or without Jessie, Steve found himself avoiding the day his wife came home. He set his schedule so he'd have to work late. He asked Gwen to pick up Jess and to spend the night, even though this was a weekday.

He was no closer to a decision now than he'd been a month ago. He'd wanted Kristina to give him advice, but she would only listen, saying he wouldn't accept it anyway--and shouldn't--because it was his decision alone.

Today was the day. He hadn't told Kristina it was, but he knew she'd sensed a change because of his behavior. He felt like the hounds of hell were jumping out of the shadows at him every way he turned. Kristina had asked him about things, and he'd avoided going into it today. The last thing he could talk about was Jess. So Kristina held his hands in the solitude of Tilly's, speaking volumes to him in just her gaze.

She'd been silent about her feelings for the past two weeks. She'd accepted this might be all they'd ever have--talking, hand-holding. He needed her so bad he couldn't imagine his life without her now. She'd told him she didn't want to be a factor in his divorce or his continuing marriage. But she was. She had to be, whether she liked it or not. His feelings for her were too strong to ignore.

As he drove home in the dark that night, he wondered what it was like there now. With Jess home. *Probably not much different.* Val talked about Kristina all the time, asking when they could see her again. Ronnie had withdrawn completely. He refused to talk to any of them. And Tom ignored his older brother. Much as his son didn't want to reveal it, Steve could see he was vulnerable and he'd tried to make more time for Tom lately. Sometimes he thought he'd never get through to his middle son again though.

The only highlight had been hearing Tom promise he wouldn't hang out with Aaron anymore, wouldn't smoke. He'd said he befriended Aaron because his life-long friend, Timothy Rushing, had been on his case about his smoking. He'd known it was stupid.

With Jess home now, all of them would be withdrawn except Ronnie, who would be begging his mom for attention. Maybe she'd give it. Maybe she wouldn't.

Steve had no idea what to expect her state of mind to be. Past experience didn't give him a clue either. She could be resentful for what he'd put her through and take it out on all of them. Or she'd convinced herself the fact that she went through the rehab program proved she'd really changed. They all knew that wasn't possible. She'd never gone through a four-week rehab like this before. But a leopard couldn't change its spots.

Evangeline's car was gone, Steve saw as he pulled into his driveway. Gwen's was there. Lights glowed warmly from inside the house. Steve willed himself to go inside.

And do what? He had no idea. He couldn't act like everything was back to normal. He couldn't forgive Jess. But he wasn't sure he could end it either.

What do you want me to do, Tommie? I know you asked me to stay with her, but what if I can't? What it kills me? What if my kids are scarred so bad from this, they'll never recover?

He wasn't willing to think about Kristina. He felt superstitious about it, as if Tommie could really hear him and take action. He'd always believed Tommie was a level above human. Even years after his death, Steve couldn't get over that feeling.

Walking into the house, he might as well have been encased in body armor. His emotions, his muscles felt strung tight with dread. The first thing he saw was Val sitting on the floor Indian-style in the living room, playing a game with Gwen and Allison. She played because Gwen had initiated it. Steve could see how uptight she was.

Jess came through the archway, stopping there to look at him as if expecting him to scream at her. He couldn't allow himself to react in any way to her.

"Where are the boys?" he asked rigidly.

"Ron's here and Tom's upstairs on his computer."

"Did they eat?"

She nodded. "Did you have dinner?"

"Yeah."

She moved into the hall, closer to him, slowly, and he forced himself to hold his ground. She looked good, but that didn't mean anything. She looked good even when she was so wasted, she was puking her guts out. Her thick, long hair was caught back in a loose scrunchie, making her look younger. In the short, swingy mini dress she wore--no shoes or socks, he couldn't help remembering her as a teenager. He didn't like the memory. She'd always tried to make him believe she was the innocent, pulled down against her own will. He would have believed anything she told him then, he'd been so caught up in her spell.

She stopped only inches from him, the scent of the musk she wore strong, and he heard his mind pointing out his options like a drill sergeant: *You either try to make this work or you end it right now. No gray areas here. You can't just do nothing. Not anymore.*

One of her hands reached out to him, capturing his jacket in her long, slim fingers. She looked up at him, guileless, seeking forgiveness. "How are you?" she asked softly.

"How are you?" he countered, wishing he could push her away. He wanted to do nothing. Hell, nothing would be so much easier than deciding the fate of five lives in one fell blow. *Maybe six. I can't think of Kristina now.*

"I'm better. I thought about you the entire time. I thought about how I could be a good wife to you. How to make it better for the kids around here. If you'll let me. If you'll just let me prove I can be what you guys need."

Steve swallowed, feeling like his throat had closed up to keep words down. Any words at all. He didn't want to face this.

He turned away, looking into the living room. "Val, it's a school night. Did you do your homework?"

"I already did."

"You ready for your bath?"

She stood immediately and came to him.

"I can help you with your bath," Jess said with a smile at Val.

Val looked up at him frantically, shaking her head. "I want Daddy or Aunt Gwen."

Steve didn't look to see Jessie's expression. He murmured to his daughter. Keeping his distance from Jess, he went up to draw Val's bath, get her a towel and robe, and lay out her pajamas on her bed. He went through the motions, stopping only to ask Tom how he was doing and if he'd finished his homework. Tom's mumbled reply and unwillingness to look away from his computer wasn't out of the ordinary, but Steve knew his son felt like he was encased in armor, too.

How much longer can we do this? If I take her back, if I grant her forgiveness and make love to her tonight, the way she'll push for, it won't last. We're going around in circles, and we can't take it anymore. Maybe it'd be easier to just go along with it or maybe I'd just be making it all worse.

He asked Ronnie if he'd done his homework, and Ronnie's shrug told him he hadn't. He'd obviously been at his mother's beck and call since he walked in the door today. When Jess encouraged him to go do it, Ronnie got started reluctantly. Steve fled to the living room, to Gwen and Allison, until Val called down she was ready for bed.

Jess offered to put her down, but Steve shook his head. Val would never get to sleep that way. As it was, she wouldn't let him leave her easily.

Just like he suspected, Jess waited for him on the top step when he came out of Val's bedroom. He could have claimed he had work to do, but Gwen would be getting Allison to sleep on the sofa bed in the living room soon. Besides, Jess gave him nowhere to go. She purposely blocked the staircase. He could either go to Ronnie's or Tom's room or into their bedroom.

"You're still wearing your jacket," she said teasingly, holding on to both sides of it and letting him feel her nails against his stomach. "Why don't you let me show you how much I've missed you? It's been four weeks. Maybe you're as ready as I am now. Or maybe you've found someone else who can satisfy you better than I can."

Steve knew her tone too well. She was trying to draw him into a fight. She wanted him to make love with her or give her a reason why he wouldn't. He wouldn't give her the satisfaction this time.

"The boys have to be in bed in an hour."

She drew in closer to him, pressing her breasts to his chest and lowering her voice. "So we'll have a quickie before that and take it slow the rest of the night."

She'd put him through hell a million times, but came back every damn time believing she didn't have to pay for any of it. That he'd take her back because she was sorry--temporarily anyway. That he'd forgive her because he couldn't refuse her, or so she believed.

Steve stared at her, his jaw tight. She had absolutely no concept of the pain she'd caused him. The pain she'd caused all of them. Their grief meant nothing to her. She never had to pay for her crimes. *He'd* paid for them. Every goddamn time, he'd paid for them while she got off scot-free.

I can't do it. I can't take her sins and make them disappear. I won't.

He pushed her away and stalked down the stairs, out of the house. He didn't slam the door, but his anger wanted him to get that gratification. He wanted to squeal out of the driveway and roar down the street like a bat out of hell, not having a clue where he was going. Just knowing he had to get out. And she'd know he didn't want anything to do with her.

But he knew exactly where he was going and he had to force his anger away. If he saw Kristina like this, he'd kiss her like a punishment she didn't deserve. He'd make love to her to get back at Jess. Knowing Kristina the way he did, she'd take it, too. She'd take anything he gave her. He'd never forgive himself if he did that.

He felt no shame or guilt when he knocked on her door, hearing movement on the other side of it. He heard fumbling, then the door flew open.

She'd been sitting just inside the door, waiting for him, Steve realized. And, God condemn him, she'd been crying.

Kristina came into his arms immediately, holding him so tight he couldn't breathe. He didn't care. He shut the door with his foot and held on to her with his eyes squeezed shut.

"I had to see her. I had to see her before I made the decision. I'm sorry I'm dragging you through all this, honey."

"I was so afraid you wouldn't come. That you were taking her back tonight," she moaned.

"It's over. I can't do this anymore. I have to tell her. Soon."

Kristina pulled back, her eyes wide, as if she was deathly afraid to hope for what she thought she'd heard him say. "I can't, I *can't* be a factor in this, Steve. Promise me I'm not."

Swallowing, he stared at her beautiful, soft eyes. "You complicate things, honey. I won't lie to you about that. But she's killing us. Even when she's better, I know it'll never last. I know I can't put my kids through this anymore. And I know I can never be with her again."

Steve cupped her face, leaning close to her until their foreheads touched. He wanted to kiss her. Not hard. Not punishing. He wanted to breathe in her soul again and feel whole the way only she made him feel.

But he knew he couldn't do that now. Until he told Jess it was over, he couldn't kiss her. He couldn't touch her in any way that crossed the line. All he could do was look at her, stroke her face and hold her in his arms.

"Steve," she whispered breathlessly, shakily.

She didn't need to say more. He knew she would wait for him. She would be here for him whenever he needed her. There was nothing she wouldn't do for him.

Oh, God.

Eighteen

Steve's parents had divorced, but he'd never asked them each step in the process. They'd divorced long after he and his sister moved out anyway. His mom had announced one day--completely out of the blue from his point-of-view, not at all a surprise from Wendy's--that she and their father were divorcing. She got the house and a shitload of money, and that was the end of it as far as Steve was concerned. He didn't know how or when they'd started the process, let alone how long it took and exactly when it'd become official. He assumed his mom left first, because the old man had a long history of cheating, then she'd filed for the divorce later.

That seemed like the best strategy to Steve as well. After the kids were in bed tonight, he'd somehow tell Jess he wanted out of their marriage. He'd slept in the extra bedroom they used for storage the night before, in a sleeping bag, to avoid entering his own bedroom and having to deal with her.

He wanted her to leave immediately--Gwen would no doubt take her in until she could get her own place. Then he'd file for a divorce soon and he'd get full custody of the kids. As soon as those things were done, he'd worry about telling the kids. *Ronnie. God.* He expected that to be the hardest part of the whole thing.

When Steve walked in the house Thursday evening, he knew it wouldn't be anywhere near as easy as he'd planned. Jess was the only one downstairs, and, when he asked where the kids were, she announced they were all doing their homework. She'd picked them up from school, fed them--delivered pizza, he noted--cleaned the house and claimed to have taken care of everything.

She smoked a cigarette and gave him an I'll-do-whatever-the-hell-I-want-in-my-own-house glare.

If Steve had known she'd call Evangeline and tell her she wasn't needed today, he wouldn't have spent an extra hour after work with Kristina at her apartment. He'd assumed Evangeline would be here to take care of the kids until he came home.

Jessie moved out of the kitchen, not guileless or seeking forgiveness tonight. He knew her expression like the back of his hand. She was looking for a fight.

"Where'd you go last night?" she asked, dragging on her cigarette as if she was only curious about it.

Hell, she'd always been murderously jealous. He'd look at a woman in passing, not with interest at all, and she'd fly into a rage. If he talked to a woman, even a cashier in a store, she'd still get furious. Yet she had no compunction about her own betrayals that went a hell of a lot further than looking or talking.

Steve stared at her hard. "I don't have to defend myself to you. I haven't done anything wrong."

She walked right up to him, surprising him when she put herself in his arms, cigarette and all. "I smell perfume on you. *Sunflowers*, to be exact. You were with another woman."

She stepped back proudly, and Steve knew arguing with her would be a waste of time. If anyone knew cosmetics, it was Jess. "I work with dozens of women," he told her.

"Yeah. Do they get close enough to you for their perfume to rub off on you? Whoever the hell you were with, she was in your arms. She touched your face with part of her body. I wonder which. I wonder what her fucking name is. It's not *Kristina* by any chance is it? Kristina is someone you work with, isn't she?"

Ronnie had told her, just like Steve expected him to. Still, hearing Jess say her name shocked him enough to keep quiet.

"Ronnie says she was in my house while I was gone. That you were out late a lot, asking Gwen to watch the kids here."

"I always work late. It goes with my job."

"You saw her in the grocery store. You went to lunch with her, with the kids. You brought Tom and Val to her goddamned apartment. So who is this bitch? Is she sexier than I am? Will she let you do anything you want to her? Will she do all the things I do to you?"

She'd never cheat on me. That I know she'd never do to me. The words stalled on the tip of Steve's tongue. Holding them back took all his control.

"Do you love her? Have you fucked her? Does she know you're married?" Her eyes flashed with rage.

"You've got no idea what you're talking about, Jess. You better stop before you say something you'll regret."

She turned away for a second to stub out her cigarette viciously. "I don't understand you. I can't believe you of all people would do this to me. I spent four weeks, twenty-eight fucking days in a prison with a bunch of whacked-out SOB's who couldn't tell their asses from their heads. I come home, wanting just to be with my family and my husband. I'm here taking care of the house, taking care of the kids, waiting for you to come home to us, and you're out banging another woman."

"Lower your voice. You'll scare the kids," Steve said, wondering if she even believed anything she said herself. "You want to talk about being in a prison, babe? Let's talk about the number of times you went off on a binge and left me all alone to take care of everything. Then you come back, wasted out of your fucking mind, expecting me to pick up all the pieces you shattered. You think doing it for a single day makes you a saint? Think again."

"You're strong. I've never been strong. I can't believe you'd throw it back in my face. Do you think I like the shit I do? Don't you think it kills me to remember everything? But I have to forget those things and forgive myself or I'll never get better."

That was what she'd learned in rehab? That she was being too hard on herself for the mistakes she'd made? That she could just neatly box her sins up, shove them under the bed, and everyone else had to do the same?

"Hell, this is what they've got you believing? You know, maybe if you felt guilty for all the bullshit you put us through, maybe *then* you'd get better. You spend too damn *much* time telling yourself you're weak, that's okay. Everybody's treated you bad all your life. You've had it harder than everybody else. Everybody else can carry you and *they* can suffer for your sins."

Steve kept his voice low, trying to hold back the emotions that threatened to break him. "Do you have any idea what it's like to swallow your pride and forgive somebody only because they're on the edge? If I don't forgive, that means I kill you, right? That's my goddamned fault, isn't it?

"Do you know what you do to our kids? Every day I ask myself if they'll make it. If they'll be okay when they grow up or they'll be so fucking scarred, they'll never recover. I don't know how to help them.

"Do you have any idea what it's like when you touch me? I look at you and I see *them.* I see the stupid bastards you fuck just because they're there. They dull your pain or something. Who knows why? Do you even know? Strangers you won't even remember when it's over. They're all there with us, and I can't bear making love with you anymore. It kills me. You're not mine. You've never been mine. And I don't want to share you anymore. I don't trust you, I don't believe a word you say. I'm not the blade you sharpen yourself on. I'm not. I can't be anymore."

She stared at him in shock, as if she'd had no idea about these things that were so obvious to everyone else. He might have thrust a spear in her she truly believed she'd put in herself first.

"I hate you!" she shouted, surprising him because he'd foolishly thought maybe he'd gotten through to her for once.

A creak on the stairs signaled Ronnie's presence. Steve didn't need to see him. He knew before he emerged from the shadows who it was.

Jessie knew it, too. She was infuriated and she wanted to hurt Steve for hurting her. "You think you're so fucking great with the kids. You're the savior and I'm the monster. Well, maybe it's time to set the facts straight--"

"Dammit, Jess, don't do it." Steve wanted to shut her up. He knew exactly what she would do.

She yanked herself away from Steve's grasp, and Ronnie backed her protectively. "You're not even Ronnie's father. He's *my* son. Not yours. So don't play the saint here."

What the hell was wrong with her? By admitting she'd gotten pregnant from some guy she didn't even remember now, let alone then, she put herself in the worst position, yet she seemed to believe she'd done the opposite. She didn't do it for any other reason except selfishness either. She didn't care if she hurt Ronnie. All she cared about was the fact that she had the upper hand for one moment.

Steve had never hated her more in his life when he saw the paralyzed shock on Ronnie's face. "Ron--" he started, but then Val called "Daddy" from the top of the stairs. He heard the fear in his little girl's voice and knew he had to go to her.

"I'm getting the hell out of here," Jess said. "And I'm not coming back this time."

Steve didn't even turn to watch her slam out the door. *Don't expect me to cry, babe.*

Tom stood at the top of the stairs with Val, trying to console her in an awkward way she accepted until Steve appeared. "Daddy, what's happening?" she asked, hugging his neck in a strangling grip.

"She's gone. It's okay, baby."

"Is it true Ronnie's not really your kid?" Tom asked in quiet shock.

Steve couldn't answer him. He held Val as long as he dared, then kissed her and hugged Tom as well. "Take care of your sister for a little while, okay? I have to talk to your brother."

Ronnie was already halfway down the sidewalk, trying to chase his mother's car.

"I wanna go with her, dammit," Ronnie shouted. Frantic tears ran down his face.

Steve caught him and held him back.

"No. Listen, Ronnie, I know what she told you..."

"If you don't go after her and bring her back now, I'll go after her. I'll stay with her. I won't stay here," Ronnie threatened shakily, and Steve knew his life would be a nightmare. There was no way he would allow his son to stay with Jess. If he had to watch him day and night, he'd make sure he didn't go there.

Ronnie gulped air. "You're not my father. You can't tell me what to do."

Steve turned him to face him. Ronnie's tears made his legs weak. "I am your father," he said softly but firmly. "Whether you like it or not, you're my son, Ronnie. The biological doesn't matter. It's never mattered to me. I've raised you. I've taken care of you all your life. I love you. You're my son. Nothing will ever change that."

Ronnie broke away from him, choking on a sob, and raced into the house.

As Steve's anger and fear tore through him, he realized it wasn't over. This was just the beginning. And it would get a hell of a lot worse before it got even a little better.

* * * *

"'lo."

"Ah shit. What time is it there?" Steve realized his mistake as soon as his sister came on the line. He'd never considered the time difference between here and California, where Wendy lived with her husband Paul.

"No. Don't worry about it. I'm awake. Working on more things Mom says she can't figure out," she said, sounding a lot less tired than her greeting had. Wendy ran a shelter for teen drug-addicted and pregnant girls in Los Angeles, an hour from where she and her husband lived. She'd helped their mom start another like it in Milwaukee years ago, but she did a lot of the work running the shelter herself from a distance. "What's going on?"

He heard the suspicion in her voice. He'd called her this late at night in the past. It usually signaled he was having trouble of one kind or another.

Steve took a deep breath. He hadn't told his friends or family anything about what he'd decided. Kristina was the only person he'd talked with about it. "I'm going to do it. I can't take this anymore."

"Do what? Where are you, Steve?" Wendy asked in concern.

"Home. Sitting here blocking the front door in case Ronnie tries to sneak out tonight." Steve looked straight down the hall to the dark staircase. He'd spent at least twenty minutes putting hardware on the back door so he could padlock it and keep Ronnie from running. He'd already checked out the window situation and figured he was relatively safe against his son trying to escape that way.

The cold wind blew beneath the door against his back, freezing him as solidly as Jessie's ruthless admission had earlier.

"I'm going to divorce Jess," he said.

"Oh, God." The shock in Wendy's voice told him a lot about *himself.* Just like Jess would be shocked by his decision, so was his sister. She knew just about everything about his life since he got involved with Jessie. She'd asked him more than once why he stayed with her. Yet she'd never expected him to really leave her.

"She told Ronnie he's not my son for no damn good reason. She comes out of that rehab, acting like she's got a clean slate. Like we're all supposed to forget everything she's put us through and take her back with open arms. Like we don't know she'll never last this time anymore than she ever has the other times."

Steve took a deep breath but knew he wouldn't be able to keep his emotions in check. He hadn't since the kids went to bed. His face and eyes felt swollen, and he ached everywhere. "Like just because I have someone to talk to, someone who's a woman, I'm guilty of a crime when I haven't done anything and she's... Fuck it, she's never respected me or this marriage."

"No, she hasn't. Oh, Steve," Wendy said softly, and he heard the tears in her voice, too. "We're so much alike. We've spent our lives trying to help other people and we rarely think about what we need. But we have to think about that."

"I haven't done anything," he said, feeling he had to. "Kristina is a friend. I care about her--"

"Geez, Steve, don't defend yourself with me. I know you. And I know Jessie. You've got absolutely *nothing* to apologize for. Sometimes I think you deserve a medal for all you've put up with. I try to understand Jess. You know I do. But nothing makes sense there."

Steve nodded though she couldn't see him. "Thanks." He closed his eyes against the shield of his hand.

After a pause, Wendy asked gently, "When are you going to do it?"

"Monday."

"Have you told Jessie?"

He swallowed. "No. She left. She dropped that bomb on Ron and walked out--"

Wendy murmured something not too nice, then asked about Ronnie.

"I don't know. He won't talk to me. He says he wants to be with her. But you know, you know, she'll only take him if it benefits her somehow. She'll use him. There's no way I'd ever allow anyone to take them away from me. Not Val or Tom either. Not Ronnie."

"Do you want me to talk to Jess?"

Wendy was the type who could influence people with mere words, but he couldn't imagine how that would help right now. Jess would be on the defensive and wouldn't listen to logic. Not that she ever really did.

"I have to do *something*," his sister insisted. "Look, I was planning to come there anyway, soon. Mom's got me doing half of the projects for Wayward Angels and it's not easy trying to run two shelters at once, especially when one is in another state."

"You don't have to--" But he wanted her to. He wanted Wendy near him during this break from Jess.

"I want to. You're going to need help with the kids for awhile because the court will hold a preliminary hearing to decide on custody fast--they're all young and that's crucial. I'll see what I can do, flight-wise."

"Thanks, Wendy."

"I love you. And, for what's it's worth, I think you're definitely doing the right thing."

He hung up, feeling like definitely was too decisive. He was sure he'd made the right decision, but things were falling apart already and would only get worse. Thinking of things in terms of definite at this point didn't seem possible.

Holding the phone against his chest, he listened. The house was silent. Val would probably wake soon. She'd already woken twice tonight. Her nightmares had stopped for awhile in Jess' absence. That break probably wouldn't happen again anytime soon.

Steve glanced at the business card next to him that he'd taken out of his daykeeper earlier. Kristina had scrawled her home phone number on the back of it years ago.

He should have told Wendy the truth about Kristina. She loved him. He more than cared for her. Complicating things ever more than they were... His head hurt. He was freezing.

He wanted to talk to Kristina.

After rubbing his face with his hands, he dialed her number, expecting it but feeling painful pleasure when she answered on the first ring. "Steve?" she whispered, and he heard the desperation in her voice.

Am I doing her wrong? Am I using her? Why do I want her so much if I am? I want to talk to her all the time. See her. Hold her and never let go.

"It's me."

"Are you all right?"

"I don't know. I didn't tell her. I planned to, but she was looking for a fight as soon as I walked in the door. She ended up telling Ronnie he's not my son and walking out."

"Oh my God." Kristina's tone was shell-shocked. "How is he? He must be devastated."

"I don't know what to do, but I'm terrified he'll run away. What if I lose him? When I tell him I'm divorcing his mom... That's it. He'll never forgive me." His throat and eyes filled again, and he pinched his thumb and index finger together at the bridge of his nose. "Maybe he's not my son biologically, but I was the first one who held him after he was born. He smiled at me first. I made him laugh. Who'd believe that now? But I love him and I can't lose him." He shook his head at the risks he was taking. They equaled those if he didn't make the final break.

"Oh Steve, I know. I know! It seems like it's all falling apart and it seems right to draw back and not take any risk it could get worse," Kristina read his mind. "Please don't think I'm trying to tell you what to do. But I need to tell you that, from my experience, Ronnie loves you. He loves his mother, and he feels in some ways that he has to choose. He's devastated you're not his biological father because he doesn't know where he fits in anymore. I know you've already assured him of your feelings for him. Just keep doing that. Right now, it might not seem like it's getting through to him, but he'll hold it close to him when he most needs it."

"You think so?"

"I believe that with everything inside me. Everything's dark now, and it'll get worse before it gets better, but it *will* get better. I promise you."

Steve closed his eyes, soaking in the words and her unspoken promise that she'd be there to remind him each time he forgot. "You're still awake," he said softly. Her voice sounded as exhausted as he felt.

"Yes. I can't sleep. I kept thinking about you and all you're going through. I knew it would be hard for you tonight. I was hoping you'd call."

"I feel like I'm dragging you down where you don't deserve to be." *Nobody deserves this. Except maybe me.*

"I want to be here for you. No matter what."

"*Thanks* doesn't cover what I feel. And it's not just gratitude. I don't want to hurt you. God, I don't want to hurt you, but I need you. I need to talk to you and-- I can't make you promises, but, hell, I want to."

He heard her inhale shakily, then she said on the exhale, "I understand. I want you to need me, Steve."

"I'm filing Monday." Somehow the words felt like a promise to *her* instead of to himself and his kids. He was filing for the promise of freedom for them. For all of them. "I wish I could see you before then."

"I'll be at my parents' tomorrow. I know you can't come, but maybe you should take the address and phone number, just in case."

Even as Steve told himself he had to stay here with the kids, had to make sure Ronnie stayed with them, he reached for a pen and jotted down the information she gave him.

"You should try to get some sleep, Steve. You'll need it for the days ahead. You know where I am."

With that promise, she hung up, and he wanted to do something crazy. Something to prove to her he wasn't using her for his own selfish needs and would drop her as soon as he got his life back. But he wasn't free to do anything right now. He had to take care of his kids and secure their future. For that, he needed to be stronger than he'd ever been in his life.

Nineteen

Kristina had been at her parents' thirtieth anniversary party for less than two hours when the desire to escape came on in an overwhelming wave. Apparently her father wasn't the only one who believed she was sending criminal kids into a system he was trying to clean up. His lawyer colleagues seemed to have the same opinion of her work--that rehabilitating teenagers and young adults with drug and alcohol addictions and trouble with the law was a utopian fantasy not grounded in reality.

After a time, Kristina stopped defending her work and walked away from a lawyer colleague of her father's with the words: "You're right. We should throw the book at young kids and make them pay to the full extent of the law instead of trying to get to the root of the problem, trying to solve it, and sending them back out where they can make something of their lives. What was I thinking?"

"Are you all right, darling?" her mother asked after dinner, coming to the corner Kristina stood in. Everyone else sipped coffee. Kristina drank a brandy, straight up.

Once again, Kristina admired her mother's beauty in the sparkling white outfit she wore. Despite the advanced state of Parkinson's Disease, her mother still retained a youthful figure, quiet sophistication, and a twinkle in her violet blue eyes.

"I'm just tired," Kristina said. She hadn't slept more than a few hours a night for the past couple weeks. Her life was on hold, and only Steve could set it into motion. The last thing she wanted to do was let him realize the weight she carried, but maybe he already knew it. She sensed he felt guilty for their relationship, partially because he couldn't give her anything in exchange. There was a better than average chance he might never be able to give her anything she wanted only with him.

"It seems like more than that, Kristina. Each time I see you, you seemed *drained* of life. You're pale. Your eyes look so wan. Is there something you're not telling me?"

Kristina started to reassure her mother with meaningless words, then make an excuse to leave, when her gaze was drawn to the oversized doors of the great room. Her heart almost stopped at the sight of Steve, who followed the directions of a waiter to locate her.

He'd come. She'd never for one second believed he would, not simply because of his obligations to his children but because it would make their relationship more public than he might want.

He hadn't dressed up because he'd had no way of knowing her parents were celebrating. Even in his usual black jeans, black t-shirt and the leather jacket, he made her heart skip a beat as he came to her.

Kristina smiled, tears filling her eyes as he arrived before her.

"I'm sorry. I had no idea--" he started, obviously embarrassed.

"Don't worry about it," Kristina told him. "It's my parents' thirtieth anniversary. This is my mother. Mom, this is Steve Thomas. He's an Associate Professor in the Music Department at Eisner University."

Kristina's mother smiled warmly, offering a shaky hand Kristina knew took effort for her to extend, with her other holding a cane, to hold her upright. Steve took it gently, not shying away the way some people did. "You seem so young to be an Associate Professor already, Mr. Thomas."

Still abashed, Steve offered, "It was a recent appointment." He glanced around before adding, "Congratulations are in order, I guess. Happy Anniversary."

"Thank you. You're welcome to stay, of course. We don't meet very many of Kristina's co-workers."

After her mother excused herself, giving Kristina a you'll-tell-me-about-this-later glance, Kristina put her hand on Steve's arm. "You came to rescue me just in time."

"I did?"

"Definitely. I'm going crazy and was just about to make an excuse to leave."

"I had no idea I'd be walking into a party in progress. This will make it hard on you. Explaining *me* to your parents."

Kristina smiled. "I'm thirty years old. I don't have to explain myself to my parents anymore."

His gaze shifted to the clingy purple velvet dress she wore that dipped low at the cleavage and ended at mid-thigh. She'd bought it for the occasion, since she rarely had reason to wear an evening gown in her regular life.

"Where are the kids?" she asked softly, and he looked up at her as if her concern for his children meant a lot to him.

"I called my sister last night to tell her. She must have made flight plans as soon as we hung up. She flew out early this morning. Got here this afternoon. She told me to go out and get a minute to myself. Ronnie will stay with her."

"That's good." Kristina lowered her voice as she drew closer to him. "I'm so glad you came here. Came to me."

"Are you ready to leave?"

The expression of longing in his eyes would have convinced her in any circumstances at all.

"More than ready. My parents sent for me, so I don't have my car here."

"Good."

She wanted to smile, but she could hardly move. "I'll tell my mother goodbye. If you want to wait outside or in the foyer--"

"Outside."

"Then I'll be right out."

Kristina made her excuses quickly, ignoring her father because she knew he would have demanded to know who Steve was. The fact that Steve wasn't wearing a suit would lead him to assume the worst. It was none of his business in any case.

After trying to get away for five minutes, Kristina retrieved her wrap and handbag.

She realized what Steve's presence here meant. While he'd had no idea there was a party going on, he'd known he would meet her parents by coming here. No doubt he'd stopped at or called her apartment before he arrived, yet he'd come here nevertheless. It meant something. She was terrified to put it together into an actual intention on his part. Not now.

Steve's car was parked out front of the house on the circular drive, and he pushed the passenger door open from the inside when she emerged. Once inside his car, she saw Steve look at her legs encased in shimmering nude nylons. She couldn't feel offended by the obviousness of his glance and the even more obviousness of him glancing away. She felt beautiful, sexy. Wanted. By the only man she wanted.

"Your mom's disease is advanced, isn't it?" Steve said gently as they drove toward her apartment.

Kristina nodded.

"I'm sorry for her. For you."

"Thanks. It's always hard to know how bad it could become. That makes it worse. Right now, she can't get of bed without help from her nurse. Sometimes, she'll be walking and suddenly she's paralyzed. It seems rude, but shouting at her is all that gets her going again. It's hard to see her like that."

Steve murmured "I bet" as he took her hand. "I met your father."

"What?" Kristina's head whipped toward him.

"He came out to the porch while I was getting my keys from the valet."

"What--?"

"It's okay. He asked where I worked. If I was married--?"

"What did you tell him?" Kristina asked in dread, apparently still the little girl who'd tried to please her father and failed each and every time.

"What did you want me to tell him? You're close to your mom, aren't you? You'll probably tell her something about me sooner or later, right? And she'd probably tell your old man. I told him the truth. I told him I've got three kids and I'm getting a divorce."

Kristina swallowed. "What did he say?"

"He asked if we were seeing each other despite all that."

Could it get any worse? Kristina wasn't sure, but she also wasn't sure why she even cared about her father's reaction.

"I said I'm getting a divorce, I care about you, but I won't be seeing anybody seriously until my divorce is final."

She nodded, stinging despite knowing all of this before. Now she had to force herself to accept the fact that before long her parents would both know she was involved with a married man and his children--a man she was serious about but who couldn't be serious about her yet, if ever.

"I think you'll forgive me if I say your old man is an overbearing, judgmental jackass who's got his principles completely screwed up."

In alarm, she glanced at him. "Did he say something cruel to you? About being married and caring for me?"

Steve shook his head. "No. He accepted that. I even got the feeling he liked me. Approved. Whatever. He said some fucked up things about you though."

"Oh." So her father had bad-mouthed her career to Steve. "The two of you said a lot in a few minutes."

"Yeah. I told him he was a damn fool if he wasn't proud of you. You're the best counselor Eisner University's ever had."

"Really? You said that?"

"Right before I walked away."

Kristina smiled, wishing she could have witnessed this conversation. "Thank you."

She'd have to ask her mother about it later.

"I'll walk you inside," Steve said after the remainder of the short, silent drive to her apartment building.

As soon as he opened the passenger door for her and held out his hand to help her out, she asked, "Will you come inside?" She felt contradictorily both bold and shy.

"If you want me to. I want to talk to you."

She stepped out on the sidewalk with him, all but in his arms. What she wouldn't give to be pressed to his heartbeat again.

"I want," she said simply, softly.

As soon as they entered her apartment, he took her wrap and her handbag and tossed them on the couch. Then he eased her into his arms. Kristina could hardly breathe as she watched him helplessly, waiting.

"I want to tell you something, and it's crazy and it's not a promise, but I want you to understand something. About me."

His hands stroked her back, not platonically yet not sensually. Her gaze locked to his, conscious that this moment would be a turning point in their relationship. Whatever he had to say would change things between them, for bad or for good. She didn't know whether to be happy or scared out of her mind.

"All right."

"I want to tell you why I couldn't divorce my wife before now. I've never told anyone else before. Not even her."

Kristina didn't speak, just let her unflinching gaze tell him what this meant to her.

"Thirteen years ago, Jessie's brother--Tommie--was killed in a car accident. I was with him. I mean, I was, but... See, we were neighbors. Best friends. We shared an apartment when I was in college. I knew Tommie all my life. I... Hell, I worshipped him. I don't know how else to say it. He always seemed like he knew exactly what was right and what was wrong and he never strayed, you know? He could solve any problem he had. Any we had. He knew how to get down to the heart of things so everything else just fell away. I can't explain it better than that. I promised Tommie when we were just kids that I'd never get involved with Jess. And I tried to keep that promise over everything else because the thought of disappointing Tommie--"

Steve shook his head, and Kristina understood, at the very least, that Tommie had been his idol. His idol had died.

"That was one thing me and Jess shared--she couldn't stand the thought of disappointing Tommie either. But it never stopped her from living life like she didn't care if she died. She was always wild, always in trouble. I was attracted to her for as long as I can remember. She wasn't like a kid or a sister. Not to me. And she did her damnedest to break my resolve. She was always on me, like it'd be laughing at fate or something, if we--

"I'm not explaining this very well."

"It's all right. Just go on," Kristina urged softly, almost understanding more from what he didn't say than what he did.

"Skip ahead. This guy I'd been talking to from Washington about starting a band together moved to Milwaukee. Moved into the apartment me and Tommie had when I was in college. Gregg Stevens."

"Your friend who's famous now?"

Steve nodded. "Yeah. Him. Anyway, this sounds kind of stupid, but it didn't at the time. Gregg and Tommie really hit it off. Me and Tommie had been best friend's all our lives, so..."

He shrugged, but Kristina could tell he'd been devastated.

"I felt like Tommie was replacing me. Felt like he was disappointed in me, like I'd failed him somehow. I didn't break my promise to him, but Jess was in trouble a lot and I bailed her out all the time. I don't know if Tommie somehow found out about that and assumed I broke my promise or what. But I got to the point where I felt like I couldn't please him. He was pissed off at me and all I was doing was helping his sister, doing what *he'd* do if he knew all the shit she was doing.

"What did it matter? Between years of wanting her and Jess teasing me, I didn't have any resistance. I got involved with her.

But it wasn't a committed thing. Not from her point of view. She came to me whenever she was at the bottom. I never knew when she'd call me. When I'd be running out in the middle of the night. When she'd show up and crawl into my bed, without even checking to see if Tommie was in the apartment."

Steve took a deep breath. Kristina could tell his life was washing over him again and it felt as black as it had then.

"This went on for a long time, and then one time she came to me. I was like twenty-four...and she said she was pregnant. I knew the kid wasn't mine. I hadn't seen her, let alone slept with her, for months. She said she didn't have a clue whose kid it was, but she wanted to get an abortion. She didn't want Tommie to know anything about it.

"I couldn't allow that, you know? I promised Tommie I'd take care of her like she was my own sister. Besides, it was a baby. Why should this innocent life suffer for Jessie's mistakes? I asked her to marry me, but she kept talking about the abortion. She stayed with me though. She let me take care of her. I kept thinking the whole time that she wasn't letting herself believe any of it is real. She hoped she'll wake up one day and it'd all be a dream or something.

"Gwen found out. Then my sister. And then Tommie. Gwen let it slip during their honeymoon. He cut his honeymoon short and showed up on my doorstep, took me for a drive..."

Steve's voice sounded strangled, and the sheen of tears came into his eyes as he summed up the memories of his life running through his mind.

"Never once did Tommie consider it wasn't me who got his sister pregnant. He just assumed I did it and I was the worst thing that could've happened to her. I got out of the car, started walking, but he tried to convince me to get back in. I didn't. I just turned around and started walking in the other direction."

"You felt betrayed by him," Kristina said.

He closed his eyes and nodded. "I couldn't get myself to look back. Not when I heard him whip the car around and come back for me. Not until I heard the semi barreling around the corner. I don't know what Tommie was thinking. I've been over it and over it in my mind, and I can't come up with what he was thinking when he did that. Was he so pissed off at me he saw red? He just whipped the car around without looking where he was going? He was a racecar driver. When he drove, it was like he was playing chess. He'd predict his moves and the moves of other drivers on the track. That time he couldn't have been thinking at all.

"When I pulled him out of the car and dragged him away, I knew *I'd* killed him. If I hadn't been so damned jealous of his friendship with Gregg, if I'd kept my promise to him, if I hadn't gotten involved with Jess or tried to bail her out of her every problem...

"He died a couple hours after surgery. His last words were to me. 'Take care of Jess or I'll come back and haunt you.'"

"You never told him her baby wasn't yours," Kristina guessed.

"I was too mad. Maybe he figured it out, and that's why he wanted me to get back in the car."

Kristina had taken her own advice for as long as she'd known Steve: She'd never offered him unsolicited advice. She couldn't stop herself this time. "Steve, you feel guilty for Tommie's death but you really weren't responsible. You realize that, don't you? Things happen that are unpredictable and unexplainable. You didn't will that semi to come around the bend at that moment. You don't have that kind of power. You can't take responsibility for Tommie's actions or reactions either."

"I married Jess. She allowed that. But she didn't forgive me for Tommie's death. Why else would she do the things she does? Why would she hurt me and herself and our kids if she's not punishing us all for Tommie's death?"

"She told you that? She told you she blames you for Tommie's death or that she doesn't forgive you for it?"

Steve shook his head in a way that was obvious to Kristina the actual words didn't matter. It was the truth in his mind nevertheless.

"*You* blame *yourself* for his death. A part of you believes Tommie went to his death thinking the worst of you. Guilt is a powerful emotion that can skew our clarity in any situation, Steve."

"If I'd died instead of him, everyone could have been happy. Jess. Gwen and Tommie's baby. Every one of our friends. Sometimes I think it would have been easier on all of us if I'd died instead of him."

Kristina wrapped her arms around his neck and held him hard. She couldn't scold him for his feelings or tell him that he was wrong to feel them. They were valid in his own mind, and people felt what they felt, whether or not they wanted to or should feel it. "I don't think anyone wishes you'd died, Steve. What happened was a tragedy. But I know my life is better with you in it. You wouldn't have had children. I'm so glad you're here. I know they are."

He chuckled, but she also felt the shudder in his chest at her words.

"I don't know how you've held up after all you've been through, my love," Kristina said as she hugged him to her and stroked his hair. He had plenty of guilt, she acknowledged, but something told her he'd left some part of it unvoiced--either because he was afraid to say it or because his subconscious mind refused to let it out into the light of day.

"You know what a lunar eclipse is?"

Surprised, Kristina managed, "Um, is that...?"

"It's when the earth gets between the moon and the sun, and the shadow of the earth falls on the moon. I feel like that. I feel like I got between the moon--Jess--and the sun--Tommie. I'm the earth, and I'm waiting for the eclipse. All I remember is being needed to the point where *I* don't exist anymore.

"I disappeared when I broke my promise to Tommie and got involved with Jess. It was all about her, because I disappointed Tommie. I want to see my shadow again. I want to live again. But I don't know how to get rid of the guilt I feel. I killed her brother. My mind believes that, no matter what I might tell myself or other people might say."

He drew back, and Kristina couldn't speak. All she could hear was that he might have changed his mind about getting a divorce.

"But the thing is, I also don't think Tommie would have wanted any of us to live like this."

Numbly, Kristina offered, "I don't know him, but from what you've said about him, I think you're right." Why else would he have asked Steve--with the final words on his deathbed--to take care of his sister? He must have realized, belatedly, that Steve was a good man. The *best* man to take care of his sister. And, believing that, Tommie wouldn't have wanted Steve and his kids to be unhappy as they suffered at his sister's hand.

Steve glanced up, closing his eyes as if summoning his courage, then he faced her again. "The reason I told you all of this is because I think I could fall in love with you, honey. I don't want to hurt you. So I can't make you any promises. I'm sorry. Until I'm completely and legally divorced from Jessie, we have to go slow. If that's what you want, too."

Kristina laughed in sheer bliss at hearing what she'd told herself not to hope she'd ever hear from this man.

Even as he smiled, his eyes held worry.

"Steve, I want you to know something about *me*: The fact that you're so concerned about making a mistake with your divorce and with us, I respect that so much. You take your marriage vows seriously. You did everything you possibly could to stand by them. You don't act out of a justified need for revenge. You act with your heart and your head. You realize your actions have consequences that affect not just you, but your family and your friends as well. If we got involved in a way, a sexual way, before you were free, that would hurt your children, even if they believed you have reason to get back at Jessie. The fact that you're worried about not giving me what I need, that you don't want to give me promises you may not be able to keep--all of it just makes me love you more. Marriage means nothing in this day and age, and sex means even less. I know I'm guilty of this, too, but people don't keep their promises anymore and they don't value commitment at all. You *do*. You do, and I only hope I'm worthy of you when you are free. Thank you for telling me all you have tonight."

"Thanks for listening."

At that, Kristina took a deep breath to give her own confession. "Steve, my relationship with Matt, what I told you before, that's over. No matter what happens between us, I won't allow it to happen again. I'm ashamed that I ignored my own principles. Loneliness is no excuse for it."

Steve pulled her close once more. "Don't be too hard on yourself for it," he advised what he'd never allowed himself. Then he added softly, "I'm glad."

****

Sunday passed without Jessie's return. Gwen and Jessie's parents had no idea where she was. She hadn't contacted them at all. Steve couldn't help wondering if she'd fallen back into old habits so easily.

He spent the day with his sister and the kids, trying to take all their minds off what had happened and what only he knew would happen the next day. Ronnie wouldn't listen to anything he said and kept to himself in his room, coming down only to make himself sandwiches and take them back up with him.

Even when Steve went into his room and tried to force him to listen, Ronnie ignored him. As Kristina had suggested, he'd just keep saying the truth and hope when his son needed it most, he'd let it penetrate. Tom and Valerie also tried to talk to Ronnie--at Wendy's urging, but they were met with an equally stony lack of acknowledgement.

Steve had called his lawyer at home on Sunday. Travis Ragsdale was actually someone he'd gone to high school with and he represented Jessie's parents' company, Nelson Industries. Still, Travis was the only lawyer Steve knew and, hence, the only one he trusted.

Monday morning, Steve met with him in his office.

That night, Ronnie surprised everyone by coming down to dinner and sitting next to his aunt. Wendy was the only one he talked to throughout the meal. When it was over, Wendy offered to play with the kids in the living room so Steve could do the dishes.

As Steve filled the dishwasher, he thought about the facts he'd learned about divorce that morning. It wouldn't be cheap and it wouldn't be easy. He'd be paying Travis more a day than he paid his nanny in a week.

They were in for a long, bitter battle. He'd have as much paperwork as his job required in filing as well. He'd started a list of things he had to do in Travis' office. With Wendy here, he'd probably be able to do all of it in a week or so.

Hell, he couldn't imagine looking forward to anything less than he did to this.

Ronnie rushed out of the living room suddenly, shouting, "Mom's home."

Steve felt the words like a premonition of disaster. He dropped the sponge in the sink as the front door opened. Ronnie didn't throw himself in Jess' arms, though anyone who knew him understood he wanted to. He waited until his mom initiated it. Surprisingly, she did, but Steve saw the wariness in her eyes. At least she didn't assume she was welcome by everyone this time.

"Come on, kids. We need to go upstairs," Wendy said.

"No," Ronnie insisted. "Mom just got here."

"Now, Ronnie. There'll be time later. Come on."

Against his will, Ronnie allowed himself to be herded upstairs with his sister and brother.

Jess stood in front of the door silently.

"Where have you been?" Steve asked, determined not to get drawn into a fight. The time for fighting had passed. The time for solving was long past.

"Do you really care?" she asked, walking by him into the kitchen. Yet, a second later, she told him, as if he'd dragged it out of her. "I have a condo on the shore of Lake Michigan. I have for years. It doesn't mean anything. Sometimes I just need a place to cool out."

Steve took in the information. If she had a condo there, her parents or the money she'd made from modeling paid for it. She hadn't used their--*his*--money. She didn't have any of her own since she rarely worked. If she kept her own place, why did she have her affairs and drug binges here so often? Steve felt yet another layer of betrayal and shame. She had to blame him for Tommie's death if she'd throw her sins in his face so blatantly.

She leaned a shoulder against the fridge. "How are the kids?"

Do you really care? Steve thought in retaliation, but said, "Not good."

"Ronnie?" Obviously she knew she'd blundered the last time she was here, but he could tell she didn't think she'd committed any great crime.

"How do you expect him to be? He's devastated."

Jess lifted her eyes to his. "I didn't mean to say it. It just came out 'cause I was so fucking pissed. I wasn't thinking. I know we agreed we'd never tell him. I can lie, tell him I was just mad and was bullshit--" She pivoted toward the stairs, and Steve realized she actually thought the worst had blown over. She'd come back to stay. He'd forgive her and they'd go on like they always did.

"I filed for divorce today," he said. "I want sole custody of Ronnie, Tom, and Val."

She stopped dead, turning her head slowly to look at him over her shoulder. "What? No, you didn't."

"Yeah. I did. I filed this morning. It's official. It's legitimate. Travis will have the papers ready soon."

"Travis is *my* lawyer."

"Not for this."

She faced him with her hands clenched into powerless fists. "You can't do this! What...! Goddammit, I went through that fucking rehab for you! You promised--"

"When have promises ever meant anything in this relationship, Jess? I've kept my promises, but I can't do it anymore."

"You promised *Tommie.* You promised him you'd take care of me."

"I know."

Footsteps hurried down the stairs fast, and Steve knew it was Ronnie from step one.

"I won't stay with you! I don't care what anybody says!" he shouted, standing next to his mother.

Steve could see he was shaken to the core.

"I want you to move out right away, Jess," Steve said firmly, not acknowledging his son's words yet wishing he could go to him. "I'll pack up your stuff and have somebody bring it to you."

Wendy joined them quietly, remaining in the shadows of the stairway.

"I'm taking Ronnie with me," Jess said.

"No."

"I'm not your son!" Ronnie insisted.

Steve faced the boy head-on, without anger. "The hell you're not. I've been more of a father to you than she's ever been a mother. I don't give a damn if it's biological. You're my son. I love you. I'll never let you go. I promise you that."

"You've got no legally binding document, do you? Until you do, I'm taking Ronnie. He's my goddamned son," Jessie said.

Steve glanced helplessly at Wendy.

"I'll go with them," she said. "Just for tonight, until you have it in writing."

Could the courts take Ronnie away from him just because he wasn't biologically his son?

Steve accepted the situation Wendy proposed. "I want the address and phone number of your condo. I want Wendy to call me as soon as you get there."

"Fine," Jess agreed peevishly.

Ronnie went up to pack a bag and get his school books.

"I can't fucking believe you did this," Jess muttered as she scrawled the information he'd demanded on a notepad. "So who are you banging?"

Steve said nothing, even as the three of them left and Wendy whispered some encouragement with her hug. As soon as they disappeared around the corner, Steve called his lawyer.

"I have to get custody of Ronnie. All my kids, Travis. I don't care if I have to drag Jess' reputation through the mud to get it. Whatever it takes."

Patiently, Travis listened to him. Then he asked, "Is there anything you want me to know, Steve, other than her lifestyle, which I well know?"

Steve took a deep breath. "Yeah. Ronnie isn't my biological son."

Travis' pause told him that fact was bad. "All right. But you're the one who's taken care of him all his life, right? You're the primary caregiver?"

"Yeah. Everybody who knows me knows that." Steve inhaled as he considered maybe it wasn't enough. "I love him. He's my son. I won't let her take him."

"Does he want to stay with her?"

"He says he does, but she won't take care of him. I know her. It'd be dangerous for him to stay with her."

"All right. Let me see what I can do to get the preliminary custody hearing set for this week."

When Steve hung up, Val and Tom came downstairs.

"Daddy, we want to stay with you," Val said, and Steve opened his arms to her.

"What about you, buddy?" he asked Tom with his heart in his throat.

Tom nodded and came to him when Steve reached for him. He held them both with his eyes shut tight. "We'll stay together. All four of us," he said in quiet conviction. "I promise. I'll never let any of you go. You're my life. I love you guys more than anything."

"I love you," Val returned.

"Love you, Dad." Tom didn't look at him, his words spoken so softly they were almost inaudible. Nevertheless, Steve felt them like a balm over all his wounds.

"Daddy, are you going to marry Kristina?" Val asked.

"Let's just get through this first, baby."

When Tom backed up, Steve asked, "Do you two like Kristina?"

"I love her, Daddy."

"She's cool," Tom said, looking down at the floor. "She'll treat you nice. You deserve that."

I'm not alone. Even if I want to protect my kids from all we'll go through, and I will as much as I can, I'm not alone. No one will ever take Val and Tom from me.

He'd face what lay ahead a little easier for that.

Twenty

"There's no way your mother will ever take Ronnie from us," Steve whispered softly. "I promise you that, Val."

"How do you know?"

Even in the glow of the nightlight in her bedroom and the moon shining in the window, he saw tears glistening on her face. This was the second time she'd woken crying tonight. Both times, she'd asked about her big brother.

"Because it'd be over my dead body. We'll be a family, Val. You, Tom, Ronnie and me. No one will ever take us away from each other. Trust me. There's nothing I wouldn't do for you guys. Believe me."

She nodded, hugging him again. Steve stroked her hair until at last she fell asleep once more. Carefully, he got up and left her room.

Tom came out of the bathroom, saw him and asked if Val was okay. Steve nodded. "How about you?"

When Tom shrugged, Steve gave him a hug, told him everything would be better tomorrow, when Ronnie was back with them.

"He'll give you hell though."

Steve nodded. "I can take it as long as he's with us. Get some sleep, buddy. We've got a long day tomorrow."

He couldn't help worrying about Ronnie, too, but Wendy was there tonight. She'd take care of things. And Travis would call him in the morning, hopefully with good news about the preliminary custody hearing.

Needing to close his eyes, Steve laid down on the bed.

He woke bolt upright, unaware he'd even fallen asleep. His hand groped for the phone. His heart was beating out of control as he demanded, "Yeah?"

"Dad?"

Steve heard tears in his son's voice. "Ron? What it is? What's wrong?"

"Mom. She's not breathing. She took something. I asked her not to, but she did it anyway."

Steve swung his legs off the bed. "What do you mean?"

"Before I went to bed, I asked her not to take anything and she seemed okay. Told me okay, she wouldn't take anything 'cause I asked her not to. Aunt Wendy called an ambulance."

"Put her on, Ronnie."

Wendy answered, sounding almost as drained as the boy did.

"What happened?"

"Geez, I don't know. She seemed fine. We all went to bed, and I heard a glass shatter. Ronnie woke, too, and we went into her room. She took sleeping pills. I don't know how many since I don't know what was in the bottle before. It's empty now, and I couldn't wake her."

Steve swore. He'd known she'd do something like this, but he thought she'd wait until she was alone at the very least. *Dammit.*

"I can't imagine what you guys have gone through all these years," Wendy said softly. "What do you want me to do?"

He'd done this so many times, his mind had already worked out the details before he was consciously aware of it. "Stay with her until the ambulance gets there. Ronnie will want to go along, but keep him with you. Follow the ambulance to the hospital. I'll ask Kristina to watch Tom and Val, and I'll be there soon."

"Kris--? Oh. Okay."

Steve hung up and dialed Kristina's number, feeling bad when he realized he'd woken her. She became alert after a minute and told him to drop the kids off on his way to the hospital.

His chest hurt as he went down to the laundry room, took the load of laundry out of the dryer he'd forgotten about the night before, and starting putting some clothes for the kids in a duffel bag.

How can I divorce Jess? She'll kill herself if I do. And I'll never be able to forgive myself for that.

As he woke the kids and told them what was happening, he felt angry and scared--like he was suffocating. There was no goddamn way to win.

* * * *

"I'll take her," Kristina said when she opened the door to Steve, two of his children, and a duffel bag. "Hi, Tom."

The boy said nothing, nor did his worn-out expression change. But he came inside.

Steve handed her Valerie, who slept on his shoulder. She woke only briefly, smiled and wrapped her arms around Kristina's neck. He set down the duffel bag just inside the door.

"Thanks for doing this."

"You told her," Kristina whispered her earlier realization. Steve had told Jessie he'd filed for a divorce.

He nodded, but clearly didn't want to talk about it now. Was he re-thinking the decision to divorce his wife based on her suicide attempt? Kristina didn't want to think about that anymore than he would talk about it. He'd called her to take care of his younger children. His worry was about Ronnie now and he no doubt felt guilty about the whole thing.

"I'll call you later. I don't know how long I'll be, but don't worry about getting them ready for school. I'll call the school and tell them there's a family emergency--" He halted as if something had dawned on him at that very moment. "I forgot you have to work."

"I have plenty of sick days I can take. I don't mind at all."

"Thanks."

He looked relieved, willing to take whatever he could get. Surprising her, he leaned forward and kissed her check. Then he kissed Val, reassured Tom with a hug and some quiet words, and left.

"You guys can sleep in my bed," Kristina said in the awkward silence that followed between her and Steve's youngest son. "Go ahead and take off your shoes and coat."

Tom complied as though programmed to obey. After both children covered up under her warm, lilac print comforter, she left the room. She wouldn't be able to sleep in the few hours left before dawn anyway.

As she set the tea kettle on the stove, she wondered what the next few hours would be like for Steve. From what he'd told her on the phone earlier, Jess had taken Ronnie with her to a condo she'd been keeping for herself along the shore. Steve's sister accompanied them there. Jessie had swallowed an entire bottle of sleeping pills, which his sister discovered when the glass of water Jess took them with had fallen off the nightstand and shattered.

Obviously, it was an attempted suicide in response to Steve's divorce pronouncement. Kristina couldn't believe Jessie was upset about the fact that Steve would get custody of their children.

Sitting down at the table, Kristina blew on her tea. A moment later, the kitchen door swung open, and Tom came in. Kristina got up and went to him. "What's the matter? Are you all right? Valerie?"

He shrugged calmly at her overreaction. "Can't sleep."

"Do you want me to warm some milk up for you?"

"Can I have it cold?"

"Sure."

As she went about getting him a glass of milk, feeling ridiculously like it was one of the most important things she'd ever do for him, he said, "Wanna play Journeyman III? We didn't get to that last time."

Kristina had summed up a small, but integral part of Tom's personality the first time he'd come here with his father and sister: Computers and games were how he coped with a crisis, much the same way Steve worked himself to the bone to achieve career goals in order to get through the stress of his personal life.

"Sure. Do you want to boot up my computer?"

He disappeared in a second, and Kristina smiled. Their common interest would help her get close to him. During the next few hours, they worked together to solve the mystery, and she couldn't help being amazed at his intelligence and logic. Tom didn't solve the mysteries of the game for her, though he could have, since he'd done so when he "was, like, eight." He gave her clues and asked her questions that led her to solve it on her own. Kristina had to wonder if his teachers even knew how smart he was. He seemed to know something about everything--art, history, math, science. Kristina was awed by him.

She also watched him both openly and surreptitiously as she marveled. He looked so much like his father. Same dark blond hair. Same style, except Tom's was much longer. Same defined features and chin. Same heartbreakingly haunted eyes.

"Are you a friend of my dad's?" Tom asked, almost out of the blue, as they waited for the last segment of the game to load.

"Yes. I'm a friend of your dad's," Kristina said, wondering what he was thinking. Another trait so much like his father--

getting close to him was a feat and a privilege few had been granted. "He talks to me. Maybe because I'm a counselor at the college. Maybe it makes it easier for him to talk because of my career. He needs someone to talk to."

Tom was silent for a few minutes as he followed instructions on the screen. After clicking on something, he said without turning from the screen, "Dad's got a lot to do. He's sad a lot. Nobody ever helps him. I want to, but..." He shrugged. "So maybe talking to someone--you--helps him. I know Ron doesn't believe it, but I know my dad would never cheat on my mom. Even if she's always done it to him."

Though Tom was a withdrawn person who liked to portray that he considered nothing a big deal, Kristina could tell he believed strongly in his father's good character. He would stand beside Steve during this ordeal with unfailing loyalty. The boy was only eleven years old, but had the maturity of someone so much older.

"Daddy?" Valerie cried from the bedroom, and Tom looked in that direction.

"She does that a couple times a night. Every night." The expression in his dark eyes--so like his father's--seemed desperate. He wanted to do something, Kristina could tell, but either didn't know what to do or if he should do it. Probably a dilemma he fought every night, a couple times a night.

"I'll go to her," Kristina said, and he nodded. She was disappointed that Tom had just opened up to her and it had to end for the time being.

Kristina turned the dimmer switch in her bedroom up slightly to see Valerie curled up on her bed, looking white as a sheet. She was so tall, thin. Frail. Her face was so pale, the blue veins under the surface stood out boldly even in the darkness.

"Are you all right, sweetheart?"

"Where's my daddy?"

"He'll be back later."

"Will you lay down with me?"

"Of course."

When Kristina slid next to Valerie on the bed, the little girl curled up beside her. Tears glistened on her cheeks, Kristina saw as she looked down at her in her arms.

"Did you have a nightmare?" Kristina asked softly.

Valerie nodded.

"Do you have nightmares a lot?"

"Uh-huh."

"Are they always different? Or the same?"

Valerie raised wide brown eyes to her. "I dream my mom is a witch. A witch under my bed who waits for me to move. If I try to get up, she'll grab me and pull me under the bed with her."

Kristina listened attentively, trying not to let Valerie see her emotions. She was a counselor. She heard horror stories every day and she'd learned to involve herself professional but not personally. She wanted to leave her job at the campus, not bring it home with her at night. She succeeded most of the time, too. Not tonight. She couldn't view Steve's children on a strictly professional level.

"Sometimes I dream she wants to stick needles into me and do mean things to me. Sometimes the guys she's with in my dreams stick needles into me, too."

Kristina forced the first painful question out because she had to ask, "Valerie, has your mother ever really put needles into you?"

Valerie shook her head, and Kristina sighed in immense relief. Valerie was telling her the truth. Kristina could see innocence in the nakedness of her expression.

"Have any of the men she was with put needles in you or touched you in any way?"

"No. I just dream that. When I'm not dreaming, Mom tells us to go, leave her alone. Except Ronnie. Sometimes she asks him to take care of her."

Kristina looked into Valerie's beautiful, haunted eyes and felt the torment this child and her siblings had suffered all of their lives.

"Do you have bad dreams about your daddy, too?"

Valerie shook her head. "No. Daddy comes and tries to push the bad dreams back, so I can sleep. I'm not scared when he's with me."

"Have you ever told your daddy about the dreams you have about your mother?"

Valerie's reaction consisted of a fierce head shake and even fiercer denial. "It would hurt him. I don't want to hurt him. Tom says we can handle some things ourselves because Daddy hurts so much already."

"I know, sweetheart, but your father loves you. Some things he needs to know."

Valerie played with the pendant on the necklace Kristina wore. "I like you, Kristina. I think my dad likes you, too. Can I call you 'mom'?"

The grief in Kristina's heart almost made her cry out as she hugged Valerie to her.

"Oh, sweetheart, I don't know. I don't know if that's a good idea right now."

"Will you stay with me until I fall asleep?"

Unable to answer past the lump in her throat, Kristina murmured and hugged Valerie as hard as she dared, trying not to give in to her own need to weep for all Val and Tom and Ronnie and Steve had been through.

Kristina stayed a minute longer to stare into the angelically sweet face that, like her daddy's, didn't know peace even in sleep. Carefully withdrawing, she found Tom asleep on the couch. She got a blanket and covered him. Then she shut down her computer.

The trauma they'd faced--the entire family--at the hands of the witch! Steve had done everything in his power to make the burdens his own, not his children's, but the damage was done. The only way for them to heal would be for the divorce to happen and for contact to be limited with Jessie afterward.

The last thing Kristina wanted to do was tell Steve the level of his kids' trauma and their need for counseling. He tried so hard to be everything they needed. But he couldn't do it all himself anymore. He would break if he did, and no one would be able to help any of them then.

Twenty-One

"Are you guys getting hungry?"

The knock Kristina had been waiting on for hours stopped their answers. Valerie was brushing Trina, making her chirp contentedly. Tom sat at her computer once more, cleaning, compressing, defragging, and otherwise making it run the way Kristina hadn't been able to since she bought it.

She rushed to the door, surprised and unnerved when she saw Steve with a woman who had to be his younger sister, and Ronnie. All of them looked as though they'd been in a wreck. They were clearly beyond exhaustion and not capable of reacting to another crisis.

When they came in, Steve hung back, taking Kristina's elbow. She'd been afraid he wouldn't touch her again, not after his wife's attempted suicide.

"This is my sister Wendy," he introduced. "Kristina Ingram." He went to greet Valerie and Tom.

Wendy smiled genuinely, though without much energy, at his introduction. "Nice to meet you, Kristina. Steve's told me about you."

He had? He'd talked to his sister about her? In what context? Or shouldn't she even wonder right now? The important thing was whether or not his wife was alive and whether or not the divorce would continue.

Steve's sister was tall, graceful and striking in an All-American girl way. She looked like the type of person everyone trusted immediately. The open honesty in her face spoke of someone always true to herself and pure of heart.

Steve joined them again and nodded toward the kitchen. He didn't touch Kristina on the way there, but as soon as the swinging door remained stationary behind them she saw the needy look in his eyes. She made the move to put her arms around him, and he held on to her desperately.

"How did it go?" she asked softly, not backing away an inch from the solid pressure of his body so close to hers. He'd called once to say they hadn't heard anything yet and that he'd called the school. Kristina had phoned work after hanging up, to tell them she planned to take the day off.

"She's stable. They said it was lucky Wendy found her when she did. She must've just taken a handful of the pills and missed the nightstand when she set down the glass."

Kristina had already formulated her own opinion about Jessie's attempted suicide and this factoid only confirmed her suspicions more.

"How's Ronnie?"

Steve shook his head. "He didn't say much. He's worn-out. How did it go here?"

"Valerie woke up once or twice. Tom and I played computer games for a few hours before he fell asleep on the couch. I don't think any of us have gotten much sleep."

He pulled back to look into her eyes. "Thanks for staying with them."

"You have wonderful children. It was no trouble at all. I'm glad you asked me."

"My lawyer called and said the preliminary custody hearing is set for Thursday morning, but--hell, I don't know what to do. About anything."

For a moment, as they looked at each other silently, she thought he would kiss her and her entire being strained for the possibility. Instead, he just stroked her face with his thumb and index finger, glancing at her mouth longingly.

"Steve?"

His thumb brushed her lips. She closed her eyes at the sensation the light touch sent through her.

"Are you re-thinking the divorce?" she asked because she had to, not because she wanted to.

The look that crossed Steve's face said it all. Kristina could hardly control the anger and fear and grief that washed over her in that one look. He backed away from her as if he didn't feel worthy to be near her anymore because of his thoughts.

Kristina took a deep breath, forcing down her tears. "She won't try suicide again."

He didn't speak, and again, didn't need to. He didn't believe her or trust her instincts in this case. His own experiences had been too well-honed.

With her teeth clenched tightly, Kristina stepped forward and forced him to look at her. "I'm a counselor. I've had so much experience with this. *Exactly* this. I'm telling you, she won't try suicide again. It was never her intention to kill herself. She was trying to make you stay with her. And it's working."

She continued without missing a beat at the guilt claiming his expression, "Let me ask you something: How many times has she OD'ed?"

Steve shook his head. "I can't-- *Countless.*"

"She's never died. She's never intended to. She's not willing to commit suicide. Whether or not she'll admit it to herself, she doesn't want to kill herself. She uses drugs, sex, alcohol, your children, your feelings, your obligations. She uses *everything* she can to punish herself or you, or punish *whatever* or *whoever* makes her feel the way she does. I can promise you this, too, Steve--she's going to try everything in her arsenal to get what she wants from you. She doesn't care who she hurts in the process either. The only way you and your children will be free is when you get through her tricks. When she has to accept that it's over and she can't have what she wants."

Kristina took a step toward him and ducked down to get him to face her fully. "Are you strong enough to handle whatever comes? Because it is going to come and it'll feel like hell. It won't be easy. But it will end."

"Ah, God, I..." He shook his head, and she could tell he felt close to collapse. The last thing he needed to hear was that this was just the beginning. "I don't know if I'm strong enough, honey. I'll never forgive myself if she kills herself."

"She won't try this again. Trust me, Steve," she pleaded, not exactly sure of herself. Right now, she could only assume at Jessie's personality, past, and intentions. Kristina's judgment was clouded with feelings for the rest of the family as well. Selfishly, she wanted them for herself. That never helped. But she knew divorce was the best thing for all of them.

Steve exhaled shakily, reaching for her without much confidence. She went to him, stepping into his arms and holding him to her with more confidence than she felt.

"I wanted this to work. I wanted to be free." His face came closer to hers. He touched his forehead to hers, his mouth so close she could almost taste the coffee on his breath. "I want to love you and share a life with you that isn't crazy. Where my kids can be happy. Where I can make you happy. And maybe I can be happy."

Kristina put her hand on the back of his head. "Oh Steve, don't let her win. Not again," she whispered frantically. "You deserve this. Your kids deserve it. And I love you. She doesn't and never will. She doesn't know how."

He laughed, surprising her, especially when she saw the tears in his eyes. "Doesn't make sense. Everything is so insane now. But..."

"What?" she asked softly, her throat so tight she knew she would cry soon, whether she wanted to or not.

Steve shook his head, easing closer to her and touching his lips to her ear. "I wish I could make love to you. It's all I could think about this morning. Commit me now."

Kristina closed her eyes so tightly, she was sure she'd fall if Steve didn't hold onto her. "Then I'd have to be committed right along with you."

His intimate confession was sad, sweet, sexy. She knew exactly why he'd thought about her all morning. It could be their last chance to be together, if he decided not to go through with the divorce. They could become one a single time and never again. On one hand, it made sense. On the other, it was the most senseless kind of love imaginable.

They held each other, every part of their bodies molded together through design as well as the solid pressure of his hands against her lower back. She felt his arousal and knew he felt hers. His breathing came harshly against her ear, adding to the pain and pleasure she felt. He didn't kiss her. And she cried silently throughout a wish they shared that might never come true.

* * * *

"It is the court's ruling to award sole custody of Ronald, Thomas and Valerie Thomas to the father, Steven Thomas. Jessica Nelson-Thomas' fitness as a mother is deemed to be unsuitable due to psychological and behavioral problems culminating in her recent suicide attempt, which could be injurious to the children.

"This ruling is only temporary. I'm assigning a court liaison to oversee Mrs. Thomas' case as soon as she's released from the hospital. There will be a continuance of these proceedings in ninety days. Mrs. Thomas has three months to get a job and keep it, to get drug and psychological counseling and to create a suitable home for the children. If this proves to be a possibility, Mrs. Thomas will be allowed supervised visits when we reconvene."

Numbly relieved, Steve accepted Wendy's hug and shook his lawyer's hand when Travis congratulated him, but it wasn't until they'd left the court room that it sunk in. "He didn't know Ronnie's not my son, did he?"

Travis drew Steve aside, shaking his reddish-blond head. Even in high school, Travis had looked like a lawyer. He'd probably worn a tie on the weekends then, too. He always looked composed, calm, unruffled. Steve got the feeling many times that the man could make a mountain into a mole-hill. Nothing ever seemed to phase him.

"Since your wife is in the hospital, her lawyer hasn't been apprised of many of the details. It'll come out, but you don't have to worry. I'm sure the judge isn't going award her even joint custody. She's got a record a mile long. A bad one. Your public conduct and reputation is sterling. Just go home and celebrate with your kids, Steve. You'll be a free man next year, as early as we can swing it. Hopefully, Jess won't contest the divorce."

But she would. Steve knew that but didn't say anything about it as Travis left the courthouse. As a matter of principle and punishment, Jess would make his life a living hell until it ended one way or another.

He didn't think he was strong enough, even with the added incentive and complication of his feelings for Kristina. Yet he'd gone ahead with the preliminary custody hearing today. He didn't tell Travis to stop the divorce. A part of him knew why he'd done it, and he wasn't sure he wanted to admit it to himself. Not yet.

"Come on. I'll buy you a late breakfast before we have to go to work," Wendy said softly, obviously seeing the conflicts warring in his expression. She slipped her arm through his.

Once in a booth at a restaurant they used to come to as teenagers, Steve asked his sister, "So how've you been? How's

Paul? I haven't asked you that even once since you got here. I'm sorry."

Wendy smiled, the easygoing one he knew so well. They were used to serving, not being served. "Don't worry about it. I understand. Paul's doing great. He'll be here tonight, in fact, and not a minute too soon. I've been going through withdrawal symptoms for him."

Paul and Wendy had been through a lot in their relationship, which had almost fallen apart after Tommie died. They'd been married for almost a decade now, and were what Steve considered the perfect couple. It didn't hurt that they were so happy with each other everyone who saw them together knew they had to be together or bust. It hadn't always been that way, but they'd survived and come out stronger than ever.

"I hope you don't mind, but we're going to a hotel as soon as he gets here. You need time with the kids, to tell them the news anyway, right?"

Steve laughed at his sister's bluntness and nodded. "Far be it for me to stand between two lovers who haven't seen each other in days."

The word *lovers* made him think of Kristina, an uncomfortable situation in public. He hadn't even kissed the woman on the lips yet, for God's sake.

"I've been meaning to talk to you about something," Wendy said, after they ordered. "Paul and I have decided to adopt."

Because of the endometriosis that had plagued Wendy for most of her adult life, she wasn't able to have kids of her own. If any woman in the world should have had kids, it was Wendy. But she'd learned to accept it, and both her and Paul had seemed content to live their lives together without kids.

"A baby?" Steve guessed, remembering how she'd looked at his kids when they were babies.

"No. I mean, I thought about it. We did. But then I met Nicole and Jason. I knew they were the ones. Paul felt the same after he met them. They're fraternal twins, twelve years old. Their mother was a drug addict who's been in and out of Hard Times Haven for years. She died two months ago. She has no family and no one knows who the father is."

"So what happens now?"

"We've already gone through the process of adopting them and..." She took a deep breath. "They come to live with us forever at the end of November."

Steve could see the happiness shining in her eyes, wondered briefly why she hadn't told him about this major life change sooner, then answered his own question. His life overshadowed hers in their conversations.

Hell, it'd always been that way. Wendy had taken care of everyone and everything since the time she was a little girl. She'd been like a mother to her family, her friends. Keeping her own problems and needs to herself had become instinct at an early age. Only once in Steve's life--when things had been bad between her and Paul--had he felt brotherly protectiveness for her. She took care of herself. He'd rarely needed to worry about that. She was a hell of a woman.

"We didn't want to tell anyone until we knew for sure."

"So what are they like?"

"They've been through a lot. And it'll take a long time for them to heal. They're used to stealing to get everything they need. They're a little wild, and they don't know what real love is. But you should see Paul with them. It's like they all understand each other. I know, I know, you're probably thinking I'm the first one who made a connection with them, but it was Paul. They worship him, and he loves them."

"What about you?" Steve asked because she'd left herself out of the equation.

"I think they're afraid to trust a women because their mother was abusive and cruel and neglected them so much. But we've spent a lot of time together, and I know it'll be fine. Two weeks ago, Jason asked me if he could call me Mom. That's a huge step for a kid who's been kicked around the way he has. I love them so much, every day until *the* day will be torture. I can't wait for you to meet them. You're still planning to come out for Christmas this year, right?"

He and the kids went to Wendy and Paul's house in the mountains in San Bernardino every year without Jess. This year they'd probably need that respite more than ever. "I hope so."

Their meals arrived, and Steve realized how hungry he was. He'd been skipping meals and eating out of vending machines or from fast food restaurants for the past two days.

"So tell me more about Kristina. She seems great. I didn't talk to her for very long, but the kids--Val and Tom anyway--really seemed to like her."

"They do. Since he was a little boy, I haven't seen Tom open up to anybody the way he does with her."

"And Val's looking for a mother." Wendy smiled.

"Yeah."

Wendy sipped her water, her eyes leveled on him. "She's in love with you."

The abruptness of his sister's comment threw him, but she laughed when he choked in shock. "You had to know that! Geez, I was in the room with the two of you for like five minutes or less and I could see it every time she looked at you. You'd have to be blind not to see it."

He'd been blind to Kristina's love for him for a long time. Had it been obvious? To everyone except him?

"I don't think you're too far behind her, big brother."

Ah hell, he'd been too obvious because his guard had been down out of exhaustion. "I'm still married."

"You know how I feel about Jessie, Steve." Wendy's tone was impatient. "She's been a burden on you since she was a teenager. She's not a wife. She's a child. A bratty, selfish, insane child. When's the last time someone cared about your feelings? When's the last time someone put you before themselves? When's the last time a woman made you feel good about yourself, made you want anything but to escape?"

Having his own sister hone in so easily and precisely on his pain was damned uncomfortable and enough to make him want to leave. At the same time, he wanted to hear what Wendy had to say about Kristina, even if he couldn't cross the boundaries he'd set for himself.

"I've got a good feeling about Kristina. She's beautiful. She's sexy. And I think she wants to take care of you, heal you and satisfy you more than anything."

"You've been away from Paul too long. You've got sex on the brain," Steve scolded.

Wendy shrugged. "That's true. That's very true. But say what you will--I worry about you, Steve. Your whole life has been wrapped up in the kids and putting up with Jessie's--excuse my language--bullshit. I've wondered how you put up with it. How you don't go crazy. I've wondered how come you don't pay her back for her infidelity. But then I know you and I know you would never do that, not unless you were in love with someone else and that affected your judgment."

"I'm still married. Until I'm divorced, I'm still married," Steve said defensively. He swallowed against the lump in his throat. "I want my kids to respect me. I want them to believe I made the right choices."

"I know. I knew you'd say that, too. You're a good man. But if I were you, I would think it was about time *I* got some happiness out of life. You gave that up when you got involved with Jess. I don't think you even realized that's what you were doing.

"Jessie's antics are known all over this city--another reason I think you're not going to have any trouble getting full custody of *all* the kids. You've always been faithful. Everyone who knows you can testify to that. If I were you, I'd see Kristina as often as I wanted, in whatever way I wanted to, and I wouldn't feel guilty about it in the least. You don't owe Jessie or anyone anything. No one would think less of you if you became involved with someone like Kristina."

Steve didn't want permission, and he told himself so many more times than he needed to on the way back to work. He didn't need to hear it was fine if he saw Kristina, if he loved her, if she loved him, and they did the things men and women in love did. He didn't need permission, but it followed him to the college. And, as he got out of his car, he knew he wasn't going to his office. Not yet. He didn't have a class for more than an hour.

Kristina was alone in her office. She stood as soon as he came in, closing the door behind him. "What happened? I thought you'd call," she said breathlessly.

"I got temporary, full custody. If Jess cleans up her act before the final custody hearing, she might get supervised visitation rights. But the judge didn't know Ronnie's not my biological son."

"It doesn't matter. You've been a good father to him. Jessie's history of drug abuse is long and documented. You'll get the children, Ronnie included. I'm so happy for you."

He anticipated her hug, but Steve already knew it wouldn't be enough this time.

"Can we close the blinds?" The words escaped Steve's mouth without conscious thought, and Kristina looked puzzled for an instant.

She was beautiful. Her *mouth* was beautiful. It could smile so sweetly at him, be filled with so much understanding and compassion sometimes. But right now all he saw were the full curves, the moist softness, and his need of their healing.

She knew what he was going to do, and he felt her shock as she stared up at him. She didn't move. Not until he lowered his head and his lips touched hers, sending electricity flowing between them. Then her mouth shifted as she sighed, holding and giving back eagerly.

"Close the blinds," he murmured his plea again, and this time she hurried to do it while he backed up and groped for the lock on the door.

She returned in an instant, looking at him with anticipation and wonder. She'd dropped her glasses on her desk somewhere between the blinds and her return to him.

"I'm going to divorce her, Kristina. Somehow, I'm going to do it. And this has to be slow. *This* has to be enough until it's final."

"Yes."

Her hands crept to the collar of his jacket, and he pulled her against him, back where he wanted to be more than anything. Her lips opened under his, sweet, satisfying every hidden desire he'd had for long, he couldn't count the loss. He savored the taste of her, the warmth of her tongue against his--not tentative, not hurried, but eager to explore.

He hadn't been with a woman for so long, with one who made him feel every single motion, feel the fire of renewal that seemed to race through his veins. He felt Kristina's hands creep inside his jacket, under his collar, felt the heat of them through his shirt. He felt her body against his, straining toward him just as anxiously as he did toward her.

Steve cradled her head, inching his fingers back through her hair. The barrette holding the silken mass back came loose, and he allowed the clip to fall to the desk. He sank his fingers into the thick waves.

Slow savoring shifted into an ache that began in his hands and worked down his body until all he could do was react to the heavy adrenaline coursing headlong through him.

Ah hell. Oh yeah. He hadn't experienced this for so long. This need, this heat, this passion. His manhood filled with a rush of hot blood that felt so damn good, he couldn't do anything but let it happen while her harsh breathing against his neck made it better and better.

He couldn't help molding her against him until she sucked in a breath that ended in a moan. Her cheeks were flushed scarlet when he looked at her, and her eyes were glazed with desire. "Steve," she whispered, her tone so full of emotions he knew she was on the edge.

This isn't slow, he thought, in the intensity of their mutual stare. But he couldn't stop it. Not when she pressed his palm to her breast, where the evidence of her arousal proved just as hard and heavy as his.

It was true, he acknowledged in a moment of pure male triumph. He'd wondered before if her breasts resembled that of the woman in the poster on his closet door as a kid. He felt the curve, like a horn of plenty, and her nipple free of any confinement beneath her shirt.

Her breath came in hard, almost painful pants, and he brought her mouth to his again, letting his hand slide away from her beautiful breast--one he'd pleasured so briefly. *She wants me. She's responding to* me. I'm *all she wants and needs right now.*

As her arms surrounded him beneath his jacket, he kissed her and satisfied himself with that wonder alone. Would it be enough for both of them? Just this for the next couple months? Could he control himself? He didn't know, but he knew he was happy. In the midst of this insanity, he had a ray of sunshine. Maybe the warmth would get him through the darkness.

Twenty-Two

Kristina stepped out of the Center, knowing Steve would expect her this time. She didn't plan their meeting so much as she anticipated his mutual desire to see her. Her entire body tightened at the sight of him coming toward her. She saw the excitement in his eyes upon seeing her.

She wanted to kiss him again. Her entire life had come down to moving from kiss to kiss with Steve Thomas. He'd only kissed her for the first time yesterday afternoon. They'd met again later, after work, and he'd taken her home. They'd spent fifteen of the shortest minutes of her life kissing outside her apartment door.

It'd given him an excuse to pick her up this morning, after dropping his kids off at school. He'd come inside. They'd been wonderfully, satisfyingly late for work. Since she'd called in sick the day before, Hillary asked her how she was. Kristina knew she didn't look sick. Though she hadn't slept or eaten much in the last twenty-four hours, her appearance had changed since her and Steve's first kiss. She knew it had, because her mother had seen the difference immediately during their breakfast that morning. Her mother guessed the shine in Kristina's eyes and the glow in her skin could only attributed to love, to Steve.

Just as Steve had predicted, Kristina told her mother everything. She'd told her more than she intended to, though she'd already known some of it because Kristina's father revealed his and Steve's meeting to her.

The shock of the whole thing was that Steve had been right in her father's assessment of him--he'd heartily approved of Steve, including his job, his personal life, even his defense of Kristina. Kristina's mother also revealed her father had begun to look at her counseling position in a new light after talking to Steve. What Kristina wouldn't have given for a transcript of that conversation. She'd left Elm Grove, certain her mother would worry relentlessly about her being hurt in this relationship.

Maybe she would be hurt. There was a better than average chance she could be. But she wouldn't stop what they'd started for anything in the world.

"Hi," Steve said when they reached each other. His tone, his tense expression, said it all. He was counting the minutes until he could kiss her again. The parking lot was too public, and many of the people milling around knew at least one of them.

The memory of each kiss was as powerful as she realized the next would be. Steve's kisses qualified as both flammable and platonic. Except that first time, when he'd made her breathlessly aware of his arousal and she'd returned the gesture, he hadn't touched her anywhere that could be construed as inappropriate.

Even still, the slightest stroke of his hands on her arm or her back, his fingers tangled in her hair, were the most erotic sensations she'd ever experienced. But it was more than that. When he'd called her late last night, the need to be with him became so overwhelming she'd actually experienced chest pains of anxiety. She'd spent the entire conversation with tears in her eyes, her body humming with each word he spoke, his every breath, Even his *silence* engulfed her.

To think she'd considered herself in love with him for years. What she felt now was so powerful, she didn't doubt for a second it could kill her or save her.

"Did you get any work done today?" Steve said as he drove without looking at her. He seemed dead-set on getting to her apartment in five minutes or less. Traffic on the freeway wasn't making that likely.

She turned toward him, her back to the door. "Yes--" She let out a shaky breath. "But if I do any more work like that, they'll probably fire me."

Steve laughed as if his tension had reached the breaking point, and she knew his work had suffered just as much.

"You can't be fired, so you're lucky."

Stopped at a light, he glanced at her. His eyes were dark and compelling. A sob fell from her throat uncontrollably. "I love you."

He leaned over. She met him halfway. His mouth fit hers so perfectly, their union made her feel completely whole for the first time since the last time they were together. They'd barely satisfied the most basic need before horns honked behind them.

Steve swore under his breath and shot forward again. As soon as they merged into the flow of traffic, he reached for her hand and brought it to his mouth. Sitting in the passenger seat, so far from him, made her insane. Her apartment had never felt a million miles away before.

"I can't stay long. I wish I could," he murmured against her palm.

She shivered under the feel of his rough stubble against her bare skin. What would it be like to be with him?

Don't think about that! Not now. I'll think about it tonight, when I'm alone and it's safer.

The nearer they got to her apartment, the harder it became for her to breathe. His hold on her hand tightened and the pressure of his mouth against her palm increased. Then he dragged her hand over his chin, down to his chest. Kristina opened her hand, and he covered it with his own, lacing their fingers. She felt his heartbeat against her fingertips, strong and hard. He rubbed her hand over the center of his chest. Touching him like that didn't feel platonic. She loved the feel of his chest, even through the cotton of his shirt. Pleasure coursed from her fingertips, throughout her body, increasing at the harshness of his breathing.

Reaching her building and parking the car were a blur to her. All she remembered later was feeling Steve, hearing him, then he was fulfilling her desire to be immersed in their own little world again. She didn't even feel the gear shift between them as he kissed her, not until he backed off, gasping, "Let's go up."

They somehow got up the stairs to her floor without letting go of each other, stopping once or twice and then moving on almost as an afterthought.

In Steve's arms, she fumbled blindly with her key in the door, his insistence to hurry unspoken but clear nevertheless as he kissed her mouth, her ear, her neck.

The door opened, closed. Their jackets dropped, magically or by their own doing. She wouldn't have been able to answer if asked how. He dropped back to the sofa and she sat over him. They kissed and her fingers cradled her head. Steve's hands dug into her sides, sliding up slowly, bypassing her breasts to press her closer.

He opened his eyes when she suddenly lifted her face to look at him. She loved his eyes--shadowed, narrow, the fierce expression there answering the question she'd needed answered.

"How will I ever get enough of you?" he asked, so quietly that she wondered if he'd intended her to hear it. While the words made her feel wanted, wanted *critically*, she knew their needs worried him.

"We'll make this enough." Her promise would be easier said than done, but they'd both be watching and being careful they didn't cross the line.

Steve brought her down on his lap and covered her mouth again. She would ache after he left, so badly she'd wonder if a person could die from need. Yet she wouldn't ask for more from him while he had obligations.

"I want you to meet my friends."

"What?"

He stroked the line of her jaw. "My friends... Gwen and my sister's husband. Brenda and Gregg. They're all here. Tomorrow, we're getting together at Gwen's. I want you to come with me."

"I thought you wanted to keep this quiet."

"I do. But they're my friends and they'll accept it. They know--"

He didn't need to finish his sentence. His friends knew about Jessie. They understood. And they believed Steve was justified, even if he was doing something wrong. They would assume he was in the right.

"Oh Steve, I would love to meet them."

"I told Wendy. She approves. She wants to get to know you better."

"Really?"

Steve smiled. "I'm bringing the kids, so...none of this."

Kristina laughed, too happy to think about how hard that would be right now. "I'll survive, I think."

Meeting his friends seemed so intimate and wondrous, she knew she'd have to remind herself of Ronnie's reaction to it to keep her feet on the ground.

"I told my mom," Kristina said. "I know I probably shouldn't have, but she knew something was going on anyway."

"Yeah?" he asked, obviously believing it couldn't possibly have gone well.

"She said she thought well of you in the few minutes of your first meeting, and my dad wants to draft you into the family as soon as possible."

Steve shook his head in disbelief. "What about your mom after she heard I'm married and have three kids?"

"She's scared for me. She thinks I'm going to get hurt. She's worried about that."

Steve's guilt darkened his expression. "So am I."

"I'll take the risk. Any risk."

Her confidence, in part bravado, didn't lighten his spirits. "You ever feel like you're glad about something, but you're also scared about the same thing? Every time I kiss you, I know I'll take any risk to be with you, but what if I can't? What if...?"

"I know." Kristina tried to save him from his own torture. "Sometimes I think it'd be better if we weren't influenced by the past and the future at all. If we just lived in the present, we'd enjoy life more. We don't know what's going to happen. I want to take the chance it'll be good in the end if we make the right choices now."

He nodded.

"So what time should I be ready tomorrow, and what should I wear?"

"Ten. Casual."

"Too many hours between then and now."

"Mhm." He kissed her again, softly and slowly this time, and Kristina closed her eyes to enjoy it thoroughly without the fears littered ahead of them getting in the way.

When he buried his face in her hair to hold her, she murmured, "I know, I know. You have to go."

"Yeah."

"Tell the kids I said hi--the ones who want to hear it anyway."

"I will. I have to take Ronnie to see his mom."

Kristina didn't get a chance to hide her reaction, and she kicked herself for her uncontrolled jealousy. Feeling jealous would put Steve in a corner and make him feel guilty or defensive.

He kissed her hard, emphatically. "*I'm* not going to see her. I'm just bringing Ronnie there."

"I'm sorry. I didn't mean..."

"I know."

He got his jacket before they walked to the door together, where he kissed her so sweetly, she didn't open her eyes until after she said, "Will you call me tonight? Anytime that's good for you?"

When he inched her even closer to him, she looked at him to see him smiling. "If I call you, I won't be able to sleep. Not without..."

Kristina swallowed hard, waiting breathlessly for him to finish her own thought.

"...wanting you to be there beside me."

She'd cried herself to sleep last night, after Steve's call, because her bed had suddenly felt as big as a continent.

"I'll call," he promised before kissing her one last time and forcing him to go.

A knock came a minute later, and she opened to him. "One more."

"I wish you never had to leave me, Steve," she said on a sigh as they came together.

His silence had her on the precipice again, awaiting her heart's desire, one he couldn't give because it would be a promise.

After a last kiss, she watched him until he disappeared from her sight, only then closing her door, wrapping her arms around herself and giving in to the sob strangling her.

* * * *

"Hi."

Kristina's eyes sparkled when she saw them at her door, but her smile wasn't as expressive. She probably didn't want Ronnie to read more into this than he was inclined to already.

"I'm ready," she said, slipping a jacket over the purple turtleneck and faded blue jeans she wore. She closed the door behind her. Valerie reached for her hand, and Kristina smiled down at her.

Steve wanted to kiss her now more than ever. Because he couldn't, he stepped in behind all of them and pressed his hand to her back. She turned to smile at him, a smile he knew belonged only to him and expressed what she'd tried to hide from Ronnie. Today was special to her, merely because he'd asked her to be with his family and to meet his closest friends.

As Steve lead them back to the car, Ronnie said nothing though his shoulders hunched as if against the world. His only defense lately was the silent treatment. He'd claimed not Steve, not the law, not *anyone* could tell him he couldn't be with his mother. But at least while his mother was in the hospital, he wouldn't and couldn't do anything about the situation.

Gwen lived in one of the newer areas of Oak Creek, in a brick, open-concept house with more room than she'd probably ever need. Steve knew it was the house she and Tommie had planned together, down to the last detail, with every intention of filling with children.

After calling greetings to their out-of-town friends from the foyer, Allison and Steve's kids went down to the fully furnished basement, which Gwen had converted into a game room any kid would love. The lower walk-out led down to the boat house and dock the kids enjoyed in the summer.

Gwen led Steve and Kristina into the great room that had vaulted ceilings, an oversized, natural fireplace and a patio that wrapped around the entire back of the house. Tommie's many trophies were encased on the west wall in a lighted cabinet.

Steve introduced Kristina to his friends, sure the pleased surprise he saw in them wasn't obvious to her. Maybe she suspected his friends would never have considered him leaving Jess, not in this lifetime anyway. Why else would she be so calm and so excited about meeting them instead of wary that they would consider her an enemy?

Gwen hugged Kristina in greeting. Brenda hugged *Steve*, with a thrilled twinkle in her cornflower blue eyes, after she said hello to Kristina. Gregg slapped him on the back and said, for Steve's ears only, "Somebody had to go on next. I'm glad it's you, dude."

Gregg was the type of guy who had an eye for every attractive woman he met up with. From the day Steve met him, he'd indulged his voracious sexual appetite like he'd never get enough. Women, unfortunately for them, found him irresistible. Yet he was unwaveringly loyal to his friends. He would never pursue anyone within their circle. He'd never come on to Gwen, Wendy, Brenda or even Jess, despite her avid pursuit. Though Gregg had to see that Kristina was gorgeous, he remained a perfect gentleman with her.

Paul asked Kristina about her work, since it was similar to Wendy's, and Steve talked to Gregg about his career. He was surprised by Gregg's shrug that disputed the "It's going good" proclamation.

"Paul's out there day and night for me."

Nevertheless, Gregg didn't sound happy with the musical career that had given him worldwide fame and recognition--the stuff Steve had spent the first twenty-two years of his life coveting with everything inside him.

As he got reacquainted with his friends once more, Steve watched Kristina interact with his sister, Paul, Gwen, and Brenda. Something about it felt right to him. She fit in here. Kristina wasn't one of those people you either liked or hated the first time you met her and never changed your mind. She was likable to everyone. Even though all his friends were also friends with Jessie, they accepted Kristina.

"I knew it," Gwen said as he came up the carpeted basement stairs from checking on the kids.

"What?"

"I saw something purple in my magic mirror. I knew there was someone in your life, even if you didn't want to admit it to yourself, let alone me." Her tone and sparkling eyes teased without making him feel uncomfortable. "She's wonderful, Steve. She'll be nice to you."

Steve wondered why that seemed so important--to have a woman be nice to him. With Jess, there'd always been an agenda. If he did something she wanted, she would treat him right, give him what she needed, always temporarily. Nice sounded like heaven to him. Kristina was heaven to him.

"Hi," Kristina said.

Steve felt paralyzed as he stepped up to her. She was here. He wasn't hiding their relationship. He could be here with her, and it was okay.

"Your sister, your friends are so nice," she said as he backed her into the kitchen. "I'm glad they care about you so much. Just talking to them, I can tell how much they want what's best for you. You deserve that."

Steve nodded. He did have good friends, the best a person could have.

He braced on the wall behind her, and she smiled almost shyly as her longing came across. Last night on the phone she hadn't been at all shy about telling him how much she loved him.

Her combination of uninhibited honesty and shyness undid him now the way it had then.

"Thank you for inviting me," she said softly.

"Thanks for coming."

He kissed her the way he'd wanted to since she opened her door that morning. She tugged him up against her until he wanted to lift her, wrap her legs around him...

"Had the feeling I'd walk in on something today," Gregg said from nearby, in a chuckling tone.

"I'll be downstairs," Kristina murmured, gliding away.

Steve wanted to groan with dissatisfaction at the little he'd have to content himself with today.

Gregg glanced after Kristina, who looked so damn good in those faded jeans and curve-for-curve turtleneck. He grinned when he turned back to say, "Not bad. Not bad at all."

"She's not your type." Steve realized with blinding relief that Kristina would never even look at Gregg that way, whether or not she found him attractive. *And face it, who the hell doesn't find the guy attractive?* Steve didn't have a single doubt Kristina had eyes for him only. What a feeling, one he hadn't had in so long. Security. Trust.

Gregg laughed. "You're right. She's got a thing for you. On the other hand, I wouldn't be required to make a commitment for a few hours' fun."

Steve shook his head at him with a scolding grin. "Someday you'll find somebody who'll change your mind about that."

"I don't know about that. I've been through them all." Gregg pulled himself up on the island beneath skylights.

"Probably feels like it," Steve agreed with a chuckle.

Imagining how someone who had as much companionship and good looks as Gregg could be lonely wasn't easy for Steve. Even if they'd never talked about it in specifics, Steve knew Gregg felt loneliness to the same depths he had.

"Have you seen Mitch at all?" Steve asked because friend get-togethers like this always made him acutely aware there were two people missing--Tommie and Mitch. Jessie came along so infrequently, he'd never felt her absence.

Years before Tommie's death, Mitch Taylor--once Brenda's lover, someone she'd considered her soulmate, and a part of their circle--had left Milwaukee and had never looked back, except to attend Tommie's funeral. Steve's friendship with Mitch had never been as strong as Mitch's history with Paul and Tommie, yet he'd considered him one of them. From all prior accounts, Mitch had fallen from grace in a major way, seemingly due to Tommie's death and losing Brenda because of his own self-destructiveness.

Gregg shrugged. "I've seen him with Paul. He's doing a two-step with the grim reaper. That never seems to change. Ain't nobody who can bring him back from the edge now."

Not since Tommie died went unspoken. Tommie had been one of the few people Mitch respected and listened to.

Steve returned to the basement, his chest heavy until he saw Kristina playing foosball with Val, Tom, and Allison. The four of them were shrieking, laughing, and having such a good time, Steve didn't interrupt.

He saw Ron sitting, alone and morose, in Tommie's race car, something Gwen had immortalized by bringing it into her basement game room and making it the center of attention. The car sat on a platform that turned in a slow revolution.

Steve didn't go to him, knowing he'd ignore him anyway.

When he returned upstairs, he walked into the great room and realized by the sudden silence he was the topic of conversation. "All right, what'd I miss?"

Gwen patted the couch next to her. "We were talking about Jess. We're worried about losing her."

They'd already lost Tommie. For all intents and purposes, they'd lost Mitch, too.

"We were also talking about you," Gwen admitted when Steve sat beside her. "We all think Kristina is the perfect woman for you, but, even if she wasn't a part of the equation, you're doing the right thing divorcing Jessie. She might not realize it now, but it's the best thing for her as well. We'll stand behind you in this, if you need anything."

Steve was surprised as he stared around the room at the faces of his closest friends, the ones who knew him better than anyone and understood what he'd been through.

"I'd be a witness against Jess, if you needed me to be," Wendy said, "but since I don't live in Milwaukee, I don't know if they'd allow me to."

"I love Jessie, but she can't win this," Gwen added. "She's no good for those children."

Steve took a deep breath at the show of support. "I hope it doesn't come to that, but thanks. I won't lose my kids. Not even Ronnie."

Gwen hugged him, and Brenda said what they all had to be thinking: "But what do we do about Jess? If she keeps it up, she'll kill herself and we can't let that happen."

Wendy nodded. "Somebody needs to teach her how to lead a productive life. She told me that last Monday, just before she took all those pills. She said she doesn't know how to live by herself. She tries to be normal and ends up even more insane. She doesn't listen to any of us. The only person she ever listened to was Tommie."

"Maybe she needs to get away from here," Gregg offered. "Maybe we should try to drag her to California with us."

Steve shook his head. "She hates California. Whenever I ask her to go there with us, she refuses. No way she'd agree."

No one knew what to do. Brenda, Wendy, and Gwen decided they'd try to spend more time with her and, hopefully, try to lead her down more productive paths than the ones she was used to following blindly.

Later that night, Steve asked Gwen if the kids could stay until he got back from dropping Kristina off.

"Why not let them spend the night? Then you and Kristina can have some time alone."

Steve had counted on her saying that and warned her Ronnie needed close supervision.

"Don't worry. I have four adult guests. We're going to go visit Jessie at the hospital. Wendy will stay here with Valerie and Tom, since they both said they didn't want to go along."

Steve nodded. When he went down to the game room, he found Valerie sitting in Kristina's lap. They were reading *The Secret Garden*, one of Val's favorite books, together. Kristina's voice was lulling, and Valerie's head rested comfortably on her shoulder.

Instead of disturbing them, he went to tell Ronnie and Tom the plan for the night. Ronnie said nothing and moved out of Steve's reach. Tom didn't. Their opposite reactions made him feel torn apart.

"My friends love you. My kids love you," Steve said softly to Kristina in the car.

In the glow of oncoming headlights, her eyes sparkled. "I feel like nothing can go wrong."

He understood what she meant, especially when he had her in his arms later and nothing else mattered except being close to her. Nothing could go wrong, he agreed silently. At least not tonight.

Twenty-Three

As soon as Gwen opened the door, Steve saw something was wrong.

"What's up?" Steve asked, once the kids were down in the basement.

She shrugged, but, as she slid onto a stool in the kitchen, it was clear from her tight expression she was upset.

"I saw Jessie today," Gwen said. "She went back to work. Actually, she didn't just go back to Nelson Industries. She took over."

Steve stared at his sister-in-law in shock. "Took over? She's never wanted to do that."

Gwen took a deep breath. "She does now."

"Why now?" But he had a strong suspicion why. "Did she tell you anything?"

When he sat on the stool next to her, she told him, "I love Jessie. I do. I've known her all her life. And it was so hard when Tommie died. For everyone. For me. But I think it was harder for Jessie even than it was for me. She worshipped Tommie. I think a big part of her died with him. Her only hold on life has been you, but she's spent the past thirteen years pulling you down with her to the grave." Gwen shook her head in frustration. "That doesn't even get into what her behavior has done to your kids. She knows it's time to let go now, but she's afraid. So she's trying to take a crash course in how to live *successfully*, I think. Maybe she believes you'll take her back or that it'll make up for all the bad years."

She placed her hand over his on the countertop. "I don't know her motives, Steve, but she told me she wouldn't let you go. She would fight for her kids. I believe her, and I'm sorry for you. She's not willing to consider letting all of you go."

Putting her chin on her propped fist, Gwen told him gently, "I think it has something to do with Kristina. She doesn't know who you're in love with, but it's a competition to her. She thinks she lost you to another woman instead of believing the truth--that she lost you because of her own actions. She's going to make it hard for all of you, Steve. I couldn't talk her out of it. I'm so sorry."

Steve shook his head, numbly telling her she wasn't responsible.

He didn't want to tell Kristina about this, but he had to. He'd promised himself he'd be completely honest with her.

She hadn't voiced any resentment over Jessie since last Friday, yet he sensed strongly that her jealousy grew along with her fear this wasn't going to work. When Travis had told him Jess was contesting the divorce and planning to drag the divorce out for a hell of a lot longer than it needed to be, he'd thought it himself. *There's a good chance this won't work with Kristina. I'll hurt her, hurt my kids, hurt myself.*

Jess had taken over the company. Hell, he couldn't imagine it. He couldn't imagine she'd continue there for long or that her motives had anything to do with forgiving her parents. But what if she did make it work? Should he give her another chance?

Even as he thought it, he wondered how he could take the risk. She'd made him thousands of promises and never kept a single one. Besides, if he turned back, he knew he'd never be able to escape.

Kristina's face glowed with happiness when she opened her door. "Hi."

Steve strode inside, listening to the door close and aware she'd sense his mood.

"Is everything all right?" she asked, concern warring with fear in her tone.

He slipped off his jacket. "Jess took over her parents' company. They've spent the last thirteen years asking her to take over, but she wouldn't. To her, taking it is like giving them the forgiveness they've been begging for since Tommie died. But she did it. Why now?"

Steve sat down on the couch, putting his arms on his knees and leaning his head into his hands.

"You're re-thinking the divorce," Kristina said--simple, soft, angry.

He shook his head, but she didn't believe him and he didn't expect her to. She stood on the opposite side of the couch with her arms crossed over her chest. Her expression was so tight, he worried she'd either cry or scream at him. He didn't think he could take either at the moment.

She inhaled, hard. "Steve, look, I know I'm compromised here. I know it, and I wish I could hide it because the last thing I want to do is make things harder on you. It's already hard enough. I want to be a shelter for you, not another complication."

"But...?"

Pressing her hand against her throat, she pursed her lips. "I didn't want to tell you this. Because I *am* compromised. Because I know I can't be rational about this...this *bitch* who's spent years tormenting you and your children. But I think you need to know something, Steve. I think, as compromised as I am, you *need* to hear my professional opinion. About your children."

Shocked, Steve's gaze darted to her. Professional opinion about his kids? He was suddenly afraid. Kristina had never offered her opinion--personal or professional--unsolicited. He'd never considered she *had* a professional opinion about his kids. Maybe he hadn't wanted to think about it.

"Steve, your children are severely traumatized. I saw it the first time I met them, and each time I see them, I know it more and more. Ronnie walks around like a time-bomb and he doesn't even know how to switch it off. All he knows is that, in order to get the love he needs from his mother, he needs to make you the enemy. *You*, the parent he *knows* with all his heart loves him and wants what's best for him. Do you realize what'll happen if he continues to feel he has to make a choice between you and Jessie?

"And Tom is desperate to reach out to someone, but he's equally terrified of losing himself or being rejected if he does. He's so withdrawn, I wonder how long before he'll be unreachable. He's eleven years old, and he has the wisdom and fear of a grown man. He doesn't want to be used by his mother, the way Ronnie is. He's afraid to hope anything will ever get better. He loves you, he wants to help you because he sees that you carry the entire burden on your own shoulders to protect them, but he doesn't know how to. So he feels helpless.

"Valerie..."

Kristina choked on a sob that proved what he already knew. As she'd said, she was compromised. She loved his children and she was a counselor with expert opinions in exactly this area. She didn't want to hurt him, but she couldn't protect him from the truth either.

"Steve, she hates her mother so thoroughly, she may never recover from that. She has nightmares about Jessie, that she's a witch who sticks needles in her and waits under her bed to prevent her from ever being free. She's trapped and can't escape. She's...she's a newborn baby. She has no independence, no confidence. She's afraid of the world and believes you're the only person who can make it better for a little while."

"Oh, God," Steve murmured ineffectually against the horrors he'd spent years praying were invisible to everyone except him. He'd wanted to protect his kids, but he hadn't done anything except make their lives worse.

Kristina walked in front of the couch and sat next to him, ignoring her own tears for his. "Don't you dare blame yourself for this, Steve! You did every single thing you could to give them a better life. But you can't save what's unsalvageable. Give yourself and them a chance to heal, I beg you. Children are resilient. In a few years, without Jessie's influence, they may heal. Without Jessie's influence."

"Help me," he whispered. "What do I do? Tell me, show me how to help them."

"You know how. And you know it's the only way."

Steve clenched his teeth against the sob of dread that broke from his throat, and she wrapped her arms around him, whispering, "I'm sorry. I'm so sorry. I didn't want to tell you, but I had to."

"Did they tell you? Did Tom and Val tell you this stuff?"

After a reluctant pause, she nodded against him. *They never told me. Val never told me what her nightmares were about, but maybe I knew. I just never imagined. And Tom... God, my kids! I can't protect them. Nothing I've ever done has helped them.*

"I love them. I bleed for them, Steve. For you. I wanted to help all of you with everything I have in my power. I love you so much, you're in my every waking thought. But I'm scared, scared that this is never going to happen and then I'll always love all of you when I *can't.*"

Steve drew back to look at her. He cradled her tear-streaked face in his hands. He knew now that he never should have started this. Or he should have waited until the divorce was final. It wasn't fair to her. He also knew it was too late to turn back now.

"I'm not re-considering the divorce," he told her, startled by the force in his own voice.

She swallowed. "You're not?"

"No. I'm not." And when he kissed her, he knew he wouldn't go backward ever again.

****

Taking a deep breath, Steve walked into Tom's room and found him staring unwaveringly at his computer screen, his ears covered with headphones that seemed to vibrate with the music screaming inside them. When Steve sat down on his bed, Tom removed the headphones. "I didn't have any homework," he said, and Steve nodded. Resting his elbows on his knees, he propped his mouth against his tightly folded hands.

"I want talk to you, Tom."

"About what?" his son asked warily.

"About the next couple months. They'll be hard. On all of us. On me."

Tom looked at him wordlessly, expressionlessly.

"I was wondering if you'd be willing to help me, buddy. Ron's, hell, we know he'll take a long time to come around. Val needs so much. I need to know if I can count on you. I won't ask too much of you, I promise, but I know you could be a great help."

In the depths of Tom's dark eyes, so much like looking into a mirror, Steve saw something flicker. Then Tom turned away, mumbling, "What do you think you want me to help out with?"

"Val. The house. And maybe, sometimes, if you want to, maybe we can talk. Maybe I can talk to you about things that are bothering me. Maybe you can talk to me, too."

"Yeah?"

Tom still wouldn't look at him, but Steve heard the broken hope in his voice, a world better than the *nothing* he gave ninety-nine-point-nine percent of the time.

After leaving Kristina's yesterday, Steve had decided he'd do this. He wouldn't pile too much on his youngest son because God knew he already had enough to deal with, but if Tom realized how important he was, that he was needed, maybe he wouldn't be so withdrawn. Maybe the newfound responsibility would help him.

"Yeah. I need you, buddy. You've never let me down."

Tom wouldn't turn, even when Steve asked, "You want to help me with dinner tonight?"

"I can do that."

Tom punched a few keys on his computer, then stood. Steve put his arm around him, feeling his heart lighten inside his chest.

Twenty-Four

"I'll be back by nine-thirty," Steve said, looking at Kristina. Valerie had attached herself to her side as soon as she'd walked into Steve's home.

Eisner University's Music Department was preparing for their annual Christmas production and that meant a lot of overtime. Over the last few weeks, Steve had been asking his sister-in-law and the nanny to stay with the kids alternately. Today, he'd asked Kristina, and she still couldn't get over how happy the task made her. Steve trusted her with his children. Even with Ronnie.

He kissed Valerie, and then, pleasing her, he kissed Kristina. "All the candy's in the kitchen. Tom will show you. I almost never let them have candy, so they can have all they want tonight as long as they don't make themselves sick."

Apparently he'd told his kids that he was going to ask Kristina to stay with them tonight before he'd even asked her. Valerie had decided she didn't want to go trick-or-treating because she preferred to spend the time with Kristina.

As Steve slipped into his jacket, he smiled at the two of them, and Kristina knew what he was thinking. He liked that she and Valerie were so close.

"C'mon, I'll show you my room," Valerie said, catching her hand.

Kristina smiled, following Valerie up the stairs. The wide hall had three closed doors, two of them Ronnie's and Tom's rooms no doubt. The bathroom was next to an open door, and Kristina knew immediately that this was Steve's bedroom. Steve's and Jessie's. The bed was oversized, with solid wood posts. All the furniture in the room matched it. The door of the walk-in closet was open and Kristina saw it was overflowing with a female wardrobe. A lighted vanity table still held make-up, jewelry and brushes. The bed had been made hastily, covered with a black satin comforter. Steve used to sleep in this bed with his wife. Whenever she was home, that was.

Kristina tried to ignore her silly jealousy and the pain she felt at the obvious. Obviously Steve had lived with his wife, slept with her, shared the things a husband and wife were supposed to share.

Valerie's room was much simpler, decorated with cream and purple colors, ruffles, lots of stuffed animals, young adult romance novels, and movie posters--all from romance films.

Kristina couldn't help noticing how happy Valerie seemed. The circles under her eyes had lightened. She seemed more confident of herself as well. Clearly, her mother's absence had been good for her.

Valerie easily convinced her to play Mystery Date in the living room until the doorbell rang with trick-or-treaters.

Tom came downstairs to help pass out the candy. Kristina watched him, noting his newly acquired purpose and sense of security since the last time she'd seen him. When she'd arrived tonight, he'd been helping his father load the dishwasher, then said he was going upstairs to do his homework. Steve had told her he'd asked Tom to help him out more, with his sister and the house. He'd also said Tom talked more, instead of spending so much time with his computer games and headphones.

He joined them for a game of Slap Jack that had them all howling with laughter at their stinging hands. In between rounds, they passed out candy to the trick-or-treaters, eating a lot of it themselves.

The laughter stopped almost guiltily when Ronnie unexpectedly appeared and answered the doorbell. Kristina was already halfway there. She watched Ronnie toss candy into the kids' bags and buckets without a word. He seemed angry.

"We're playing Slap Jack. Do you want to join us?" she said with a welcoming smile.

Ronnie slammed the candy bowl down on the foyer table. When he looked at her, she knew for a fact he wasn't merely angry. He was furious. "You don't fool me. You may fool them and my old man, but you don't fool me."

He was only a few inches shorter than her. Kristina could have felt intimidated by him if she hadn't faced some of the biggest and baddest in her career. "I'm not sure what you mean, Ronnie." She spoke honestly, hoping she sounded calm.

"You're a homewrecker. You don't care about my mom or me or anybody as long as you get what you want."

Kristina wanted to flinch, but she knew she couldn't at this pivotal moment. He'd come out of his withdrawn silence and depression enough to confront her. "You're right that I don't care for your mother, Ronnie. But I do care about your father and his family."

"You're not part of this family. My mom is. You never will be."

Hearing Tom and Valerie get up and creep toward the doorway of the living room, Kristina wanted to send them back. She didn't want to cause dissension between the kids. "I understand the way you feel, Ronnie. I really do. You're scared and uncertain about the future. We all are. But your family needs you--your dad and your brother and sister. Your father is doing everything he can to keep the four of you together."

"He's doin' everything he can to tear us apart. He's not really my father, so what right does he have to take me away from my mom?"

"I know this is hard for you to understand, but your mother isn't capable of taking care of you. Your father is. He loves you and he would never do anything to harm you. It really doesn't matter what's true biologically. He's been with you from the moment you were born. He needs you as much and Valerie and Tom do."

Ronnie leaned closer to her, his expression twisted with fury as he jabbed his finger toward her face. "You don't know anything about my mom. Don't pretend you do. Admit it, bitch, you just wanna fuck my old man. That's *all* you two want."

Kristina's face flushed at the harsh words. She'd never been over the professional line before and didn't know how to respond, not until Tom said, "Mom told you that, didn't she? She told you to say that. You're so whipped, man. You'd jump off a cliff if she told you to."

Seeing it coming, Kristina threw herself between Ronnie and Tom. Only inches from Ronnie's face, she said firmly, "All right, Ronnie. You want the truth, so I'm going to give it to you. Your father is a good man. He's divorcing your mother because she's destroying all of you. He's not divorcing her *for me.* I want to make love with your father very much. I won't lie about it. But we haven't and we won't take that step until he's legally free, when this divorce is final. He doesn't want to cheat on your mother. He wants his children to know he was always faithful. He deserves your respect."

She didn't know whether saying all that was wrong or right, but she had to say it nevertheless. Her face burned, and she saw the color creep into Ronnie's cheeks as well. Then he snorted, as if he refused to believe anything she told him. But she heard the doubt in his voice just before he turned and fled upstairs.

Valerie slipped under Kristina's arm. Still abashed, Kristina smiled down at her awkwardly. Valerie seemed utterly thrilled as she hugged her and Kristina stroked her hair.

"Sorry 'bout him," Tom said unexpectedly. "He doesn't know you. He'd never say that if he did. He's just..."

Kristina nodded, cupping Tom's chin in her hand. "I know, sweetie. I know, and he's entitled to feel what he feels. Thank you for standing up for me."

He shrugged just as she expected him to. The doorbell rang, and Tom went to take care of the tricker-or-treaters to avoid the intensity of the moment. They returned to their game of Slap Jack with less enthusiasm. A half-hour later, Tom said that Valerie should have her bath and went up to get it started. Kristina read a couple chapters of *The Secret Garden* with her once she had on her pajamas.

Valerie cuddled next to her with her head on her breast to listen. "I love you, Kristina," she said when Kristina eased out of bed.

"Oh, Valerie. I love you, too." Kneeling beside the bed, she pressed a kiss to Valerie's pale forehead. "Never forget that, sweetheart. No matter what happens."

"I won't," Valerie promised confidently, as though she knew what would happen.

"Sweet dreams."

Valerie smiled a secret smile they shared, closing her eyes.

Tom was in the living room, flipping through channels, when she came back in. He turned off the TV after she sat next to him on the sofa. As he turned to her, she was surprised at the way he stared directly at her. Always in the past, he'd turned away or averted his eyes.

"I haven't told Dad something," he said. "Mom's been coming to school every day at lunchtime to see Ronnie."

Kristina frowned at the news. "But hasn't your dad informed the school that she isn't allowed to see any of you?"

"He doesn't sign out. He just goes out to the parking lot behind the school and they sit in her car for about twenty minutes."

"Why haven't you told your father?" Kristina asked gently, also wondering why Tom had chosen to tell her.

"'Cause I know if I do, he'll put a stop to it. I think that'll make it worse. Right now, they just sit in the car and he comes back in the school. If he wasn't allowed to see her at all, he'd be sneaking around, you know? He'd skip out of school or he'd sneak out at night. And then he could get in a lot of trouble. I figured I'd watch them. Make sure she doesn't try to take off with him. I'd call Dad right away if she did, but she hasn't."

Kristina couldn't help smiling at him. "You've got the wisdom of a sage," she told him, and a ghost of a smile crossed his lips. "But you should tell your father--and tell him just the way you told me. You have to understand that right now it's illegal for her to see Ronnie. Until the final hearing, that's the way it has to be. Even if your father agrees with you, he can't allow it to continue."

Tom sighed, yet nodded. He turned back and started flipping channels on the television again. After a few minutes, he said without looking at her, "I think it's cool--that you and Dad haven't."

Kristina's face flamed. Then Tom glanced at her, and they both laughed out loud.

"I just mean...what you said--I respect that, you know? Especially since I know you both probably want to and all."

"I've been in love with your father from the moment I met him, Tom. I don't know if you want to hear that, but it's true. To me, five minutes spent with him is all I'd ever ask for. But I do want to spend the rest of my life with him. I want to make him happy. And I...I want you and Valerie and Ronnie to be happy, too. That's very important to me."

"What about you?"

"If the four of you are happy, then how could I not be happy? That would make me the happiest person in the world."

Tom stared at her as if she'd turned into an angel before his very eyes. But her motives weren't altruistic. She loved them. She wanted to love them. She wanted to be loved by them. She wanted to be as important to them as they were to her.

"Do you mind if I hug you, Tom?"

The embarrassment flooded his expression again, but he shrugged. When she put her arms around him and held him close, he hugged her back--more in the end than the beginning. Just as she figured he would, he said goodnight and went upstairs as soon as soon as it was over. She didn't mind. It made her smile and love him even more.

* * * *

"Come here."

Steve grabbed her jacket and pulled Kristina outside.

"What--?" she started, but quieted when they stepped off the front porch onto the sidewalk. "Oh, it's snowing!"

After helping her get her jacket on, Steve put his arms around her as they looked up at the large flakes falling all around. They hit the ground and melted.

Jess had never liked to watch the first snow with him. If it was still light out, he used to bundle the kids up when they were little and bring them out to watch. Or the next morning, they would all go outside if it hadn't melted away.

He glanced at Kristina and saw her enraptured smile. Then he kissed her. She turned to him fully, wrapping her arms around him and giving of herself wholly. Steve tasted chocolate in her mouth, teased her about it, but went back to kissing her a second later. Why did she seem sweeter than ever tonight?

"How did it go?" he asked softly, not moving more than a half inch back from her.

Her eyes glistened as bright as the stars, the moon and the snowflakes falling on them lightly. "Oh Steve, I can't help it, I'm so in love with them I wish I never had to leave."

Tears tracked down her cheeks. *Happiness?* Steve cradled her face, brushing the tears back with his thumbs, before he caught her lips again. She moaned, and he couldn't stop his body from reacting to the sound, let alone the wet heat of her mouth. She shivered against him, yet didn't seem to notice the cold any more than he did. "Let's go in the house."

She nodded, glancing up at the velvet sky once more before they went inside arm-in-arm.

"Do you have any photo albums? Pictures of the kids, and you, when you were all younger?" she said as they both slipped out of their jackets.

"Yeah." He couldn't help noticing her nipples were hard under her light sweater and wondering if he'd had anything to do with it. "They're in the storage room. I'll show you while I look in on the kids."

She followed him upstairs, and then he opened the door of the storage room, next to the bathroom. "This box. There are a lot of pictures. Most of them aren't in albums."

He left her to pick the ones she wanted to see and crossed the hall to the kids' bedrooms. Valerie was smiling in her sleep, and he couldn't help the ache he felt when he saw it. The last time he'd seen her do that was when she was a tiny baby. Ronnie slept, turned toward the wall. When Steve kissed him, he tasted salt on Ronnie's cheek. In the dark, he couldn't tell if Ronnie had been crying. He'd known it would be hard for Ronnie, having Kristina here where he thought his mother should be.

Tom lay half-awake, as though he'd been waiting up for him as best as he could. He told Steve about Jessie coming to Ron's school every day, further worrying Steve about his older son. "Thanks for looking out for your brother. I'm glad you told me."

"You're going to make her stop, aren't you?" Tom asked without censure.

"You're right that it's probably safer to allow it, but she's ignoring a judge's orders. It can't continue."

Tom nodded, and Steve hugged and kissed him before standing up.

"Dad?" Tom said, lying back again.

"Yeah, buddy?"

"I...I like Kristina. I think she's good for you. Ronnie'd see that, too, if Mom didn't have him brainwashed."

Surprised, Steve asked, "Did something happen tonight?"

Tom shrugged. "Ronnie said some nasty stuff to her. She stood up for herself and you. But she didn't do it so, well, she didn't tell him he was wrong for feeling like he does. She did it real nice and easy."

He'd have to ask Kristina about it as soon as he went downstairs.

"I respect you," Tom said. "I used to wonder what that meant, but I understand now. I know you were good to Mom, even when she didn't deserve it. But Kristina will never treat you like that. She'll make you happy and you'll make her happy. She cares about all of us. Even Ron, and he's never given her a reason to."

Steve's first instinct was to tell Tom not to get ahead of himself with Kristina. But then he realized Tom couldn't get any more ahead of himself than Steve was on his own.

Tom sat up when Steve went back to hug him again. "You make me proud, Tom. Of you."

Kristina was waiting in the hall when Steve emerged. She turned from his bedroom guiltily.

"She still hasn't come to get her stuff," Steve said softly. "And I told her I'd box it up and send it to her. I haven't had time with this production at the college."

"I-I can help you do it."

Steve laughed, and she blushed, knowing he'd guessed her thoughts of jealousy that Jessie continued to inhabit this house--even if just her clothes. But then he wondered if Kristina was thinking about something else. Him in bed, where he dreamed about her almost every night after talking to her on the phone.

"I'm sorry. It's just a bed," she said in a whisper. "It's stupid. Why should that bother me at all?"

"My bed?"

"It was your bed, the one you shared with her," she clarified, then shook her head again.

Steve eased her closer to him and put his mouth right against her ear. "When I call you, I'm there. You're all I think about in this bed. All night."

When Kristina glanced up at him, she had tears in her eyes again, but she smiled.

They went downstairs, and Steve got a drink while she went to the living room and started looking through the photo boxes she'd brought down. She laughed and cried and oohed and ahhed over each picture.

"I looked like *I* just gave birth in these," Steve chuckled. "The ones when the kids were just born." He handed her back a picture Wendy had taken only days after Valerie had been born. He'd looked completely wiped out.

"But look at the way the two of you look at each other. It was love at first sight," Kristina said. "You're such a good father."

Steve popped the last bite of a candy bar in his mouth as she snuggled closer against him.

"Your wife isn't in most of these," she said softly.

"No. She left the hospital less than two hours after Tom and Val were born. She was good about it after Ron was born. Called him 'the twenty-four-hour need factory'. She didn't do any drugs or even drink while she was pregnant with him. But she was insane when she got pregnant with Tom. She hadn't even begun to deal with Tommie's death at that point. Not that I did either. I couldn't control her at all. She didn't take care of herself and sure as hell didn't think about taking care of him inside her. It's a miracle he was born so perfect. I was so pissed off at her all the time."

Steve shook his head, remembering it so well because he'd gone through it more than once.

"I threatened to divorce her, but after she had Tom, she got pregnant with Val. I think she did it so I'd promise not to leave her. I was taking care of both Ron and Tom, trying to keep my job and I couldn't take care of her the way I tried to the last two times. I know she didn't take care of herself, but she stayed home most of the time. As soon as Val was born, she left and got wasted. Put herself in the hospital on a three-day binge. I didn't know where she was and I didn't have time to care."

"My God," Kristina whispered in horror. "You were taking care of a toddler, an infant, and a newborn and she didn't even have the decency-- Steve, you're a saint! Only a woman possessed by a demon wouldn't cherish the day she met you, the day you blocked out the sun and became the center of her world. What woman wouldn't want to burrow into your arms and never leave!"

Steve brushed her hair back from her face, smiling at her fierce expression that seemed to want justice and want it immediately.

"'Something happen between you and Ron tonight?" he asked because he didn't want to talk about Jessie. He wasn't applying for sainthood. All he wanted was to be happy, make his kids happy and make *this* woman happy.

Kristina told him, in what sounded like a word-for-word account, and Steve felt her love again. A love that embraced Ronnie and Tom and Val.

"I can't believe you had the guts to say all that, but...thanks."

"I love you. And I think Ronnie needed me to be honest instead of trying to befriend him. He's scared and he feels protective of his mother. She's manipulated him to the point where he feels that, when she loves him, he's done the right thing and, when she doesn't, he's been bad. He feels you're betraying her with the divorce and if he takes your side, his mother won't love him ever again. He also feels like Tom and Valerie are betraying their mother by not holding the family together. But I think deep down he knows it's not what's best for any of you. I didn't want him to believe the divorce has anything to do with me. It doesn't and it shouldn't. Right?"

Did it matter? At this moment, it didn't matter in the least to Steve *why* he was divorcing Jess. It was necessary. That was all he needed to know. It seemed to matter to Kristina though.

"Right."

She stared at him, her eyes wide and blurred with tears. He had a strong sense she was satisfied with his reply, even if she didn't really want it.

After he showed her baby pictures of himself that seemed to move her to tears as well, he told her he still had work to do tonight. E-mail, lecture notes for next week.

"I'll go then."

"Thanks for staying with the kids."

"It was my pleasure."

At the door, after a long kiss, she asked, "Will you call me? Before you go to sleep?"

"Could be late."

"I don't care."

From the porch, he watched her drive away, then booted up his computer. He cleaned the house while his e-mail poured in. Garret had gone through it, but Steve still felt drained just looking at the volume he had to handle.

"Are you in love with her?"

Steve glanced up from the computer screen to see Tommie standing next to him with his arms crossed over his chest the way he always did. His black hair was still long, the way Steve's used to be when he was in college and Tommie was on the racetracks all the time. Steve noticed the heart tattoo on his arm he'd gotten for Gwen when he was a teenager still drew attention. His dark brown eyes saw right into Steve's mind. He couldn't hide the truth.

"I'm afraid, man." Right now, he was afraid instead of sure. He'd made Tommie a promise he couldn't keep any more than he'd been able to keep the first one he'd made to him.

"It's just e-mail," Tommie shrugged.

Steve recognized his trademark sense of humor. It was something Tommie had abandoned with Steve and Steve alone when he got involved with Jess.

"Why are you scared?" he asked a moment later, seriously.

"'Cause if I disappoint you...hell, you'll never forgive me."

"You've been taking care of Jess a long time, Steve," Tommie said, picking up a framed picture of Ronnie*, looking at it with a grin, then putting it back carefully. "So long you can't remember the last time you took care of yourself."*

"I tried to make it right, Tommie. I broke my promise to you, but I wanted to make it right. Don't hate me."

Tommie leaned across the desk, meeting him eye to eye. "Steve, listen to me."

Steve did. He couldn't do anything else. He saw the depth of Tommie's gaze and it left him naked.

"Take care of yourself, *Steve."*

Steve lifted his head from his arms, resting on the desk. His heart thudded like a jackhammer in his chest. A dream. Just a dream.

He was crying.

Twenty-Five

"Oh God, what the hell are you doing here?" Jessie asked. She sat behind a desk and looked more out of place at than Steve could have imagined. Jess was suited for centerfolds, fashion shows, motorcycles. She didn't fit the mold of a businesswoman. "Isn't there some law against a husband *suing* his wife for divorce and seeing her during it?"

Steve shook his head, not venturing past the open doorway of her office. "No. But there is a law against you seeing our son when a judge has ordered you not to."

Jess paled, but kept her composure as she rose from her chair. "I can't believe Ronnie told you."

"He didn't. Tom saw the two of you in the parking lot at school."

"The judge had no right to forbid me from seeing him. He's *my* son, dammit, not yours. Maybe if I'd been allowed to attend the hearing, he would've known that."

Steve's eyes narrowed on her in disbelief, but he forced himself to be calm. "Yeah. Too bad you tried to kill yourself the night before to punish me."

Jess came around the front of her desk. After crossing her arms over her chest, she asked coolly, "So what are you gonna do about it?"

"I'm going to offer you a deal and you're going to take it."

She glared at him, her over-generous mouth grimacing.

"You stop seeing Ronnie now. You call him and tell him you can't see him, that he can't see you until the final hearing."

"And if I don't?"

"I'll have my lawyer tell the judge you've been seeing Ronnie against his orders and you may never see Ron again. I don't want that, but if you want to play hardball that's what will happen. What do you say? Do we have a deal?"

She looked so angry, he was surprised she didn't let him have it both verbally and physically the way she always did when she knew she couldn't win. "Fine," she said between her teeth.

"Good. We'll be home tonight at five-thirty. You can call around six to tell him."

Steve had already alerted the school when and where Jess might show up, and today would be no exception if she was pissed enough. If she did anything out of spite, he'd consider it a deal breaker, regardless of the severity of it.

He went through the rest of the day with his ear open for a page or phone call. He also spent the rest of the day haunted by the dream he'd had about Tommie the night before. It was a dream, had to be. Tommie would never let him off the hook so easily.

"Your mom come to school today?" Steve asked Tom when he got home from work that night.

Tom shook his head.

While Tom started dinner and Val did her homework, Steve went up to Ron's room. "I saw your mom today," he said, knowing his son wouldn't ignore him this time.

"You did? Why?" Ronnie asked suspiciously from his desk.

"Because she's been coming to school and seeing you."

"That little dork Tom told you, didn't he?" Ronnie sneered. He glanced away as Steve advanced further into the room.

"It doesn't matter how I found out," Steve said, standing over him. "What does matter is that the judge made a decision based on your mom's suicide attempt and her background. I had nothing to do with that decision. But if your mom doesn't obey it, she'll get in a lot of trouble. There's a chance she might never be able to see you again--"

Steve went on without heeding Ronnie's incensed protest. "I don't want that. I know you won't believe it either, but I don't want to cut any of you off from your mother if she's willing to clean up her life and you want to see her."

"So why'd you see her today?" Ronnie asked sullenly. His anger had seemed to be missing lately. In its place was this sullenness. Steve didn't know which emotion was better.

"To tell her she can't see you until after the final hearing in January. She'll call you at six and tell you that herself. Do you understand why we have to do it this way, Ron?"

Ronnie nodded, turning away. Steve started to do the same, wishing he could get his older son to talk to him the way Tom had been lately.

"I'm not really your son," Ronnie said suddenly, forcefully. "Why do you care so much? Why do you wanna keep me? Why don't you just let her have me without a fight? It'd be easier for everybody."

Steve shook his head. "You think that, Ron? It wouldn't be easier for anybody. It'd be harder."

"Why?" Ronnie asked, his tone quiet and hoarse.

Steve sat on the bed next to Ronnie's desk. "Your mom was about seven months pregnant the first time we felt you kick. She barely looked pregnant. She had this little..." Steve made a small motion to indicate the practically non-existent size of Jessie's pregnant form. "She was asleep with this sheet over her. She was always too hot or too cold, never just right, when she was pregnant. But the sheet was moving. I mean, something was moving under the sheet. I could see it, and I sat up and lifted the sheet off her, and there you were." Steve smiled at the bittersweet memory. "You must've had your hand or your knee or your foot--I've never figured out which--thrust forward, like you were trying to get out. I could feel the shape of that limb beneath her skin."

Steve laughed and felt tears in his eyes at the sentimental emotion pressing on him. "You also hiccupped all the time while you were in your mom's belly. At least three times a day, her whole stomach would be jumping up and down 'cause you had the hiccups. God, she hated that. She said it hurt, but..." Steve shook his head on an exhale. "Maybe it's hard on a woman, being pregnant. I don't know. You were so alive, even inside those protective layers, and when you'd be kicking up a storm, or hiccupping, or using your mom's ribs for a jungle gym. I could hardly wait for you to really be there with us."

"I can hardly wait to get this thing outta me." Steve remembered Jessie's reaction to pregnancy just as vividly as his own. Of all the kids, Ronnie had been the most aggressive in the womb. Tom and Val had been quiet a lot, and Jess had endured a lot of ultrasounds to prove each one was still doing fine.

"I'll never forget the day you finally came either. You were screaming yourself hoarse while they measured you and dried you off and did all that stuff they do after a baby is born." Steve laughed faintly, but he was there once more, in the delivery room, where he'd fallen irrevocably in love with his son. "I rubbed my hand over your foot like I used to when you kicked inside your mom's belly. I held your hand in mine, and you opened your eyes. You calmed down, just like that. Like you recognized me as the one who'd been holding your foot or hand or knee and trying to calm you when you were inside."

"What about Mom?" Ronnie asked even hoarser now.

Steve looked at him, swiping the back of his hand over his eyes. He couldn't say it. He couldn't say Jess had hated being pregnant and she'd been happy the day he was born--happy because she was finally rid of him. She'd never needed to say that. She hadn't wanted anything to do with her child. Though she conceded to breastfeeding, she'd ended up pumping and letting anyone else who would feed him and take care of him--"the twenty-four-hour need factory"--do the work.

"It never mattered to me, Ronnie, that you weren't mine the way Tom and Val are. I've loved you from the moment I felt you moving beneath my hand."

Shocking Steve, a sob broke free from Ronnie as if he couldn't have held it back for anything in the world. Shocking Steve even more, Ron allowed Steve to pull him into his arms. He didn't speak. He just wept while Steve held him and felt useless to offer more comfort. Giving in to his own tears was all he could do.

When the phone rang, Ronnie tore out of his embrace and raced out of the room without looking back.

* * * *

"Copy these notes on the blackboard. Here are the worksheets. I need about twenty-five of each."

Garret nodded, making notes for himself.

"I'll be back in about an hour."

"Tilly's?"

Steve nodded.

"Counselor Kristina Ingram?"

"What?"

Garret grinned at him. "Come on, dude. *Everybody* knows about you two. No wonder you didn't want me going after her."

Steve had no idea his and Kristina's relationship had become a topic of conversation--or rumor--at the college. They drove to school separately now. The only place they were seen on campus was the parking lot, then only in platonic situations, and at Tilly's. But even there, they'd been circumspect. He visited her office occasionally. She came to his. They were friends. His colleagues didn't know anything about their relationship outside the university. Daniel Cook, his mentor, knew about the divorce. He'd been discreet about the information, Steve was certain, especially since he approved of the action wholeheartedly.

Garret stared at him like he had a lot of nerve being surprised by the news he and Kristina's relationship was out in the open. "I've seen the way you two look at each other."

"How? Where?"

"Tilly's. And out there in the lot between DeSmet and the Drug Center. You're not fooling anybody."

Garret's tone remained teasing. Nevertheless, it affected Steve. He'd been very careful. He knew a lot of people in Milwaukee. The last thing he wanted was Jessie, her lawyer or someone else to start some lurid rumor about the nature of his and Kristina's relationship.

As it was, the divorce was dragging out. Every Marital Settlement Agreement Travis drafted was ripped apart by Jessie and her lawyer. She'd agreed not to see Ronnie again until the final custody hearing. Ron had abided by it, too. Nevertheless, in the three months since Steve filed for divorce, they'd accomplished nothing to get him closer to freedom. Jess didn't want to end the torture. Whatever she had to do to drag it out, she did.

When Garret saw his expression, he backed off, saying in a wounded voice, "What's the big deal? You're getting a divorce anyway, right? I've never heard of anybody not dating, and more, during a divorce. Nobody expects you to put your life on hold until the official decree is handed down."

"I'm not sleeping with her. I'm not sleeping with anybody," Steve insisted.

"Then shame on you."

"I mean it. You tell that to anybody who whispers about it behind my back."

Garret stared at him in shock until Steve left his office.

Kristina was in their usual booth when he slid in on the opposite side of her. "You're getting rave reviews," she said, holding up just one of the many local papers that had reviewed the Christmas production last night. "But then you probably already know."

She looked up to smile at him, but frowned when she saw his expression. "What's the matter?"

"Everybody's talking about us."

"What? Who?"

"On campus. On my side of it anyway."

Kristina set down the paper she'd been reading before he arrived on the stack next to her, then faced him across the table. "My side, too. Hillary tends to love gossip. And I'm apparently ripe for some."

"I wish we could, hell, go somewhere where nobody knows us. And just..." Steve shook his head.

"So do I."

"Yeah?" he asked. Now was the time, but he couldn't help being afraid of the prospect of having the freedom to be with Kristina. Freedom in a place where no one would gossip about them.

She nodded.

"My sister called last night. The kids and I go to San Bernardino every year. Skiing. Christmas. The whole thing. We're there for a week."

Winter break was coming up in little more than a week. His family usually spent a full week with Wendy and Paul. A full week without Jess.

Kristina looked devastated and obviously wanted to hide it.

"She invited you, too."

Wendy hadn't simply invited her. She'd already bought the extra plane ticket, and flat-out asked Steve if he wanted her to make up one or two bedrooms. Even after he insisted again that he wasn't sleeping with Kristina, she'd asked how they could possibly hold out.

Hold out he had, though, but this trip worried him. God only knew how long the divorce would drag out. Regardless, he wasn't sure how much longer he could restrain himself, especially if he and Kristina were in a place where the people around them not only accepted them, but encouraged them to take what they wanted.

"Really?" Kristina asked happily. "Do *you* want me to? Oh, but what about the kids?"

"I already talked to them about it. They want you to go. Even Ronnie said he 'didn't care.'"

"What about you?"

You'll be tested. Your mettle. Your morals. Your self-respect. You could fail. But there's no way you'll say no.

"I want you to come with us, honey, if you want to."

"I want to," she said softly. "With all my heart, I want to."

Twenty-Six

Steve kept expecting to wake up from the dream because he hadn’t felt this level of excitement for so long. The kids, even Ronnie, had gotten up that morning eager. Everything had been packed into the car the night before, so they showered, picked up Kristina and had breakfast at the airport while they waited for their flight.

Steve was on edge the entire time and couldn't decide it if it was a good feeling or a bad one. He just knew every time he looked at Kristina--whether she was interacting with his kids, eating, smiling, talking with him or staring out the window of the plane--he wanted to kiss her and never stop.

"He's starting to accept the situation," Kristina whispered to him. "I think he's decided to trust you."

Steve glanced at her, unsure what she meant. She put her mouth to his ear again, and her warm breath and nearness sent a jolt straight through him. "Ronnie."

"You think?"

Ronnie had changed in the last few weeks, since they'd talked about why Steve fought to hold on to him. While he remained sullen, he wasn't angry, and Steve saw glimpses of the life-loving enthusiasm Ronnie used to reveal as a baby.

"That's my professional opinion, yes," Kristina said, smiling softly.

Ronnie *could* accept a new life without Jess and with Kristina. It made Steve happy to think maybe there a light shone at the end of the dark tunnel they were all in.

He took Kristina's hand, and they laced their fingers. *Tell her. Tell her you're not sharing a room.*

But he couldn't get himself to do it. Not now. While he knew she'd taken his invitation, *Wendy's* invitation, as a step up to a higher level in their relationship, he didn't want to hurt her if the level they entered into wasn't the one she expected.

* * * *

Wendy waited at the baggage claim, and hugged everyone, including Kristina, enthusiastically.

Steve realized suddenly that the last time she'd been in Milwaukee, his sister had said the adoption of the twins would go through soon. "Did you get the kids Nicole and...?" he asked, feeling like a heel for how wrapped up he always got in his own life--to the exclusion of all else.

"Jason. They came home with us on November thirtieth." Uninhibited tears filled Wendy's eyes. "I can't wait for you to meet them. They're really excited about having all of you spend Christmas with us."

"You don't think it's too much stress for them?"

Wendy shook her head as they hauled their luggage out to the truck. "With all these kids to play with and all the plans we've made, I doubt it. They've spent their lives alone, with little or nothing, including love. They're part of our family and so are you."

Wendy and Paul's property in the snowy San Bernardino mountains was surrounded by a massive gate controlled by remote. The house itself had belonged to Wendy and Steve's father's best friends, missionaries who'd sold the house to Paul and Wendy years ago, literally giving up a palace for a mud flat. Wendy had loved the house and their honorary aunt and uncle as a kid, and had spent summers in this house. Steve spent his summers playing in bands and never felt the connection Wendy did here. Since it'd become Wendy and Paul's property and Steve had started bringing his kids here for a week or so in summer and winter, he understood her love for the house.

Paul was waiting for them, with two kids who could have been their own, based on their appearance. Nicole was thin, tall, with blond hair as brilliant as Wendy's and a sweet and shy and pure smile. Jason was the opposite--dark hair, dark eyes, just a little withdrawn and wary, which described Paul to a T. At least it'd described him before he fell in love with Wendy.

The kids bonded almost immediately and ran off to play while the adults brought in the luggage and Wendy revealed the sleeping arrangements in her mini tour of the upstairs. Steve realized his sister was playing matchmaker when she showed him and Kristina the rooms they'd be staying in. She gave them the rooms that she usually gave the kids, connected by a bathroom.

Kristina picked up her luggage and went into the nearest one.

"I'll let you guys get unpacked. We'll have a late lunch in about a half-hour. Then we'll decorate the tree if everyone's up for it." Wendy winked at him before going downstairs.

Steve brought the kids' suitcases into the rooms Wendy had assigned, for them to unpack later, and took his own into the room connected to Kristina's.

The bathroom doors between the rooms stood open. Kristina glanced up at him when she saw him on the other side.

"I'm sorry I didn't tell you--" he started.

She shook her head, smiling as she walked to the doorway on her side. "I assumed we wouldn't be sharing a room. This is a gorgeous house. Every room, every hallway. I feel like I'm at the Ritz!"

Steve laughed.

"This feels like a dream to me. If I pinch myself, I might wake up at home in bed. And I think I'd burst into tears if I did."

He crossed the bathroom to her. "I think my sister's going to play matchmaker while we're here," he warned.

Happily, she came into his arms. Her eyes sparkled at him. "We can handle it."

Sighing, Steve eased her closer, until their foreheads touched. "I'm not so sure I can."

"You don't think so?"

He shook his head. "No. Everything back home feels like we're under a big microscope. We're accountable to everybody. But here, here we're free and people accept that we're together. They think we should be together. Sometimes too much freedom can lead to regrets."

"I won't let that happen," Kristina surprised him with the firmness in her tone. "I love you, I want to be with you, but I couldn't bear it if you regretted anything we did together. I'm not expecting anything. I'm not asking for anything but the chance to be with you and your family."

Even as Steve kissed her the way he'd wanted to all day, he wondered what *he* might ask for.

To hell with all this worry. Maybe it's time to be happy. I won't ruin it.

* * * *

"She's got a wicked fastball," Steve shouted to his comrades from behind their barricade. When he peeked out, Kristina aimed another soft snowball, which hit him in the face. Valerie, Wendy, and Nicole laughed uproariously, congratulating her.

The guys were getting few snowballs past their barricade. Valerie and Nicole made the ammunition for Kristina and Wendy to fire faster.

Valerie shrieked in laughter. Kristina turned to see Steve sneaking up on them with a couple snowballs. They pelted him immediately, and he fell back in the deep snow pretending they'd taken him out.

A few minutes later, Ronnie, Tom, Paul and Jason found them laughing as they buried Steve, who was such a good sport about it, Kristina wanted to kiss him.

She'd never had a more magical Christmas in her life. The night they arrived, they'd all decorated the tree together while listening to jolly holiday music and sipping eggnog. The adults had a spiked version. After the kids went to bed, the adults stayed up talking and Steve had played one of Paul's acoustic guitars for them. The song wasn't one any of them had ever heard before, and he told Kristina why hours later, after he'd kissed her at her bedroom door. He'd composed it himself. Kristina would never forget the haunting refrain.

Christmas Eve followed with last-minute shopping in Los Angeles, then home to wrap presents and take a very unseasonable dip in Paul and Wendy's pool, enclosed for the winter and heated. That night at bedtime, Steve had kissed her at her door for almost fifteen minutes--not nearly long enough for either of them, Kristina suspected.

The children woke early and everyone opened one present before Paul and Wendy's spectacular housekeeper, Grace, served a breakfast that would go down in Kristina's mind as the best meal she'd ever eaten in her life. Steve told her Grace had been the housekeeper in his parents' home as long as he could remember. After his parents divorced, Wendy brought Grace home with her, as she had no family of her own left in Milwaukee. They'd come outside to work off the meal by building a snowman. Tom had initiated the snowball fight.

"Hate to break this up, but our guests will be here in about an hour. We better get showered and dressed in warm, dry clothes," Wendy said.

Still laughing and tossing the occasional snowball, the kids followed Wendy and Paul in the house.

Kristina held her hand out to Steve to help him up. "You better be the first to shower--" she began, seeing he was soaked to the skin.

Steve yanked her down to him instead of rising with her help. His lips felt like ice against hers, but Kristina didn't mind in the least, especially since they warmed so quickly.

"No! I'd definitely say they don't need help!" Paul shouted from behind them, and Kristina and Steve turned guiltily. Paul grinned at them, close to laughing. "Might need some privacy though. Carry on," he added, for their ears only, saluting them before he followed everyone else around the corner and into the house.

Steve chuckled, drawing her back for another kiss before they got up and went into the house arm-in-arm. A lump formed in Kristina's throat as she glanced surreptitiously at him. He looked so happy. She'd never seen him so open, uninhibited, and free. His expression proved it. His easy manner when he laughed and played with the kids proved it. The way he looked at her, taking every opportunity to touch her or put his arms around her proved it. He didn't seem to care if anyone else noticed his affection.

Ronnie noticed their lack of inhibitions here. Kristina noticed he noticed it. He said nothing about it. Kristina wondered if Steve was aware of the significance of Ronnie noticing their affection and not becoming sullen or angry in response.

All of his children seemed happy, again in a way Kristina had never witnessed from them before. Ronnie was as open, uninhibited and free as his father, quite possibly because his mother wasn't anywhere near to make him feel like he couldn't be so happy.

All Kristina knew and cared about was that she was a part of this beautiful family, just for now or, *please God*, forever.

Twenty-Seven

Steve followed the sound of Kristina's footsteps with his eyes shut, as if knowing exactly where she was in her room would carry him there with her.

He'd heard her enter the connecting bathroom. She hadn't closed his door for privacy. The intimacy--and lunacy, he supposed--of hearing her pee made him think of those lazy weekends when he'd been in college. He and his current girlfriend--and he'd always had a girlfriend, faceless as they were now--would sleep in, she'd get out of bed to pee, and, when she came back out, they'd make love until the hunger for food called a halt to the festivities.

As ludicrous as it sounded even to him, the sound of a woman peeing had become an intimacy to him that made his nether regions surge with hot blood. He'd spent the night wanting Kristina, knowing his door was ajar, her door was ajar. No one in the house would know if he went to her. No one except the two of them. In the heat of the night, the reasons why they couldn't seemed as vague as the furniture cloaked in shadows around his lonely room.

Steve glanced at the clock on the Amish nightstand. It was barely five a.m. Everyone had gone to bed late last night. They'd sleep in late.

Kristina hadn't gotten into bed. He didn't hear the rustle of sheets, blankets, the shift of her body beneath them as she got comfortable again. She'd tossed and turned all night. She should be exhausted, too. Yet she hadn't returned to bed yet.

Steve sat up, shoving back the covers as he did, to look at his own body. The loose drawstring pants he wore stretched like a tent from his erection.

They couldn't make love. Not yet. If he knew that, why couldn't he lie next to her and watch her sleep?

You'd take any excuse, wouldn't you? Never know when a meteorite will hit right here. Might be safer in her room.

Steve tamped down on the laughter that rose in his throat. He was going in, damn the consequences.

He went into the bathroom, waiting until his erection subsided, then used the facilities. He avoided his own eyes in the mirror as he took a swig of mouthwash and spat it in the sink, just like Kristina had when she'd been in here.

When he nudged open the door to her room, she turned from the window as though she'd been waiting for him. Her expression looked as tense as her body.

Her body... Steve would have had to be dead not to notice how aroused she was. She wore simple white cotton pajamas. Her top was long-sleeve, loose and ended at her midriff in ruffles. The matching pants dipped low on her sleekly rounded hips. Her nipples stood erect, pulling the top tight across her chest.

"You're awake, too," he said softly, not emerging from the doorway because he was afraid to move, now that his body rapidly returned to the state it'd been in for most of the night.

"I don't want to miss a minute of this, even for eight hours of sleep," she told him what he knew was only half the truth. The slow, sweep of her gaze over his body told him the rest. She swallowed with obvious difficulty as she caressed his bare chest with a look that slid farther down. And stayed there. Her next breath hitched in her throat at the evidence of his hunger for her.

Even as he told himself no, he strode halfway across the room to her.

She turned to him with an expression of agony.

"I know. I know we can't," she whispered as if the words killed her. Tears of frustration he well understood filled her eyes. "I wanted to...I got up to... I thought, if all I can ever have of you is lying next to you, listening to your heartbeat, I would be the most satisfied woman in the world. But I couldn't get myself to do it. I can't be the one to make you lose your self-respect."

"You wouldn't be the only one."

She nodded, dancing closer to him, her hands coming in contact with his bare middle and holding there as if for dear life.

Steve sucked in his breath at her inhibited caress, his stomach muscles quivering.

She drew back.

Just this. This is all I'll allow. He brought her hands back and put his arms around her.

"I was afraid to sleep. I was afraid I'd dream about you and wake up, feeling..." She glanced up at him, her eyes naked with her own honesty. "Just kissing you sometimes, Steve, I'm so close..."

She swallowed the words he understood without hearing. When they kissed, he knew she was on the edge of an orgasm. *God.*

"And, at night, dreaming of you, I've--I *have...*" She swallowed hard, "...without touching myself at all."

Steve swore under his breath, closing his eyes as he gripped her harder than he intended to. Maybe she shouldn't have told him, but hell, he wanted to know. It'd been so damned long since he'd made a woman want him like this. Made her want him with no incentive at all.

She shivered, and he saw the goose bumps on her arms and belly. For some crazy reason, her confession made him feel in control. She understood his reasons for denying them. She accepted them. If he could satisfy her without compromising himself physically, that was all right. That was ideal.

"You're cold, honey. Get under the covers."

"I'm not cold. Will you hold me? Under the covers?"

He knew she wasn't asking for more than that. As she'd said, if all they could have was holding each other, it was enough.

"I love being here. I love your family. I love the kids," she said as soon as he'd eased under the blanket with her, drawing her body parallel with his. She felt warm, and her body fit against his like it belonged there. "I love them as much as I would my own."

"Do you want kids?"

"I always have. But now..."

She lowered her gaze to his chest, where her fingers tangled in his chest hair.

Tears clung to her lashes when she looked up again. "Last night..." She pursed her lips as though holding back a sob. "...Valerie hugged me goodnight. And she called me Mommy. 'I love you, Mommy,' she said."

Steve smiled when she buried her face against him. She laughed and cried a second later. "My mom was right. I am going to get hurt here. I tell myself to slow down and wait. See what's going to happen. But I can't control how feel, what I want."

"I'm sorry," Steve muttered, not feeling so in control himself anymore. He'd promised himself he wouldn't hurt her, but he didn't see how it was possible. If he walked away from her until the divorce became final, he'd hurt her. If he made love to her along with a thousand promises, he'd hurt her. If they went on the way they had been, he'd hurt her, someway, somehow.

Kristina glanced at him, face covered with tears yet smiling. "Don't worry. I'm losing my mind, but I wouldn't change a thing right now. Except to have your divorce over this very minute."

She was as happy as she was miserable, mixed up, but he understood it. He was going through the same thing.

"Tell me things," she requested enthusiastically, but she didn't give him the opportunity to even ask 'What things?' Her mouth covered his. He understood this, too. She didn't want to think about the misery. She wanted to be happy in this moment.

Steve closed his eyes and gave in to pleasure. The softness of her lips, her tongue, her body close, but not close enough. *Hmm, there.* Her breasts met and yielded sweetly to the wall of his chest.

She bled a moan through their kiss, one that lingered when his hand covered her hip, snaking to cup one cheek of her rear end. He hadn't felt the softness of a woman in such a long time. He hadn't tasted the softness of a woman possibly in a lifetime. The thought had him squeezing harder, aching to fill his mouth with her breasts and fill her body with him. He remembered that intimate surrender like a far-off reality he'd walked away from.

His fingers stole to her belly, and he touched the ring pierced there. "When did you get this?" he asked as he played with it.

"College," she murmured breathlessly, barely opening her eyes. "I thought it was sexy."

Steve uttered agreement in a groan. "You don't wear a bra."

Her eyes opened now, as if she hadn't expected him to notice. "I can't find any that fit my, well, shape."

"I know."

"You know?"

"I know. I've spent most of the hormonal years of my life fantasizing about a woman with your shape."

"*You...*? You have?" she asked weakly, her face flushed.

Steve pressed a kiss to her lips, her jaw and then her ear. He whispered, "My mouth has been watering since I realized it." His teeth gently captured the lobe of her ear.

"Oh God, Steve, don't kiss me! If you do, right now, I'll..."

"I'm tempted."

"Tell me something. Quickly! Tell me how your family celebrated Christmas when you were young."

Steve couldn't help chuckling, especially when he saw her pained smile.

"About two weeks before Christmas, Wendy and I would decorate the tree with Grace's help, while my parents got drunk on spiked eggnog. On Christmas Eve, we'd go to the Nelson Industries annual Christmas shindig. My old man is Vice President of the company. Every year, he'd write a check for $100,000 to some charity. His parents were missionaries, and I think it was his way of not feeling guilty for his own money-driven lifestyle."

"Nelson Industries is your wife's company? The family company?"

Steve nodded. "Five hundred people and their kids. Wendy and I never thought the party would end. But on Christmas morning, we'd always try to beat each other getting up first. We'd shake every present under the tree for us and try to figure out what was in each one. When my parents came down, we'd open the presents, and Grace would have this huge brunch ready for us. Then we'd go to Jess and Tommie's for an elaborate Christmas dinner. I couldn't wait 'til the day I moved out and didn't have to do any of it anymore."

"What did you do for Christmas after you moved out?"

"See my friends. Wendy. End up making myself eggs--the only thing I could cook myself back then--since I didn't want to make anybody work on a holiday. If I had a steady girlfriend, we might do something together if she didn't insist she had to be with her family.

"What about you? What were Christmases like in the Ingram household?"

Kristina smiled tightly. "Dull, just like yours. My dad would drag us to how many holiday dinner parties before the actual day arrived. We stayed home for Christmas dinner, and it was this totally uncomfortable meal. Dad would work most of the day. He works every day of his life, I swear. The best part of the holidays was decorating the tree with Mom. Going caroling around the neighborhood. Going to the Christmas Eve service at church." She looked up at him. "This is the best Christmas I've ever had.

This is what the holidays should be about. Families, children. Being together."

"My best ever, too."

Kristina smiled at him. She laid her head on his chest and snuggled closer. After a few minutes, she murmured happily, sleepily, "Mhm, your heartbeat is lulling me."

Steve tilted her chin up to kiss her. "Sleep then, honey."

* * * *

When Steve asked her if she wanted to attend a concert with him, Kristina thought only of being with him and agreed. Jason insisted on going along with Paul, and Ronnie, who'd made fast friends with Jason, wanted to go as well.

The drive to Los Angeles, where their friend Gregg Stevens was playing a sold-out concert, seemed long this day. Paul and Wendy had bought a mini-van in preparation for being parents. Jason sat in the passenger's seat, near his dad. Ronnie sat nearest the door. The two boys made as much noise as would come from a stack of speakers at a concert.

Kristina barely noticed, though Paul and Steve asked them to keep it down repeatedly and to no affect. Steve sat with his arm around her, ignoring Ronnie's mild reaction to it. He told her all about Gregg. How they'd met through an ad in *Rolling Stone* when Steve was twenty-one and Gregg wasn't yet out of high school. Gregg had lived in Seattle and had been in negotiations with a major record label. The deal fell through at the last minute, and Gregg quit school and went to Milwaukee to hook up with Steve. They'd formed a band, which had changed members many times before Steve dropped out to become a music teacher.

Paul had tried to get Gregg a record deal. Failing that, he'd formed his own company, Randall Records, and produced Gregg's first album himself. That very first album had put both Gregg and Paul on the map. Gregg now had four multi-platinum albums out, all produced by Randall Records. He had become a star the world over.

Steve told her about some of the other groups Paul represented, as well as a handful of songwriters he worked with. Paul wanted to keep his company small and personal. Because many of his groups were at the top of the charts, keeping things manageable wasn't easy, so he'd recently hired additional staff.

The conversation reminded Kristina of three years ago, when she and Steve had met at Summerfest in Milwaukee. A month earlier, he'd mentioned to her his friend Gregg Stevens would be playing at Summerfest. She'd gone and hung out near the stage where Gregg would be performing.

Steve had been there for all of five minutes. He'd gotten a call on his cell phone, something she'd known was an emergency by the way he'd left in such a hurry, barely uttering a goodbye to her as he'd disappeared into the crowd. She'd been hurt by that encounter, silly as it'd been to feel that way, because she'd spent so long looking forward to it and preparing for the possibility they might spend the day together. She'd forced herself to forget it until now.

"What made you decide you wanted to be a teacher instead of a musician?" Kristina said.

"Reality. I realized I was holding Gregg back. I figured it wasn't fair--"

"Hold on," Paul said from the front seat, readjusting the rearview mirror to look at Steve. "Did Wendy tell you that?"

"Tell me what?" Steve asked.

"That *you* were holding Gregg back?"

"Why would *she* tell me? I knew. Back then, I knew. I knew he lost representation from other producers and managers because he wouldn't ditch the rest of us in the band. I knew you wanted to take him on personally."

Paul seemed chagrined by this news.

"Once I got used to the idea, I realized if I hadn't made anything of myself in eighteen years trying to be a rock star, I never would. And now I think it was all meant to be. Don't worry about it."

Kristina realized by the stunned sorrow in Paul's expression that he'd never believed Steve had what it took to be a rock star, not the way Gregg did. It must have hurt Steve to realize his friend believed he wasn't good enough and to accept he had to give up his own dreams to make two of his friends' dreams come true.

"Seriously, man, it's no big deal. I mean, at the time-- But I had enough problems then without making it more than it was. I don't regret it." Steve slapped Paul on the shoulder in an affectionately male gesture of consolation. Kristina assumed Paul accepted it when he readjusted the rearview mirror a minute later.

She couldn't regret Steve's decision to become a teacher. She never would have met him if he hadn't given up those early dreams of grandeur.

At the concert, they were allowed backstage, something she had never experienced before and now felt extremely lucky for the honor--at least until the concert started and her ears felt much too close to the stage. She'd gone to operas, orchestras, musicals, pop artist concerts. She'd never been to a hard rock concert indoors before, and it came as a shock to her system.

"He could play in a coma," Steve said loudly in her ear. She heard the reverence in his voice and saw it in his eyes as he watched Gregg play his guitar. Maybe he didn't notice what Kristina did--Gregg's eyes looked different than they had in the dressing room earlier. He looked, well, he looked *wasted* now. He kept his eyes closed most of the time as he played, but when he did open them, she recognized the drugged look. It faded temporarily when he sang and when he charmed the crowd, who alternated between swooning and screaming at the top of their lungs for their hero.

Gregg was a consummate showman. He never missed a note. He played his guitar as though it was the most intimacy he would ever have. The instrument responded in kind, seeming to beg for his touch--a touch that only he could give and a desire only he could satisfy.

Drugs and the rock star lifestyle were synonymous. Maybe the music and his passion for it made Gregg react and resemble someone high on some chemical. What did she know? She just couldn't imagine Steve would sit back if Gregg, someone she knew he considered a close friend, was a drug addict.

It was late when they left the concert. The boys were sleepy, but neither seemed shaken by the abrupt quiet. Kristina's ears rang hollowly and her body seemed to reverberate at the trauma of the last, loud hour and a half.

"You mind if I sit in the front? I want to talk to Paul," Steve said.

Kristina nodded, afraid to speak for fear she'd end up screaming because she couldn't tell the difference between a whisper and a shout at the moment.

Jason got in first, taking the seat by the window. Not knowing what to do, Kristina waited for Ronnie to make the next move. He went next, wordlessly and without looking at her as she sat next to him. Jason fell asleep, his head resting on his balled jacket against the window, within five minutes of hitting the road.

Kristina listened to Paul and Steve talk to each other. Although their voices were hushed, she picked up most of it, especially the end of it when her hearing recovered.

"Gregg's eyes looked drugged," Steve commented.

"He's not over Tommie's death yet. He drinks constantly and I know he's got his addictions, though I have yet to catch him in the act of taking anything. Other than that, he's been going through women like he's looking for a disease."

"Nothing unusual about that--he'd been that way since we met him.

"He's quitting," Paul said, and Kristina couldn't help glancing over to him in the driver's seat. "He told me a couple weeks ago he's getting outta the music business."

"What?" Steve murmured in disbelief.

"I've done everything I can to talk him out of it. Wendy even talked to him. He won't explain why and he won't back down. We'll make it public on New Year's Eve, just before he plays his last concert."

"Maybe he'll come back. In a couple years," Steve offered a minute later.

Paul shrugged with what seemed like an utter lack of hope.

Kristina felt Ronnie's head touch her shoulder and glanced at him to see he was asleep. A minute later, the pressure increased and she couldn't help smiling at how innocent and sweet his face looked in sleep. Just as he had in his baby pictures.

Ten minutes later, his head began to slip and Kristina either had to embrace him or he'd nod off the seat altogether. He didn't jerk away when she slipped her arm around his shoulders. He didn't wake at all until the position made him uncomfortable. Then he twisted slightly, easing himself further over on the seat. His head rested on her lap.

Kristina watched him in surprise, afraid to wake him fully, afraid he'd wake up when they arrived at Paul and Wendy's and be angry with her.

She couldn't worry about it, not when the opportunity to be close to him was so near and would flee so quickly. She stroked his hair. He seemed much older than he was when awake and aware. Maybe he really was young enough to recover from this. Maybe he could someday be as happy as he'd been over the past few days. Maybe he could like her just a little, the longer they were together as a family.

Paul nudged Steve in the front seat a half-hour later, and Kristina saw him jerk his thumb behind them. Steve glanced back. Astonishment gave way to a sentimental smile, one Kristina shared with him.

When they arrived at the house, Steve came to get Ronnie and picked him up without waking him. He wouldn't be embarrassed or angry. Kristina could cherish the memory of him sleeping on her lap so peacefully.

Together, they went upstairs with Ronnie. Steve pulled off his jacket and shoes and tucked him in. They visited Tom and Valerie after, and Steve kissed her when they came out.

Wendy and Paul emerged from Nicole's room, and smiled upon seeing them. Wendy said quietly, "Start thinking about what you guys want to do on your date."

"Huh?" Steve asked for them both.

"We're taking the kids to Bear Mountain Ski Resort tomorrow. Brenda and Gregg are coming along. The two of you will have the entire day together. Grace is being treated to a luxury spa and won't be back until Thursday morning. So the whole place is yours."

Kristina was so overwhelmed she couldn't speak. Though the resort wasn't far from the house, she sensed Wendy planned to keep the group away as long as possible for them. A part of her expected Steve to say they'd prefer to join all of them. It would be safer. But he didn't say a word.

Wendy hugged them both before she and Paul said goodnight and retired to their bedroom. Only then did Kristina glance at Steve.

"We've never been on a date before. Tilly's doesn't count."

Kristina couldn't help laughing. "No, I guess it really doesn't."

"Then we'll have to make it special."

A date. A *real* date with Steve. She wouldn't sleep a wink tonight. Her anticipation at the possibilities would make it impossible.

Twenty-Eight

"It's a good thing he didn't wake up, or he'd have been mad at everyone."

"Especially himself," Steve added.

Early the next morning, while everyone else slept, Steve had told his sister how Ronnie fell asleep on Kristina's lap last night. Ronnie was a light sleeper. He'd always been. He woke at the slightest sound and disturbance. Steve was convinced he'd known exactly where he'd been asleep. He'd allowed himself something he never could have consciously. He could get away with accepting Kristina under the pretense of sleep.

"I don't imagine it's going to be easy for Ronnie to accept her," Wendy said, "but I'd say that's progress. Unconscious progress anyway."

Wendy set a steaming mug of black coffee in front of him, and leaned across the breakfast bar. "I love her. I love seeing you together. Even Paul said he's never seen you happier." She poked at his chest, and Steve glanced at her. "You've been tangled up with Jess for so damn long, I really can't even remember the last time I saw you happy. Kristina's good to you. She's good *for* you. And Val and Tom love her."

Steve was surprised by the intensity in her voice when she said, "God, I hope this works out for you." It sounded like there were tears in her eyes. But she pivoted away to get herself coffee instead of facing him.

Paul wandered into the kitchen, muttering a greeting to Steve as he passed behind the counter. Wendy set down her full mug as Paul caught her around the waist and said something in her ear. Steve cleaned up the coffee that sloshed on the counter.

She laughed, twisted toward her husband.

Steve watched them kiss feeling embarrassment and envy. Like they deserved to be, they were free, to be together in every way possible for two people who were in love. He had the feeling, even when he was finally divorced from Jessie, he'd never really be free. He'd divorce her, but his guilt would never go away. Not when he knew he'd disappointed Tommie by breaking another promise. A deathbed promise.

"Good morning."

All of them turned at Kristina's otherwise soundless entrance. She stood at Steve's elbow, smiling at the warm greeting she received. As she eased onto the stool next to Steve, he felt a twinge of guilt. He'd come down here, not willing to test himself again this morning by getting into bed with her. Seeing her tenderness with his older son last night already had him vulnerable.

He suddenly wished he hadn't been so noble. This week of freedom might be the last he shared with her until the divorce became final. They were both aware of the limits. Why was he inadvertently punishing her for his weaknesses?

Rotating his stool toward her, he leaned forward and kissed her, knowing full well his sister and her husband would watch the whole time. He didn't care. When he eased back, he saw Kristina didn't care either. She didn't look away from him even when Wendy surreptitiously set a mug of coffee in front of her.

"If you want, we can get you reservations at Le Rendezvous here in the city for tonight. They've got great food and atmosphere," Wendy said. "We can get you a good table. Or you can just go off on your own, wherever you want. I highly recommend Le Rendezvous though."

Steve glanced at Kristina, and she shrugged. His thoughts exactly. He didn't care where they went, as long as they were alone together.

"Sounds good."

Wendy laughed. "Unless *you're* a good cook, Kristina, I wouldn't recommend having a romantic dinner here."

"Hey, hey, hey, I cook," Steve defended at his sister's teasing good-naturedly. "I don't open a can and eat over the sink anymore. Neither do my kids."

Kristina giggled, her eyes twinkling as if she was trying to imagine him doing that. "I'm not crazy about cooking either. I lived on boxed mac and cheese and breakfast cereal when I was in college. I eat out most of the time now. Why go to all the trouble of cooking for just one?"

"I'd probably starve without Wendy or Grace, or take-out," Paul added, still wrapped around Wendy like a cobra. He bit her earlobe, and she scolded him without any censure at all.

Kristina and Wendy started talking about clothes for the date and soon they disappeared upstairs.

"She's sweet," Paul said unexpectedly. He wasn't one to make a comment like that.

Steve nodded, sipping his coffee.

"How old is she?"

"Thirty."

Paul leaned on the counter with his elbows. "She's of-age and there's nothing she wouldn't do for you. You're divorcing Jess. So what's the hold-up, *mi amigo*?"

Wendy had obviously told him they were refraining and not simply to put in an appearance for the kids.

"I'm already skirting the line I've drawn for myself as it is," Steve said softly. "It's harder to tell myself I can't here."

He didn't expect Paul to understand that, yet his brother-in-law said "Oh" in a way that made Steve glance up.

"What?"

Paul straightened, crossing his arms over his chest. "Nothing. Just...I know Tommie made you promise to take care of Jess before he died. But I know Tommie. If he knew what Jess has been putting you through, no way he'd hold you to it, man. You put in the time. More damn time than she deserved. I think Tommie would've liked Kristina."

Steve thought of the dream he'd had, asleep at his computer: "*Take care of yourself.*" Then he remembered Tommie's anger and immediate assumption that Steve was the cretin who'd knocked up his sister. No. Tommie wouldn't have let him off the hook.

"Look, you know I don't like to get involved in your personal business. *¡Mierda!* Wendy tells me stuff. I know you believe Tommie didn't think much of you at the end there. 'Cause of all that shit going on with Jess, and you made promises to him. But you know the guy had a blind spot when it came to his baby sister. He wanted to blame somebody other than her, and you were an easy target. I don't think he realized until the very end that she didn't give you a choice and the promise you made to him didn't give you any leeway. In one breath, he's asking you to look out for her, take care of her, and the other he's dissing you for getting involved with her at all. You were damned if you did and damned if you didn't. You've given enough. Maybe it's time to let it go and let yourself believe Tommie'd want you to do the same. We all believe it."

Steve couldn't get himself to believe it. Not now, when he'd turned his back on a promise. Even if he could accept what Paul and all his friends wanted him to, he couldn't get past the obvious. "I let go of Jess and of my promise to Tommie. But she cheated on me. More times than I can count. I hope you never have to feel what that's like, man. I know you won't because Wendy loves you too much to even look at another guy. But if I can't walk out with anything else, I want to know I kept my own self-respect. I didn't make love with another woman from the start of our marriage and I won't at the end of it. I need to know that." *It's all I've got. And I'm terrified I won't be able to hold on to it for the duration.*

Paul nodded his understanding. "Jess was lucky and she didn't know it. And so is Kristina."

Slapping Steve on the shoulder instead of sticking around to hear his gratitude, Paul left the room.

Two hours later, after the ski equipment had been packed into the mini-van, Steve and Kristina found themselves watching everyone clear out. They glanced at each other. He offered a smile. "Now what?"

"Wendy invited me to go to work with her tomorrow," Kristina said as they wandered into the living room.

"We'll probably go with Paul. That'll work out."

She smiled. "She says Le Rendezvous is fancy. I tried on some of her clothes, but she's a lot taller and thinner than I am. I don't know what I'm going to wear."

They took Paul's Corvette into town and went shopping, then came back to the house for a light lunch. Between the two of them, they managed to cook an appetizing enough meal for themselves.

"I haven't been on a date in, hell, since I was in college," Steve told her while they did dishes by hand instead of running the machine.

"What did you do with your dates back then?"

"Went to concerts. Sometimes I'd bring them to my gigs. Went to a nightclub or out to eat. It's crazy, but I remember myself as being kind of a romantic guy, even if I don't even know what I did that was romantic now."

"What were you like when you were younger?" he said, after she let the water out of the sink and handed him the last dish to dry.

"As a teenager, something of a geek. I had braces until I was eighteen. I never went to the prom or danced with a boy until my senior year. My braces came off mid-year and the boys started asking me out. I was really uncomfortable with dating. When I was in college, I realized why. I had all these male friends, and they would start to become more romantic. I preferred being friends with someone for years before it turned romantic. Otherwise, I didn't trust them. How could I? I didn't know them."

She set the sponge in the holder and turned to him. "Did you have a lot of sexual experiences before you got married?" Her cheeks flushed slightly as he handed her the towel for her hands.

"Yeah," Steve told her, leaning against the counter. "I had my first girlfriend when I was fourteen and every one of them from that point on came with plenty of it."

"You liked being in relationships that were committed and complete?" Kristina said, really more of a statement or a good guess than a question.

He nodded. "It's hard for me to believe now, but that was me."

"I'm glad you got that. And that you look back at it nostalgically."

Surprised, he asked, "You're *glad*?"

"Because you've been in this loveless marriage for so long. I'm glad you had good relationships, even if they didn't last. I'm glad you considered yourself happy at some point."

She'd stepped forward, nearer to him, and he reached out and eased her all-the-way close. "I'm sorry you take so long to trust a guy. Your daddy do that to you?"

Kristina shrugged, her chin resting on his chest as she looked up at him. "Maybe. I was never close to my dad. He was always letting me know, one way or another, I didn't live up to his standards. Maybe he wanted a boy and I lost that one early. I don't know. I just know I'd give him what he wanted, then he'd find something else to work on--he said that all the time. 'You have to work on this, missy. This world doesn't allow second chances. You want success, you have to be the best, first out of the gate.' I couldn't compete, I couldn't win, so I stopped caring."

Steve covered her mouth with his and kissed her, comfortingly at first, until she didn't seem to be holding herself up anymore. He was all that held her up.

"What was that for?" she asked when he eased back and looked down at her.

"Because my old man said and did the same thing to me. I didn't like it, and I don't like the thought of something making you feel the way I felt."

She exhaled, laying her head on his chest and hugging him close. "Your father, too, huh?"

"I haven't seen him since Tommie's funeral. We didn't say a word to each other then."

"What about your mom?" she asked without moving. "Are you close to her?"

"No. Not close. But I see her a lot. She takes the kids."

"I want you to meet my mom."

"I have met her."

Kristina looked up. "I know. But that was before she knew you. I want her to know you the way I know you. I don't want her to worry about me because, once she meets you, she'll understand you're a good man. She won't be able to doubt it."

Steve felt a strong sense of impending failure, swallowed it, and kissed her again with his hands cradling her face. "I want to be everything you ever need, Kristina Ingram," he told her, taking her mouth under his once more before she could even open her eyes or acknowledge his words.

Her grip on his biceps tightened even as her legs seemed to give out. Five minutes later, he found himself over her on the wide Mission sofa in the living room. Her hair spread out on the dark leather behind her like a glowing fire. He couldn't remember them coming in here. All he could remember was the taste of her mouth, her tongue tangling with his and her body melting against his.

She turned slightly, raising her leg over his, and he wondered what it would feel like to touch her skin. All of her skin. Just run his hands over every bare inch from shoulders to heels. Ah hell, what he wouldn't give just to *look* at her that way.

How would he control himself then? Especially since Paul and Wendy wouldn't be back until late?

"I want to see you," he whispered. "I can't."

"I want to see you, too. More than anything." Her face was suffused with passion, her eyes dark and moody. Without a hint of aggression, she eased up the hem of the Henley shirt he wore and he didn't stop her. He yanked it over his head, watching her expression as her hands touched his bare flesh. His nipples tightened as soon as her fingertips came in contract with his ribs, his stomach.

Telling himself not to and willing to go to hell on his own refusal to listen, he kissed her, hissing, then groaning as she stroked his nipples.

Oh no, oh hell, he couldn't trust himself. He wanted her tongue there, along with her teeth, biting, licking, sucking. He wanted to open her shirt and play with her exactly the same way. But just her fingers on him killed him. He hadn't been this close to an orgasm in years. Even in his own hand, he lost his erection before he ever reached that point. Today wasn't the day to test the reliability of his impotency, no matter how badly he wanted to.

He also knew he wasn't being fair. Kristina whimpered, kissed him breathlessly, stopping for seconds only to come back, draw his tongue into her mouth and suck and lick it the way she seemed to want to elsewhere. He felt her desperation reaching the point of no return and he couldn't ignore it.

Steve notched himself between her legs, reaching down with one hand at a time to draw her legs higher against his thighs until she was open to him. With two sets of denim between them, they were safe. To a certain point anyway. He had to keep that denim between them no matter what.

He rocked his hips against hers. Her back arched, her mouth fell away and her eyes squeezed closed even tighter. Steve kissed her chin, the line of her jaw, all the while sliding his erection back and forth against her core. She cried as she held him, guiding him and gasping beneath his kisses.

The heat of the friction they generated grew, and Steve knew it could last this time. If they made love now, he wouldn't lose his erection.

She sobbed as her orgasm claimed her. Steve watched her, afraid to breathe because he was just that close, too. He couldn't allow it. He couldn't stop himself if he took release. He'd have to be inside her.

"Did you? Did you, too?" she begged as she clutched him like she'd fly into a million pieces if she didn't.

"I can't. I want you too bad, honey. I'm too close not to finish it the way I want to."

Her tears ran down into her hair as she shook her head in frustration. "Then finish it alone. Please. I don't want-- I want to know you're satisfied. Do it for me."

"No."

She gritted her teeth, letting out a sob that told him all about her shame. He'd wanted to satisfy her, not make her feel like this.

"Please, Steve."

He sat up, and she followed.

"If I do, I'll walk out of a shower and you won't be able to look at me."

"No, I'm going to be waiting to put my arms around you and tell you I love you, that the first time we make love after your divorce is going to be the happiest day of my life." She put her arms around him now and whispered again, "Please."

Steve felt like a stupid teenager as he went to the bathroom he and Kristina shared, stripped off his clothes and got into the shower. He shouldn't have started this. He barely remembered how it'd started. But then he realized they had so many hours to get through. How could he be with her without being *with* her?

He lost his erection trying to rationalize a way to do it without doing everything. If he was going to do this, he wanted to do it with Kristina. And he couldn't do it without losing his last ties to self-control. That was all.

Just as she'd promised, Kristina waited outside the door when he got out of the bathroom. She put her arms around him. He wouldn't tell her. She didn't need to know.

"I love you. I want to make love to you, in every way possible, but I can wait." She smiled, easing the awkwardness he felt with her light touch. "It might kill me, but I can wait. Solemn promise." She kissed him, murmuring, "Thank you. Thank you for... Do you want me to tell you...? I've never felt anything so incredible in my life."

The color in her cheeks made him grin. "Yeah?"

"Yeah. I can only *imagine* how incredible..."

"I know." He wanted to hear her reaction, but he didn't want to think again about how good it would feel to be inside her.

"Do you not want to talk about kisses, touches?" she asked, and Steve pulled back to look at her.

"Talk...?"

"Just touching you--" Butterfly-light, she touched his nipples. "Just touching you here, I could have. God, I could have!"

"I'm hard again," he muttered painfully, unable to stop himself from matching her honesty.

Her cheeks flaming, she glanced that way. "I want to know that," she said breathlessly. "I want to know how you feel, how *I* make you feel, even if it turns me on until it hurts. Do you?"

"I'll be walking around like a high school kid. No control whatsoever."

She laughed so sweetly, he had to kiss her.

"We better do something else."

"I saw some games in the den."

So they played games, they laughed, they stole kisses, made confessions that would make any priest write them off, and Steve spent most of the next few hours semi-erect. Then they got ready for their date. When he emerged from the shower for a third time that day, Kristina called through the door, "Thank you for the flowers."

He'd set up the delivery of the roses while they were in town earlier. Steve realized, from her gratitude, that maybe part of the romantic he'd considered himself in college still lurked in him.

Kristina came out of her room twenty minutes later dressed in a long-sleeved, white knit dress that followed her every delectable curve. It ended mid-thigh and revealed nude legs long enough to stop seven o'clock traffic. All he could do was stand there staring at her and mutter, "Oh God."

"You like?" she asked like an adorable little girl.

"Like...? The only thing I can imagine liking better than you in that dress is you--"

He didn't need to finish. She knew he was imagining her out of that dress, then she told him he looked incredible.

The restaurant was all Wendy and Paul claimed it'd be, but Steve wasn't interested in eating or in the atmosphere. He couldn't wait to get Kristina in his arms again, where he could touch her. The dance floor was a perfect excuse.

I would have made love to her without a qualm if I was still the same person I was all those years ago. I can't imagine I'd let her get away as easily as I let the others get away.

Hours had passed since their aborted lovemaking in the living room, yet getting back to the same place took only seconds when they returned to Paul and Wendy's house. All he knew was he could kiss her forever and it would never satisfy him. He wanted her more than he could remember ever having wanted a woman--including Jess. And that was damn ironic, considering his lust for Jess was what had screwed up his entire life.

Unceremoniously, they dropped his coat, then hers in the living room. She kicked off her shoes.

"You feel so good."

"So do you," she murmured, and he had an image of himself naked while she wore only the knit dress.

"I want you. God, I want you."

"I know. I want you, too. We can stop. I promise."

He'd heard and made that promise before in his life. He'd never needed to hold to it. He had to keep himself in check now, but how?

He didn't have a clue and pulling her down on his lap wouldn't help him figure it out any easier. But she was there, and he felt so damn greedy.

"I love your body," he told her between clenched teeth. He ran his hands over every inch of her.

He saw that she had trouble breathing, and he realized why when he kissed her and she rose on his lap to meet him. With her bottom cradled in his hands, the dress only barely covering it, she shuddered and he closed his eyes until he thought he'd go blind on the realization. She wanted him. She had all night. Her panties would prove it if he touched her. At the moment, he couldn't imagine anything sexier than feeling that wet silk.

"I'm crazy. Can a person die from wanting? I don't even know my own body anymore. It's yours. It's just yours. It's not mine anymore," she said in the pathway between pleasure and pain. Her tone revealed her torment.

She'd been with another man in the past, but she hadn't reacted to him the way she did to Steve--that was what she was telling him. While Steve had never considered himself the type of guy who needed to be the only one ever, right now he liked knowing her reactions were new to her. She belonged to him.

He had to be careful with her, he understood more so now. She wasn't a woman who gave herself easily. The other guy she'd been with had taken what he wanted without her consent, at least the first time. Amazingly, she'd continued the relationship against her own will, and she felt shame for it. He didn't want her to ever feel ashamed for giving herself to him.

Somehow, he'd be worthy of the trust she gave him. He just hoped it wasn't another vow he'd end up breaking.

* * * *

Hard Times Haven was a thriving community, Kristina saw in amazement. The shelter had been set up over two decades before for teenager girls who were drug addicts, pregnant or both.

"This is where the Jumpstart Project began, isn't it?" Kristina said as Wendy took her to the second floor, where girls were learning to use computers and various software programs. Everything in the room had been donated by various businesses in the community.

Wendy nodded. "You've heard of it?"

"I'm a counselor at the Drug Crisis Center on Eisner University's campus. I try to work with as many other community programs as I can. Wayward Angels in Milwaukee is one of the best I've come across. The Jumpstart Project they use is one of the few I've ever seen actually work."

From what Kristina had read about the program in the brochures, statistics proved at least half of the girls who came into a shelter like Wayward Angels returned within a year or two. Because many shelters took on the responsibility of providing a productive life for its participants, always on a temporary basis,

Jumpstart took over where the shelters left off. Since the girls had deeper problems than drug addictions, unplanned pregnancies or abuse, they often went back to the same situation once released from the shelter. The Jumpstart Project taught them how to live productive lives themselves, with the hope that it would be permanent. Funding for it came from state and federal grants as well as community donations and free workshops offered by local schools. Jumpstart had become the basis for long-term rehabilitation of underprivileged girls around the country.

"I wish there was some way to implement it at the college. I've just been referring Wayward Angels as much as I can."

"Your supervisor doesn't want to go to the trouble?" Wendy guessed.

Kristina laughed in surprise. "How did you know?"

"I've heard it before. It is a tremendous amount of work to set up The Jumpstart Project. And you can't do it without having annual fundraisers that bring in decent financial support. A lot of people are intimidated by the idea of asking businesses and community leaders to open their wallets or checkbooks to them. It's a lot of work. It took me more than two years to get this first one really started. I did most of the work getting Wayward Angels in Milwaukee set up, too. That wasn't easy. I was flying back and forth between here and there for most of a year."

"I bet. You know what I'd like to see?" Kristina said as they walked around the room. "Something like Wayward Angels for boys within the city. Right where they are."

Wendy nodded. "So would I. If I could find the right guy to do it, I would be interested in helping get something started. I might even move back to Milwaukee for awhile for it. Do you know anyone?"

Kristina shook her head. "But I'll keep it in the back of my head. See if I can think of anybody. I might start the groundwork for The Jumpstart Project at Eisner, but the fundraiser couldn't be set up until this summer."

"Let me know if you need help."

"Thanks," Kristina said, squeezing Wendy's hand in gratitude.

As they got back on the elevator and the doors slid closed behind them, Wendy glanced at Kristina. "So, did you and Steve have fun yesterday?"

Kristina saw the teasing sparkle in Wendy's eyes--eyes so much like Steve's, only not haunted--and couldn't help the blush that crept into her face. "Yes. Thank you. It was like a dream come true." Most of her dream anyway. "What was Steve like when he was younger? He said he had a lot of girlfriends. He's so good looking. But in some ways, I can't imagine him being the womanizer I think he might have considered himself."

"Oh, he wasn't a womanizer at all. He did go through a lot of women though." Wendy smiled. "They almost always broke up with him instead of visa versa. He never talked about why. He just moved on. I suspect the truth was that he wanted more commitment than they were willing to give him. He wanted everything--heart, body and soul. Girls in college are usually looking for fun and experience. Not something exclusive and binding."

"That's the way I imagined him."

They stepped off the elevator, and Wendy asked her if she'd like some coffee. Kristina nodded.

"Can I ask you something else?" she asked Wendy in the cozy break room they had to themselves for the moment.

"Sure. Ask away."

"Was Steve...? Did he used to be less uninhibited?" Kristina took a deep breath. "I mean, I never noticed this until recently, but he's *so* controlled. I used to think it was just part of his personality, and I loved that about him because I've never met a man so dark and mysterious. But the more I get to know him, the more he tells me about how he was *before*, the more I think he wasn't always that way."

Wendy shrugged, mixing liquid creamer into her coffee. "In some ways, he has always been controlled. More than most people. But I think what you're really saying is that he always puts everyone else's needs before his own. And there you're right. He used to do more for himself. To think more about what he wanted instead of what he had to do and what others wanted or needed him to do."

"Years of protecting his kids," Kristina said softly, sadly.

Wendy nodded. "You really seem to understand him. Jess never tried. She never really cared."

Kristina couldn't speak. After all, Jessie was their friend. She wanted to know how any of them could remain friends with Jessie after all the horrendous things she'd done to Steve.

As though reading her mind, Wendy met her eyes levelly. "I wish I could tell you I understand Jessie, but I can't. She's insane and she has been as long as I've known her. For a long time, I made excuses for her. For awhile, I hated her for what she's done to Steve and to the kids. But now…now I guess I just accept her because she's a part of all of us. That'll never change."

When they sat down at a table, Wendy touched her hand to Kristina's knee for a second. "I'll admit something to you though. When Steve told me he was divorcing Jess, I was so happy. I know that sounds terrible. I knew it wouldn't be easy, but there's no other way. And then, when he told me about you, well, he deserves something good, after all he's been through."

Kristina smiled.

"Will *you* tell me how this all happened between the two of you? I know you both work on the campus, but what changed?"

"Nothing. Nothing for me anyway. I met Steve my first day of work at the Center. I came out, slipped on the ice, and he was suddenly there, helping me up and asking me if I was all right. I fell for him from that very moment."

"You'll have to tell Val that story sometime. She's such a romantic she'll eat it up. So you've been in love with him for what? Five years? And who knew he'd ever leave Jess? So what happened then?"

"I did all the things a schoolgirl would do. I scheduled my life to fit his, so I could see him as often as possible. He always talked to me when I showed up unexpectedly."

Wendy burst out laughing, obviously thrilled at the one-sided love story that had grown into a two-person drama.

"I knew he was married. I knew about the kids. And that things were bad at home. I knew that because I could see it in his eyes. The storm cloud was always there in his face. He was a gentleman with me. Everything, every moment with him, made me love him more. He started to tell me about things at home. You can't imagine..." She shook her head. "Suffice it to say that there's nothing I wouldn't do for him. In September, this past September, he almost kissed me. He didn't, but the next day he told me he couldn't see me anymore."

Kristina couldn't help closing her eyes at the pleasure and pain of the memory. "I was miserable. I knew he was right because I couldn't keep doing what I was doing. I either had to tell him or never see him again. When he came back and told me he couldn't stop seeing me, I knew I had to tell him the truth. I did, around the time I met you. Just before that. I don't know if hearing the truth of my feelings changed anything for him, and I really don't want to be a consideration in his divorce."

"And now you're together," Wendy said, tears swimming in her eyes.

"We're together, but then we're not together."

"You mean because...?"

Wendy knew they hadn't made love. Why did that make Kristina feel like her relationship with Steve wasn't real? She couldn't say, but she felt defensive, the way she always did with Hillary, to the point where she avoided her boss as much as possible now. All those years Hillary had known she loved Steve but couldn't have him. Kristina felt silly and stupid and vulnerable because things were no more solid than they had been all those years. Hillary never failed to remind her of that either.

"That, in part, but I understand Steve's feelings," Kristina said to Wendy. "I respect that we can't be together fully until the divorce is final. I don't want to be either, deep down. I mean, we're together, but sometimes, *lately* I feel like it's all a dream I'm going to wake up from and it'll all be over. Or I'll realize it never happened and it *won't* happen."

Kristina couldn't stop herself from telling someone what she'd realized it yesterday, in the stolen time she had with Steve. "I think he's been wounded for so long, he may never heal."

"He cares for you. I know he does. He wouldn't just turn his back on you," Wendy insisted, clearly dumbfounded at Kristina's assessment. "He cares for *you.*"

Yes, but there's a big difference between caring and loving someone.

"You don't understand just how in control he is. He's *always* in control. Even when he's out of control, he's in control."

Wendy looked confused, but Kristina couldn't tell her about yesterday. Yesterday had gotten seriously out of hand, more than once. Yet Steve remained in control. He hadn't lost it, even though he'd slipped. She knew for fact he hadn't finished things himself. She'd known it, but kept it to herself. He hadn't wanted to lose himself, even alone. She'd lost herself body, heart and soul, and she had no idea if Steve had really taken the love she'd given him.

"I don't know, maybe there's something I don't know because I've never felt like this with anyone except Steve. But I think to fall in love, you have to let yourself go. You have to let go of your heart completely. You have to let it go and trust it's in good hands. I'm not sure if Steve is capable of doing that. And, if he does, that he won't run for cover afterward."

Wendy couldn't give her the reassurance she needed, though she tried when she said, "The reason Jess is so jealous of Steve being with another woman is because she knows it would have to be serious for him. He would never have a meaningless fling the way Jess does. If he's revealed his feelings for you, then it is serious. You just have to give it time. Let him straighten out his life before he jumps into something new."

Kristina knew Wendy was right. She also knew time was running out for her. She could feel it and hear it with everything inside her. And the only thing she could do about it was close her eyes against it. start here

Twenty-Nine

"Everything okay?" Steve asked after his sister and her husband once again loaded all the kids into the van with Grace and headed off for a day at Disneyland.

Kristina turned to him, slipped into his arms and shook her head. "We have to leave tomorrow." Their flight back to Milwaukee was mid-morning.

"Anything else?"

"Why do you ask?" Kristina couldn't imagine Wendy had divulged anything they'd talked about in confidence yesterday to her brother.

"You seem sad."

She smiled. "I'm tired. I didn't sleep last night."

"At all?"

"At all. But that's all right. I can sleep on the plane tomorrow."

"I heard you leave your room."

She'd thought he would, quiet as she'd been. She'd had no choice but to go. If he heard her crying, he would have come to her and what could she tell him? *I'm afraid I'm a transitional woman for you. The one who helps you get through your divorce, but you'll never really love, even if you don't know it yourself now.*

In the insane limbo she lived her life in, she'd convinced herself that, despite her respect for the choices Steve made, the only way she could be sure how he felt about her was if he lost all control--if he made love to her, spoke his love for her, spent the night in her arms, and, most importantly, didn't run away from what they'd done sooner or later. And then she'd become the other woman in the sense of the word she most despised. There was no way to win.

"Will you play a song for me? On guitar?"

"You sure you're okay?" he asked again.

She was afraid to meet his gaze. He might see her desperation for some kind, *any* kind of validation of her feelings. She put her arms around his shoulders, tucking her face into his neck, and murmured, "Hmm."

He held her tightly, yet she knew he sensed her fragility. He didn't understand it. Maybe he really didn't want to understand. But he knew something lurked there. A part of her wanted to shout: *Hold me. Break me. Shatter me. I don't care. Just don't treat me like I'm fragile, even though I am. I want you to feel me, deep inside, as deep inside as I feel you. I don't want you to hold anything back. Because I know you're so afraid of hurting me, you'd rather protect me than give me what both of us want.*

"Play me something you wrote," she whispered without lifting her head. She felt safe in his arms, the only place she could feel that way.

They went to the den. She sat on the plush carpet in front of the footstool and listened to him strum the same haunting refrain he had the night they arrived. This time he sang softly, words that put a hard lump in Kristina's throat.

There's a point in time
when love can't change all the wrong.
When love just seems to stand in the way
for a lifetime too long...
You stand there with all you ever hoped for
ripped out of your arms,
screams blocked in your throat.
Even when I hold you, the storm never seems to break.
I took the life from your soul with my unforgivable sin.
And I don't think I can ever
make you love me again...
There was a time when I might have missed how I cry
just to see your smile
Now I look at you, you look away,
and there's nothing I can see
that could make you love me.
I'd give my life to walk back to where we've been.
I'd give everything I have
just to make you love me again...

"I wrote it for Jess after Tommie died," Steve told her without looking up from strumming chords. "I stopped playing for myself after that. I play to keep in shape because I teach music. But I haven't played for myself since I decided to be a teacher."

"You're so good," Kristina whispered.

He shrugged. "I can play. But I don't have what Gregg does. I don't even have what Paul has and he doesn't even do it for a living. I understand that now, but I didn't then. Then I thought because you could play, because you love to play, that's all you needed. But now that I teach it. I can always tell the difference between a student who's working for a credit, likes it and is even passionate about it, and one who loves music because *it* loves him just as much. It's something inborn. You either have it or you don't. I don't have it."

"You play beautifully. You sing beautifully. That song you played for us has haunted me since. I'll never forget it."

Steve stroked the underside of her chin with his fingers. "Thanks."

She listened to him play another song, then he set the guitar aside. "They'll be back too soon. I want to put you in a bubble bath."

"*What?*"

Steve laughed. "A bubble bath. A bubble bath in the evening is supposed to relax you so you sleep well that night."

"It's afternoon."

"Close enough."

He stood, holding his hand out to her, and she couldn't refuse. They went up to the bathroom they shared and Steve started the water and poured in bubble bath from the fancy jar on the counter. Kristina watched him gather a towel and washcloth, not knowing what she was supposed to do, if anything.

Once the tub was filled with fragrant, steaming water, he turned to her, surprising her with a kiss. "Go ahead and get in. I'll be right back."

The truth was, Kristina would take any loophole at all that brought her intimacy with this man. If he wanted to put her in a bubble bath, she'd go along with it start to finish.

She stripped off her clothes, not hurrying, then put her hair up to keep it out of the water. She'd just slipped under cover of the bubbles when Steve came in with a glass of what looked like white wine.

She'd had a glass of wine the night she and Steve had dinner together at Feng Shui, so he knew she drank. She hadn't had any alcohol since their relationship had changed. He didn't drink. Was he trying to get her drunk? The last thing they needed was her more out of control and him in his usual state of total control.

"If I drink this, I might be asleep before seven o'clock."

"That's okay."

He sat on the stool next to the tub, facing her, watching her while she sipped and soaked. Between the wonderful heat of the water and the alcohol spreading through her insides, she would have felt relaxed enough to sleep if not for Steve's presence. His fingers dangled over the edge of the tub, stirring the water and the bubbles floating on top of it. She had no idea how much he could see, especially when the bubbles began to disperse. He took the thick washcloth and washed her. The cloth slid over her skin, and his hand followed in its wake, massaging and draining away all of her inhibitions.

Moaning, she closed her eyes and allowed him to take care of her. Her skin danced, but the nerves beneath it were completely out of step. He touched her feet, and her legs quivered. He touched her legs, and her core tightened and coiled. The washcloth passed over her stomach, and her nipples hardened fiercely.

Kristina feared opening her eyes as he lifted one of her arms. She was so aroused. He had to know it. She knew she was exposed. She wanted to know he was aroused, as well, and nothing else. She didn't want to hear why he couldn't act on it, not again, nor that he wanted her but refused to lose himself.

Tears slammed into her eyes and slid down her cheeks.

"Kristina," he whispered.

She opened her eyes, and looked at him, now standing beside the tub. Her breath crammed into her throat, not knowing whether to go up or down, when she saw his erection straining the fly of his jeans. Then she saw he held a towel for her.

He would see her completely naked. He was *asking* her to show him herself. She was aware that anything could happen here, despite her promise yesterday she would be as strong as he was.

She rose on shaky legs and stepped out to him. He lifted the towel over her head and put it around her shoulders instead of wrapping it around her front to hide her. Even pulling it as close around her as she could, she couldn't cover herself from him and didn't try.

Not when he put his arms around her and whispered, "You're my fantasy."

He kissed her, his hands blotting the wetness from her back as he held her tightly. But he couldn't seem to keep them where they were safe. He slipped forward, clutched the edges of the towel, touched her bare sides. Kristina opened her eyes when his mouth abandoned hers. He stared at her, his eyes dark and turbulent. Hot tears slid down her face, ones she thought he'd question, but he only cradled her cheek, kissed her, kissed the salty tears.

"I can't stand," she murmured. If he hadn't had his arm around her, she would have collapsed. Exhaustion and need overwhelmed her. She couldn't imagine how much longer she could hold out.

"C'mon."

She followed his voice like the children followed the Pied Piper's flute--helplessly. When Steve pulled back the covers on her bed, she got under them, shedding the towel and waiting for him. His shirt was wet from the bubbles and water that had been on her chest when he'd held her earlier. Her body coiled more at the realization, the way he tore his shirt off, unsnapped his jeans to relieve some of the pressure, and rose over her on the bed.

He had to be in control. He had to, because she couldn't be. She wanted and needed his love, and nothing else seemed to matter right then. Not even a rejection or a regret that might come as a consequence.

Kristina wrapped her arms around him, opened her thighs to allow him. She kissed him wildly. Stroked his soft-yet-hard nipples and the hair covering them, covering his chest and a narrow strip on his stomach leading below. She felt his muscles quiver under her touch and his groaning response only made her want to touch him more.

"Mhm, ahh..." he muttered harshly between clenched teeth when she cradled his denim-covered erection. His eyes closed, his expression proved his agony.

She looked at him, and tears tore out of her in joy. It wasn't fair. He was losing control and she'd never loved him more because of it. She brought her hand to his jaw, urging him to look at her.

He did, and his gaze slid down to her breasts. Never in her life had she felt so sexy to someone as when Steve loved her in a single, prolonged glance. *She* was his fantasy. Not his wife, a woman at least half of the world must have lusted for.

"I can't wait to make love to you," he said when his eyes met hers again. "I can't wait to touch your breasts. Put my mouth on you. You're so beautiful. I've never seen anyone more beautiful in my life."

She sobbed at seeing and hearing his vulnerability, his spontaneousness. He didn't need to touch her. She felt his touch with the words he'd said and the sweet hunger of his mouth on hers. Almost at the same time, their bodies shifted together, closer, tighter, rocking in a rhythm so magical the rest of the world fell away. They were in their personal heaven, where everything was right and good and perfect.

Her climax claimed her in seconds, as shattering as it was satisfying. She expected him to put a stop to anything further, but, as she rose on another wave, his mouth fell away. His body jerked hard, she saw his release in the torment of his expression. She felt a scalding heat on her stomach, closed her eyes knowing what it was and loving him for it. Shudders slammed through him over and over, and he cried out.

Gladly she took his weight and consoled him until reality returned, slowly. Silence filled the space. A grandfather clock somewhere in the house chimed the hour, then the silence descended again.

She wanted to tell him she loved him, but she had no idea how he felt. So she said, "I need a bath." For a minute, while he laughed with his cheek scraping erotically against her chest, she thought she'd said the right thing. But he shuddered again, and she realized with alarm that he was crying.

Because she felt terrified to do anything else, she simply held him in the endless minutes that followed.

"I never loved her," he said suddenly, gasping it out like he couldn't keep it in for a second longer. "I never said that to anyone before. I never said it to *myself*. Ah, dammit."

He'd never loved *Jessie*? He'd stayed with her for thirteen agonizing years. Longer.

"I wanted her. I wanted her so damn bad, in any and all ways she'd let me. There was nothing she wouldn't do. I knew that. But that's all it was.

"Does that make you think less of me? Makes me think less of myself. And I promised Tommie, so I had to stay with her. Take care of her. I had to. I was obsessed with her and she was my obligation. It was never about love, but I believed I had to love her. I wanted to. But I never did."

Everything made complete sense to Kristina for the first time. He'd stayed with Jessie because he couldn't forgive himself for using his best friend's sister for pure, base lust and not loving her. If he couldn't love her, he couldn't leave her. As mixed up as that was, it made sense.

He rolled to his side, and Kristina followed instinctively. He'd covered his eyes with his hand. "Then Tommie died, and my addiction was over. My obligation started. For the past I don't know how long anymore, when we made love, I gave her what she needed, but I didn't feel it. I didn't feel anything but anger and disgust. This is the first time..."

Helplessly, Kristina put her hand on his arm and urged him to look at her. When he did, his eyes were naked with emotion. He was a haunted man, a wounded one with a long way to go before he healed. The night he'd told her about his vow to his wife's brother, he'd said he could fall in love with her. What right did Kristina have to want him to tell her he did love her now? She couldn't ask it of him. But she selfishly wanted to.

"I know you don't believe this, Steve, but it's all right. You've paid for what might have been a mistake a thousand times over. You have absolutely nothing to be ashamed of. Especially not with me." She kissed him softly, kissed his tears, and waited. When she didn't get what her heart cried for, she accepted his arms around her, tucking her against him tenderly.

"I love you," she whispered. He only held her tighter.

* * * *

Ronnie remained in the backseat, avoiding the scene, as his brother and sister got out of the car to hug Kristina. Steve removed her luggage from the trunk.

"Take care of your brother and sister, okay?" he asked of Ronnie after Tom and Val returned to the car. "I'll be right back."

Ronnie nodded as if it didn't matter to him in the least. Steve knew he'd do it though.

When he turned with Kristina's luggage, he noticed tears filling her eyes. Again. Each time he looked at her since yesterday she looked minutes from crying. Her eyes seemed haunted, as if she felt afraid and lost. He wasn't sure why, and each time he brought it up or caught her attention, she seemed fine.

Putting his arm around her, they walked into her building. If she felt weird, he couldn't blame her. He felt the same way, yet he didn't regret anything they'd done. He would later. Hell, he would, but he didn't want Kristina to know it.

She cried silently all the way up to her apartment, but laughed at herself when she faced him before her door.

"Don't cry," he begged.

"I can't seem to help it."

"I'll see you tomorrow." He made it a firm promise with his tone.

"I know." She nodded, gliding into his arms as soon as he set her down suitcase. "Call me tonight."

Steve laughed.

"Will you?"

He drew back to look at her, cradling her face as he nodded. "No problem. I would've, even if you hadn't asked."

She smiled. When they kissed, his body reacted readily, eagerly the way it had every time he touched her, looked at her, kissed her since he'd discovered he wasn't impotent.

"I better go or I won't be able to walk out of here."

Her smile was a combination of sensual and dread. She nodded. "Thank you for inviting me. Thank you for everything."

She said it as if she'd never see him again.

"We'll do it again next year."

"We will?"

He grinned. "If you still want me around by then, yeah."

"I want."

One last short kiss and her sweet words of love, and he forced himself to walk away.

"Oh. Don't call within the next two hours. I have to pick up my animals from Hillary's," she called.

He looked over his shoulder from the stairs.

"If you were planning to, that is. I wouldn't want to miss your call."

"I'd call back."

Her lopsided smile told him she thought herself silly, but she murmured, "All right. Bye."

"See you, honey."

When he glanced back from the next floor, she stood at the top, looking down at him with her hands against her mouth. She waved, and he saw the sheen of tears sparkling even in the distance. Had he done something wrong? Something to hurt her? He'd wondered a thousand times if he was losing her, already, but she gave no indication of it except in the moments she thought she was alone or not being observed.

"You guys as tired as I am?" Steve asked when he got in the car and found Ronnie in the front seat, where Kristina had been.

Murmurs of agreement went all around.

"Let's just order in for dinner tonight."

The kids scattered as soon as they got home. Steve saw Gwen had not only had his walk shoveled, but she'd also brought his mail. He didn't have the energy or the inclination to call and thank her. What he really wanted to do was bring Kristina home, lie down with her in his bed, and fall asleep with her in his arms.

I don't want to dream. Not like yesterday.

He and Kristina had fallen asleep in her bed after they'd, hell, after they'd found the loophole that would allow them intimacy without compromising his stance. What had happened later was a dream. He knew it was a dream. But it hadn't felt like a dream at the time. He'd opened his eyes, and Tommie had been standing near the bathroom door, looking at them.

"You love her," he'd said. Not a question this time. A statement that couldn't be refuted, not with her wrapped in Steve's arms, her nude body warm and pliant against his.

Steve had wanted to deny it. Everything inside him rebelled against admitting to Tommie he did love Kristina. *Kristina.* Not Jess. Never Jess.

"I took care of Jess. For more than thirteen years," Steve had said softly.

"I know you did, man. You brought home the bacon. Took care of the kids, too." Tommie had come into the room and stood over the bed. "Even Ronnie."

"He's my son."

"You took care of everybody and everything. Now it's time to take care of you."

"I can't stay with Jess. I'm sorry."

"Steve."

"I tried, Tommie."

"Steve, take care of you."

Steve had convinced himself he had to be dreaming, even when Kristina stirred against his side, he'd looked down at her and Tommie disappeared. With her hand on his chest, her nipples hard against his side, Steve's guilt had become monumental as his manhood swelled again in hot anticipation.

Tommie would never come to him and tell him it was okay with him that he loved Kristina and was leaving Jessie. Tommie would never allow him freedom. Not when his last words in this world had been to Steve about his sister--not to his wife about their unborn child. To Steve.

While the kids took naps, Steve did laundry, caught up on his e-mail and wondered when he could call Kristina. One by one, the kids got up, came downstairs and everything was back to normal. He just didn't feel normal. He felt like the house was missing someone, someone who'd only been here twice--once to help him bring in his groceries, and once to watch the kids.

"I wish Kristina was here," Val said in the living room, after she started a movie that didn't seem to interest her. She also had a book on her lap that she kept picking up and putting down. "Do you miss her, too, Daddy?"

Steve nodded.

"I wish she could live with us. If you marry her, she can. Maybe we could move to another house then."

"If he married her, he'd go to jail, dork," Ronnie said from the doorway, a glass of milk in his hand. "It's bigamy."

Val made a face at him. "I meant when Mom's divorced."

The phone rang, and Ronnie moved out of the room to get it in the kitchen. He brought it to Steve, then sat on the couch.

"Travis here. Just thought I'd check in--"

When Steve hung up, Tom had pushed into the room, sat in the middle of the couch between his siblings, and put his feet up on the coffee table. Travis's idea of checking in was something Steve wished he'd called California with as soon as he'd found out.

"That was Travis. My lawyer," he said, and the kids glanced, without seeming concern, at him from the TV. "I guess on Thursday--I don't think it's a big deal, but--the judge wants the three of you to talk to him in his chambers. He wants to ask you individually--" Their casual indifference had altered, despite Steve's attempt to downplay what made his heart beat uncertainly. "--where you want to live."

Travis seemed to think it was standard procedure or purposely conveyed it that way, but Steve couldn't consider it that. Ronnie would say he wanted to stay with his mother. What if the judge took that into account despite her history?

"Do we have to?" Ron asked, surprising him.

Wasn't it what he'd wanted all along--the court to take his wants and wishes into consideration, despite what was best for him?

"Yeah. It'll only take a minute or two."

"I'm scared," Val said.

"Don't be, baby. I'll be right outside the door."

Tom shrugged coolly. "I'll do it. Maybe they'll let me go in with Val."

"Yeah. Maybe."

Abruptly, Ronnie left the room, and Steve wasn't sure of his mood.

"I'll have to tell the school, since I'll have to take you out for about for an hour or two," Steve said on automatic.

Tom got up and picked up the basket of folded laundry, saying he'd put it away. Steve nodded.

"Can I tell the judge I want Kristina to be my mom?" Val asked in the minutes after Steve considered what Thursday could mean for him.

"No. No, I don't think that'd help, Val." *My case anyway.*

"Okay."

When he left the room, he heard Tom and Ron talking in the hall upstairs and strained closer when Kristina's name floated down.

"Don't be stupid. Even if it weren't for her," Tom said, "the judge knows all about Mom. And you know Dad hasn't done anything wrong anyway. You tell the judge about Kristina, it doesn't change anything. Mom's done a million times *worse*, a million times *more*. I can tell the judge all about that, too."

"Don't," Ronnie said so softly, Steve couldn't be sure of his tone.

"Then leave Kristina out of it."

Hearing footsteps coming near the stairs, Steve ducked into the kitchen. His hands shook when he considered what would happen if anyone, the judge, found out about Kristina. He hadn't told Travis about her because, whether or not she was involved, he would divorce Jess. But Jess' lawyer could make her a factor. Ronnie had told his mother about Kristina. There could be fallout because of it, and Steve knew he had to prepare his lawyer for the possibility. Still, he hesitated, remembering the years he'd been the victim of gossip at the college. He didn't want to face that again, let alone make Kristina a fellow victim.

Right now, he didn't care if every single one of their friends testified against Jess, in favor of him. He didn't want his name or Kristina's dragged through the college gossip mill, a public forum, or into the courtroom.

Stop seeing her. Until the divorce is final.

The alternative had crossed his mind, more than once, but he hated it each time. Kristina would consider it punishment. She'd consider it goodbye. She wouldn't understand because she believed no one was cruel enough to sling mud or tell lies. At the very least, she didn't believe anyone would be stupid enough to believe the worst of him.

He called her later, after the kids were in bed, and she answered on the first ring. He heard tears in her voice and knew he couldn't tell her they had to postpone their relationship until his divorce was official. Not now. Just as he'd known she would, as soon as he told her about the kids scheduled to meet with the judge in his chambers, Kristina had a convincing argument.

"It's a formality. The judge has seen all the evidence against Jessie. He wants to see if there's any for a relationship between the kids and their mother. Even if Ronnie does tell him he wants to stay with his mother, his wishes are only a small part of the criteria the judge will use to determine whether or not she's a suitable mother. With everything else against her, I really don't think you have to worry."

"What if Ronnie tells the judge about you?"

"What do you mean?"

"I mean, what if he says I'm with you. That we're sleeping together or whatever. Any mention of me and you will hurt my chances of getting full custody."

Surprising him, she laughed, though he sensed anger in it. "Steve, think of it this way, the way the judge will most likely view it, I'm sure. Jessie has spent a lifetime in this city, making a reputation for herself that is utterly *notorious*. So she's cleaned up her act for a couple of months? Obviously she's putting on a good face, one that may or may not last, considering her history. And, considering her history, it probably *won't* last. Ronnie tells the judge he wants to stay with her. If this judge has any intuition at all, he'll realize exactly why Ronnie is saying what he is--Jessie has manipulated him into doing whatever she asks of him. Even Ronnie's desire to stay with his mother speaks poorly of her. Then there's you. At least two of your children want to stay with you. You're respected in the community. You've not only held down a steady job, but you've excelled at it *while taking care of your children and your deadbeat wife*. You have a girlfriend? Who is she? Is she the town harlot--?"

"I didn't mean--" Steve injected, but she continued without pause.

"No. She's a counselor at the Drug Crisis Center. Her colleagues will most likely all say nice things about her without anyone having to twist their arms. She has no priors, let alone a reputation around the city. Her parents are notable citizens.

"I'm not claming I'm an asset to you in your divorce, Steve. I know the courts want to hear that each of us is a saint, but they wouldn't believe it even if all appearances pointed to that, the way they do in your case. They know we're all human. What I'm trying to say is that, even if the judge found out about me, in light of everything else, he would have to award you full custody of the children. He might even wish us well, being that he's human as well."

"Is this your professional opinion?" Steve asked with a smile.

"Yes, it is. But it's also logical."

It did sound logical. He wanted to believe it, too, but he knew it would gnaw at him regardless.

"I miss you."

"I miss you, too. Val wants you to live with us. In a new house."

"She does?"

Steve put his hand between his pillow and his head. "Yeah. Tom defended you."

"When?"

"I overheard him and Ron. Ron must have said he was going to tell the judge about you and Tom said if he did, he'd drag out all the dirt on Jess."

"Oh God," Kristina said in awe. "I love him for it, but I don't want them divided over me."

"They are. For now."

"I know."

"How are your pets?" Steve asked.

"I think they missed me. Hillary was a little too eager to have me take them home. But at least I didn't bring any new ones back with me."

He chuckled, wished she was in the room with him still.

"Dream of me," Kristina said softly.

"Count on it."

"I love you."

"Don't stop. Please."

She sighed or choked back a sob.

"Don't worry about that. Goodnight, Steve."

"'Night, honey. See you tomorrow."

"All right."

He knew when he hung up that she would cry and he couldn't do a thing to comfort her.

Thirty

"Traditional Blues is based on a twelve-bar pattern, or sometimes an eight- or sixteen-bar, like in this song. The root chord is played for the first four bars, then they switch to the four-chord in the fifth bar."

An inordinate number of his students had shifted their attention to the door instead of the sheet music on the overhead. Steve glanced that way, expecting to see someone coming in seriously late. Instead, Jessie stood in the doorway passively, even when one of the males in the room let loose with a catcall. She was dressed as she'd been the last time he saw her in her office. In a sexy business suit that fit her like a glove, even if the professionalism it implied didn't.

His mind immediately shifted off his topic and he knew it wouldn't return until he found out why she was here. Luckily, he'd only had ten more minutes of his lecture to go.

"We'll end here for today. Go over the next chapter," Steve dismissed his class and shut off the projector.

The kids filed out more silently than they ever had, yet Steve knew exactly when he was alone with Jess, without turning to look. "What are you doing here?" he said as he continued to gather his lecture notes.

She came into the auditorium, her heels clicking and echoing back. "I took over Nelson Industries."

"I know, Jess. I saw how you looked behind your big, fancy desk." He looked at her. "Out of place."

She ignored the barb. "I just landed the biggest model account in the history of the company."

"Good for you," Steve said, neither friendly nor unfriendly. He didn't look at her as he took the slides from the screen and put them into the envelope.

"I've been clean since that stupid night I tried to kill myself."

She was so close now, across the desk, he smelled the musk of the perfume she preferred.

"You won't get Ronnie," Steve told her evenly.

"I know. And I know living with me is insane. But I'm better, Steve. If I wasn't, would I have taken over my parents' damn company?"

"You want custody of Ronnie and you'll do anything to make it look like you're fit to be a mother. Nothing you do can change my mind or the judge's mind."

She took a deep breath, and he waited motionlessly. He didn't trust her for a minute.

"I don't want Ronnie all for myself. I want us to be a family again. We haven't gone too far with this divorce shit. We can still turn back."

She rounded the desk to ease between it and him. Steve took a step back, but the projector blocked him from going farther.

"I'm not gonna do anything stupid again. I realized that I need to be in charge of the company. I need to have my family around me. I need you."

She touched her hand to his chest. When she glanced up at him, her eyes were naked with longing. She always believed herself, even when he knew she was putting on another act just to get what she wanted. "You know that's what Tommie would have wanted for us, baby. You know that. Give me another chance."

Steve shook his head. "No, Jess. Tommie never wanted us to be together. *You* know that. I have to deal with the guilt from going against him in the first place. So do you. But we can't help each other do that anymore. We can't be together. Maybe someday I'll forgive you, but right now I can't take your pain anymore. I don't want our kids subjected to it ever again."

He walked around the desk and started getting his briefcase together again.

"Is it because of *her*? Kristina Ingram? How precious. Do you think you're in love with this bitch?"

Ronnie had told her--Steve knew that. He didn't like the idea that his son had even told his mother Kristina's name and God only knew what else.

"Are you fucking her?"

"No. And it's none of your business. She's not a factor in my decision to leave you."

"So you say," Jessie said with narrowed eyes. "Fine. Then it might interest you to know that Jon Rushing came to me recently. He wants to marry me and he wants to take his son."

"*His* son?"

"Don't tell me you never suspected that Jon is Ronnie's father?"

No, it'd never had occurred to Steve. Jon Rushing was a part of Jessie's past. She'd known him since she was a teenager. He was another idiot who came panting every time she crooked her finger at him, regardless of the number of times she'd dropped him without so much as a "See ya later." Steve had believed Ronnie's biological father was Mexican or Hispanic, given his dark coloring. Jon Rushing wasn't dark, Ronnie didn't resemble him, but Steve was acutely aware it didn't rule out Rushing.

She leaned across the desk, and her suit jacket parted enticingly. "I can promise you, baby, she'll never satisfy you. Not the way I did."

Steve didn't dwell on the ridiculousness of her statement.

"If you're sure you don't wanna give me another chance, then I guess I'll take Jon up on his offer. You know I can't stand to be alone."

"You'll have to divorce me to marry him," Steve pointed out. "I don't care if you marry the Pope, you won't get Ronnie."

Her smile was calculating, cruel. She stroked his cheek with the tip of her nail, then she walked confidently out of the room. All he thought was that Jon Rushing--*Jon Rushing*, a man who knew all about Steve, his kids, yet had never been able to resist Jessie enough to refuse her when she came to him--was planning to take Ronnie away from him. He'd never allow it to happen.

"You dismissed early," Garret said, coming into the auditorium to take care of the projector.

Steve grabbed his briefcase off the desk. "Cancel my last class today."

"You've got a meeting with--"

"Cancel it. Reschedule it."

Jerry Gordon. Jerry Gordon would know where Jon Rushing lived now. He'd know where Rushing was right this minute.

It wasn't until Steve left the building that he realized there was a good chance Jon Rushing didn't live in Milwaukee anymore. In fact, he remembered Jessie taunting him with where she'd been for two weeks without a word to anyone long ago. He just couldn't remember where Rushing had moved.

Then he saw Kristina getting out of her car in the parking lot. She had a ready smile at his approach.

"Can you do something for me?"

"Of course," she said, sounding startled.

"Evangeline will pick the kids up after school and she'll stay there until you get there."

"You want me to--?"

She started to smile, but he said, "Yeah. Will you stay until I get home? I'll call Evangeline and tell her to expect you."

He turned away and jammed his keys into the door of his car.

"Steve, where are you going?" Kristina called.

"I don't know."

"When will you be home? They'll ask."

"I don't know. I'll call you. It could be late. I'm sorry."

"I don't mind. I just--"

She was surprised when he kissed her full on the mouth in the parking lot, but she'd become speechless.

"Thanks, honey."

He didn't have time to answer all her questions. He didn't even have time to feel bad that the kids would be bombarding her with them, and Ronnie would look at her with suspicion when she couldn't answer them. He had to confront Jon Rushing right now, before he and Jessie did something stupid, something Steve would fight tooth and nail against.

Jerry Gordon was the owner of Rainbow Nights, one of the most popular nightclubs in Milwaukee. When Steve was in college, it had been one of his many hangouts and one he and his bands had played. He knew Jerry Gordon well. He also knew Jerry was like a father to Jon Rushing and to his friends. He'd know where Rushing lived. Maybe he'd wonder why Steve wanted to know, since he probably also knew what Rushing and Steve shared.

"He's not in Milwaukee," Jerry said. He stood behind the bar, his perpetual cigar clamped between his teeth. It was still early in the afternoon and there weren't many customers. "He'd drop by if he was. Usually calls before."

"Where does he live now?"

"Stevens Point. Got a bike shop there with Blackie and Rod. You know 'em, don't ya?"

Steve had met them. Right now he didn't care. Whatever got the information out of Jerry.

"Yeah," Jerry went on. "Blackie sold his share of the shop to Rod and Jon. He's an artist now."

"Where is the shop in Stevens Point?" Steve asked.

"Church Street."

He'd be able to find that easily. "He live near there?"

Jerry told him Jon's phone number, and Steve committed it to memory knowing he wouldn't get more.

"Somethin' goin' on with your wife again?" Jerry asked in a sympathetic tone. He was well versed in Jessie's antics.

"Yeah. You could say that. Thanks, Jerry."

If Steve had given him the chance, Jerry would have defended Jon's off-and-on relationship with Steve's wife, probably citing Jess for "havin' problems".

The three-hour drive to Stevens Point gave Steve plenty of time to think what would happen if Jon claimed Ronnie was his son. He'd called Travis as soon as he got on the road, and Travis insisted they'd have to prove it with a paternity test first and foremost--like it was a hurdle or something.

Steve didn't see it that way. If Jess went through with making this public, making it a factor in the divorce, it had to be true. She wasn't stupid. And that meant there was a chance he'd lose his son. If Jess only recently told Jon he was Ronnie's father, then Jon had a damn good excuse for not taking care of him for twelve years. The courts would sympathize with a man with no idea he was a father.

By the time Steve was in Point, searching Church Street for the bike shop, his heart felt like it'd gone through a wringer and his mind was too insane to plan out what he'd say. He already knew how it would go down when he walked in there and saw Rushing. He'd kill him before he let Rushing become a father to Ronnie.

The place was called Hog Heaven. Steve cursed impatiently when he saw they had customers. He didn't want to stand in line. As soon as he saw Jon Rushing, he wanted to threaten his life until he gave up the idea of Ronnie.

Jon swore when he saw him. He stepped away from the counter, where he'd been with a customer, and called, "Rod, get out here."

As soon as Rod appeared, Rushing said, "Take care of this," then motioned to Steve to follow him. He seemed annoyed, not afraid or intimidated. So did that mean he was already set in his decision?

Jon closed the door of the office behind Steve. "You know, there was a time when I would've been scared shitless to have you show up here."

Steve finished bitterly, "You mean when my wife left our bed and crawled into yours?"

"Yeah," Rushing said, sucking in his breath.

Steve *could* be convinced Jon felt guilty for his association with Jessie. He'd met him at least a dozen times. Technically, Jessie had been Jon's first. He'd been obsessed with her from day one, something Steve came to understand only too well. He understood just as well that, even if you want out of an obsession, it wasn't always easy to escape.

"Look, she was here," Jon said, facing him from where he perched on the disorganized desk. "A couple days ago. I told her to go home."

Steve stared at him in disbelief. "You did?"

"Yeah, I did. You two really need to learn how to solve your own problems."

"I'm divorcing her."

Jon's expression said it all. Now *he* was locked in disbelief. But then he nodded, as if something made sense now. "So that's what that was all about."

"What?"

"She told me your older boy is my son."

Steve couldn't say a word as he waited with his teeth clenched.

Jon laughed, seemingly at him. "It's not true, man. Do the math. We'd been apart for more than a year before I heard she got pregnant." Jon glanced down the way a kicked puppy might. "You must've known or maybe it's been so long you forgot. I was sure you always knew when she was with me. He's not mine, Steve. If you need me to do a blood test to prove it, I'd be happy to."

Much as he'd hated it and Rushing all those years, it didn't matter at this point. "So she lied? You don't want to marry her and take Ronnie?" he asked.

Jon looked up, shaking his head. "No. Hell, no. I'm marrying someone else." He added. "I'm finally outta the black hole called Jess Nelson."

Steve sank onto the couch behind him, covering his face with his hands. *God, thank God.* Another one of Jess' goddamn, last-minute bluffs.

"Look, I'm not...I mean, shit, I know I don't deserve absolution here, Steve, but I'm sorry about all that shit with her. I'd like to give you a grand excuse for why I screwed around with a married woman, especially when I halfway liked her husband--"

Steve shook his head without looking at him. "Forget it."

Taking a deep breath, Rushing nodded. "I hope you find a woman like the one I found. I think that's the only cure for what we had."

Steve didn't like the idea of understanding even one in the long line of Jessie's extramarital lovers. But he knew Jessie had used Jon to boost her self-confidence, then dropped him as soon as she got what she wanted from him. Steve understood that intimately. She'd done the same to him. The only difference between him and Jon was that she'd had kids with him and lived with him legally at least half the years they'd been married.

Steve left the shop, started his car, and headed home. She'd lied--did she think he wouldn't try to find out the truth? How far had she planned to carry the bluff? Did she think he'd be too embarrassed or too afraid to face Jon? Did she hope he'd give Ronnie up? Or did she just like watching him twist under the misery she gleefully caused him?

At that moment, he hated her so passionately he wanted to scream. He wanted to find her and make her pay for her goddamned selfish games. She'd wanted to hurt him again. She'd wanted to and she had.

It was after nine when he pulled into his driveway. Kristina's car was parked on the street in front of the house, and she came out to the porch without her jacket. "What's going on?" she asked when he came to her and rubbing her bare arms.

Steve put his arm around her and led her into the house.

"The kids are upstairs. Valerie and Tom are asleep. Ronnie said he had some homework. Maybe he's asleep now," she told him.

"I have to see them."

Val and Tom were safe in bed, not stirring, when he whispered he loved them. Ronnie was still awake at his desk. Steve had no intention of telling him what'd happened today, but as soon as he saw his older son, his fears rose up and strangled him. He sat on the bed and covered his eyes. For a long minute, he couldn't do anything except sob wordlessly.

"What's going on?" Ronnie asked warily, shocked by his tears.

Steve heard the fear in his voice. "I thought I lost you today." He glanced up, and Ronnie's face shuttered.

"Why?"

"Because your mom wanted me to believe I had. She told me your biological father wanted to marry her and take you away from me."

Ronnie stared at him, stunned. Steve could see it in his eyes. But all he said, softly, was, "So what did you do?"

"I talked to the guy she claimed was your father and found out she lied. She doesn't know who the hell fathered you. She doesn't know, but she wanted me to think she did."

Steve reached for Ronnie's arm, expecting him to pull away, but he allowed him to draw him over to the bed. "Even if it'd been true, I wouldn't have let you go. I swear it. I think I could kill anybody who tried to take one of you kids away from me. I could do it as easily as falling asleep. I know you won't like this, but I'm getting a restraining order against her. I can't risk any of you again."

Ronnie stood rigidly in Steve's fierce embrace. He didn't shift away, even when Steve kissed him and told him he loved him, called him son. He nodded when Steve said, "Get some sleep."

Kristina stood in the hallway when he closed Ronnie's door behind him. From the horror on her face, he knew she'd heard everything.

Steve pulled off his jacket as he went into his bedroom. She followed him and closed the door behind her. "Every time I think she can't sink another level..." She paused. "*Why* would she do something like that, something so cruel and something so easy to prove false?"

"She knows she's losing. She wanted to hurt me. She knew exactly how to do it, too."

"She had to know you'd find out the truth. She must be desperate. Or her arsenal's low."

Kristina sat beside him on the bed. She put her arms around his shoulders, leaning her head near his. "I wish you'd told me. I can't imagine what you've been through in the past seven hours."

He wanted to turn to her, hold her. He wanted revenge on Jessie so badly right now, nothing else seemed to matter. But he couldn't give into the impulse. There was too much to lose--he knew that only too well after what she'd put him through today.

"Have you eaten anything?"

Steve shook his head.

"I can make you--"

"Look, I-- I could've lost my son today. There's still a chance I could lose him. And I can't take that chance. I have to do everything in my power to make sure I get my kids. Do you understand that?"

"Of course!"

He nodded. "Then I need you to understand that this, *us*, could be used against me. There's nothing she wouldn't do to hurt me. And every time I'm alone with you, I lose control faster. I want you too much. If I don't back off now..."

Kristina sat up straighter, her face suddenly pale. "What are you saying?"

She understood exactly what he was saying. He knew it. She wanted him to voice it. "I think we should back off from seeing each other--"

Tears filled her eyes as she sprang to her feet. She wasn't going to let him say more, not right now. He didn't have the energy to follow her and explain.

"Jessie wins again," she said. Then she fled.

Regardless of what he could say to her, it was all the same in the end. He couldn't see her. It was too damn dangerous.

* * * *

Steve's car remained parked in the lot between DeSmet and the Drug Center, Kristina noted whether she wanted to or not. It was Thursday. His kids were supposed to have met with the judge today. At ten-thirty this morning. So why was Steve still at work?

It's none of your business. Remember, he's backed off. You can't care.

But she did. She wasn't made of stone. The past four days proved that. She was a mess. She couldn't sleep, couldn't eat. *Can't get through five hours of the day without crying.* She'd been working late each night, trying to set the groundwork for The Jumpstart Project at the Center herself, as much as she was trying to avoid her own misery.

Just as Kristina reached the sidewalk in front of the Center, Hillary came out. "You've got a visitor. I told him he could wait in your office, since you'd be back from your meeting at five. You're a half hour late, so I'm not sure if he's still there."

"He?"

"Don't give me that, girl. I've known you for five years. There is only one he with you."

Steve's car was still in the lot. Hillary claimed he'd come to see her, might still be in her office. Kristina had never expected it, not when he believed custody of his older son might be at stake. A part of her had hoped she'd run out of his house before he'd said everything he intended to say Monday night. She'd been too upset to stay for anything, even to hear he hadn't meant they needed to back off forever, just temporarily.

Everything she'd dreaded for weeks had come to pass. What more was there to say? Even if he tried to promise her their separation was temporary, he didn't know what would happen. Jessie could lure him back into her cage somehow. Even if the divorce went through, Steve could realize his feelings for Kristina were simply misappropriated.

He was suffering. She sympathized with him. He needed someone who was completely on his side. There was a very real chance Steve didn't love her at all, which would explain why he'd never been able to say it. Only once had he said he could fall in love with her, not that he had or would. He hadn't even said it in the heat of the moment. That alone could make a case against true love.

The Center was quiet, as most of the employees had already gone home for the night. Kristina walked through the dark hallways to her office, her throat filled with both anticipation and dread.

Her office door stood ajar, the lights off, and she walked in feeling tears well in defeat. *He left.* But Steve occupied the chair behind her desk. All the blinds had been drawn and he sat almost in darkness.

"I need you to understand that what we have, what we've done and what we could do if we don't stop for now, could be used against me in this divorce. There's nothing Jessie wouldn't do to hurt me."

It sounded as though he continued a conversation, the *very* conversation, they'd been having before she ran out on Monday.

"I think we should back off from seeing each other for awhile. Just until the divorce is final."

Kristina closed her office door and flipped on the lights.

Steve stood. "I know you didn't want to hear that on Monday, but that's what I meant."

She set down her bags as he came around her desk toward her. "I know that's what you want it to mean now, Steve, but we can't predict the future. I don't want you to make any promises you can't keep."

"I'm not making any promises. I wish I could. I told you from the start I didn't want to hurt you. I think the best thing, the thing we should have done, is not start any of this until the divorce was final. But I couldn't. What man would refuse what you offered me?"

She hadn't offered everything she was and everything she had to just any man. She'd offered it to Steve. She understood that his kids had to come first. She understood what she'd offered him had never gone out with any strings attached--he knew that. Maybe that was why he'd temporarily taken what she offered. He could walk away from it at any time, knowing he had no obligation to give her what she wanted in return. Because she would have taken anything from Steve. Anything or nothing.

Surprising her, he put his arms around her carefully, willing to let her go at any time she initiated it. "I'm sorry, honey. I wish I could tell you this is all temporary, it'll be over soon and we can be together and everything will be great, but I don't know. Just like you I said. I don't want to lose you, but I can't do anything to jeopardize getting custody of my kids."

"Did something happen to make you believe it will happen that way?"

Steve glanced down, inhaling sharply. "It's not over, but the kids met with the judge and all of them--even Ronnie--said they want to be with me. Ron told the judge he wants to see his mom, but he knows she can't take care of herself or him."

She'd thought she might have been imagining the change in Ronnie Monday night. He hadn't been friendly to her, but he'd been worried about his father. He'd stayed with all of them most of the night because he was a part of the family, because he believed he had to take care of his sister and brother. Kristina knew he'd been lying when he said he had homework. He'd wanted to wait up for his dad.

"I knew it," Kristina said simply.

"I didn't. I didn't expect it at all."

Because she was afraid he would make a promise he might not be able to keep, Kristina stepped away, walking to the other side of the room from him. As they had constantly in the past few weeks, tears rampaged down her cheeks. When she turned to him, she said in pieces, "I never asked for anything from you, Steve. Never. I never will."

He stared at her with a helpless, wounded expression. Yet he made no move to come to her and comfort her.

"I never expected anything from you either. Never expected anything to come of this. So I don't blame you."

"Oh God, don't say that."

He couldn't change anything. She knew he wouldn't even try now. It had to be this way. He believed that.

"Don't you believe that, Kristina."

He understood her, she realized, and somehow his distance made the truth even harder to take. He could never love her. She was to blame for loving him so much it'd never mattered if he'd return it someday.

"Steve, can I ask you something?"

He nodded.

"Have you ever asked your wife if she blames you for her brother's death? I mean, I know you've assumed all these years she blames you for it, but have you ever asked her?"

She could see he'd expected her to ask him something else. "No," he said softly.

"Then you should. Maybe you'd be surprised at her answer. Maybe you wouldn't be. But you should ask."

Thirty-One

"You're not put on this earth to serve others, Janine," Kristina reminded the young woman sitting before her desk. Janine agreed with her almost every time she came here, yet couldn't seem to incorporate what she knew into the reality of her life. "You've given everything you can to this man. He refuses to stop his addiction. It's time to think of *yourself*."

"What if he kills himself?" Janine sobbed.

"Janine, is it your fault he shoots up three times a day? Do you force him to do it? Put a gun to his head? Do you do anything to make him feel like he can't handle his life because you're in it?"

Janice shook her head wildly. "I know, I know."

"If it's not your fault he does it, it's certainly not your fault if he kills himself over it. You can't make it your responsibility. You need to get on with your life. The only responsibility you have is to yourself. You *can't* change him. The only thing you can change is what *you* do.

"Do you remember I told you we have some allocation funding for this? All you have to do is fill out a few forms--it won't take you longer than ten minutes, and you'll be able to use this money to move out, get a new place to live and continue your education. Do you want to do that?"

Janine stared at her helplessly, and Kristina knew exactly what she was thinking. They'd been through this so many times, she also knew exactly what Janine would say. And she did: "He can't live without me. He *can't*."

Kristina sat back in her chair, folding her hands together. She'd always felt compassion for Janine and her situation before. Today, she felt angry.

Coolly, she said, "No, Janine. The truth of the matter is, *you* can't live without *him*. Your need to be needed is so overwhelming, you can't separate yourself from his addictions. If you give him up, you give up your own sense of worth.

"You keep coming here, telling me you need help because Samson's addiction is killing you. You do need help, but not with Samson. You already know what you need to do about him, you've known all along. You need to be counseled on why you feel so worthless when you're alone. People can't use you without your permission. Do you understand that? Samson uses you because you let him. He takes everything you give him because you don't have the strength to attach strings to it. If you come back here, Janine, I want you to come on the right pretense. Because you need help. There's nothing else I can help you with until you admit that."

Janine let out a small cry of alarm as if she'd never expected the cold water Kristina dashed on her without sensitivity.

As Janine fled the room, Kristina played back her words, only she said them to herself: *You can't make Steve your responsibility. You need to get on with your life. The only responsibility you have is to yourself. You can't change him. The only thing you can change is what you do. The truth of the matter is, you can't live without him. Your need to be needed is so overwhelming, you can't separate your desires from his. If you give him up, you give up your own sense of worth. People can't use you without your permission. Steve took everything you gave him because you didn't have the strength to attach strings to it.*

Oh, that's great. She'd driven a patient out of here because of her own issues. She knew Janine wouldn't come back unless she called, refuted everything she'd said, and returned to the former pretense. But Kristina couldn't do that. What she'd said to Janine was accurate. She just shouldn't have gone about it so callously.

Someone knocked on her door, and Kristina looked up to see the door open. A woman stood there, a woman who looked vaguely familiar to Kristina, but she wasn't sure why.

Kristina stood. "Can I help you?"

"Are you Kristina Ingram?"

Puzzled, Kristina rounded her desk. "Yes."

The woman entered the room. "I'm Jessie Thomas. Steve's *wife*."

Oh my God, oh my God, oh my God! Steve had said his wife might find out about them and use the information against him in court. He'd never once said his wife not only *already* knew about them, but also knew her by name. Shell-shocked, Kristina realized Jessie had made a point of using her married name instead of "Nelson-Thomas", as she was commonly known as.

Jessie blatantly enjoyed the power she had at the moment. She smiled almost sweetly, saying, "I thought we should talk. Do you have a minute?"

Kristina could only swallow. Jessie closed the door and came fully into the room, to the chair Janine had vacated only minutes ago.

Kristina couldn't move as she stared at Jessie. A part of her wanted to be childish and pick out all Jessie's physical flaws to make herself feel better. There was no way to do that though. The woman was stunning. Everything about her was breath-taking, as if she had stepped right out of the pages of a glossy magazine. No wonder Matt had said there was no way Kristina could compete. Why would Steve leave Jessie? She was every man's fantasy, a woman no other could compete with.

Wishing she could withdraw into a shell, Kristina forced herself to go to the chair behind her desk and hide behind it as much as she could.

"I didn't expect you to be beautiful," Jessie said, and Kristina stopped breathing in shock. "I didn't think Steve cared about that anymore. He just wants someone to be on his side. Any schoolmarm hag would suffice for that."

Then it was true. Steve had just needed a cheerleader to get him through the divorce. He'd never felt anything for her outside of that.

"So what are we going to do about you?" Jessie said.

Considering all the things Kristina knew about this woman, how could she be intimidated by her? Yet what woman wouldn't be? She forced herself to back off from the situation personally, as if Steve had been nothing more than a patient to her. "We don't need to do anything. Steve and I were just friends. As you said, he needed a friend. I'm a counselor. It's what I do for a living."

Jessie touched her index finger to her full bottom lip as though confused. "So when I saw you and Steve together in the parking lot on Monday, saw you kiss, that was what? Just friends?"

Without thinking, Kristina started to say she and Steve had broken up. She stopped when she realized she and Steve had never really been together, not in the sense that Jessie implied. After all, how can you break up when there's no commitment?

But what business is it of hers? How dare she question what we're going to do with me?

"Is there something I can do for you, Jessie? I really don't know why you're here," Kristina said with the same cool she'd leveled at Janine. This time, she felt proud of herself for the control.

"Steve and I have been together for more than a decade. Even before that, he was always mine. Do you understand that? I allowed him to have his little girlfriends, but he belonged to me throughout. He always returns to me. He will this time, too, even if means we have to drag all the dirt out for the public. There's nothing I won't do to get him back."

Kristina stared at her in shock. Who was this woman? Who did she think she was? The reigning queen of the world? She could beat the hell out of everyone around her and they were still expected to remain faithful?

Scooting forward, Kristina forgot her intimidation. "Look, if you know enough about me to be here, you know Steve has told me everything about you. I mean, my God, I've worked with people who are a little mixed up. I've worked with those who genuinely have no idea of the damage they're doing or have done. I've also worked a lot of nutcases in my life. But you-- I've never met anyone like *you* in my life. Your nerve astounds me. Don't you ever feel guilty for the crimes you've committed against a man who wanted nothing except to take care of you? You've scarred your children so badly, it's going to take years until they're whole, *if* they ever are. Doesn't it bother you that your little girl is *terrified* of you? How can you hurt those beautiful, wonderful children? *How?*"

She was saying too much. Kristina knew it, but she couldn't seem to slow the tide of anger. This wasn't just a case she could leave here when she went home at night. This was Steve and his children.

"How could you cheat on Steve?" she asked, choking on a sob. "He's...God, there's nothing he wouldn't give to the woman he loves or commits himself to. There's never been another woman since he married you. He's faithful to his vows. How can you throw all your sins in his face the way you do and still expect him to forgive you? I can't understand that. I can't. I can't understand how you wouldn't fall in love with him from the moment you laid eyes on him and then do everything in your power to hold on to him. You don't love him. You don't love anyone except yourself. I don't understand how you can't just let him go now, let them all go and let them be happy for once."

"With you?" Jessie asked in trembling fury.

Sobs broke free in Kristina's chest at her outburst. "No! Not with me. I don't matter in this. *They* do. They're all that matters. Anything that gets them away from you is good for them. For once in your life, Jessie, do something for *them.* Let them go forever and wish them well. I'm begging you."

Jessie stood, her lush mouth twisted in a grimace. "How dare you talk to me like this! You have no fucking idea what I've been through. You don't know shit about me. I love Steve. I love my kids. I'm just trying to keep my family together."

"If you stay, you'll tear them all apart."

"My lawyer is gonna drag you through the mud, you bitch. I'm gonna enjoy every minute of it, too. I *will* win."

Kristina pulled off her glasses and covered her eyes with her hands. She couldn't look at this woman for another instant. "You're evil. It's the only thing that makes sense," she whispered. Seconds later the door to her office slammed.

Now she understood. She understood why Steve was so afraid of losing to this woman. Kristina had been convinced from the very beginning there was no way Jessie could ever win in this divorce. But now she concluded that Jessie had the devil on her side. And when she went to hell, everyone around her would go down with her.

* * * *

Hell, he couldn't concentrate on this right now. Steve pushed the stack of books away from him and pressed his hands against his eyes. All he could think about was Kristina, standing there crying in her office and saying she'd never asked for anything of him, that she never expected this to work out anyway. He knew she believed he'd just used her to get through the divorce, get through his pain.

The truth was, he had run to her every time *he* needed something. Now she needed something--needed him to tell her they'd be together forever as soon as his divorce was final--and he couldn't give it to her. He couldn't even argue against her belief that he'd never loved her. Everything had to be put on hold. It had to. She couldn't understand that, he couldn't help her to, and he had no damn right in the world to ask her to wait for him. But, God, he wanted to ask promise more than anything.

What would he do if she didn't wait for him? He couldn't give her three simple words that would make the wait easier for her. The only way he could do this thing was to risk losing Kristina until he became free to go to her with no chains.

His phone rang, and he reached for it on a sigh. "Steve Thomas."

"Steve?"

He sat up straight in his chair, instantly recognizing her voice. "Kristina?" She was crying.

"Your wife was just here." She pushed the words out on a shaky exhale.

"What? Jess was--? What happened? Are you okay?"

"I don't know. I don't know why she came. But she left pissed off."

"Why?"

After a pause that Steve strained to hear her answer, she said softly, "You know why, Steve. I thought I should warn you."

She was going to hang up. "Wait a minute," he pleaded. "Wait."

She did, and he knew he was back where he'd tried not to be. "Are you okay? Should I come over there?"

"I'm not your problem, Steve. You have no responsibility to me. I accept that."

He closed his eyes to the torment ripping through him. "Honey..."

"No. I didn't call to change your mind. Your wife is a vindictive, selfish bitch. But you already know that. She's angry because I made her look at herself in a mirror. She'll punish you for it."

"She threatened you," he guessed.

"She can't punish me. I have no dirt in my life. I've never cheated on my taxes, robbed a convenience store, or starred in a porno flick. The closest I've come is falling in love with a married man and his children. I couldn't have them, so I really don't think it'll make much difference to anyone, including a judge."

"I'm so sorry, honey."

"So am I," she said sincerely, in a way that made his chest tighten. "Take care of yourself. I know you'll take care of the kids first and foremost, so I don't need to say that."

"Don't say goodbye," he begged.

She laughed humorlessly over a sob. "All right. Then I'll see you around." She hung up.

Steve swore. He sat holding the phone in his hand for a minute before he realized this couldn't go on. The longer it did, the longer Jessie believed she could win. He wouldn't allow it this time.

It was still early in the day. He didn't have any lectures, just research that could wait. Without packing his briefcase, got his coat and left his office. While he walked out to his car, he dialed Gwen's number on his cell phone.

"Are you doing anything?" he asked as soon as she answered. "Now?"

"Uh, no. Why?"

"I need to talk to you, if you'll be home for awhile."

"Of course."

"I'm on my way."

Thirty-Two

"What's going on?" Gwen showed concern as she let him into the house. She was uncharacteristically dressed in old, paint-splattered clothes. "I was painting."

"I need to ask you something."

"You can ask me anything. Do you want something to drink?"

He shook his head, and she led him into the Great Room. He sat down, looking at his hands. Kristina had told him to ask Jessie this, but she wasn't the only one he needed to ask.

"Steve, you're scaring me. Is everything all right?" She leaned toward him from where she sat on the couch.

"I never asked before because..." He laughed and broke off abruptly, glancing at her delicately enchanting face. Why did he see Tommie there again, the way he had for months after Tommie died? "I never really wanted to know the answer."

"To what?" she asked gently.

"Do you blame me for Tommie's death, Gwen?"

Yeah, he wanted her to laugh out loud like it was insane. He wanted her to burst out immediately with "No!" She didn't do either. Instead, she slid closer to his chair. "I feel many things about Tommie's death, many things that I've never told anyone, but I have never blamed you, Steve. Not then and not since."

She laced her fingers with his, squeezing until he met her soft, vulnerable gaze. "Tommie was so damn headstrong. He wouldn't listen to anyone when he got something into his head. You know that. When I was fourteen--the year I fell in love with him with all my heart and then some--I had a dream. Not a dream, but a *vision.* I saw our wedding. I saw our honeymoon. I saw how happy I was. All my dreams had come true. And then we were flying. We were flying so fast, I was so scared. Even when we landed, I was terrified and it wouldn't go away. I begged him over and over to go back with me. He wouldn't listen to me. He left. He left with you. Through the window, I saw the taillights of his car, the one you were with him in. I watched until you disappeared. And I knew I'd never see him again."

"Oh God." He'd known she had visions of Tommie's death. All of them knew that, but she'd never told him what she'd seen in those visions. How the reality came to pass.

"I broke up with him when I was fourteen and I spent the next almost ten years trying not to love him. Because I thought if we never got married, he'd never go away from me. My vision would never happen. He knew about it. I told him. I told him over and over. I begged him to listen to me. But he thought I was being silly. He refused to listen, and I..."

She drew in a shaky breath, as though she had no idea tears rolled down her cheeks without end. "I've had a hard time not blaming Jessie for being so stupid. I blame Tommie for feeling like she was his full responsibility and she had none to herself. I blame myself for being so in love with him, I let him convince me we could be together forever. I blame myself for not telling you about my vision--maybe it would have been different if I had. But I've never blamed you, Steve. You don't deserve any of the pain you've had to deal with since you got involved with Jessie."

Sliding off the couch, she kneeled before him, cradling his face in her hands. "Steve, I knew you were blaming yourself for his death and I've tried to do everything I could to tell you that you shouldn't. I guess you weren't listening."

He laughed, and she rose up on her knees and hugged him. Holding her hard, he realized he'd spent so much time feeling like he had to atone for his sins, he hadn't considered more than superficially the hell she lived with every day. Her life was just as saturated with Tommie now as it'd been when he was alive. She hadn't healed.

"I wish I could help you let him go," he said, and she sat back, looking at him silently for a moment.

"He's never left me," she said softly, another confession he believed she'd never told another soul.

"What do you mean?"

"I mean, he comes to me. He comes to me in dreams. In visions. He comes to me and tells me to let him go. To let go of my anger and grief."

Steve swallowed the horror in his throat. Tommie had come to him, too. He'd come to him twice, recently. Maybe he'd always thought Gwen and her magic mirror were part of her eccentric personality. But she'd been right so many times. She'd had visions about so many things that often came true. She seemed to know things that had happened to her friends when she couldn't possibly know. Maybe she did have a connection to the spirit world. Maybe she did see Tommie.

"Has he ever talked about me? When he comes to you?" Steve asked.

Gwen nodded. "Yes. A lot. Especially in the past five months."

Sitting before him, she looked like an omniscient gypsy. He couldn't doubt for a minute what she said was valid. "What did he say?"

"He said that you're not healed, that you blame yourself for his death. He knows he was wrong to ask you to take care of Jessie. He realized the truth about you in those minutes before the accident. He realized Jessie wasn't pregnant with your child, but you were willing to let him believe you were."

Steve sucked in a sharp breath. He'd never told Gwen about that. Wendy might have revealed part of it, but she didn't know it all because Steve had never told her everything. The only person who knew was Kristina. And Tommie.

"He knows about Kristina, too. How you feel about her. That you don't believe you should leave Jessie and be happy with Kristina. He's come to you, hasn't he, Steve? He's told you all this, too."

Steve lowered his head into his hands. Tommie wouldn't come to him. Tommie believed Jessie needed him to take care of her because she didn't know how to take care of herself. Tommie would never--

"Steve," Gwen said softly, putting her hand on the back of his head, "he's coming to you because he wants you to let him go. He wants you and the children to be happy, even if it means divorcing Jessie. She'll learn how to live on her own. It's not your responsibility anymore. It never should have been your responsibility in the first place."

"What happened to her? Why is she the way she is?" Steve asked, overwhelmed with the need to know. "Why can't anyone help her?"

When Gwen didn't answer, Steve realized she knew something about Jessie he'd never known. Maybe she had the answer to Jessie's problems.

Yet she offered the disclaimer, "I don't know much. Tommie could never find out the truth either."

She sat on the couch again. "Tommie told me that when Jessie was eleven years old, she went to spend the summer with her mom's sister and brother-in-law in San Francisco. They didn't have children. I supposed Jessie thought it would be fun to be alone in a big city with such a cool couple.

"That was the year Tommie discovered racing. I think he never wanted to admit he was a little relieved to have the summer off from taking care of Jessie. Even back then, she was a handful. Her phone calls home decreased, but he was so busy he didn't notice it until later.

"When she got back home, she was withdrawn. Tommie described her as shell-shocked. She cried all the time, for no apparent reason. She couldn't be away from him for more than a few minutes. She'd insist that nothing happened in California and she really didn't seem to remember *anything* about those weeks she was there. Tommie thought maybe she didn't want to divulge the truth, but he asked her about it years later, and he came to the conclusion that she didn't have any memories of that time.

"In any case, this aunt and uncle she stayed with got a divorce only weeks after Jessie came home, so finding out anything from them was impossible. The aunt disappeared and the uncle didn't want to talk about her at all. Years later, he told Tommie vaguely that his wife had had a horrendous childhood and she had a nervous breakdown that summer. He'd been traveling for weeks, so he didn't know if something happened to Jessie while she was in his wife's care.

"Jessie's antics got worse after that summer. To Tommie, she seemed like she was in a daze. He couldn't understand anything she did. He never found out what really happened, and since Jessie doesn't even remember being there, she can't tell anyone anything. Maybe this has nothing to do with the way she is, or maybe it has everything to do with it. In any case, I'm not sure there is anyone who can help Jessie. Not even you, and God knows how you've tried."

"Have you ever asked her about it?"

"Yes. And she was angry at me for asking and told me to never talk about it again."

Her jaw tightened. Her eyes darkened. "Don't ask me that," she said in a low voice that revealed anger, fear. "Don't ever ask me again."

In the silence that followed, they stared at each other, neither yielding.

"I can't help what I am. I know it's not fair to you or them--" She indicated the kids with a jerk of her shoulder. "I get depressed and I stop thinking. It doesn't mean anything happened. It just means I need to avoid getting depressed."

"Maybe she does remember," Steve said softly.

"Or maybe she's afraid to. I don't think it's our place to force her to tell us or to face it herself. Some things are better left in the dark, where we can't face the horror that could destroy us."

She knew something, Steve realized. Gwen had had a vision or something about Jessie and the event that made her what she was. If she advised everyone--including Jessie--to leave it alone, it had to be bad.

"Go to Jessie," Gwen said. "Ask her the question you need to ask her and trust that it'll set you all free."

Steve nodded, getting to his feet at her encouragement. At the door, she hugged him and whispered, "If Tommie comes to you again, listen to him, Steve. Really listen. Hear what he says. Talk to him. And do what he asks."

He walked to his car, telling himself Tommie had never come to him. He'd had dreams that he probably would never have again.

* * * *

Jessie was at her condo, the way he figured she would be after her defeat with Kristina earlier.

"Are you here to lambaste me about your little girlfriend?" Jessie turned from her open door to let him come in on his own. "I don't know how you'd live with her. She throws everything in your face, the very things you could spend a lifetime apologizing for and not get anywhere."

"You had no right to go to her. I told you she's not a factor in this."

"Not a factor?" Jessie hooted. "She was drooling all over you. She's drop-dead in love with a married man with three kids. I sat there *insulting her* and she sat there *defending you.* You're involved with a fucking lapdog."

Steve grabbed her arm and yanked her toward him with more force than he'd ever used on her. "Kristina is not a lapdog. She has something you'll never have--compassion. I don't want you to see her again. I don't want you to talk to her. And I don't want you to assume anything between me and her is any of your goddamn business."

"Is that why you're here, baby? To defend her? Or do you wanna fuck me one more time?" She blew smoke in his face.

Steve shoved her away from him. "The only thing I want is for you to let this divorce happen."

"That's all? That's *everything*, sweetheart. Everything I've got. Are you sure that's all you want?" she asked, sweetly sarcastic.

"And I want you to tell me something."

Her eyes narrowed as she looked at him. "Tell you what?"

"I want you to tell me..." He swallowed, looking away for an instant. "...if you blame me for Tommie's death."

Her mouth opened, stayed open, then she took a shaky breath before veering away from him. She stubbed her cigarette out in the crystal ashtray on top of the bar.

"I blame myself. I always have. I took Tommie away from everyone. From all of us. Gwen. Allison. You," Steve said. She didn't care. She had no reaction whatsoever. "I'm asking you if you agree with what I've always believed--that *I* should've been the one who died in that accident. Then everyone could've been happy."

"Oh my God," Jessie said under her breath, so quietly he almost didn't hear her. Her back to him remained rigid. Her silence stretched across the room like an ear-splitting gavel pronouncing him guilty.

"That's what I thought," he whispered.

He started to leave, but she spoke as he opened the door. She didn't face him. "I never blamed you. I blamed myself. *I* killed Tommie. I fucked everything up. I made him furious because I always had to do everything he told me not to. He was only trying to protect me. You were trying to protect me. If anyone should've died, it's me." When she laughed, pivoting just enough for him to see her face. He was startled to realize she was crying.

"But you know Tommie. He always took my punishment for me. So did Jon. Ronnie. And now you want out of taking my punishment, too. What's a girl to do? There's no one left but me." She walked out of the room, and he heard a door close behind her.

Thirty-Three

Complacently numb, Kristina closed her eyes, listening to the shower run in her bathroom like a lullaby. All she wanted to do was sleep and forget this whole night had happened. She'd deal with everything else later.

She woke suddenly, her ears straining for some noise. The shower was off. She reached up and felt her hair. Still wet. She couldn't have been asleep long.

Then it came again. A knock on the front door.

Who was that? Hillary? It was still early. Only eight p.m. And Hillary knew she was a mess.

Carefully, Kristina put her feet on the floor and stood as soon as the dizziness passed. She didn't even have the energy to tighten the belt on her robe. Her mind felt like it swam in a cesspool of whispering, tormenting ghosts.

Robe gaping, her hair was a tangled, wet mess, she grasped the doorknob, a lifeline, and pulled open the door.

Not Hillary. Not Hillary. Steve. Not Hillary.

"Are you--?" His gaze flew past her.

Kristina couldn't have turned if she wanted to. She didn't need to. Not when Matt said, "Hey."

Steve's expression hardened.

Knowing Matt, she was sure he'd walked out of her bedroom in just a towel.

Without a word, Steve turned and stalked down the stairs.

Kristina called to him, but all she could manage was a whisper. From the top, the staircase looked black and fuzzy. If she didn't have such a hard grasp on the railing, she would have fallen.

She could barely see Steve, just his outline. He'd stopped.

"Please. I can't follow you unless it's the hard way. Don't walk away, Steve."

She had to sit down. Weakness and overbearing heat washed over her. She put her head against her knees, drifting until she felt Steve's hand on her head.

"Are you sick?"

She nodded vaguely, averted her head from her lap. She squinted up at him and could make out the tightness of his face.

"Who is he?"

"Matt," she whispered.

"The guy, the one...?"

She nodded again, closing her eyes because she didn't have the strength to explain all this away.

"Did you sleep with him?"

He had no right to ask. He had to know that. His tone was vulnerable, not accusing, so she knew he was aware it was none of his business.

"No!" she said, too hoarse to deny it the way she wanted to. She wanted to scream the denial until it echoed off the walls.

"But you have in the past. The last time he was in the city."

Kristina lifted her head limply, shaking it and making herself sicker in the process. "You have no right to throw that in my face. It was different then. I was sick tonight. I got sick, and he was... Suddenly he was there. He just showed up. I don't know why."

"He has a key?"

"What are you doing?" she cried listlessly. "What are you doing to me? I'm not..." Tears flooded into her eyes. "I'm not an old coat. One that you can take off and put on at your leisure. Maybe it's my fault. Maybe I do that. Maybe I look like a rest stop to guys. They stop in, get what they need, and then pull out without..."

Steve drew her against him suddenly, and all she knew was that it felt so good to be in his arms again. "Don't say that. You're not a coat or a rest stop. Not to me."

It sounded so ridiculous, she started laughing. She didn't have the energy to continue. She just wanted to sleep. Right here in Steve's arms.

"So why is he here? In nothing but a towel? Why are you sick?" Steve asked, and she still heard the jealousy in his voice, soft as it was.

"I wanted to sleep. Not cry. I can't remember... I had a glass of wine. I think I took some sleeping pills. I just wanted to sleep. I can't remember. Then I had more wine. I was so sick. Matt was there. I puked all over him. He thought I was trying to kill myself."

"Because of me?"

"I wasn't-- I didn't mean to..."

Steve stood, pulling her with him, and she cried out as her legs gave out completely. He held her though. He lifted her in his arms like a child, like a bride.

"Don't leave me," she begged.

"I'm not staying here if he's here."

She closed her eyes against his chest, feeling movement, hearing voices. The familiar comfort of her bed greeted her ten seconds or ten minutes later. She clutched Steve tighter, knowing he would let her go now. Again.

He tightened the belt of her robe, tucked her under the covers securely, but she sat up and locked her arms around him once more.

"Don't do this again," he whispered in her ear. "Not over me. I'm not worth it."

He backed off, gently but forcibly loosening her arms and holding them on her lap. His eyes were dark and unreadable. Kristina didn't care if Matt stood there watching them. She just waited for Steve to say or do anything. Maybe all this was a dream.

When he leaned forward and kissed her, she knew she had to be in deep sleep. Steve wouldn't make such a show of possession. Of demarcation. Claiming her so Matt would have no doubt who she belonged to. He wouldn't. He was still married and could possibly be married forever if his wife had any say in it.

She opened her eyes and found herself completely alone in the room. She'd been dreaming. That explained Steve's presence here. Had he really been here?

Why had he come? He'd never said. The only reason he would come back would be if his divorce was final. And she knew he wasn't coming back for her. He didn't love her.

"So that's him, huh?" Matt said, appearing in her bedroom doorway. He had pants on now at least.

She hadn't been dreaming. Steve had really been here. He'd been jealous, he'd carried her into her bedroom, kissed her in front of Matt. Why?

"I can't see you anymore, Matt. You have to go."

She remembered puking her guts out--projectile-like, all over her bed--sending Trina running. She remembered Matt appearing like a figment of her imagination, swearing, just seconds before she'd puked all over him as well. He'd taken her to the bathroom, stayed with her until even the hot bile that followed stopped coming up. Then he'd put her in the shower, cleaned up her bed, and put her in it. All while he'd had the disgusting vomit on him.

"I'm sorry. Thank you for taking care of me, but you have to go."

"Because he saw me here?"

She nodded.

"So he's getting a divorce? He's divorcing his wife for you?"

"I have nothing to do with his divorce. He's divorcing her for himself. For his kids."

Matt entered the room, his gait annoyingly cocky. "So why was he here?"

"I have no idea."

"The two of you are together? Not together? What? Did he tell you he loves you or ask you to wait for him?"

Kristina turned on her side, pulling the covers up under her chin tightly. "Not together," she said softly because Matt had walked around the bed, sat down and stared at her like everything was so obvious. Pitiful.

"That's what I thought," Matt said softly. He brushed the hair back from her cheek. "But you are waiting, babe. You're as committed to him as marriage. What makes you think he won't go back to his wife? Because if he hasn't told you he loves you or asked you to wait for him, he's *not* committed to you. It's not nice of him to come around to make sure you're still dangling on his wire while he's not taking any risks for you."

It's not like that, Kristina's mind defended automatically, but she couldn't say it. She didn't think that was why Steve had come earlier. He wouldn't make her dangle.

Matt was right. She was making herself sick for love when there was no reason in the world to hope it would ever work out. Steve wasn't taking any risks, and if she convinced himself the reason he wasn't was because he didn't want to hurt her, she'd be completely lost. She had to let this go. Somehow. Soon.

* * * *

Steve took a deep breath as he walked into the Drug Crisis Center. He knew Kristina was in her office. He'd seen movement inside her windows not five minutes ago. He recognized her shape.

It'd been a damn long time since he'd been a romantic. Where once he'd smoothly glided into every romantic gesture, now he stumbled like he didn't have a clue what he was doing. And he really didn't. Not anymore. He'd been sure of the women he'd bestowed romance on way back when. He wasn't sure of Kristina.

Not anymore.

Her co-workers stared at him as he strode down the hall. Some of them probably recognized him, knew the only person he'd come here for was Kristina. He carried a big white florist's box with a purple bow. Yeah, he had no doubt he looked like an idiot. But if it worked, he didn't care.

Her office door was open, yet she wasn't in sight. He suddenly felt so stupid, he decided he'd do it another way. Go to her apartment tonight.

Earlier, this had seemed like the perfect idea. Val and Tom's encouragement had made it seem like the right thing to do, the sooner the better.

Steve entered her office and set the roses on the couch. He started writing a note, and knew he wouldn't leave it. Nothing he could say on paper would sound right. It'd be hard enough to say it to her face.

He crumpled up the note and tossed it in the trash. She'd been right here five minutes ago, dammit. The thing about nerve was, once you pushed forward only to get stalled in the process, it'd be harder to work it up the next time.

Steve took a deep breath and turned around, planning to leave. *Come back later.*

But she was there. In the doorway. Tears were rolling down her face. How long had she been there?

"Is it over?" she asked, before he could say a word.

She looked thinner, pale, and he wondered if she'd been making herself sick over him in the last three weeks. Was she alone? Or involved with the cretin who'd taken her virginity without permission, but took care of her when she was sick almost ten years later?

"If you mean the divorce, yeah. It's been final for two weeks now."

"Tom called me that day you came to my apartment. He told me why you were there. That Jessie conceded defeat and it would all be over soon."

"He did?"

Tom had never said a word about it to him. It was that very day that Steve had planned to tell Kristina about the strange call he'd gotten from his lawyer only twenty minutes after he left Jess' condo with absolution of the kind he'd never expected from her.

Jessie had given up completely. She'd told her lawyer to push the divorce through as fast as he could and to give Steve everything he'd asked for in the first Settlement Agreement he and Travis had drafted--everything he'd asked for and more. As in the whole of their relationship, Steve didn't understand why she'd done any of it. He'd probably never know, but that wasn't his concern anymore. He'd had to let go of his responsibility for her.

Kristina nodded, swiping her cheeks with the tips of her fingers. "He asked me not to give up on you. That if I respected you before for your decisions, then I should continue to trust them."

"He said that, huh?" Steve felt humbled at his son's faith.

"He did. So what happened?"

"I have sole custody of Ronnie, Tom, and Val. Jess has supervised visits once a month as long as she keeps her job and stays clean."

She took a deep breath. "I'm glad you got everything you wanted. I'm glad it worked out. You deserve it."

He'd planned this moment down to the letter, but all his intentions scattered. All he wanted to do was put his arms around her and lay an explanation on her that would take the next two hours. He didn't want to leave anything out. He wanted that, and he wanted to just kiss her until she knew wordlessly exactly why he was here.

"I *didn't* get everything I wanted. Still one thing that's not worked out."

She held a folder in her hands so tight, her knuckles were pure white. He took two steps toward her, then three.

"Me?"

Steve laughed, taking the folder from her and setting it on her desk. She'd taken some baby steps forward, but he closed the distance. "Yeah, you."

Her eyes went wide, almost feverish. He knew she'd cry and, if she did, he wanted her to do it because she was happy.

"I love you. I'm sorry I put you through this, especially if you plan to tell me to get out and never come back--"

"I wanted to hate you for dropping me the way it felt like you did. I wanted to believe you didn't really love me, that you were using me. I was some kind of transitional person for you while you got over your wife. But I couldn't believe it of you. I couldn't believe you didn't feel everything I do for you."

"I wasn't...would *never*...use—"

She put her hand over his mouth, shaking her head and dislodging tears. "It took me a while to accept it, but I know you would never use me. I think everything that happened the night you came to my apartment was your way of showing me you loved me and didn't want me to give up on the idea of us being together. I told Matt he had to go and that I couldn't see him ever again. I didn't sleep with him."

"I know. I had no right--"

"You were jealous."

"I could've killed him with my bare hands." He'd never forget how he'd felt when Kristina opened her door, her robe gaping open so enticingly, her hair wet. Then Matt had stepped out of the bedroom in a towel, his hair as wet as hers. Steve had gone blind in the next few minutes, until Kristina called him back in a mere whisper that pierced him almost as much as the thought that'd he'd lost her completely. It was his own damn fault for needing to get his house in order before he committed himself to anything new.

"But you kissed me instead."

Steve drew his thumb over her bottom lip. "What kind of flogging does a man get for wanting a woman to be his, even if he knows he can't have her?"

"The worst kind. Life sentence at least." She touched her lips to his. They held there together. He was back, right where he'd wanted to be for what seemed like a lifetime. He breathed, she breathed.

"Life, huh? I think I can handle that," he whispered, then he kissed her again. Her body drifted closer and he pressed her as close as she could get. Her mouth was as eager as his. He never wanted to go this long without kissing her. Never again.

From outside the office, cheering erupted, and Kristina laughed against his mouth. She turned, still smiling, and they faced her colleagues for a few seconds before Kristina pushed her door shut and came back into his arms. The cheering outside the door got louder, and Steve laughed as they kissed.

"Come home with me," he whispered, moments later, when their laughter had dissipated completely and he knew this office wasn't private enough for him. "After work? Tonight?" He molded her hips to his, gratified by her moan. "Now?"

She didn't even open her eyes. "Mhm, now? I--I have a meeting in an hour."

"Later then."

"Now."

She looked at him.

"Now?"

She nodded. "Now."

"I want you to stay. Spend the night with me. Gwen's picking the kids up from school. We'll worry about your car later."

Her face suffused with color and a happy glow he couldn't wait to see spread over every inch of her body. "Yes."

She took her flowers, and they left her office, where she told her supervisor, without an ounce of embarrassment, that she planned to take the rest of the day off. Smiling, Hillary said she'd cancel her appointments herself. They dropped by her apartment to get an overnight bag and fill her pets' food and water dishes.

Steve was as eager as a kid on his first date. He and the kids had spent all of last weekend cleaning the house. Boxing up Jessie's stuff, getting rid of all the clutter. Preparing eagerly for possibilities. Though Ronnie hadn't commented on any of it, he'd pitched in as much as everyone.

"Wow," was the first thing Kristina said when she walked in the front door and glanced in the living room. "I can see your desk."

Steve laughed, nodding.

"Did you--?"

"*We* did it for you. All of us."

"Even Ronnie?"

"Even Ronnie."

He led her up the stairs, and she looked into his bedroom just like he'd planned for her to. "Why are all these boxes in here?" she asked in surprise. Everything that had been in the storage room was now in what had been his bedroom. He and Jessie's.

Past the room, the bathroom and to the last bedroom, he led her. The storage room had been completely re-done. He'd even taken all the furniture from his old bedroom to Goodwill. Everything in this room was new. New carpeting. New pale purple walls. Two new dressers. New bed. One side of the closet held his clothes. The other was empty, the hangers waiting to be filled.

But she wasn't looking at any of the furnishings. She looked at the center of the rose petal-covered bed.

"Marry me, Kristina. Be a part of our family."

She glanced up at him as if she believed everything in front of her was a mirage she couldn't trust. "Am I dreaming?"

Steve reached over and took the velvet box off the new, purple flowered comforter. As he slipped the ring out and put it on her finger, he asked, "You tell me. Are you dreaming?"

"Don't wake me up. Please."

"You have to be awake for what I have in mind."

She smiled with tears in her eyes. "I love you. I love your family. Wake me up, Steve. I'm ready to live."

Thirty-Four

Steve's breath hitched in his throat as her clothes came off, slowly, a little uncertainty, onto the bathroom floor. Maybe a two-person bubble bath wasn't such a good idea, after all. He wanted her now. Right this instant.

She was so small, delicate, and yet there was a glow to her skin that kept him feeling like he'd hurt her if he even touched her.

The blush in her cheeks spread down her neck to her breasts. The most perfect breasts he'd ever seen in his life.

"You're almost unbearably sexy, honey."

She swallowed, looking impossibly more self-conscious. "Really?"

He didn't want her to feel insecure, especially if she was comparing herself to his ex-wife. This was a moment he'd waited for endlessly. One she had waited for longer than he had. He didn't want to disappoint her.

Drawing her against his half-clothed body, he tilted and held her chin up so she faced him. "The sexiest woman I've ever seen. You're my fantasy."

"Reality," she whispered, putting her arms around him and kissing him as if throwing away any lingering insecurities.

Steve ran his hands down her back to cradle her rear end in his hands. Hot blood filled his lower region. How long could he make this last, especially when her hands reached past the waistband of his jeans and tugged?

"Take these off," she insisted. "I want to see you, too."

As he obeyed her command, she backed toward the bathtub. She halted at the edge of it, watching him with fire in her violet blue eyes.

Whatever cocky confidence he'd had about his own appeal as a man had dissolved to nothing over the years. Kristina resurrected it in a single, scalding look, one that seemed to affect her as much as it did him. Tears filled her eyes, and she murmured, "I want to be with you more than I want to take my next breath."

She reached for him, his mouth covered hers, and she let out a shaky sob as their mouths opened together, tongues touching, licking wildly.

Steve lifted her over the edge of the tub, pulling back from her only long enough to join her. Then they lowered themselves into the warm water and bubbles.

She surprised him when she crawled over his legs on her knees and wrapped her arms around his head. He couldn't wait another minute to explore her.

His kissed the line of her jaw, down her throat until she lifted her head to allow him full access. Her breasts rose with the movement, the rosy tips hard as they pointed toward the ceiling.

Steve sucked in a harsh breath at the sight of a life-long fantasy, all his for the taking. His hands curled around the top curves of her breasts, closing so only her nipples showed through.

She looked at him, at herself, and whispered throatily, "Put your mouth on me, Steve, before I die."

His manhood tightened until he was afraid he couldn't hold on, but then she gently urged his head to her. He opened his lips against her, licked her, and his instincts took over. He hadn't forgotten what he was doing here.

Long and hard, he sucked on her nipple against the roof of his mouth.

"Yes!' she cried.

His fingers stroked the other nipple for a minute before he drew back and greeted that one enthusiastically, too.

"Oh Steve, I'm going to--"

He looked at her passion-drugged eyes and felt a surge of masculine power, such a foreign thing for him when once upon a time it'd been as natural as breathing. Only Kristina could give that back to him.

He slid his hands down her to rear end again, eased his fingers there and lower, imagining his mouth exploring her here soon.

She reached between them and rode his erection against her center as her body shuddered. He almost lost it, but seeing a woman so on fire for him, *only* him, kept him in control for the moment.

"Bed," she panted when her climax subsided. "Please, Steve, please take me to bed and love me. Lose yourself in me the way I do in you. I love you so much."

Had he expected her to be sweetly submissive? He couldn't say, but he was so aroused he didn't think it could get any better until they were out of the tub and back in the room. After he dried her, she took the towel from him and dried him, slowly, following the cotton with her own mouth, down his back, his sides, lower. Then she came around him and started there, over his chest, his nipples, his contracting stomach muscles...

He fell back on the bed with an agonizing groan. Lifting his legs, he reached down and held her head, guiding her as she brought him to an explosive climax that somehow left him wanting her even more when he dragged her up to him and she looked at him with triumph and love warring in her eyes. She'd enjoyed making him lose control.

"I came," she murmured as he shook violently. "Again. With you. But enter me now. I want you so deep inside me, I can feel you everywhere. I don't want to dream anymore."

He rolled them until she was under him, and reached down to slid his fingers into her, full length. She was still contracting. And his erection was as strong now as when he'd watched her undress for him in the bathroom.

While she wrapped her legs around his hips, he said, "I planned this moment. I have condoms, but I want you to make the choice if we use one now or not." Steve shifted, bringing his arms up to bracket her head and pressing his erection where his fingers had been. They both groaned.

"What do you want?" she asked, looking slightly surprised.

"I want to get you pregnant."

Their eyes met, and then she smiled. "I want to get pregnant."

Steve smiled along with her. Keeping his gaze locked with hers, he eased forward, her back arched, her knees rose, cradling him.

It was so easy. Nothing had ever felt so easy, so good to him before pushing himself inside her body. She had tears in her eyes when he went as far as he could go.

"I love you," she murmured happily.

"I've never loved any woman except you, honey."

Steve kissed her as he rocked against her. She met him each time in glorious friction. He couldn't hold on, not now that he had everything he wanted. When it'd been so long since he'd felt anything at all. Felt so much love and desire.

Her mouth fell away as she accepted him, closing her eyes as she cried out helplessly with each thrust. "More," she murmured, as if she didn't want it to end.

Steve closed his eyes, holding her even tighter when he felt heat racing through him where he'd been incapable before. He couldn't stop the force now. Even more so than last time, his ejaculation seemed to rip him apart. It felt like the first time, the only, the best.

His muscles came close to collapse, so he rolled them until she was on top. She rose only slightly, and her breasts came close to him. He drew her down the rest of the way, sucking at her the engorged tips again.

She rode him wildly, shifting from trying to hold back to giving in uncontrollably, without a single inhibition.

Watching her flow over him, he wanted her again, even if he didn't think he could move. She was crying when she collapsed on his chest.

"I love you," he said, and she curled up on top of him with a joyous peal of laughter.

"Mhm, I could listen to you say that forever and never get sick of it."

"I couldn't say it before. I couldn't even think it," he panted. "A married guy who says 'I love you' to another woman is cheating on his wife. I didn't want to cheat on Jess, but I think I did. Just by kissing you. More--the things we did in San Bernardino. Wanting you more than any women I've ever known. I danced on the line too often with you as it was, and that's why I had to back away. I wanted you so bad, I knew if I didn't remove myself, I'd take it all the way. And then I'd lose everything."

"You're the most wonderful man I've ever known in my life. I promise you I'll never forget that. I'll never betray your trust. I'll be worthy of your love."

The words settled over his heart like balm. "I'll be good to you, Kristina. I'll be good *for* you. Everything you ever need..."

"...is right here. I know. I know you."

She smiled, and he smiled back at her. "I don't think I'll ever get enough of you."

"We can try. Now. Again. Please."

He laughed. He didn't feel any guilt at all.

* * * *

"It's quarter to twelve. We're supposed to be there in fifteen minutes," Kristina called to Steve when the shower went off in the next room.

She dug through her make-up bag until she found a tube of purple lip gloss. They'd called Gwen last night, talked to the kids, but they hadn't told them the good news yet. Kristina suspected all of them already knew, but they would make it official at lunch today.

She couldn't wait to see them. Ronnie's reaction might not be everything they could hope for. Steve insisted he'd be okay about it. He'd helped the rest of his family clear out his mother's things and put in a whole new bedroom set for another woman. That went a long way in proving that he would probably be "okay about it."

Yet she couldn't deny a feeling that she didn't belong here. What they'd shared in the hours since he brought her to this house felt both right and illicit, as if she was taking something that didn't belong to her.

She'd tried to tell herself this house was a part of Steve and his family. She loved the four of them for working so hard to make her a part of it as well. She couldn't tell them the truth. Jessie's presence lingered here, like a specter that showed up unexpectedly to insist that Kristina was taking what belonged to her alone.

"I don't think I'll ever be able to look at you with clothes on again. Not without--"

He pressed his body against her back, and Kristina felt exactly how he reacted to the sight of her with clothes.

"--remembering..."

His hands snaked under her skirt. Kristina closed her eyes at her immediate arousal as he rubbed against her behind. For once, she'd gotten next to no sleep for positive reasons. As many times as they'd made love, it was still so new, she became paralyzed with longing each time he touched her. Each time he merely looked at her with his eyes so dark, so intense, so naked with love, she was completely lost.

As he peeled away the barrier between them, she saw herself in the mirror and thought of his ex-wife. She turned to him quickly and kissed him until the tears in her eyes cleared.

No, she could never admit to him that the pleasure he gave her was interrupted at the worst times with reminders of another woman using the bathroom, putting make-up on while he showered, making love to him whether he'd enjoyed it or not.

"We have to go."

"They'll understand," he said, pushing back the blouse he'd unbuttoned in seconds and burying his face in her naked breasts.

"Do we want them to understand?" she laughed and groaned at his consummate mouth.

"This is probably the last time we'll have the house to ourselves until the kids are in college."

It was such a domestic thing to say. This would be *their* home. This was *their* family. He offered her everything she'd ever wanted, and she felt Jessie's eyes on them from every direction.

No, she wouldn't let anything spoil this. Kristina flung aside any pretense of worry that they'd be late and made love to him, feeling like she was trying desperately to one-up someone.

Until, panting, Steve drew her down and kissed her gently, sweetly, whispering his love, she couldn't get rid of that feeling and just let herself relax in the arms of the man she wanted to spend her life with.

* * * *

When Valerie cried, "You guys are late!" at nearly twelve-thirty, Kristina and Steve glanced at each other, laughed and kissed before they were enveloped with hugs by Valerie and Tom. Gwen stood back and watched them, a knowing smile on her lips.

Ronnie kept himself apart until Steve pulled him into the fray. He didn't hug Kristina, but it didn't matter. He looked her in the eye for the first time without anger or jealousy. He looked at her and said, "Hi" almost shyly.

Kristina's heart somersaulted at the tiny step of acceptance. "Hi, Ronnie."

She'd missed them, all of them, more so because she'd believed she might never see them again.

Steve hugged Ronnie again, and Kristina couldn't help stroking his dark hair. Someday she could hug him and tell him she loved him. Someday he might even return it. But he wasn't ready yet and that was all right. The fact that they'd gotten this far was a miracle in itself. It could have gone completely the other way with Ronnie, her professional expertise told her. According to Steve, Jess had told her son to trust Steve because he loved him and would take care of him better than anyone else in the world. If Steve wasn't such a good father and Jessie hadn't let Ron go, he could have hated them and become self-destructive because everything he'd feared had come to pass. Kristina had witness the scenario happening too often not to realize the fact that it hadn't happened this time was a miracle they should cherish for the rest of their lives.

The kids didn't let them go much, but enough that Gwen could hug them both and tease softly she'd expected them to be even later getting home than they had been.

"Daddy!" Val said as they crossed the threshold of the front door at last. Kristina could hear the urgency in her tone, the expectation.

Steve ruffled Valerie's silky hair affectionately. "You can't wait another minute, can you, baby?"

Valerie shook her head frantically.

Steve chuckled. "Yeah. Yeah, Kristina said yes. She's going to marry me and put me out of my misery."

"I knew it!" Valerie beamed, throwing her arms around Kristina again. "Now you'll really be my mom."

Kristina hugged her with the tears still holding in her eyes. She saw Tom smile, glance at his brother and something passed between the two of them, something that made Ronnie nod, look embarrassed, then he smiled. She knew at that moment everything would be all right. They would truly be a family. They would heal.

"When can Kristina move in, Daddy?" Valerie demanded.

Steve pulled Kristina against him. They'd already talked about it last night. "Moving day is today," he said before he kissed her.

Epilogue

Steve locked his office door behind him, waved to the colleague who called good night, but didn't stop to chat. He had too much to look forward to.

When he stepped out of the DeSmet Building, the sun seemed to pull him into its spotlight. He smiled, immediately looking for Kristina coming out of the Center. Her welcoming smile had him striding toward her without conscious effort. All he knew was that everything he wanted was right before him and he had to get to her.

"Hi," she said with her whole heart in her eyes.

"Hey."

In full view of the campus, his colleagues, her colleagues, the world, he brought her into his arms and kissed her the way he'd been waiting to for the last five hours.

She'd been his wife for a month now, and every day of his life--ordinary as some might see it--was something he looked forward to. He woke up with Kristina every morning. They got the kids ready for school, themselves ready for work, and they came home together every night to their family. A normal, average family who loved each other, helped each other, worked together like a team. And, after the kids were in bed, they became a man and a woman who lived for their moments alone. He didn't think the things they did together would ever become commonplace to him. Now he thought about her, and instantly became filled with pleasure and the pain of wanting her. When he closed his eyes for the night, she was wrapped around him, her head against his heartbeat, content. He was happy.

Steve had set the guilt free. Tommie had come to him on his honeymoon. Steve had expected it as much as he'd wondered if Gwen was right--Tommie would ask him to let him go.

Kristina had been in the bathroom. The sun had just started to come up through the patio doors, where they'd left the blinds open and made love in the moonlight the night before for the first time as husband and wife. She'd kissed him, whispering she'd be right back. His entire body came to life at the promise in her voice and her eyes.

"You love her," Tommie had said from the shadows of the room.

"I love her."

"Good. She deserves it. So do you."

"Jessie will have to learn how to take care of herself."

"She will. And you don't need to worry about it anymore."

Steve nodded.

"Only thing one left, man." He leaned against the bedpost. *"Are you ready to let me go?"* He said it like it should be the easiest thing in the world. But then what had ever been hard for Tommie? He could do anything.

Steve swallowed, remembered Tommie--broken, dying, whispering, "Take care of Jess or I'll come back and haunt you." He closed his eyes against the memory and the pain that still remained. A part of him thought, *How can I ever let Tommie go? How?* Even as he opened his eyes and the tears came, he nodded to Tommie. He would let him go.

"I loved you, man. You were my best friend. I'll never forget you," Steve promised.

Tommie nodded. *"I forgot that for a minute and you suffered for it. I was hard on you, harder than I would have been on anyone else. You were right about that. Because it was* you. *I trusted you more than anybody else. You mattered more."*

Steve closed his eyes on the sob slamming through his chest.

Tommie gave him a light punch on the arm. He sat on the bed and waited for Steve to open his eyes. *"Now I want you to be happy, Steve. Don't ever forget you were my best friend and I loved you, too, but now you have to let me go. There's no more guilt. Let the eclipse come, so you can see your shadow again. You're free."*

Steve nodded. "'Bye, Tommie."

"'Bye."

Steve had almost been about to let go of the breath that seemed to be suspended in his lungs when Tommie said, *"Oh, and when that little girl comes next year, don't call her 'Tommie', man. I'm begging you. You've already got a Ronald Tommie Thomas and a Thomas Nathan Thomas. Enough already."*

By the time Kristina had come out of the bathroom, Steve had been laughing, damn near delirious from it.

He looked down and saw his and Kristina's shadows meld together on the sidewalk. She sighed, an everything-is-right-in-the-world sigh, when he looked at her.

Steve slid an arm around her shoulders. "Come on, honey. Let's go home."

* * * *

"Steve, you missed the exit," Kristina warned as they sailed past on the freeway.

He just turned and smiled at her.

"What are you up to?" she asked, seeing the playfulness in his eyes.

"Nothing. Just hold your horses, honey."

"We're supposed to have dinner with my parents at seven. The kids--"

"--will be with Wendy until then. She's picking them up after school."

Wendy and Paul were in town with their kids. Wendy had been helping her prepare for the Jumpstart fundraiser as well as setting up a Wayward Angels for boys in Milwaukee. Their friend Gregg Stevens had given up a mega-successful music career, gone through rehabilitation of his own volition, and would be leading the new Wayward Angels. Everyone agreed that if anyone could reach boys heading down the path of destruction, it was Gregg.

Kristina waited with insatiable curiosity as they followed the freeway, exiting at Oak Creek, where Gwen lived. When she looked at Steve questioningly, he gave her that hold-your-horses-honey look again, but refused to put her out of her misery.

They didn't follow the usual route to Gwen's house, and she began to feel like a kid with her nose pressed to the glass as they passed gorgeous homes, into a section of town that spoke of domestic tranquility.

Did he want her to meet someone? Who did he know that she didn't?

"Steve--" she said again, impatience making her crazy.

He pulled up to a two-story home with a façade that combined both brick and wood. Another car was parked in front of the two-car garage. A For Sale sign on the gorgeous lawn.

When she turned to him again, he put a finger to her lips then his arms went around her.

"You haven't said it, and I've been so damn happy I don't think I would have noticed if Tom hadn't said something."

Frowning, she couldn't begin to imagine what Tom might have told Steve about her.

"I thought if I moved our room into what was the storage room, put in a new bed and all new furniture, it would make it a whole new place for us. But you've been uncomfortable there, haven't you? She's still there for you."

Tears filled her eyes. She made an attempt at an apology he silenced once more.

"This doesn't have to be the one. I've lined up a couple different choices, but this is the one I liked as soon as I saw it."

"Steve, I'm sorry. I just, I don't want to feel it, but sometimes it's like everything I do there is to spite her. To prove to somebody that I won, not her. And I hate feeling it. I love you and the kids. It's never been a competition for me. I'm not surprised that Tom is the one who sensed it. I tried so hard to hide it. I have everything I want. How can I complain?"

He grinned and told her it was all right for her to feel the way she unwillingly had. "No wonder you were so relaxed on our honeymoon."

"What did Tom say?"

"Nothing really. He just said the house was getting crowded. Too many kids. Too many pets. He asked if we could afford to move into a bigger house where you'd be more comfortable. That's when I noticed you didn't feel like you belonged in our house. You told me once you wanted a big house you could fill with a family and your animals, didn't you?"

The fact that he remembered touched her. "*Can* we afford to move?" she asked, turning back to the gorgeous house in front of them. "This looks so expensive."

He eased her back to kiss her until the excitement inside her at the prospect of having a home, a place Jessie had never and would never be in, filled her as much as her love for her family did.

"We can afford it. You want to look?"

She nodded, eagerly jumping out of the car and snuggling into Steve's arm when he came around to join her. Kristina couldn't breathe as the realtor--a friend of Brenda's--took them from room to room. The inside of the house was huge, with cathedral ceilings, a raised hearth fireplace in the great room, a backyard big enough for dozens of pets and kids, five bedrooms upstairs and a master bedroom with its own balcony and whirlpool bath.

"You could have an office at home," she murmured, and Steve laughed.

"You like it?"

Like it? "Can we buy it?" she asked, as happy as a little girl at Christmas.

Steve laughed again, looking glad that she loved his first choice as much as he did.

"You're sure?"

Kristina wrapped her arms around him at his side, putting her mouth near his ear. "Let's christen it. Now," she whispered.

He looked at her with instant fire in his eyes before he said to the realtor, "We'll take it."

"Just like that?"

"Just like that. Get the paperwork ready. We'll have a down payment for you in the morning."

The realtor left them in the house at their request, looking startled. Kristina burst out laughing as Steve locked the bedroom door behind the man.

Steve reached for her blouse, too excited to waste a minute. Her laughter subsided as soon as he lowered her to the bare carpet, his mouth closing over her nipple.

She moaned, gathering him against her as close as she could get him. Though she'd had no official confirmation, she wanted to share her suspicion of the last week with him. "Oh Steve, this house has so many rooms, we could have a nursery."

His head lifted, a look of blown-away seriousness in his expression. "He knew. He told me."

"What? Who?"

"Tommie. We're going to have a baby. Another little girl."

Emotion crammed into her throat. Steve believed in premonitions. In destiny. Kristina nodded with tears in her eyes. She had everything she needed. This house would be a physical symbol of Steve moving on to a new life without the memories of a painful past with a woman who gone out of her way to destroy him. The children could get past their scars without the constant reminder of what they'd gone through. And having a child with the man she'd loved from the moment she'd met him was another glimpse of the benevolent side of destiny. She sighed at the prospect of a fresh start for all of them. "Yes, Steve. We're going to have a baby."

Her life could finally begin.

Karen Wiesner's Wounded Warriors Series in electronic formats from Uncial Press; paperback from http://stores.lulu.com/karenwiesner

Reluctant Hearts, Book 1 reissue (Contemporary Women's Fiction) Available now
Mirror Mirror, Book 3 reissue (Paranormal Suspense Women's Fiction)
Available now
Wayward Angels, Book 4 reissue (Inspirational Women's Fiction) Coming March 2010
Until It's Gone, Book 5 (Mainstream Romance Suspense) Available now
White Rainbow, Book 6 (Inspirational Women's Fiction) Coming Summer 2010

About the Author

Karen Wiesner is an accomplished author with 70 books published in the past 11 years, which have been nominated for and/or won 92 awards, and 7 more titles under contract. Karen's books cover such genres as women's fiction, romance, mystery/police procedural/cozy, suspense, paranormal, futuristic, gothic, inspirational, thriller, horror and action/adventure. She also writes children's books, poetry, and writing reference titles such as her bestseller, *First Draft in 30 Days* and *From First Draft to Finished Novel {A Writer's Guide to Cohesive Story Building}*, available now from Writer's Digest Books. For more information about Karen and her work, visit her Web sites at http://www.karenwiesner.com, http://www.firstdraftin30days.com, http://www.falconsbend.com and http://www.JewelsoftheQuill.com. If you would like to receive Karen's free e-mail newsletter, *Karen's Quill*, and become eligible to win her monthly book giveaways, send a blank e-mail to KarensQuill-subscribe@yahoogroups.com.

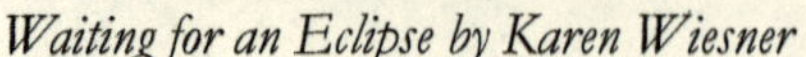

www.ingramcontent.com/pod-product-compliance
Lightning Source LLC
LaVergne TN
LVHW091020080826
845145LV00002B/313

* 9 7 8 0 5 7 8 0 3 1 5 2 1 *